I0690770

Spinning Through Time

By

Barbara Baldwin

Books We Love
A quality publisher of genre fiction.
Airdrie Alberta

Print ISBN 9781771457071

The Carousel

From afar, she heard the music,
A slow waltz from another time.
And the horses danced to the tune
They could not hear.
The carousel spun round and round,
Painted horses galloped freely.
And magic wove a wondrous spell
Through the silvery night.
Proud heads held high, the horses pranced,
Chasing mystic sounds to the past.
Seeking a world of fantasy,
They lured her through time.
Yet when the music ended,
And the horses finally stopped.
The magic still coursed through her,
Love had found her heart.

Chapter One

Dallas, Texas — Present Day

"Damn!" Jaci let the expletive escape without thought as she scrutinized the negatives in her darkroom. Positive her camera lens had been clean and the film fresh, she developed several prints to determine the problem. No matter in which position she had taken the photos, an image existed behind the black carousel horse. Although faint, the figure appeared to be a man, dressed darkly and with dark features.

She called Mackey, the carousel operator, and arranged a meeting the next morning. When she showed him the pictures, he shook his head, reiterating what she knew — no one had been around when she took the pictures. Anxious to get on with her assignment, she shot several rolls of film, making sure the black lead horse appeared in some, but not all, of the photographs of the restored Dentzel carousel.

"For Pete's sake." This time when she developed the film, the man's image appeared much more distinct. Jaci studied the proof sheets under a magnifier, chose several and made enlargements. Gray eyes seemed to mock her, as though defying her to find the source of the problem. Yet in another photo, shadows surfaced; dark brows bunched over haunted eyes. Jaci had spent most of her twenty-six years studying people, if not interacting with them, and she felt this man's pain.

She grabbed the photos and closed the door to the darkroom.

"Mandy, take a look at these." She tossed the photos on the coffee table in front of her younger sister. Logically, she knew there had to be a problem with her camera. She would just have to narrow down the options.

"Now?" Mandy peered over the top of a dog-eared romance novel. Sliding her glasses up the bridge of her nose, she frowned.

"Now." Jaci's command received a big sigh, but Mandy did pick up the prints.

"The horses are very nice, Sis, but the good looking hunk in the background is sort of out of focus."

"There is no good looking hunk."

"But he's right here in this—"

"There was no body; man, boy or otherwise. I must have a smudge on my lens." As she talked, Jaci stuck her head under the coffee table in search of her tennis shoes.

For the moment ignoring her sister, she shoved her feet into her shoes and jerked at the laces. She didn't even know why she had asked Mandy's opinion. Her younger sister was a hopeless romantic and would find a handsome man in the middle of any photograph, even if Jaci knew better.

She stopped to look at Mandy when her sister heaved the big sigh. Mandy had schooled her face in a serious expression, turning wide eyes to Jaci and allowing yet another sigh to escape.

Jaci pulled on a hooded sweatshirt. She flipped the hood off her head and ran her fingers through her short blonde bob, making a face as she headed for the door. "I will not fall for your theatrics."

"Fine, be that way," Mandy replied. "Why did you ask me to look at them if you won't listen when I have something to say?"

"Geez, Mandy, you sound like...Okay. Let me hear it, but make it fast."

Mandy bent over and retrieved the photos from the table. After studying them for several seconds, she grinned. "My theory? How's this? There's no doubt this man is a hunk. Judging by his clothes, I'd say he's actually a gentleman from another era."

Jaci rolled her eyes at the explanation even as she wondered why she hadn't noticed the difference in the clothes.

Mandy hurried on. "He looks very unhappy. Perhaps he's lost his lady love, and must spend all eternity floating around trying to find her. Or maybe he's finally located her, and is making his presence known before he sweeps her off her feet and carries her away to his manor." Mandy hugged a pillow as she pretended to swoon, giving one last dramatic sigh. "They will, of course, live happily ever after."

"Good God, Amanda Elizabeth Eastman! That tops anything you have ever said. Are you trying to tell me I took a picture of a ghost?" Why had she thought Mandy would be serious? Jaci didn't even wait for an answer. She slammed out the door, trotted down the steps and out into the night.

Running would clear her mind, and she now wished she had kept to her regular workouts for the past weeks. The time alone in the quiet night seemed a precious commodity. As much as she loved her sister, she could be a trial.

Unlike Mandy, Jaci felt love and romance were fairy tales for children and had no place in her life. While Mandy was a dreamer, Jaci often stated if she couldn't photograph it, it didn't exist.

She sucked in a lungful of crisp night air and slowly exhaled, hoping at the same time to expel the doubts from her mind. But tonight it didn't work. The further and faster she ran, the more his image came to mind — dark features, strong hands wrapped around the center pole of the carousel horse, or was it a cane? And his eyes — shimmering silver beckoned her; begged her for something. Understanding? Help? What did he want?

The strenuous exercise of her body did nothing to eliminate the confusion in her mind. The only resolution was to start again at the beginning.

* * *

7

Jaci rose the next morning determined to exorcise whatever gremlin existed with her work. Knowing the fall weather in Texas, she dressed in layers, figuring she could peel off garments as it warmed up. She pulled on worn blue jeans over Lycra running shorts and grabbed a sweatshirt to wear over her tank top. She never consciously thought about her clothes, and being a freelance photographer, she dressed as she pleased. According to Mandy, that was exactly the reason she never had any dates.

"No pizzazz to your dress," Mandy would say.

Jaci looked at herself in the mirror as she brushed her teeth. "Whatcha mean, no pizzazz?" She made a face. What could possibly be wrong with a sweatshirt emblazoned with the words photographers do it better in dark rooms?

She grinned; who was she kidding? She had no desire to date and perhaps she dressed to deliberately ward off proposals.

"Yeah, right," she told her reflection. "Like you've had so many of them." She snapped on her fanny pack, putting an end to her inner conversation.

In less than half an hour, she punched the lock on her car and headed for the carousel. She had chosen to arrive later today when the ride was full of people. Setting her camera on a tripod, she softly whistled to the tune of the Wurlitzer. Mackey was already taking tickets and helping youngsters aboard the brightly painted horses and menagerie animals.

Tucking her hair under a cabby hat to keep it out of her eyes, Jaci adjusted the focus, and then turned the timer to automatic so she could study the carved animals as they slowly revolved. She tried to imagine the Dentzel carousel before the turn of the century, in the heydays of amusement parks and county fairs. Prancers and jumpers would have carried laughing children round and round to the tune of a pipe organ. The carved and painted frieze edging the upper facade of the carousel was as ornate as the horses themselves. Even the kiosk, the part containing the

8

operating equipment, was encrusted with carved figures and scenery panels.

Any artist would be in awe of the craftsmanship of this bygone era. But like too much of America's history, the original carousels had practically disappeared before anyone became concerned. Jaci Eastman was pleased her name would accompany pictures of the restored Dentzel for Life magazine. Her photo essay would remind people of an artistry which only existed in our modern world as a part of the past.

She reloaded her camera, keeping an eye on the ride. Round and round — speed up — slow down — stop. All riders off. New riders on — round and round again.

Nowhere did she see anything, or anyone, remotely resembling the image in her photographs. Perhaps he wasn't here today, although why he had appeared for the last two days, she couldn't say.

"Oh, lord, I sound like Mandy," she chastised herself. She couldn't believe she was thinking of the blur on her negatives as a real person. Quickly adjusting the camera, she watched the riders debark.

While the carousel cleared, Mackey stood in the middle, smiling and waving at the youngsters as they happily begged their parents for another ride. Suddenly, he clutched his chest and doubled over.

Yelling, Jaci raced to the carousel, which Mackey had set in motion as he fell. She jumped onto the moving platform and tried to make her way to where he had fallen within the kiosk. Holding to reins or pommels, she zigzagged in and out of the horses as they moved up and down.

Feeling intensely dizzy, she stopped for a moment to clear her head. She grabbed the cool, wooden mane of the black horse, closing her eyes to clear her vision. An intense electric shock raced up her arm, paralyzing her motion. She felt the carousel spin faster and faster, the motion throwing her against the horse. She moaned, knowing she was going to be sick. She clutched at the horse's neck, but that didn't prevent her from falling.

*** * ***

Shrill whinnies brought Nicholas and his trainer, MacAdoo, on a dead run from the side of the barn to the exercise arena. Sam, the stable boy, running from the opposite direction, collided with Nicholas as they both rounded the corner. MacAdoo, though older, surged ahead to locate the problem while Nicholas tried to untangle himself from the gangly youth.

By the time he reached the turn-around where they exercised the horses, MacAdoo had untacked Wind Dancer. The trainer handed the lead rope of Nicholas's prize black stallion to a stable boy. One by one, the other thoroughbreds were released and led away as he cautiously watched their movements.

It took some time for his heartbeat to return to normal. His entire livelihood centered on the thoroughbreds he raced and the colts they sired. He couldn't afford to have even one of them injured.

"What should we do with him?" MacAdoo asked, bent over an inert form lying face down in the mud, right in the middle of the exercise ring.

"Good God in heaven," Nicholas muttered in vexation. "How on earth did he get under the horses? He's quite lucky not to have gotten hurt."

MacAdoo agreed as he turned over the unconscious lad. "What should we do with him when he comes to?"

Nicholas Westbrooke, Pennsylvania born gentleman and horse breeder, had no idea what to do with some wayward youth, although he was curious as to how he had ended up in the horse pen. "Since it appears he likes being under foot of the horses, we could put him in the barn shoveling manure." Even in the most trying situations, his humor usually came through.

"Boss, I don't think that would be a good idea."

Nicholas flashed a glance at the youth but his real concentration remained on the horses, reassuring himself none had been hurt by the haphazard appearance of the lad into their midst. Suddenly, an abundance of blonde hair registered in his mind, and his gaze snapped back to the limp figure on the ground. He quickly skirted the tack to kneel beside his friend.

"Well, I'll be damned. It's a girl?"

"I think — hard to tell with all the mud on her face."

But Nicholas knew. The strange shirt she wore, though much too large, still outlined the high, firm curve of her breasts. As he gently wiped the mud away, his handkerchief revealed a straight nose, high cheekbones, and full lips. Feathery eyelashes lay against pale cheeks, concealing the color of her eyes.

Disregarding the mud now splattered on his lawn shirt and buff riding breeches, he gently lifted her from the muddy ground. Long strides carried him to the house, where he called to his housekeeper while climbing the stairs.

"Mrs. Jeffrey, come to the guest room at once. And bring warm water and clean towels."

The housekeeper quickly appeared by his side, five year old Amanda peering around her skirts. She placed the necessary supplies on a table before she even glanced at the bundle Nicholas placed gently on the bed. When she did, she inhaled sharply.

"Mister Nicholas, pardon my saying so, sir, but wouldn't it be better if you, or Mister MacAdoo, were to do this?"

"Why on earth would I want to do that, Mrs. Jeffrey? It would seem to me this falls under your area of expertise. Amanda can help get these dirty clothes off and find some sleep wear." He stood back, surveying the unconscious form.

"Amanda, sir? I must put my foot down. No child of her tender years and sensibilities should—"

"What are you prattling about?" He scowled across at his housekeeper, who was normally a sensible woman.

"Why, sir, I did powder your behind when you were just a wee little thing, but you were family. I don't think it at all proper for me to bathe this young lad, not knowing him, if you see what I mean." Nicholas watched her blush fiercely as she placed the pitcher of warm water on the table near the bed.

"Young lad?" He laughed. "If you look closely, you'll see you are mistaken. This boy is a girl, or rather a woman, I would imagine. She is dressed rather strange, though, don't you think?" He fingered the odd cap that had covered her very short hair.

As soon as she realized her mistake, Mrs. Jeffrey wasted no time shooing Nicholas out of the room. He turned toward the door, hearing her cluck like a mother hen over the girl, though she remained unconscious.

He couldn't fathom why any woman would wear the odd looking trousers and shirt this one had on. No explanation came to mind for her extremely short hair, either. Certainly her unusual mien, not to mention her sudden presence at Wildwood, indicated she was no lady. He sighed, knowing his questions would have to wait for answers.

As he closed the door to the guest room, he heard Amanda, her voice full of curiosity. "She looks like a fairy princess, Mrs. J. Will she disappear if we leave her alone?"

Nicholas would have to make sure the impressionable five year old didn't spend too much time with the strange, but beautiful, golden-haired woman. Not until he found out more about her.

* * *

Jaci tried, without success, to open her eyes and move her limbs. The fall on the carousel may not have broken anything, for she didn't hurt other than a headache, but she felt as though she floated on a cloud. Through her half-conscious state, she heard voices, and tried to concentrate

12

on their sound although the accent sounded foreign to her ears.

"We found her. Can we keep her, Uncle Nicholas?" A child's voice, full of enthusiasm and excitement, made Jaci think of Mandy many years ago.

"Of course not." The rough, deep timbre of a man's reply reminded Jaci of the giant in Jack and the Beanstalk. She tried not to flinch or react in any way that might indicate she was awake, for she didn't feel ready to confront the person who owned that particular voice.

"But we kept Sir Lancelot."

"A dog is different. You don't keep people, child." The male voice, still deep and distinguished, was now laced with humor. Jaci thought perhaps he was not an ogre after all.

"She looks like a fairy princess. Maybe if you kiss her, she'll wake up."

"A-m-a-n-d-a."

Jaci drifted back into a void, the stern voice creating images of dragons and swamp monsters in her mind.

* * *

The buzzing in her head finally quieted, though it still hurt abominably. She cautiously opened her eyes but found it difficult to adjust her vision to the darkness of the room. Turning her head to the side, she searched for a night light beside the bed. Instead, she found herself staring into the curious gaze of a little girl.

A memory floated to the surface of her muddled brain — a child's voice requesting a kiss to awaken the sleeping princess. Jaci smiled. The child's countenance immediately changed from studied intensity to brilliant sunshine as she returned the smile. She silently offered Jaci a glass of water.

Jaci slowly scooted to a sitting position, careful not to move her head any more than necessary. Even so, the pounding continued.

The child shifted from one foot to the other as Jaci scrutinized her over the rim of the glass. She wore a bright blue dress that came clear to the tops of her shoes, covered by a somewhat wrinkled white pinafore. Of course, it didn't help any that the little girl kept twisting the cloth between her chubby hands as she watched Jaci with wide eyes.

Her long hair reminded Jaci of Shirley Temple — all ringlets and curls — much too much hair for a youngster.

Jaci's gaze darted from object to object around the room. She sensed there was too much of everything here. The room contained an abundance of fancy furniture, frills and lace. The bed even had a ruffled canopy.

The little girl glanced nervously at the closed door. She turned back and burst into rapid speech, as though afraid of not saying all she needed to before someone caught her.

"Hello, my name is Amanda. Did you know you look like a fairy princess? I wish I could cut all my hair off like you, but Uncle Nicholas would be so angry." She popped her hands to her mouth, eyes wide. "I must get him. He said I could sit here as long as I called him immediately upon your waking." The girl turned to leave.

"No...wait." Jaci reacted without thinking, leaning forward to grab the child's arm. "Augh!" She fell back against the pillow, squeezing her eyes shut to block out the pain.

"But he said—"

"Please." Blindly, she held out her hand. Think, she chastised herself as she sucked in a breath. She couldn't believe such confusion resulted from simply falling off a carousel. Nothing made any sense — the girl's clothes, her speech, this room and its antique furniture.

There had been talk of building a reenactment village to draw more tourists to State Fair Park. Had she been taken there? If so, Jaci mused silently, why did she have the instinctive feeling that something was terribly wrong?

14

Since the child appeared less threatening than an adult, Jaci wanted to question her.

She softened her tone. "Please stay; just for a moment."

The child hesitated, glancing over at the door before looking back at her. "All right."

Jaci took a deep breath. "Where am I?"

"Why, Wildwood Manor, of course."

Was that the name of the reenactment village? Jaci couldn't recall. "Why is all the furniture old? Why are you dressed oddly?" Her breath came in short gasps; her hands trembled as panic clawed its way to the surface. She concentrated very hard on the pattern of the coverlet until her vision cleared.

"Is not old! Uncle Nicholas just bought this bed because he's going to marry soon."

Jaci moaned and rolled her eyes at the little girl's story.

"Amanda, I thought I told you not to bother our guest." The gruff voice came from across the room.

Amanda's back stiffened, but her eyes still held a pixy light. In a whisper she said to Jaci, "He likes to use his big voice, but not to worry, he really is a very nice person." She made a dash for the door, only pausing briefly to curtsy before the tall figure.

Jaci's gaze followed the pixy as she scampered across the room, but now she studied the man who remained leaning against the doorframe. Her gaze slid up neatly tailored trousers encasing long legs, a trim waist, and arms crossed over a chest covered in a brown brocade vest, snowy shirt and darker brown jacket. His clothes, like those of the girl, appeared quite old fashioned.

That thought flew as her gaze reached his face. His eyes held a hint of anger and his stance was anything but relaxed, and still she couldn't help noticing how handsome he was. He also looked familiar. She knew she should recognize those gorgeous silver eyes, his dark hair and finely chiseled chin. Her artistic eye noted the contradiction between his youthful face and the gray threading its way through the darker hair at his temples. His full lips, puckered in thought, now gave way to a voice as dark and intriguing as the man himself.

"Good afternoon. My name is Nicholas Westbrooke. I suppose I should welcome you to Wildwood, though you most certainly dropped by in an unexpected manner."

Jaci had felt the tension increase the moment Amanda left the room, and would have called her back if only her brain would function properly. She tried to speak, but her mouth pinched in a terrible grimace and she squeezed her eyes shut in pain. Her manner must have appeared unduly strange, because when she finally opened her eyes, she saw him hesitate.

"A lady will most usually return a gentleman's introduction by at least acknowledging it, if not by allowing him the pleasure of her name in return."

She nervously plucked at the bed covers as she crossed and uncrossed her ankles beneath the sheets, but she still didn't speak.

"You clean up quite pretty." The comment must have slipped out on accident, because she saw him clamp his lips quickly together.

The panic she had felt earlier quickened. Her gaze flickered from him to the window and back.

"I doubt you would get far."

Startled, she stared at him. How could he possibly know she contemplated jumping to escape his presence?

"I'm sure you're right, since I don't even know where I am." She finally spoke, feeling the panic curl into a tight knot in her stomach before slowly creeping upward, threatening to choke her

"Here, drink this." The strange man handed her the glass he had brought in with him. Without thought, she downed half the water, hoping it would ease her cottonmouth.

"How did you get here?" His question seemed innocent enough, but it still confused her.

"Where, exactly, is here?"

"Here is Wildwood Manor, precisely sixteen miles west of Philadelphia, Pennsylvania. Here is Monday, the fourteenth day of October in the year of our Lord 1874. Exact enough?"

"There's no reason to be rude." What he said made no sense, and she didn't like his tone. She tried to get up, determined to leave this room and go home.

"I may have bumped my head when I fell, but I'm not crazy. I know what year it is." Funny, but her limbs didn't want to cooperate. Try as she might, she couldn't get out of bed.

"I must leave now to be home in time for dinner." Even as she said the words, she laid back, her brain a muddle. Perhaps she should rest a little longer.

The man who called himself Nicholas Westbrooke stood beside her. He took away the glass and set it on the table. She squinted, trying to concentrate on his face. He wasn't quite as frightening now. In fact, a gentle smile lifted the corners of his mouth and softened the lines around his eyes. His change in expression made her feel bad about yelling at him.

She started to apologize but his image faded. When she tried to bring him back in focus, the thought haunted her that she should know him. His dark brows come together over silver eyes as he scrutinized her in turn. Just as she faded into unconsciousness, she realized who the man was. Yet before she grasped the memory, the connection disappeared, leaving her in blackness.

Chapter Two

The annoying buzz in Jaci's head gave way to voices; fuzzy at first, but gradually becoming more distinct. Two men spoke, their accent more eastern than her slight Texas drawl. She focused on the more gentle of the two voices, the rhythm of his words reminding her of the soft cadence of the carousel.

Even as she listened, she couldn't rouse herself enough to speak. She recalled weird dreams — children asking for kisses to wake princesses, a very handsome, but strange man, pretending to be someone from another century. She did recall falling on the carousel, and must have hit her head harder than she thought.

"MacAdoo keeps asking about her, though why he would ask about a stranger is beyond me," a gruff voice commented.

Oh, dear. Mackey. Wondering how he fared, she opened her eyes, but wasn't given the opportunity to speak.

"Ah, you're awake. Now, if you will tell me your name and why you fell into Wildwood's exercise ring with my prize thoroughbreds, my patience will be rewarded." It was the swamp monster voice. Jaci couldn't remember his name, but she did recall his brusque attitude from earlier.

"I fell on a carousel," she softly replied, unable to raise her voice to match the anger she felt at this man's highhandedness. In both their conversations, he had spoken as though she had invaded his precious space. "Why do you keep referring to State Fair Park as Wildwood?"

"We've had this conversation before."

Listening to his voice, she finally recalled his name — Nicholas Westbrooke. She watched as another man, shorter and fair-haired, pulled Nicholas aside, the conversation now in muted tones she strained to hear.

"...late eighteen hundreds and modern advances of medicine, you would think you could find some way of getting the truth from her."

"What time is it?" Her ear caught the numbers. She blinked several times as she tried to focus on the other man, who at this point appeared much friendlier. When she turned her head, however, intense pain shot up her neck to the base of her skull. She groaned.

"The time? Odd question, truly, but it is half past three in the afternoon." This time, the younger man answered, his voice soothing and calm.

She was confused. "But didn't he say it was six something?"

"I beg your pardon?" Nicholas answered, this time his harsh voice not matching the concern she saw in the soft silver of his eyes.

"You know, six o'clock — eighteen hundred hours?" Having flown all around the world at one time or the other, Jaci's mind automatically switched from regular to international time.

"How odd a comment. The blow to your head must have spilled your wits." Nicholas's dark brows came together over assessing eyes.

She watched in fascination as his full lips moved in speech but she had a hard time understanding. Her ears rang and vision blurred, and she knew if she closed her eyes, she would wake up in her own bed. Immediately, she squeezed her eyes shut. It's all a dream, she repeated to herself — all a dream.

"Nicholas, really. There's no sense scaring her wits out of her," the soft voiced man defended. "I've never heard of such a thing — hundreds of hours. My dear girl, 1874 is the year, not a time of day."

Jaci's eyes flew open to see his frown and note the concern in his gaze while his words assaulted her brain. Her own eyes blurred with tears while her logical, systematic mind shifted to overload and allowed her the only possible way out. She fainted.

Nicholas turned to Thomas, his friend and a practicing physician. "Why would she keep losing consciousness? She doesn't appear to be that delicate."

Thomas listened to the woman's heartbeat, lifted an eyelid, and scrutinized her breathing. "This time she is only in a faint. The blow to her head, while leaving a nasty bump, is apparently creating a pain serious enough to cause her distress. I'll leave laudanum for her. I have no doubt she'll recover quickly."

"Well, if you're sure she's out of danger, I'll leave her in Mrs. Jeffrey's capable hands and travel back to Philadelphia with you. I have several business transactions to conduct that I've been putting off."

Thomas chuckled. "Business? I swear, Nicholas, you are the only man I know who would leave a beautiful woman alone in your bed to conduct business. I doubt there's much hope for you." Shaking his head in mock sadness, Thomas left the room, still chuckling.

Nicholas remained beside the bed staring down at the creature who had mysteriously appeared in his life. In their two short conversations, he had determined she had a strong will and stubborn streak, both of which were traits he admired.

For reasons he didn't have time to dissect, he felt drawn to her. Something in her green gaze held him spellbound; her speech, a slight drawl he couldn't decipher, intrigued him. His brother, Cameron, would call this attraction fate, but Nicholas didn't believe in fate, or luck.

"Cameron? Damn," Nicholas swore, leaving the room and closing the door softly behind him.

As he gathered his things and called for his carriage, he thought about his younger sibling. Cameron was the main reason he must go to Philadelphia. It was time his brother took responsibility for his life and those who should be a part of it. While in the city, he would also do a little investigating into this woman's strange comments about historical reenactments and carousels.

Nicholas and Thomas traveled in companionable silence in Nicholas's carriage; Thomas's horse tied to the rear. Even as he traveled away from Wildwood, he couldn't keep his mind off the beautiful young woman he had left lying in a bed in his home. Why did she speak in so strange a manner? Where did she call home?

She dressed curiously, asked very intriguing questions, and had the most wondrous green eyes full of mystery. He wondered impulsively if her lips were as soft to the touch as they had looked when she nervously licked them before speaking. He was inexplicably drawn to her vulnerability and the fear she had tried to hide, and would have gladly stayed at her side if not for urgent business.

"Will you see Lycinda while in town?" Thomas questioned idly.

Guilt immediately gripped Nicholas as he thought of Lycinda Edwardson. "Yes, of course." In silent atonement, he promised himself to call on her after he visited with her father, who also happened to be his banker.

* * *

Jaci didn't know how long she had slept. She recalled her strange conversation with the even stranger man, and was determined to get dressed and go home. Her head felt much better, and she knew if she didn't make a quick phone call, Mandy would probably have the police looking for her. She swung her legs over the side of the bed to get up when the little girl bounced into the room.

"Oh, I'm glad you are awake. Before he left, Uncle Nicholas forbid me to bother you, but you slept for days, and I thought you might never wake."

The little girl still pretended to be something else, even though they were alone. She decided to get to the bottom of this, once and for all. "You're from a reenactment village, right?"

"I don't understand that word. I'm only five, you know."

21

"You dress up and pretend to live in a different era, ah, time period." She defined the word.

Amanda looked quite taken with the idea, as though she had never thought of it before. "I don't know why someone would want to do that. I like it right here where I am."

Jaci sighed, trying to convince her. "It's just for fun. You know, pretend; make believe?"

Amanda shrugged, bounced off the bed and headed for the door. "Well, I suppose. Uncle Nicholas says sometimes people pretend to be what they're not. Is that what you mean?" She never even waited for an answer, assuming Jaci would agree with her. "I'll get Molly to bring you something to eat."

Jaci finally relaxed, knowing she hadn't flipped out. She had apparently hit her head pretty hard. The strange dreams must have been caused by her fall or from the medicine that man gave her to drink.

She turned toward the door when a petite young girl of about sixteen came in, carrying a tray laden with a silver coffee pot, cup, and a dish of toast and jellies. Considering the circumstances, Jaci didn't think it at all strange for this girl to be wearing a long black dress, white apron, and a starched white cap set primly on top her head.

Her stomach growled at the thought of food, and she couldn't remember the last time she had eaten. She would eat something so not to appear rude, before going home to see Mandy and get back to the normal humdrum of her life.

"Hello, there." At the sound of Jaci's voice, the maid clattered the tray to the small desk. Spinning around, her wide eyes flickered to Jaci then down to the floor. Her hands nervously twisted her apron.

"I brung — brought — you some coffee, miss." The girl curtsied as she spoke, still not looking directly at Jaci.

"Thank you, but I'd much rather have my clothes."

"Excuse me, Miss?"

"My clothes. That man — the one who thinks he's in charge? He didn't take them with him, did he?" She felt a moment of panic at not having her possessions.

"Goodness, no. Mister Westbrooke, he wouldn't let us throw them away, strange though they be. Says your belongings are your belongings, and we was — were — not to bother them." The maid curtsied again and scooted across the room to a large cupboard on one wall. "Here they be, Miss, right here in the wardrobe. Cleaned them up the best we could, considering you fell in the middle of the horse pens and all." The girl almost smiled, thought better of it, and curtsied again.

Jaci rushed to the cupboard, relieved to see her faded jeans and sweatshirt. She grabbed them close and buried her face in the denim. It was a dream, after all.

"Mister Westbrooke; is he here?" She didn't particularly want to see the man again, but felt she owed him thanks for taking care of her.

"No, Miss, he went to the city with Dr. Stillwell. Said he'd be back late today, perhaps."

She assumed Dr. Stillwell was the other man who had faded in and out of her consciousness. She glanced out the window. Considering the lateness of the day, she dumped her clothes on the bed, anxious to get dressed and out of this very strange place.

When she noticed the maid coming over to help, she stopped unbuttoning the nightgown she wore. "I don't need any help. You can go do whatever it is you normally do, but first—" Jaci hesitated. "First, can you tell me where the bathroom is?"

"Bathroom, Miss?"

"Yes, the bathroom. You know, to — ah —" She snapped her teeth together in frustration. In her mind, she formed a letter to the administrator of this place, suggesting the employees be a little more helpful and a little less authentic.

"Oh." Recognition must have dawned on the maid, for she moved forward, this time bending over and removing a china chamber pot from beneath the bed. "There you be, Miss. I'll leave you to your morning toilet."

Jaci's mouth dropped open as she stared. The maid curtsied yet again before leaving the room.

23

"This is too much," she muttered as she jerked on her clothes. She splashed water on her face from the china bowl sitting on a commode. Boy, would she have a story for Mandy. She'd have to bring her sister back to the village; it was the kind of thing Mandy would like.

Leaving behind the frilly room and unbidden memories of the tall, handsome stranger, she descended a wide curved staircase to a marble foyer. The size of the house was impressive and Jaci certainly hoped the State Fair Board could recoup their money from this extravagance. She spied a boy dressed in knee breeches, shirt and vest near the door and assumed him to be part of the tour.

"Would you please call me a taxi?" She asked when she drew near. He screwed his face into a frown, apparently not understanding.

"You know — a taxi, a cab, a hack?"

"Oh, yes, Miss. I suppose that would be possible, but why would you want one?"

"To go home, of course." She sighed; tired of this game everyone except her seemed to enjoy playing.

"But, ma'am. If I was to travel the sixteen miles to town to find you a hack, only to get him to travel the sixteen miles out here to collect you, wouldn't it be easier if you took Mister Westbrooke's carriage into town straight-away?" The boy eyed her strangely, as though she didn't make sense but he did.

She thought she would laugh out loud at the absurdity of the situation, but from the boy's look, he wouldn't think it funny. Instead, she decided to play along.

"Okay, fine. We'll take Mister Westbrooke's carriage."

"Well, I'm afraid you can't do that."

"Why not?" She screeched at the youngster, unable to suspend her anger at his stubborn insistence on playing his role.

The boy straightened to his full height, and Jaci realized even though he appeared years younger than her, he was definitely much larger.

"I'm sorry," she said. "It's just that I must get home."

"Yes, well, be that as it may, you still can't take the carriage."

"And the reason?" This was worse than playing twenty questions with Mandy.

"Mister Westbrooke took the carriage to Philadelphia, and besides, he doesn't allow anyone to take it without his permission. What other reason might there be?" The boy gave his answer like she was the muddle-headed one. For a minute, Jaci actually considered she might still be under the influence of whatever drug they had given her earlier.

"This is ridiculous," she muttered, jerking the door open on her own. "I can find a phone by myself." The brightness of the late afternoon sun assailed her the minute she stepped through the door. She raised a hand to shade her eyes, squinting in all directions to gain her bearings.

Nothing appeared familiar. A paddock full of horses was visible off to the right, but the carousel had completely disappeared. She moved her gaze more slowly from place to place. She saw no phones or admission booth. There appeared to be no curio shop selling souvenirs of the recreation of history. All around her, leaves had turned bright yellow and red, where this morning — or was it yesterday? — they were still green, though fall hung heavy in the air.

She skirted the chairs on the porch and skipped down the steps, racing along the dirt road that ran parallel to the fence. Where was the asphalt? She strained her eyes to find some familiar landmark, but nothing was as it had been. Veering to the left, she ran faster, trees and scenery blurring as tears welled up and spilled over.

Her heart pounded in rhythm with her feet. The varied conversations of the people here echoed through her mind as she ran. She recalled the girl's belief that she lived in this period of long dresses and formal manners; the doctor and Nicholas conversing about the date. What had they insisted — 1874 was the date, not a time?

"Dear God, please don't do this to me," she moaned aloud to the heavens, her footsteps never faltering as she flew down the tree-lined path. If what they said was true, she doubted she could run far enough or fast enough to get back where she belonged.

* * *

Nicholas remained frustrated and restless as Stephen drove him back to Wildwood. It had taken little time to conduct most of his business, but Cameron had gone to sea with the latest shipment to England, and now it would be months before he returned. What was Nicholas supposed to do with his niece, Amanda, since her governess had left?

His thoughts came to a jarring halt as the carriage swerved to the right then came rapidly to a stop, almost unseating him. He opened the door and stepped down as his driver jumped off the high box seat to come to his assistance.

"What on earth is the matter with you, Stephen?"

"Lordy, I'm sorry, sir, but the horses spooked when that...that person flew by." His driver waved frantically past the back of the carriage and Nicholas turned to look.

"What?" He stared after the apparition running as though the very devil were on her tail.

"Wait here," he instructed his driver, before taking off after the vanishing figure.

For two days this female had been constantly on his mind, even as he dined with Lycinda and her family in Philadelphia. As he had sat across from the demure and dainty Miss Edwardson, images of flashing green eyes had come to mind. A full, womanly figure beneath the muddy fabric of an overlarge shirt and men's trousers had transcended his vision as Lycinda entertained at the piano after the lavish meal.

He had quickly conducted the most pressing of his business, had bid her and her father good-bye, and had rushed back to Wildwood. Why? He couldn't say except he felt a sense of responsibility toward this strange woman and there had been an instant attraction impossible to deny.

26

Now he had to race like the wind to keep her from escaping before he could determine the cause of the attraction. Finally he slowed to a trot, coming up behind her as she bent over to catch her breath. A dozen or more questions played in his brain as he eyed her curved bottom in the strange blue trousers she wore.

"Why are you running away?" He voiced the first thought that came to mind.

She screeched, spinning around at the sound of his voice. He realized immediately she verged on hysteria, for her eyes were wide and wild, her breath coming in short gasps. Cautiously, he held out a hand, approaching her as quietly as he would a frightened filly.

Her reaction was immediate. Racing toward him, she pounded on his chest with her fists, tears streaming down her cheeks and sobs choking her with their intensity.

"Go away! I don't want you; I don't need you! I only want to go home, don't you see?"

He curled his arms around her, hugging her close to stop her tantrum. With her arms trapped between them, she could no longer hit him, though the blows were hardly dangerous. Nicholas tried to soothe her, cooing soft words as he often did with Amanda, but she would have none of it.

"Let me go. I only tried to help Mackey. You have no right keeping me prisoner." She leaned back as far as his circling arms would allow, the green fire of her gaze searing him. Even with her short blonde hair blowing wildly about her face, Nicholas thought her the most beautiful creature he had ever seen. As she ranted at him, he felt the blood stir in his veins. Her heaving breasts against his chest created sweet torture for him.

"I'll let you go if you calm down." He kept his voice pitched low and soft.

"I am calm!" she hollered.

He smiled at the contradiction and began to relax his grip when she brought her fists up and smacked him under the jaw. He fell back a step, his arms going completely slack. She twisted around and sprinted towards the trees.

27

"Stop it!" He grabbed the back of her pants and jerked her to a halt. She twisted around, but he didn't give her a chance to hit him again. His strong arms tightened around her. She opened her mouth to scream, and Nicholas decided it was time to put an end to her tirade.

His kiss demanded her total acquiescence, but once he began, he realized the mistake would cost him dearly, for he surrendered as well. She was soft and hot, her lips molding perfectly with his. As he tasted her sweetness, she melted against him. The heat and scent of her penetrated his senses and sent them reeling. He slid his hands down her back, pressing her to him.

Passion raged within Nicholas, but apparently the woman in his arms didn't feel the same. She began wiggling to get away from him instead of closer to the fire he blamed her for starting. He cautiously raised his head, steeling himself for her outraged reaction.

Instead of hysteria this time, she took a calming breath and looked him straight in the eye. "Please. Take me home."

Nicholas released her and took a step back, willing his body to cool down; hoping his ardor didn't show too easily on his face. "My carriage is at your disposal, but since Philadelphia is over sixteen miles away and night is approaching, perhaps you would consider waiting until morning."

"This is Dallas! I live in Dallas." Her voice became softer, yet he could hear the rising note of despair. "1419 Tatum Drive — in Dallas." When she looked at him, her eyes full of tears, his heart turned over. A woman's tears had always been his weakness, but for some reason this particular woman's anguish tore at his heart.

"You never have told me your name," he whispered. It seemed vitally important to him at the moment; perhaps in fear she would disappear from his life and leave him no way to trace her.

"Jaci Eastman. Now, I thank you for your assistance, but I must get home." She dismissed him quite effectively and turned down the road. Without a backward glance, she walked away from him, but he wasn't about to let her out of his life that easily.

He signaled Toby, his young footman, who came running. "Watch her, but don't let her know you are," he whispered his orders, positive Jaci Eastman would return once she realized they were miles from nowhere and there weren't any neighbors to help her out. Nicholas wanted to give her time alone to cool down, but he didn't want her to be alone. He didn't intend to hold her hostage, but neither did he want to let her go just yet.

It was well past the dinner hour when the front door quietly closed. He didn't leave his chair by the fire in the library, but listened intently for signs of her passing. Not long after her footsteps faded, Toby popped his head around the partially opened door.

"She be home, now, sir." The boy grinned, knowing he had done his job well.

"Thank you very much, for looking after her." Nicholas flipped him a coin. "If you hurry to the kitchen, I believe Delta still has some dinner warming for you."

Toby caught the coin, smiling his thanks before rushing off to feed his growing body. Nicholas sighed in relief; thankful the lady had returned unharmed and had not stayed out in the chill weather all night. He closed the book he had on his lap and extinguished the lamp, heading up the long flight of stairs to his room.

For whatever reason, Jaci Eastman had fallen into his life and now it was up to him to do something with her. As far as he could tell, she had no relation and no place to go. Her strange story about a home in some place called Dallas didn't ring true, and he would send a message into the city and check it out. In the meantime, he would allow her to remain at Wildwood. As for himself, he would make sure he kept his distance, for she did strange things to his insides.

He stopped at the door to the guest room, tilting his head to the side. In the quiet of the night, he heard her crying. Without thinking about his actions, he opened the door. Moonlight washed the room in silvery light.

She had not undressed, though her strange shoes lay helter-skelter on the floor. She hadn't even turned back the coverlet on the bed, but lay curled in the middle, weeping with such anguish Nicholas thought surely her heart was breaking.

He couldn't fathom what possessed such a beautiful lady to ache so, but as a gentleman it fell to him to comfort her. Trying not to frighten her, he spoke softly as he sat on the edge of the bed. He reached out to touch her shoulder.

She didn't push him away, but instead cried even harder. She wouldn't answer his whispered questions and he soon gave up. His hand smoothed her hair away from her face; his thumb continued to wipe at the tears. Gradually she quieted, but he knew she didn't sleep, for her body remained taut as a bowstring.

Much later, she spoke. "I can't go home, can I? I'll never go home again."

Although she asked a question, the resignation in her voice implied she didn't expect an answer. It seemed that speaking the words out loud had been answer enough, for almost immediately, she fell into a deep sleep.

Recalling Amanda's initial statement about sleeping princesses, he thought maybe the child was right. Perhaps the strange and beautiful Jaci Eastman was theirs to keep.

Chapter Three

Jaci curled into a tight ball in the window seat, tears coursing down her cheeks as silently as the rain streaking the windowpane. She tucked the voluminous white nightgown around her feet, unable to get warm. She closed her eyes and dropped her head to her knees in despair. What had she ever done in her life to deserve being thrown back into some forgotten piece of history?

She had run the first day until exhausted, but she found nothing — not one solitary thing — that looked even vaguely familiar. The lush foliage and tall trees didn't belong to the super city of Dallas.

A bone chilling fear had overcome her and she had collapsed on the ground, so deep in misery that she hadn't even reacted when a hand touched her shoulder. Somewhere in a more sane part of herself, she had realized the boy standing over her must be from the reenactment.

Or rather, from Nicholas Westbrooke's home. She would have to get used to thinking that. When she finally realized she had no recourse but to rely on his hospitality until she figured a course of action, the boy quietly guided her back to the house since she had lost her bearings.

She remembered crying herself to sleep, surprisingly comforted by Nicholas' gentle voice and touch. When Jaci allowed her thoughts free rein, she recalled the power of his kiss and the way she responded to the seductive aura surrounding him. In her dreams he always came to her — handsome, strong, and very masculine. Her reaction to that one kiss frightened her to death, so now she slept very little. Besides, the turmoil in her brain refused to let her body slow down enough to rest.

She didn't have to accept her situation permanently, she reminded herself. She had accidentally fallen into this world and she could just as well find a way home. Nothing would prevent her from returning to Dallas, Mandy, and her nice, safe life. If she only knew how.

Jaci knew she wasn't being held captive, yet a prisoner she remained, locked in a world she didn't understand for reasons she couldn't begin to fathom. To keep from dealing with questions that had no answers, and a world gone awry, she refused to come out of her room. She wouldn't see anyone except the maid, whose name she learned was Molly.

"What, no tea and scones?" She asked as Molly set the tray of coffee and cookies on the desk. Even though she didn't read historical novels, Mandy did, and often carried on about the social life of the past. Once, she had even found prepackaged scone mix and brought it home to try. Didn't everyone back in this time period eat them?

Molly laughed at her question and gave her an incredulous look. "You must be living in the wrong century, Miss."

Jaci's coffee cup clattered to the china saucer. A fellow time traveler; someone to help? Her heart thudded recklessly as she sought to find out. "How did you know?"

Molly's brows came together in a frown. "T'weren't hard, Miss. We ain't — haven't — drank much tea since the War for Independence, and that be almost a hundred years ago."

The maid shrugged as though it was no big deal, but Jaci's heart plummeted. She would drive herself crazy with questions, assumptions, and useless, wishful thinking. Angered by the feeling of naivety, she stubbornly remained silent whenever the maid brought her a food tray, and she continued to refuse to see anyone else.

For two days, no one interfered with her plan. Today proved different.

First the little girl, Amanda, tried to come in, but the last thing in the world she wanted was to talk to anyone who reminded her of her own sister.

So she had locked the door.

The next morning the tray service rattled as the maid put it down outside the door; probably hoping Jaci would eventually eat.

She refused.

"Molly has duties other than waiting on you, especially when you appear sufficiently recovered to come downstairs for your meals." Nicholas's voice jarred her out of her musings when he waltzed into the room as though he owned it.

Jaci groaned, forgetting he did own it. "How did you get in here? I locked the door."

He smiled. Balancing the tray on one hand, he held up a key. "The master of his home must be master of all of it." He placed the tray in front of her, and then moved across the room to the wardrobe. "Upon my request, Dr. Stillwell, who took care of you, sent a few of his sister's things for you to wear. Since it appears, Miss Eastman, that you are temporarily stuck here, I have taken it upon myself to supply at least the necessities."

She stared at him.

"Miss Eastman, do you understand?"

"What's going to happen to me?" She asked in a whisper. "I have no clothes, no money, no way to get home."

"Well, shall we start with breakfast? After you eat, find something to wear, then join me in the library and we will discuss your future." He turned to her once more. "Are we agreed?"

She looked out the window to a world foreign to her in every way. She contemplated making a wisecrack, but she was in no position to argue, even when he treated her like a child.

"Agreed." She stated without preamble, turning her attention to her breakfast tray.

* * *

Jaci found it impossible to dress herself, something she'd been doing for more than twenty years. Finally, she pulled the cord to summon Molly. As the maid fastened what seemed like a hundred buttons up the back of the high necked dress, she chatted gaily about the household staff, and how glad they all were for Jaci to be part of them.

She didn't know where Molly got her information, but didn't correct her. No sense borrowing trouble when she didn't have a plan.

She slowly descended the stairs, feeling quite different than she had the night she tried to leave. Her long skirt kept tangling in her legs, and the slipper-like shoes Molly had laced around her feet were at least a size too large. Her hand ached from gripping the banister. She wondered when blue jeans had been invented and whether the nearest store might have any.

"Good morning, Miss." A stately man bowed low as she approached the closed door. "Mister Westbrooke is expecting you."

"You must be Selkirk." She recalled only one male name in the list Molly had recited earlier.

"Yes, Miss Eastman, that would be me." He neither looked at her nor smiled.

She had the feeling the man didn't want her here to disrupt the smooth flow of his household. Well, it wasn't like she wanted to be here, either.

Without another word, Selkirk opened the library door and ushered her inside. When the door softly clicked behind her, she felt she had been thrown to the lions.

"Please, have a seat," Nicholas spoke as he rose, moving to assist her to a chair directly in front of his desk. His library was bright, several floor to ceiling windows filtering the light and breaking the monotony of the book lined sections. A huge, unlit fireplace took up most of one wall.

"Well, Miss Eastman, what are your qualifications?" He wasted no time; his attitude now brusque as he questioned her. He returned to his seat behind a huge desk, fingers steepled in front of a frowning mouth.

As she had eaten breakfast, Jaci had come to the conclusion that she was stuck in this place, and with this family, at least for the time being. To that end, she must rely on their good graces. At least she hadn't bounced back into slavery days, or fallen into some sheik's harem.

"I can cook," she stated, wondering if recipe books had been invented yet.

He laughed, and for a moment Jaci thought the interview concluded before it even began. She breathed a sigh of relief when he explained.

"You would have to fight Delta for the privilege, and I doubt you could win. She's been here much, much longer than you and I combined. Perhaps you could be Amanda's governess."

"Governess? I'm not a baby-sitter."

"There's much more to the task, such as teaching proper etiquette and manners."

She shook her head, knowing she didn't have the patience. "I'm not a teacher."

"What, pray tell, are you then?"

She straightened her spine and proudly tilted her chin at the hauteur in his voice. "I'm a professional photographer. My pictures have been in the world's leading magazines — Harpers, Life..." Her voice trailed off as he lifted a brow, apparently not impressed with her credentials.

The man behind the desk smiled in sympathy, shaking his head. "Perhaps it was the blow to your head; perhaps some other ailment you haven't told us about? I'm sorry, but I've never heard of such a thing as a female photographer."

Her posture collapsed as she realized she had no place in this world. Nothing in her life — not her college degree or professional achievements — prepared her to live in a world over one hundred thirty-two years prior to her actual existence. She bit her lip as tears formed. Damn, she had to quit crying at every little thing. She stared out the window to keep from blinking.

"Can you read and write?"

35

"Of course I can!" She snapped her head around, for a moment forgetting to be contrite. This man seemed to take great delight in making her mad.

"Can you play the piano, embroider, run a household and set a menu — all those things it would be required to teach a young lady?"

"No." This time, her answer was barely audible.

"No? What have you done with your life? How is it a woman of your years doesn't know proper decorum for a lady?"

Jaci's cheeks burned, but with anger rather than embarrassment. "I spent my time working and taking care of my sister. You have no call to talk to me that way."

"Ah, a sister. And where is this sister, now, may I ask? No, don't bother answering." He waved aside her attempt to speak. "She is no doubt married and being a good wife, unlike you, who seem to have no direction, much less education to bare the responsibilities of a family."

She wanted to hit him. What an overbearing, pompous ass. She stood, slapping palms down on his desk and leaning forward, almost nose to nose with him. "Listen carefully, Mister Westbrooke. My sister and I were orphaned when I was eighteen. I raised her, went to college nights, and worked during the day. I had no time for frivolous ladylike activities such as piano and dance, much less the money."

"College? Work? And why, pray tell, aren't you doing it now? How did you end up in my exercise yard, dressed like a stable boy?"

"Because somehow I was...I'm not supposed to be..." How could she make him understand she didn't belong here; that she didn't want to be here? He'd never believe her story; she didn't believe it herself. Even when she woke each day still in the wrong century, she kept telling herself it was all a bad dream.

With a furious toss of her head, she turned toward the door. There was no use trying to explain. It would be better if she found a job in the nearest town and learned to support herself until she could locate a way back to her own time.

"Wait." His voice softened; the harsh tones he had used earlier gone.

She turned back to find he had moved around the desk and now leaned casually against it. The sunlight glinted off dark hair that he hadn't tied back today. It curled boyishly about his tan face, and Jaci ached in places she had suppressed years before.

Standing with his hands in his pockets and a perfect GQ smile on his face, he could make the cover of any fashion magazine. He had some indefinable mystic which would have captured the hearts of thousands of women everywhere. Her stomach tightened.

"For some unfathomable reason, Amanda's governess has left with no notice at all. It is impossible for me to conduct my business and try to supervise an energetic five year old. For the time being, since it appears you have nowhere else to go?" The question hung in the air until she nodded in agreement. "You might as well stay here and make yourself useful as Amanda's companion. Perhaps by the time she's ready for the more ladylike pursuits, I'll have found a replacement. In the meantime, you can help her with routine instruction."

His insinuations galled her. She knew more about life than she was sure he wanted Amanda to learn, but since she was temporarily stranded, it seemed prudent to acknowledge her place and hold her tongue. She wondered spitefully what he would think if she instructed Amanda about women's lib, space flight, and Woodstock.

She forced herself to return his smile, keeping her gaze on his face. She didn't want to scrutinize the tight cut of his trousers or the well-defined shape of his chest beneath the coat he wore. Every time her gaze wandered over him, butterflies attacked her stomach. Anxious to get away from his piercing gaze and her startling reaction to him, she cleared her voice. "Well, if my job is to look after Amanda, I'd better get started. Where is she?" She crossed her arms against her stomach to settle the butterflies.

"I believe you'll find her in the kitchen. She usually sneaks away there. Her ambition of late is to make cookies as wonderful as Delta's." Nicholas smiled as he spoke.

Her gaze again fell to his lips; lips she recalled kissing her with searing intensity. Another hot flash coursed through her. She had to clear her throat before she could speak. "Yes, well, it doesn't hurt for a girl to know how to cook."

"Why? While Amanda must learn what type of sauce to have served with meat or fish, she will most certainly never have to actually prepare the food herself."

How many times would she say the wrong thing, she wondered. How could she possibly know all the differences between his century and her own?

She tried to remain vague. "There are some things, Mister Westbrooke, that all women should know."

Miss Eastman's green eyes sparked fire as she turned and left the library, and Nicholas congratulated himself on a job well done. It wouldn't do to have her moping around day after day. Even though he could have easily hired a governess, and one with quality credentials, he felt she and Amanda would deal well with each other. Regardless of what he had said, he recognized in her all the qualities of a lady. His brusque manner had been to help her shake off the doldrums, not because he didn't credit her with any wisdom. Hopefully, his instincts would prove correct.

* * *

Jaci found it a lot tougher adapting than Nicholas implied. Of course, he thought she was simply transplanted from Texas, not from another century. By careful observation as the weeks passed, she managed to learn the basics of how to address people and walk without tripping over her skirts. The real trouble came from trying to do too much. She had been raised to share responsibilities. Since her parents' deaths, she did what needed to be done without thinking much about it. She couldn't believe helping out would get her in trouble, but it had that very morning.

Molly came upstairs as Jaci dusted the pictures hanging in the hallway. The maid had an absolute fit, tearfully spouting nonsense that because Jaci was doing her job, she'd soon be out on the streets. Before Jaci could stop her, Molly fled down the stairs, hollering for Mrs. Jeffrey.

In less than fifteen minutes, Selkirk appeared to advise her that Mister Westbrooke would see her in the study — immediately. She swore she saw a smile on the old butler's face for the first time since her arrival. She bet he enjoyed walking her to the proverbial gallows.

"Don't you like your position here at Wildwood, Miss Eastman?" Westbrooke asked the minute she stepped through the doorway.

She decided if he was going to chastise her, no one else need hear. Turning, she poked Selkirk in the chest with a finger causing him to step backward and closed the door in his face, giving him a smirk as she did so.

"Yes, I do enjoy taking care of Amanda. Why do you ask?" She could hold her own with any male she knew, and long ago had decided not to take any guff, but her situation had changed rapidly. She didn't care for Selkirk's, or Westbrooke's, chauvinistic attitude. At the same time, she couldn't get herself dismissed from this house. Regardless of whether she wanted it or not, Wildwood was her anchor in a storm of uncertainty.

"If you like taking care of Amanda, why are you interfering with Molly's position?"

"Interfering? I was helping." She couldn't believe she would get raked over the coals for doing more than her assigned duties.

"Miss Eastman, this household runs quite efficiently because everyone knows what they are to do, and each person performs his or her duty." He must have read something in her expression, because his voice softened. "I realize you are new, but I can't have Mrs. Jeffrey coming to me every few hours with a complaint. It will help me immensely if you take care of Amanda, and let the rest of the staff take care of Wildwood. Is that clear?"

"Perfectly," She answered and turned to leave, knowing she had been dismissed. As impossible as it seemed, she would have to try harder not to work. For starters, she went to the kitchen for a late morning cup of coffee.

* * *

Several days later, Nicholas requested her presence on a trip into Philadelphia.

"We won't be gone long, and I thought you might like to purchase a few things."

She guiltily glanced down at one of the few dresses she had found in the wardrobe. She had never properly thanked Nicholas for them, and that made her feel all the more guilty. She hated depending on anyone. She had learned to take care of herself and her sister, and found it difficult to ask for anything. Now, here she was, without a job or money except for this man's generosity.

"Thank you, but I'll stay here."

"Miss Eastman, it wasn't a request." As though he read her mind, he added, "Besides, you have wages coming that should be sufficient to purchase what you need."

Jaci wondered if she had earned enough to buy a ticket back home.

She quickly changed to a dark brown skirt and white blouse, topping it with a snug, cropped jacket. She was brushing her hair when Amanda came bounding in.

"Can't I go with you and Uncle Nicholas?" she asked, her words lisping together because of a slight cold. Jaci placed a hand on her forehead. Though her face was flushed, she showed no signs of becoming feverish.

"Sweetie, I don't want you outside. Especially not since you already have a cold."

"Please?"

Jaci hated it when they begged, for she was a soft touch. She knelt beside the little girl, still wrapped in her long flannel nightgown and furry slippers.

"If you stay here and take care of Delta and Mrs. Jeffrey, and Selkirk, I promise to bring you a treat."

"Promise?"

Jaci kissed her cheek and rose, smoothing a hand down the long skirt. She kept telling herself she was playing dress up, as she had originally accused Amanda of doing. Otherwise, panic threatened to swallow her whole. Everything from the clothes to the tooth powder she used in the morning kept reminding her that she didn't belong. It was the same world, if over a hundred years prior to her existence, yet it might as well be a different planet.

"Only a hundred years," she scuffed at her logic as she descended the stairs, Amanda racing before her to extort another surprise from her uncle for having to stay home.

When the young footman opened the door, Jaci cautiously walked out into the sunshine. She held her breath in suspense, perhaps hoping she would see her familiar Dallas. Wishing apparently didn't work, and she slowly descended the steps towards a large black carriage.

She hadn't been outside since she arrived, except for one fruitless foray. She now turned to study the house, a gasp escaping at the magnificence of Wildwood.

The house was white; a large two-story structure with additional windows jutting out from what might be an attic or third story. Huge columns rose from ground to roof, and lined up across the front and sides. Intricate metal railings ran at the edge of the second story balconies, which appeared to parallel the porches all the way around the house.

Close cut green shrubs edged the porch, and as her gaze followed the row of bushes, she spied a gazebo off to the side, away from the main building. She slowly turned in a circle, trying to absorb the wealth and splendor she saw before her. This was no recreated facade based on some artist's rendering. This was a real house, built with love for a family of real people, and somehow she had been plopped right into the middle of it.

A horse's neigh caught her attention and she turned to the right of the house. A large paddock contained several beautiful horses. Two fences surrounded the area of green, an oval dirt track sandwiched between the enclosures. A racetrack, she thought, recalling Nicholas's comments about raising racehorses.

"Are you ready, Miss Eastman?" His deep voice interrupted her thoughts and she turned a startled gaze toward him.

"You have a beautiful home, Mister Westbrooke."

He nodded his head in thanks, before indicating the carriage with a wave of his hand. She strolled past him to the door, ready to climb aboard herself, once she figured out how to collect her long skirts and hoist herself up at the same time. Before she had the chance, he circled her waist from behind and deftly lifted her inside.

She almost stumbled trying to keep her skirts untangled and get herself seated. She had learned to walk with yards of material swaying around her ankles; stepping and sitting were other lessons entirely.

As with everything in this world, the ride in a carriage was a unique experience for Jaci. The lurch of the horses as they started threw her head back, banging it against the wall of the carriage. She felt terribly awkward, and was afraid Nicholas would renege on his choice of a companion for Amanda when he saw her clumsy movements. She needn't have worried, because he appeared to forget he'd invited her as the miles slid by.

She sat on the seat opposite him and couldn't see what he read. The sheets of paper were full of heavy black ink and studying them made frown lines appear on his forehead. Jaci gave a sigh and settled back to enjoy the view.

All around them, deep crimson, mustard yellow and dusty brown dotted the landscape and Jaci wished for her camera. Even though she needed no more evidence, here was yet another indication she was no longer in Dallas.

There were too many hills, too many trees, and no concrete or asphalt anywhere.

"We'll arrive in a few minutes. Is there a particular shop you frequent?" Nicholas's voice pulled her from her wayward thoughts. He had put aside the papers and had his arms crossed on his chest, the flaps of his coat thrown back over his shoulders. The dark colors he wore only served to accent the silver in his hair, yet Jaci didn't think he was as old as the gray made him appear.

"How old are you?" The question popped out before she could stop herself, and he looked as surprised as she felt.

"You are very outspoken, for a female. Why do you want to know?" He returned her question with one of his own.

"Because the gray in your hair contradicts the youthful lines of your face. I don't think you're all that old."

"If that were a compliment, I thank you; I think." He smiled at her and her heart squeezed. Regardless in what century this man resided, he was devastatingly handsome. "To answer your question, I am thirty years of age. I dare say the gray is due to putting up with a rapscallion brother like Cameron and his pixy daughter, Amanda."

She had wondered about that relationship and why Amanda lived with an uncle, yet she had hesitated to ask. Now, as they pulled into the outskirts of Philadelphia, Nicholas answered her unspoken questions.

"I realize it doesn't appear quite the thing to have a young child, especially female, living alone with a bachelor uncle. Of course, that will change once I marry, but it doesn't explain the occurrences up to now."

"Of course." She didn't know he was going to marry. She started to wonder what would become of her when he did, but soon forgot her own plight as he told the sad story of Amanda's parents.

"My younger brother, Cameron James, married Sarah when he was only twenty-two; she only seventeen. Though both families begged them to wait, they would hear none of it for they were terribly in love."

He sounded so cynical, she couldn't help asking, "You don't believe in love, Mister Westbrooke?" Of course, she didn't, but often thought herself alone in that regard.

"Yes, Miss Eastman, I believe in love, but not the all-consuming love Sarah had for my brother. There is such a thing as loving someone too much." He paused and turned to look out the window. she wondered if perhaps he wished for that precious commodity, even as he said he didn't want it.

"Anyway, within a year of their marriage, Sarah gave birth to a daughter, Amanda. Though the child was born healthy, Sarah was too young, and the birth difficult. She bled to death." He said the last with such finality, Jaci shivered, thinking how backward medicine must be in this century.

"Cameron, of course, blamed himself for Sarah's death, and no force on earth could keep him at Wildwood, nor get him to take responsibility for a baby daughter. To allow him time to recover, I gave him control of the family shipping business. That was five years ago. He comes home, but not often. Amanda reminds him of Sarah, and it's very hard on him."

"But you would have only been twenty-five; too young for responsibility of that magnitude."

"As you so eloquently told me that day in the library, sometimes there's no time for frivolous activities. I had been managing Wildwood since I was twenty."

Nicholas began to pull on his gloves, and she realized the story had ended. It would seem they shared a common background. She wondered about his family; what kind of parents he had that shaped his personality even now. How strange for Nicholas to allow Cameron to wander the world while he raised his brother's daughter. As she continued to study the man across from her, she realized Amanda couldn't have been placed in better hands.

Nicholas was confident, strong, and had a good deal of responsibility on his shoulders. It appeared he had a sincere commitment to family for he saw to Amanda's needs and protected her, even though that responsibility should be his brother's. In fact, he provided her the same safety. She sighed, a longing for something more surfacing unbidden to her mind.

"Are you ready, Miss Eastman, or would you rather wait out here? I'll only be a moment at this first establishment." When he spoke, Jaci realized the carriage had stopped, and he had already alighted. She had no desire to stay outside in a strange town with no protection. She hurriedly gathered her skirts and scooted across the seat. This time, he held out a hand and she placed hers in the warmth of his gloved one.

"We must remember to buy you some gloves," he commented as he tucked her hand in the crook of his arm. He led her through a large wooden door into what appeared to be a furniture warehouse.

"Ah, Gustav, how are you?" Nicholas left her side to step forward, shaking the hand of an older, broad chested man.

"Wilkommen, Nicholas," the man answered in a heavy accent.

Nicholas turned and pulled her forward. "Miss Eastman, I would like you to meet a dear friend of mine, Gustav Dentzel. Perhaps you know of his work?"

"The cabinet and carousel maker, of course," she replied automatically, nodding at the introduction.

"Oh, my God, that's it!" she shouted as the connection sank in. Both men backed up in astonishment.

She grabbed the older man's arm and shook it. "Mister Dentzel, where are your carousels?" Her heart pounded and her palms became damp with the realization she could get back to her own time if she could find the carousel — the Dentzel carousel she had been photographing.

Nicholas, of course, didn't understand her agitation. "Miss Eastman, please." To his friend he added, "You'll have to excuse her, Gustav. She's newly arrived from the south, much excited to see the city. She tends to forget her manners." He slanted a meaningful glance toward her, but she ignored him. She was far too excited about getting back to Dallas.

45

"Ja, ja." Gustav nodded his head, apparently pleased with Jaci's interest in his animals. He pulled her by the hand, chattering in German as he led her to a workroom behind the front of the store.

Jaci quickly glanced back to see Nicholas following, a frown on his handsome face. She would miss him, she supposed, but the thought was fleeting. She had found her way home.

Scattered around the workroom in various stages of production were a menagerie of wooden animals. She squealed with delight as Gustav pulled her through the door. She jerked her hand free and raced to the first horse. Nothing happened.

She flitted from shape to shape, touching the horses but ignoring most of the other animals. Each time she touched one, she closed her eyes and held her breath, hoping that would be the horse to transport her back to Dallas and her own life. Each time she opened her eyes, she felt as though a great hand squeezed her throat, making it difficult to breath.

Her steps faltered and she stumbled, but grabbed her long skirts and continued on. There had to be at least one horse in this room that could recreate the magic she needed. She had to find the correct one and get back where she belonged.

She had no idea the strange sight she made; nor did she care. By the time she touched each and every animal several times, tears spiked her lashes. She stood dejected in the center of the workroom, sobs silently shaking her shoulders. When Nicholas touched her arm, she turned into him, burying her face in the soft wool of his coat.

His strong arms wrapped about her, but she could find no comfort there. She knew he couldn't comprehend her need. She felt him take a breath to ask, but she spoke first, her voice quivering.

"Don't you see? It was because of the carousel that I came through—" She glanced at Mister Dentzel, whose avid look told her he understood more than his broken English revealed.

"Remember the day I arrived at Wildwood? I was at a carousel, taking photographs." She knew she wasn't making any sense, especially since Nicholas didn't have any idea that she had come through time. "I had just touched the black—"

She turned sharply to Mister Dentzel. "Black; you have a black horse?" She swiveled around, frantically searching the horses again.

"Nein, nein." The woodcarver scooted in front of her, waving his hands in a negative gesture. "Gustav's horses are never black. We use only the pretty colors. Look." He grandly swept a hand toward the horses his workmen were completing. He was right, of course. She scanned the jumpers and steppers, but none of them were black.

Nicholas took her firmly by the arm. "Thank you, Gustav. I am sorry for any inconvenience we may have caused. You will have Amanda's chest finished by Christmas?"

"Yes, of course, Herr Westbrooke." Gustav bowed low as Nicholas led her out of the workroom.

She turned to speak, but Nicholas squeezed her elbow in warning.

"Miss Eastman. I would suggest you leave with me quietly." He spoke in a low voice. "Gustav is a good man, but he may be inclined to think you more than eccentric if you continue to barrage him with questions about some strange horse he does not have."

She hung her head in defeat. Once inside the carriage, she stared out the window, seeing nothing.

"Miss Eastman?" A pause. "Jaci?"

She turned.

"You can't return home on a wooden horse." His tone was light, and Jaci knew he thought to tease her out of her mood.

"Why not? That's how I got here." It didn't matter what she said; she didn't care what happened.

"Who are you?" This time his voice sounded hollow and haunted. Still, she didn't have the answer she knew he wanted.

"You can't possibly understand. I came from another century. I don't know why, or how, except that I'm sure the Dentzel carousel had something to do with it."

His voice turned brusque. "I believe you hit your head harder than Dr. Stillwell claimed. I probably shouldn't have brought you to town."

"It doesn't matter. He doesn't have the carousel horse I need." Totally defeated, she wanted to scream her outrage. She had been positive the horse would work.

An unsettled look crossed his features. "Perhaps I should take you to the doctor again. I'm normally an easygoing person, but you're spouting nonsense. I do not want you repeating this foolishness in front of Amanda. Do you understand?"

Jaci knew better than to argue. At present, she had no recourse but to accept his charity, and his dictates. It didn't take a genius to realize she was better off at Wildwood than in a mental hospital, if such institutions even existed in 1874.

She nodded in acceptance.

Nicholas reached behind him to a small door that opened to where the driver sat. "Take us back to Wildwood, Stephen. Miss Eastman has taken ill."

Chapter Four

Nicholas enjoyed routine and a reasonable certainty about what would happen each day. That was the way it had always been. The arrival of Miss Eastman at Wildwood had disrupted the normal flow of his life, and he wasn't sure he liked it.

After the incident at Gustav's, he became even more wary of her. When she had tearfully turned to him in the furniture shop, instead of feeling anger at her strange actions, his desire had steadily risen. She had soft curves which fit him perfectly, and she smelled extremely sweet and feminine.

All in that one suspended moment in time he had wanted to protect her from harm, fix whatever was wrong, and kiss her senseless. Such conflicting emotions had left him frustrated to the point where he had almost lost his temper in the carriage.

Perhaps he shouldn't have offered her the job as his niece's governess. He couldn't let his emotions cloud his thinking where Amanda's welfare was concerned, and Miss Eastman's presence definitely did that.

To assure himself he had chosen correctly, he kept a close eye on the governess. He noted her comings and goings, and everything she said to Amanda. As he observed her, he could see no evidence of a recurrence of her strange behavior. Each evening before Amanda went to bed he would sit her on his lap and question her about her day.

"What did the two of you do with yourselves today while I worked the horses?" he asked, knowing he should feel guilty. For Amanda's sake, however, he had to be sure of Miss Eastman's mental stability.

"Oh, Uncle Nicholas, Miss Eastman is the most marvelous person. We walked under the trees and she told me a story about why the leaves turn colors." Amanda snuggled deeper against his chest, and he hugged her tight.

"I will judge if you learned your lesson well. Tell me the story about the leaves."

Amanda squirmed around to see him better, her face animated. "You see, a very long time ago, when something died, it was put in the sky as a star picture. One picture is of an Indian hunter. I don't remember his name. Since he was a hunter he still had to hunt in the sky, you know, so a big bear was put up there, too. When the hunter shot the bear, the blood dripped down and turned the leaves red. And when the hunter cooked the bear, its fat splattered all over and turned other leaves yellow."

"Miss Eastman told you all that? I shall have to speak with her about telling you such lies."

"Oh, you can't do that. It's a—" She screwed up her face in thought. "I don't remember the word, but it's a story from long ago. It's not something that really happened, you see." She spoke with such sincerity Nicholas almost smiled. In the span of a few short weeks, she had apparently developed quite a fondness for Miss Eastman.

"I believe the word you want is legend, Muffin, and I'm glad you realize the story is pretend. We don't have Indians in the sky hunting bears anymore."

Amanda giggled. "I know that, but it does make the bestest story. Tomorrow I will have to find Toby and Travis and tell them."

Amanda yawned and snuggled closer, and he sat, content to hold her. It amazed him that Cameron didn't want a family. How could a person not long to share and converse with others, teach them values, and love them?

He recalled the love that had surrounded him and Cameron as they grew up. Even when he rebelled against his father and left home for awhile, his parents had supported his right to venture out on his own. Lately, he had often wished for his mother's presence; she would have been much better for Amanda than he.

Even with Amanda in his home, he longed for a family of his own. The Westbrooke name and thoroughbred

50

tradition must be considered, but he knew his desire stemmed more from the void that had developed close to his heart. The emptiness gnawed at him constantly, and was compounded today when he had received a message from Lycinda. She had begged off going to the Opera that very night. Though she pleaded a headache, Nicholas wondered if there were more to it.

Of late, he felt a hesitancy on her part whenever they conversed. He made a point of riding into the city often to see her because he didn't want her to feel neglected. Now, as he contemplated things, he couldn't envision Lycinda marrying him and being content to live out here at Wildwood.

He carried Amanda upstairs to bed and wondered idly if Miss Eastman was tucked in for the night. She had been rather stand-offish lately and seemed hesitant even to talk to him. He would have to find a way to draw her out, for he found he missed her smiles. Oddly enough, that brought his thoughts back to Lycinda.

He wasn't officially engaged to Lycinda Edwardson. Their families had known each other for years, and it had always been expected that the two of them would marry. Because of his parents' deaths and Cameron's disastrous marriage, Nicholas had never actually asked her, but neither had he told her he didn't want to marry her.

However unofficial his association with the Edwardson family, it still demanded he not act on the desire he had begun to feel for Jaci Eastman. Honor warred with desire and indecision, soon giving him a headache. He knew it would be inappropriate to focus his attention on Amanda's governess, but there was something inherently vulnerable and extremely desirable about her that drew him like a moth to a flame.

Nicholas rubbed his forehead, determined not to think any more about the women who lately were playing havoc with his life. It's no wonder he had hesitated all these years to marry.

* * *

Jaci stretched lazily towards the sun, amazed that this nice weather came their way as November crept quickly into December. As long as it remained unseasonably warm, she couldn't force herself or Amanda to remain inside. They had completed a little science experiment with shadows before she chased Amanda off to play and she had sought the shade of the side porch.

She breathed deeply of the clean, crisp air. Not a day passed when she didn't think of her sister, Mandy, and prayed for her welfare, but she had finally closed that chapter of her life. Though still adjusting to her new life in 1874, she realized her attitude had subtly changed. She had quit grieving.

Pleased that she now walked without tripping in her long skirts, she no longer hesitated when putting layer after layer of clothes on each morning. The lack of a shower still bothered her, but Molly never complained when she requested water for a daily bath. The most pleasant parts of any day were the meals where they ate wild things like quail and pheasant and venison which was shot in the woods on Wildwood property. She often visited with Delta as the old colored cook prepared scrumptious delights in what Jaci had once considered a very antique and backward kitchen. It amazed her that such light and fluffy bread came out of a wood burning stove.

At times, she knew the staff considered her a nuisance. Although she no longer tried to do anyone else's job, she did follow them around and ask questions about the estate. She wanted to learn everything, and she now considered Amanda, Mrs. Jeffrey, Delta, and the rest of the staff her family.

The only person she still had trouble with was Nicholas, because she couldn't determine how to act around him. Though technically his employee, he didn't treat her as such. Some days he appeared to regard her like family; say, Amanda's maiden aunt or some such thing.

Other days she would catch him staring at her, his eyes dark with passion and she knew he wanted to kiss her. While that confused her, it also made her ache with desire.

She shook her head to clear it, opening the newspaper in an effort to get her thoughts off her very handsome employer. She anxiously looked forward to the delivery of the newspaper and mail. Since she knew there would never be any letters for her, she was usually the first to latch onto the paper.

"Hmmm, at least I landed in the right era," she mused out loud as she scanned the latest news from Philadelphia. Labor reform for women and children was a hot topic, as was Temperance. The beginnings of Women's Rights must be right around the corner. She read a short article about Mrs. Annie Wittenmyer of Philadelphia, who was named president of the Women's Christian Temperance Union. The article reported the women hoped to achieve national temperance by holding demonstrations and through education.

"Yeah, right. Good luck on that one, ladies," Jaci chuckled, thinking of Carrie Nation and the many other women who had tried, unsuccessfully, to control the distribution and consumption of alcohol.

She started to close the paper when she spotted a notice that the Philadelphia Zoo had recently opened at Fairmount Park. If the weather continued to be this mild, perhaps a trip into the city was in order. The zoo would be a marvelous excuse for a field trip.

She realized how much she enjoyed teaching Amanda, and wondered if she should look into becoming a school teacher. That way if Nicholas ever got around to marrying, at least she would have a job. She frowned at the thought of leaving Wildwood.

"Miss Eastman, hurry! He's going to eat them!" Amanda's cry of anguish brought Jaci out of her chair and racing around the side of the house.

She scooted to a halt by the back door of the kitchen, clapping her hands to her mouth. She didn't think Amanda would appreciate her laughter. There, sitting in Sir

Lancelot's dog dish, were three tiny kittens, their eyes barely open. Their soft mews could barely be heard over the whines from the large Irish Setter, who lay close to the bowl. He didn't look the least bit ferocious, but rather intimidated by the tiny balls of fluff.

Amanda, however, hopped from foot to foot in agitation. Every time Jaci stepped sideways to see around her, she jumped right back in the way.

"Amanda, what in thunderation is the matter?" Nicholas appeared from the opposite direction and now stood beside Jaci.

"Help them, help them! Oh, Uncle Nicholas," Amanda wailed, flinging herself at Nicholas's knees, almost knocking him over. Jaci allowed a giggle to escape, for he looked almost as helpless as Sir Lancelot.

She knelt beside the dish, scooping the kittens one by one into her skirt. "I don't think Sir Lancelot intended to eat the kittens for lunch, sweetie." She smiled at the little girl who still clung to Nicholas' leg.

She thought how right Nicholas looked with Amanda, and wondered why he wasn't already married and a father. He patted her on the head, patiently listening and never raising his voice to her. Jaci, who had never considered herself maternal, ached with a feeling of closeness at the picture they made.

"What do you suggest we do in this situation, Miss Eastman?" Humor etched his words.

"You can't let him eat the kittens," Amanda cried again.

"Of course not." She still squatted on the ground, trying to balance squirming kittens in her lap and keep Sir Lancelot's nose away from them. He seemed to sense they talked about him, for he sidled up to her and nudged her on the arm. The movement tilted her balance just enough that she plopped onto the ground, kittens and all.

Nicholas started laughing until Jaci slanted him a glance. He quickly pinched his lips together, but humor still twinkled in his dark eyes making him look incredibly handsome.

"That's not very chivalrous of you, Mister Westbrooke." Even as she reprimanded him, she couldn't stop from laughing.

The twinkle remained as he answered. "You are right, Miss Eastman. Please, allow me to assist you." He untangled Amanda from around his knees and put out a hand. She allowed him to pull her to her feet. A tingle shot up her wrist where his hand, warm and callused, held her.

He must have felt it, too. As soon as she was safely on her feet, albeit still slightly unbalanced with the kittens collected in her skirts, he let go quite suddenly. They stared, her gaze caught in his for endless minutes.

"The kittens." Amanda jerked on her skirt, bringing her attention back to the situation at hand.

"Let's take the kittens down to the barn where they'll be safe. Then, we'll place Sir Lancelot's food dish where he can eat, but the kittens can't reach. Will that do?"

At Amanda's enthusiastic nod, they turned, leaving Nicholas standing alone.

"How does she do that?" He mumbled aloud as he watched her walk away, Amanda skipping merrily at her side. She had been sprawled on the ground in a most undignified fashion, laughing too loud for a proper lady, and yet she had his insides twisted in knots. If Amanda hadn't been there, he would have kissed her; on the lips; in broad daylight; right in the middle of the yard.

Instead of thinking about settling down with Lycinda and starting his own family, his thoughts more and more often had been on Jaci Eastman. An enigma in his world, somehow not quite fitting into the scheme of things, she made him wish there was a way to help her. He had hired her to watch after Amanda, and now he spent entirely too much time watching her.

* * *

Days later, Nicholas walked by the library on his way to the stables. Hearing voices, he peeked his head into what used to be his sanctuary. More recently, Miss Eastman had taken it over during the morning hours for Amanda's lessons. He watched unobtrusively as she spoke to Molly about a point of grammar. Molly replied politely and curtseyed before turning to leave. It was then both women saw Nicholas, and the look Jaci leveled on him made him feel like a spy in his own home.

"Is there something you need, Mister Westbrooke?" She used a tone of voice that made him think of his mother every time he had done something bad.

"Why did you speak to Molly like that?"

"What do you mean? I wasn't being disrespectful. She asked a question."

"Molly is to do her job. She doesn't require your regard. She is, after all, only a servant." He raised a brow to challenge her, and as he thought, she accepted.

"She's a human being. As such, she deserves our respect for doing her job, just as you or I would." She had risen from the chair by the fireplace and advanced toward him, head held high and hands on hips. Nicholas almost ducked his head in reproof.

"I'm glad you feel that way. Here at Wildwood I won't have an employee who doesn't feel the same." She looked as though she didn't believe him. He hurried through his contrived explanation. "After all, the war has been over for almost ten years, but there are those, especially from the south, who feel things should remain as they had always been."

She now stood directly in front of him, not the least bit cowed by his height or position in the household. She squared her shoulders for a fight, her green eyes flashing with anger. Nicholas thought her beautiful.

"Are you implying that being from Texas, I might be less than fair in my dealings with your employees, even though I happen to be one?"

"Of course not, but I have spoken to some acquaintances and it seems parts of Texas are less than civilized."

"That was a hundred years ago," she replied, then bit her lip as though she had espoused a government secret. Before he had time to question her comment, she went on the offense.

"Why are you always testing me, Mister Westbrooke? I've been here weeks, yet every time I turn around, you're questioning my methods with Amanda, my relationship with your staff, and my very manner."

"I do not," he defended himself.

"Oh? What about the time you stormed into the nursery when I was teaching Amanda her numbers?"

"You were using gaming cards."

"Cards have numbers on them, and learning games like solitaire make it easy to remember the number combinations. Did you honestly believe I would teach her to gamble?"

Nicholas knew she was right. It would be easy to say he was concerned for Amanda. Privately, however, he acknowledged it was his desire to be around her and to listen to her soft drawl, that prompted him to act like an ass. Her comments at Dentzel's shop still gave him pause, and the fact that she had appeared at Wildwood in a rather strange manner, with very peculiar clothes, showed she had a secret. Yet her care of Amanda, and more recent behavior, led him to suspect nothing untoward. Since it didn't appear she would willingly share any information about her past with him at this time, he would allow her privacy. Eventually though, he would discover what Jaci Eastman didn't want him to know. It was a challenge he couldn't resist.

"I apologize," he stated as he bowed low. "You are correct, and I stand before you contrite. I will cease spying on one condition." He grinned, and as expected, she returned his humor with a smile of her own.

"Of course, I might have known."

57

"You must go riding with me. I would enjoy showing you Wildwood, and for whatever reason, Mother Nature has smiled on us. For November, it remains very mild and without a lick of snow yet on the ground."

"I'm sorry, but I don't ride. It was one of those childhood pleasures I had to forgo." She gently rebuked him for the time he had brought up her lack of a proper childhood.

"Well, then, I must impose another condition." As he spoke, he took a step in her direction. She quickly backed up more than one step. Wary — that was good. One of them had to keep their wits about them, and whenever she was close, Nicholas couldn't be sure he was capable of doing so.

"Call me Nicholas. Every time you say Mister Westbrooke, I think of my father."

"I don't know as much about your society as I should," she spoke hesitatingly, "but I'm sure that wouldn't be proper. After all, I am a servant."

"A governess doesn't fall under that category, Miss Eastman. Try; it shouldn't be very difficult."

"I will agree to your condition if I may have one of my own," she stated matter-of-factly.

He raised a brow. "Oh?"

"If I am to call you Nicholas, you must call me Jaci. Miss Eastman makes me sound like an old school marm."

"But that is what you are." Sometimes she spoke circles around him, and his Harvard education did him no good at all.

She waved away his objections with one delicate hand. "Whatever. Do we have a deal?" She put out her hand. Shaking hands with a woman was a totally unique concept for Nicholas. He clasped her warm hand in his, squeezing lightly. She shook his hand and tried to pull away, but he wouldn't let go.

"Yes, I believe we do have a deal, Jaci." Before he released her hand, he bent low and placed a light kiss on the back side. He felt the slight quiver race through her warm skin, and wondered at her thoughts.

Nicholas considered himself a strong and independent man, and he had very particular notions as to how women should behave. They should be soft spoken and know their place. They were the weaker sex and it was a man's responsibility to protect them.

Jaci refuted all those ideas and yet he fell under her spell anyway. He wondered why as she nervously tried to remove her hand from his. He studied her pretty features, and felt the disguised strength in her arm.

Knowing he could ask no more of her today, he released her and she gathered her skirts to leave. As she slipped away from view, he caught a glimpse of her shoes — those same strange, boot-type shoes she had worn the day of her arrival.

* * *

Today was Saturday. Jaci sipped another cup of coffee in the kitchen, visiting with Delta, when Amanda burst in, feet and tongue both going a hundred miles an hour, as usual. Molly was supposed to be watching her because Saturday was Jaci's day off, but that never stopped Amanda from seeking her out. Besides, what did Jaci have to do on a day off, anyway?

"Mrs. Sullivan is here and you must see what she has. Trunks and trunks of the most marvelous stuff," Amanda practically shouted right in Jaci's ear as she scooted to a stop in front of her.

She had to grin at the child's incongruous use of the phrase marvelous stuff. For a five year old, she had an excellent grasp of the English language, probably from all the adults in the house talking to her all the time. Every once in a while, she would latch on to a word and use it in almost every sentence, sometimes regardless of whether it actually belonged there. Thus was the case for the word marvelous.

"Well, what is all this wonderful treasure, and who is Mrs. Sullivan?" She questioned with a smile, for Amanda's good humor was always contagious.

"Mrs. Sullivan is a seamstress from the city," Molly answered the question, having followed Amanda into the kitchen. "She says that Mister Westbrooke requested her presence to see to your wardrobe." Molly puckered her lips and fluttered her eyelashes, and Amanda burst out laughing. Jaci knew Molly teased, but was also implying there must be something going on between herself and the owner of Wildwood. Why else would he order clothes made for her?

She rose quickly from her seat. "I didn't ask for clothes, and I don't see that I need anything until I can afford it." She said this more for the servants' benefit than her own. She could use some dresses that fit better, but she didn't know how she would pay for them.

"You can't send her back. Uncle Nicholas wouldn't like it very much at all." Amanda pulled on her skirt trying to get her attention, but Jaci had already made up her mind.

"There are some things over which your uncle should have no say." Leaving Molly and Delta with their mouths hanging open and Amanda propped on the huge wooden table in the middle of the kitchen, Jaci left to find the master of the house and give him a piece of her mind.

* * *

Two hours later, she had been poked and pinched and measured and embarrassed until she could take no more. Amanda giggled in delight, sitting in the middle of the bed surrounded by yards of ribbon, satins and lace. Molly smugly helped with whatever Mrs. Sullivan requested of her.

Obviously, she had lost the argument with Nicholas and still fumed at his high handed attitude. She hadn't liked being called a responsibility, even if she was. And while he had refused to even discuss the cost, Jaci swore to herself she would pay back every cent. Now, as she surveyed the sea of colored cloth over every conceivable object in her room, she wondered how many years that would take.

"Honestly, Mrs. Sullivan, I don't need this many clothes." She tried to step down from the footstool, but the seamstress would not tolerate it.

"Nonsense, my dear. Every young lady needs at least this many and more." She had already measured Jaci and draped a variety of materials around her, trying for the right color combinations and trims. The pile of patterns she had chosen lay scattered at her feet.

The matronly woman had explained as she stripped Jaci to the bare essentials that her wardrobe would be made back in the shop because with the new sewing machines, it could be done in half the time of having Molly sew by hand. However, she had brought a few ready-mades with her, and after trying them first and making minor adjustments, handed them over to her assistant to alter on the spot.

"The more delicate undergarments, of course, will still be sewn by hand," Mrs. Sullivan assured her as she continued pinning fabric at her shoulders, "and the corsets, of course, will—"

"No corset!" Jaci hadn't won her argument with Nicholas, but surely she could overrule this woman.

"My dear, you have a well-developed bust, a tapering waist and large hips, all of which are points recognized as combining for a good figure. But it wouldn't hurt to enhance it with a good corset."

Jaci looked down at her body, what she could see of it. Exactly what did the woman mean — large hips?

"And besides, a postilion skirt just will not hang right without one."

She shook her head. "Post — what?"

"A bustle." Molly replied, secretively pointing to the hump which stuck out from Mrs. Sullivan's backside.

Jaci's eyes popped open and her mouth dropped. That was part of the dress? Here she thought poor Mrs. Sullivan had a gross deformity. Surely women didn't wear something like that on purpose.

"I haven't seen anyone with something that weird, er, a bustle, around here."

"Of course not. Servants have no need of formal clothes. Have you not been to the city at all?"

"Well, actually, no," she replied, but hurried on. "It doesn't make any difference. I'm a servant and I don't need a posti. . .a bustle any more than they do."

"But Mister Westbrooke said you should be dressed in style."

Jaci gritted her teeth to keep from telling these women what a chauvinistic pig she thought their employer. "Mrs. Sullivan, do you recall recent news items regarding the Women's Temperance League, and the new labor laws for women and children?" At the woman's nod, she continued, pointing a finger at her as though preaching from the highest pulpit. "In the not too distant future, you are going to see more changes in this society. Women will become doctors and lawyers and politicians; and they will vote in the elections. And best of all, they will not let some man decide what they are to wear!"

All the ladies in the room gasped at her remarks, and Jaci couldn't tell whether it was because of her unladylike outburst, or because of the information she had imparted. She didn't care; she wasn't going to torture herself with bindings.

"Nonsense," Mrs. Sullivan finally replied, shaking out a piece of trim and went about her work as though Jaci hadn't spoken at all.

She hoped she had gotten her point across, but to prevent any misunderstanding, she looked the seamstress right in the eye and said, "No corset; no bustle."

Apparently willing to allow her this small victory, Mrs. Sullivan was still out to win the war. She gathered up a variety of ribbons, feathers, flowers and sequins and turned to her. "Since you spend most of your time here in the country, I will concede the other, but you must allow me the trim. A good Sunday dress has at least fifty yards of trim."

It was too much; Jaci hung her head in defeat. Another two hours passed before Mrs. Sullivan felt vindicated enough to let Jaci dress. Her wardrobe now hosted several bright colored dresses, altered to fit. The rest, Mrs. Sullivan assured her, would arrive within a fortnight.

Jaci didn't even ask what that meant.

* * *

Nicholas strolled past the parlor door where Jaci and Amanda were in lessons. They laughed together over some silly thing Amanda said, and Nicholas felt jealous; left out in a way he had never felt before.

After their argument over her wardrobe, in which she insisted he take the cost out of her earnings and he insisted she accept the clothes with good grace, he had thought things would settle down. However, it appeared the two of them were only temporarily involved in an uneasy truce.

Jaci tried to stay out of his way. When they met by chance, she always had Amanda in tow and refused to converse with him. Nicholas longed for a way to convince her he meant no harm. He hadn't wanted to create such a scene over a thing as simple as clothes, for he was only doing his duty as a man by taking responsibility for her.

She proved as stubborn as he, and several days passed when he didn't see her at all. Days which proved entirely too long, and far too lonely, he thought, as he dined by himself at his very formal table.

In the past this never bothered him, for he usually had ledgers, stud books and lineage papers scattered about him on the huge table and worked as he ate. Knowing Jaci enjoyed dining with Amanda and the household staff rather than with him burned in his gut. Of course, it would have appeared inappropriate if he had asked her to join him, for although he considered her a lady, she was a member of his staff.

It pleased him greatly, therefore, when she followed him into his study to ask that Amanda begin taking her meals with him. If the child sat at table that meant her governess would have to sit there also, instead of hiding away in her room. Of course, it wouldn't do to let her know how much he favored the idea. She might decide against it if only to be contrary.

"A five year old child has no business sitting at table with adults." He loved to bait her, for her eyes sparked with defiance and her cheeks glowed with color.

"She must learn table manners, and what better way than to model the behavior of her elders."

He moved closer, for she smelled of springtime even though heavy frost had hit the meadows last eve. He watched her lips as she spoke and recalled the one time he had kissed her. It had begun more to calm her, though passion lay beneath the surface, and now he wondered what she would say if he kissed her again. "Are you saying I'm old?"

"You know that's not what I meant." Her blush grew brighter.

"Dinner is a place for adult conversation. Perhaps instead, you would care to join me?"

"I, well, that is…"

Nicholas thought he had pushed her too far when she gave a sigh and turned away. It appeared she needed only to collect her thoughts, for in a moment she turned back, her eyes once again full of fire.

"I will consent to dine with you, if Amanda can, also. The opportunity will be there for her to listen and learn from adult conversation. Besides, she adores you and doesn't see you except for riding lessons."

Now that was hitting below the belt, he thought, for he loved his niece, and wanted only what was best for her. To retaliate, he decided to see how far Miss Eastman was willing to go to obtain her desired objective.

"Are you, perhaps, afraid to spend time alone with me?" The question brought him closer.

"No, of course not." She took a step back, coming to a stop against the wall.

"Do you think I might take advantage of you?" He raised a hand to each side of her head, bracing them on the wall behind her and effectively blocking her escape.

"No, I'm sure you wouldn't do that. You're a gentlemen, after all." She said the words, but he didn't think she quite believed them. Her gaze darted all around, looking for a way out.

"Even a gentleman might be tempted," he breathed close to her temple, intoxicated by her essence. He turned his head a fraction and kissed the soft skin of her forehead. She trembled, but when a tumultuous sigh escaped, tickling his neck, it was his undoing.

One hand remained braced against the wall, holding him steady and slightly apart from her. The other gently tilted her chin. As he lowered his head, he caught the glint of passion in her eyes and smiled. Not a smile of spite, for he didn't want her on opposite sides from him. He smiled for joy that she shared some of the same feelings that had been tormenting him throughout the past months of her employment at Wildwood.

Her lips were as he remembered; hot and soft and sweet. He ached to move closer, but deliberately held himself back; keeping a very thin barrier of air between them, until she stepped away from the wall, wrapping her arms around his neck. He groaned, circling her waist and pulling her to him. Passion ignited quickly and he couldn't have said who started it; only that he didn't want it to end.

He slanted his mouth across hers; his tongue traced the softness of her lips. When his hands slid down to her buttocks to tighten his hold, she didn't pull away from the evidence of his passion. She didn't even gasp. Instead, she moved her hips in a subtle but erotic motion and Nicholas thought he would make love to her right there on the floor.

"Good God, how did you ever learn to do that?" He gasped the feverish words against her brow as he kissed his way to her ear.

"Do what?" Her breath tickled his neck. Her hands were at his shirt front, plucking at the buttons before he was even aware of what she was doing. Hot lips peppered his skin with kisses and a flash fire of passion exploded in his loins.

He pushed her back against the wall to maintain the pressure of his hips against hers, and to allow his hands more freedom. In a frenzy, he jerked at the buttons of her blouse, all the while kissing her with a force which alternately frightened and exulted him.

Never in his experience had he encountered such a giving, uninhibited creature. To have her respond to him in such a manner went beyond his wildest expectations. Though he had never tried to kiss Lycinda in such a manner, neither had she exhibited the desire to share passion with him.

Lycinda.

Like a gust of cold air, reality swept through Nicholas, effectively dousing his passion. He stepped away from Jaci and quickly turned his back.

In a voice more steady than his still rigid body should have allowed, he said, "Forgive me. That was unpardonable." He forced himself to stay turned, knowing if he looked into her eyes, he would kiss her again.

A hesitant sigh floated toward him. When she spoke, her voice sounded as strained as his own. "I don't understand the customs here, but you don't need to apologize for kissing me."

"It was much more than a kiss," he stated forcibly, "and would have gone even farther if—" He stopped, feeling guilty and afraid of saying the wrong thing.

She laughed hoarsely. "You're right, it was definitely more than a kiss. But the only unpardonable part was not finishing what you started."

Her comment shocked him, but when he jerked around, she had disappeared.

Chapter Five

If anyone had asked Jaci what she would miss by not living in the twenty-first century, she would never in her wildest imaginings have said sex. It had never seemed that important, but suddenly it became something she thought about more than pizza and popcorn and mystery movies on TV. Actually, she didn't even miss television.

"This is crazy," she sputtered as she paced the width of her room, frustrated and restless. She had refused to eat dinner with Nicholas last evening after their disastrous confrontation in the library. She had merely wanted to request he spend more time with Amanda, and she had ended up seducing him.

She recalled the hard contours of his body as he had pushed against her. Man, she hadn't felt that horny since high school, and even now the intense ache between her legs wouldn't abate.

She pressed her forehead against the cold window glass, staring into the pre-dawn. Night shadows were fading, and soon it would be time to start another day. If only she could relive the last one. Relive, or change? The question haunted her as she dug through the wardrobe in search of very specific clothes.

She had always tried to be honest, at least to herself, and Jaci knew without a doubt she would have liked nothing better than to have spent the night in abandoned lovemaking. Nicholas had kissed her with a great deal of enthusiasm, but she didn't know how he felt about her. Given her circumstances in this century, she wasn't at all sure she should start a relationship she had no intentions of being around to finish.

Still muttering to herself, she stealthily crept down the stairs, grabbed her wool cloak from the peg by the door and stepped out into the crisp morning air. As she trotted slowly around the side of the house toward the barn, she sincerely hoped no one else rose quite this early. She didn't know why she hadn't thought of this before. It would have relieved a lot of stress if she had kept to an exercise routine from the very beginning.

The well oiled door gave way beneath her hand and she stood on the threshold gazing at the huge indoor arena. She hadn't been out here before but Amanda had talk about where she had her riding lessons. Admittedly it made sense to have an indoor exercise ring considering the length and coldness of Pennsylvania winters.

Overhead, huge windows turned hazy pink as dawn slid across the land, and Jaci decided if she was going to run, she'd better get to it. She doubted many people would understand if they came across her dressed as she was now. Actually, probably only Nicholas would throw a fit, for he appeared to be a man with a touch of prudishness and a whole lot of honor.

She tossed her cloak over the railing and quickly unbuttoned her jeans, kicking them into a pile. She slid her hands down her Lycra covered thighs to touch her toes, then swiveled her shoulders from side to side to loosen unused muscles. The barn wasn't all that warm, so she decided to leave her sweatshirt on for a while. She giggled as she stretched, recalling how different it had felt to slide into her bra and tank top this morning.

Her old clothes now felt foreign next to her skin after lacing herself into a shift and undergarments and petticoats and shirtwaist and pinafore, all of which seemed a necessary part of the daily ritual of dressing. She had drawn the line at wearing a corset, although Mrs. Sullivan had insisted she be fitted for one to wear beneath her Sunday dress and other special clothes.

Jaci had also been informed if she dared appear at a dance without a corset she would never be considered a proper lady and all the men would take advantage. When she had asked Mrs. Sullivan exactly how the men would know if she wore one or not, the older lady had blushed red with embarrassment. It didn't matter one way or the other, she thought, as she climbed through the low railing and trotted along the dirt track. She still hoped she wouldn't be around for any fancy dress balls and Sunday outings.

Gradually, she built speed around the track. The brisk mustiness of the air inside the arena smelled good to her, and for once she didn't even miss the smog-tinged air of Dallas. She tried to brush all thoughts from her mind and concentrate on the steady rhythm of her feet on the track, knowing if she hit that invisible wall, she could run a long time and not worry about her present situation.

Nicholas stood in the shadows at the far end of the track, eyes narrowing as he watched Jaci slow to a trot and run in place as she jerked off her overlarge shirt and dropped it onto the pile of clothes by the post. He involuntarily sucked in his breath, very aware of the havoc she created in his body. He had intended to exercise Wind Dancer early this morning to take his mind off Jaci Eastman, but instead he stood there, feeling as guilty as a school boy peeking into a side show at the circus.

Lord, was she beautiful. Sleek and muscled like a race horse, she flew around the track. She wore the skimpiest of costumes; her glistening blue leggings cut off above the knee and skin tight; the white sleeveless camisole clinging to her curves like a second skin.

His groin throbbed in rhythm with the pounding of her footsteps; his hands itched to cup her breasts, which jiggled enticingly as she ran. She might as well be naked, he thought, his gaze feasting on her slim waist and tight buttocks as she ran past him and on around the track. The snug way her strange clothes fit — well, he understood why she didn't need a corset beneath her normal clothes.

He had chastised himself last night for taking advantage of her. For reasons which were still a mystery to him, she appeared unfamiliar with their customs and was much more forward than any female in his acquaintance. That forwardness, in some women, would rarely bother the men in his society, gentlemen or otherwise, and Nicholas was no different. It wouldn't have taken much for him to carry her upstairs to his bedroom. As it were, he had let a simple kiss get quite out of hand. He still hadn't decided what to do about Miss Eastman and his growing infatuation with her, and had decided an early morning ride would help him think.

Now that idea was shot to hell. He stepped further into the shadows as she rounded the curve yet again. She seemed oblivious to her surroundings, and he continued to observe her, by now past the guilt which should have averted his gaze.

He should be happy that his instincts had proven correct as Jaci dealt well with Amanda. It freed him to pursue his business. But lately, every time he traveled to Philadelphia, he searched for an excuse to take Jaci with him. That would not do, of course, since her primary reason for being there was to care for his niece. Then, because she couldn't go with him, he got rather irritated, frustrated, and generally disagreeable.

His mind became tangled with unrelated thoughts, excuses and misbegotten reasons for his actions. His body continued to throb, and he realized if he persisted in watching, he wouldn't be responsible for his actions. When he couldn't take any more of what he considered teasing, even though she had no notion of his presence, he stepped onto the track. When she came around the curve again, she couldn't help but see him.

Nicholas was surprised when she almost ran into him before stopping. It took a few seconds for her gaze to focus on his face, and he was aware of a gradual change — as though she just now came back to the present. She continued to trot in place for a few minutes, her breath ragged, her very skin quivering. He couldn't tear his eyes away.

"What on earth are you doing?" The question came out curt, but he decided it behooved him to act with authority, for his own sake as well as Jaci's. Otherwise, it was hard telling what he might do, he thought, as he watched her chest heave with exertion.

"Exercising." The single word bounced at him as she blew her breath upward, cooling her face and causing her bangs to wave.

"What?"

"Exercise isn't bad for you, you know."

"Exercise is a walk in the garden or a ride on a horse. It is not running around half naked and —" His voice squeaked as he watched her heaving breasts, barely covered by the scooped neck of the top she wore. "Miss Eastman, you are — sweating."

"Don't women in this century sweat, Nicholas?"

He ignored the familiar use of his name. He was too fascinated with the shimmer of her skin and the animal-like lust he was experiencing.

"Heavens, no. I mean, perhaps on the hottest days, they may perspire, but they truly try to prevent it." He watched as moisture trickled down her chest to disappear into the valley of her breasts.

She stepped closer. Her smell — musky, but definitely female — attacked his senses. "I'm sorry, Nicholas, that I came out here to exercise, dressed like this." Her voice dropped an octave, soft and seductive, but he paid more attention to her hand, which slid across her chest at the top of her thin camisole, creating a sheen across her entire upper torso.

He grabbed her arms and jerked her to him, crushing any further words with his kiss. Beneath her hot skin he felt her pulse throb. She was making him crazy, the thought fluttered across his mind and then was gone, leaving behind a hunger for more than her sweet kisses.

She returned his kiss with equal fervor, and that fact seeped through his dazed senses faster than if she had merely acquiesced. He recalled her abandon last night, and while he told himself he should take her to bed if only to prove a point, he wasn't clear as to what the point was. She had a power over him that no woman before had ever claimed, and that frightened him. He was used to a nice ordered life, and kept telling himself he didn't care for the way she constantly intruded on his thoughts.

Her fingers slid to the nape of his neck, gently massaging, before tangling her fingers in his hair. She opened her mouth and his reaction was immediate, deepening his kiss until he claimed her soul.

Regardless of the sensations coursing through his blood and firing his passion, Lycinda's image once again came to mind. At that moment, he hated himself for acting dishonorably. He jerked away from her, stepping back and immediately regretting the loss of contact. He averted his gaze from her heaving breasts for he longed to take her back in his arms. Damn her for bewitching me, he mentally cursed.

He turned his anger on Jaci for making him want her, and causing him to forget honor in order to partake of the glorious intervals of passion he had never known existed.

"No decent woman would dress like a local wh—" he couldn't force himself to say such a debasing word, even in anger, "—a tavern wench. Unless, of course, you want to be treated as one." She gasped at his words, but he didn't retract them.

"Look, Mister Westbrooke, I don't know why I'm here, but I refuse to give up my lifestyle just because I got thrown into your life."

She tried to get by him, but he reached out and grabbed her arm. The heat from her skin burned through him, momentarily melding them together. Slowly he raised his gaze to her face, only to see the fire of anger flashing from her eyes, not remorse or tears as he would have thought.

"No gentleman of your time would handle a lady in such a manner. Would he?" The insinuation in her words was clear.

"Are you a lady, Miss Eastman?"

"I've never tried to be a lady. I doubt seriously that I even want to be one," she snapped. Jerking her arm from his grasp, she hurried over to where her clothes lay in a pile.

The turmoil within Nicholas grew stronger as he watched her bend over and jab her long legs into trousers. Damn, she had him tied in knots, but regardless of the consequences, he had to get close to her one more time. He walked up behind her as she slid her large shirt over her head, momentarily blinding her to his approach. He gently pulled the bottom hem of the shirt down and her head popped out the top. Instead of releasing the material, he used it to pull her back against him. He tucked his chin over her shoulder to further pin her in place, whispering very close to her ear.

"Forgive me, sweet Jaci. You are lovely to the extreme, and I sometimes forget myself." Knowing that her closeness would only be torture for his own body, he released her and turned, once again becoming part of the shadows.

Jaci refused to cry. She had decided days ago that crying was a waste. It hadn't brought her mother back all those long years ago, and it wouldn't change her circumstances now. But, oh, she was mad.

Nicholas's words rang in her ears all the way back to the house. How dare he comment on her inadequacies as a lady. How dare he take advantage of her, kissing her senseless, yet getting mad at her simply because she had responded to him.

It was Saturday, so she needn't worry about talking in a civilized manner to the five year old Amanda. Instead, she sputtered the rest of the morning alone in her bedroom. She paced back and forth, only stopping to glower at herself in the mirror before storming off again. Gradually, though, she began to cool off, and tried to look at the situation in a more rational manner.

Lately, she had begun to feel like part of the family. Amanda, because of her age, loved her unconditionally, and it helped keep Jaci occupied and less frantic to know she had a job. Mrs. Jeffrey, the housekeeper, was always friendly, as were Delta and the twins, Toby and Travis.

Only Selkirk remained solemn and aloof, refusing to have a conversation no matter what she said to him. Well, it was his loss. She mentally patted herself on the back for trying.

She especially valued her time with Nicholas. They managed to get into quite lively discussions if he happened to catch her alone while Amanda napped. She avidly read the newspaper and, of course, took up the cause for women's rights that were beginning to take root in the cities. While she tried to confine her comments to the current state of affairs, sometimes she would slip and say something that only a person from the future would. The result, like the time she told Nicholas not to have a cow, was funny in retrospect, but took fancy talking at the time to make it believable.

She had thought they were becoming friends, and friends didn't slam each other the way he had this morning in the barn. His comments stung.

To tell the truth, there had never been any time in her life to truly be a woman. For all the years when Mandy was young, she had been too busy being mother and father, supporter and breadwinner. Did she even know how to be a woman — a lady — here in the nineteenth century? Things were so different. What if she tried, and he laughed? She gasped as she realized how much Nicholas's opinion mattered.

She dug through the closet, this time looking at the wardrobe Mrs. Sullivan had fashioned for her. Regardless of her protests, Nicholas had insisted she accept everything Mrs. Sullivan made. Now, as Jaci surveyed the rainbow array, she was glad.

She held up a silk stocking and recalled her days of pantyhose. Suddenly memories she had boxed away came bursting forth — Mandy at her first high school dance, Mandy going on her first job interview. Jaci hoped Mandy had learned all the important lessons of life she had tried to teach her; the lessons that would insure she survived on her own.

She rubbed the silk stocking against her cheek, deciding that stockings and garters were much more sexy. While she had never consciously thought about being feminine and frilly before, now desire to see approval in Nicholas's gaze prompted her to act.

"If Nicholas wants a lady, I'll give him one. Then we'll see how he reacts." She raised a stubborn chin as she rang for Molly.

The day flew while Molly tried to turn her into a lady. Amanda sat on Jaci's bed, happy to watch for awhile before she fell asleep.

"Miss Eastman, you don't got — don't have — any reason to worry about being a lady." Molly reassured her for the umpteenth time. "'Sides, there ain't — isn't — anyone here to impress except Mister Westbrooke, and he don't — doesn't —" Molly sighed, not even finishing her sentence.

Molly sat with Amanda quite often as Jaci gave grammar lessons, and was trying hard to improve herself. Sometimes it seemed an insurmountable task. Jaci knew exactly how she felt when it came to insurmountable.

"Mister Westbrooke doesn't what, Molly?"

"Well, he doesn't seem to care. After all, he's practically engaged to Miss Lycinda, and so what good will it do to catch his eye?"

Jaci started to deny wanting to catch Nicholas' eye, but decided to let the comment pass. She thought it strange how everyone kept referring to Lycinda, but never actually labeled her a fiancée. Were they going to marry, or was it some kind of game? And if so, on whose part?

"Practically engaged, Molly? Can you please explain that for me? After all, I wouldn't want to put my foot in my mouth tonight." When Molly had come upstairs to help Jaci, she had informed her that the Edwardsons would be at the table for dinner this very night. That, of course, had set Jaci's stomach quivering.

"Well, Miss, it seems the Edwardson and the Westbrooke families have been friends for longer than anyone can remember. That being the case, it was only natural that Mister Westbrooke and Miss Lycinda would marry."

"An arranged marriage? I didn't think they did that anymore." Jaci mused out loud.

"Well, of course, that's done; in the finest homes and families, that is." Molly appeared surprised at her comment.

"So, when is this magical wedding to take place?" What right did Nicholas have seducing her if he was going to marry another? She conveniently forgot that she had already known this fact when she threw herself at the man.

"That's the strange part," Molly whispered, as though she had a secret. Jaci lifted a brow in question and the maid continued. "It's been ten years since his parents died, and five since sweet Miss Sarah passed on. That's plenty of grieving time for a body, and yet he's made no move to marry the lady."

Lady. There was that magical word again. Aloud, she stated, "Perhaps he's waiting for the right moment to ask her."

Molly snorted. "The right moment. Tell me there ain't been no right moments in the last five years." She didn't bother to correct herself, but looked Jaci straight in the eye, her face serious. "I don't think he consciously wants to marry her. I think he likes it fine here with his horses and races and our sweet little angel, Amanda." Molly nodded her head as though to emphasize her words, and Jaci felt a tiny glimmer of hope.

Well, why not? If she was stuck in this century, she might as well enjoy herself. At the moment, that meant finding a way to make an impression on the master of the estate, Nicholas Westbrooke.

"I think Miss Eastman should marry Uncle Nicholas." Amanda's voice surprised both women and Jaci turned to the bed.

"Oh, dear." She wondered how much Amanda had overheard.

"Sweetie, your uncle is going to marry Miss Edwardson." She brushed at the girl's wayward curls.

"No." The five year old shook her head and stated the single word as though even the heavens listened to her.

Jaci smiled. "And why not?"

"Uncle Nicholas looks at you funny, like he does his horses. He looks at Miss Edwardson different; like squash for supper." As with most children, Amanda spoke the truth as she saw it, regardless of feelings and attitudes. Five year olds didn't usually display tact.

Molly burst into laughter and slipped out the door, leaving Jaci to find a way to change the subject.

"Your uncle will decide who he wants to marry, no matter what you think. We'd best let the subject drop."

"But Miss Eastman," she protested, "why don't you want to marry Uncle Nicholas? You would be the bestest wife. You're funny, and you help a lot around here, and I love you."

Jaci knew it made perfect sense to Amanda, which made it more difficult to argue against.

"Honey, I love you, too, but the two people getting married have to be in love. That's what counts."

"Don't you love Uncle Nicholas?" Amanda pleaded with her eyes and her voice and Jaci would have loved to contemplate that particular notion. She simply could not.

"Please. He's handsome, and strong, and he has lots of money."

Jaci laughed, releasing the tension. "I appreciate all those virtues, but—"

"He must be a good kisser, too. I saw you kissing him the oth—"

"Amanda Westbrooke!" Jaci's cheeks burned at the thought she had been spied on. But looking at Amanda's innocent face, she realized the girl was being honest in a way adults feared. She said what she thought, not what others thought she should say.

She decided it best to change the subject. "If you want to eat dinner with the grown-ups tonight, you had best go have Molly help you change. It wouldn't do for you to be late."

"I really get to eat at the big table?" Her attention effectively caught elsewhere, Amanda scooted off the bed and raced out the door.

Jaci breathed a sigh of relief, or was it trepidation, for the events of the evening yet to come?

Later, she entered the parlor, surprised to find it empty. Apparently Nicholas's guests were late arriving. She walked to the windows, taking the time alone to compose herself.

She ran a nervous hand down the front of her dark green, velvet dress, hoping she had chosen correctly for this dinner occasion. The silk of her underthings whispered as she walked, and she felt totally decadent with lace garters tying her silk stockings just above her knees.

Molly had assured her she looked beautiful, and Amanda called her "totally awesome." Jaci mentally flinched, hoping the phrase Amanda had picked up from her wouldn't be repeated around Nicholas.

The thought of him brought her right back to the conversation which had taken place while Molly and Amanda helped her dress. What difference did it make, she asked herself, who Nicholas married? She wouldn't be around to see it.

She gasped softly as she glanced out the window, all thoughts of Nicholas fleeing. The ground was covered with glistening white snow; huge, wet flakes continued to float downward in an ever increasing storm.

"Penny for your thoughts," Nicholas said from the doorway.

"We don't have snow in Dallas," she replied without thinking, "at least not like this." She turned to smile at him. She gasped again as she took in his appearance.

Dressed in formal black attire, he appeared as the devil himself, wickedly handsome and deadly as sin. He had slicked his hair back in a queue, but it refused to obey and a wave curled over his brow. He sauntered into the room like the king of England, and she repressed the impulse to curtsey.

"Does this look all right to you?" He questioned as he tugged on the cuffs of his white shirt, barely visible beneath the cut of his vest and coat.

"All right?" He was much more than all right. Jaci let her gaze drift down the length of him and back up.

"Yes; you know." Nicholas waved his hands up and down, encompassing his clothes. "Damn, I hate dress up affairs. I don't know why I even suggested it."

A frown marred the sculpted planes of his face and she longed to smooth away the lines with a kiss. Instead, she settled for a light touch to his bow tie and a brush of her hands across his shoulders, as though straightening that last little bit.

It worked; the frown replaced by a smile which made Jaci hold her breath in wonder. Could anyone be more charming and...more out of her league than this man? She turned back to the window.

"You speak of Dallas as though it were the garden spot of the entire world. From what I hear, Texas is a heathen country full of Indians, wild cattle, and wilderness." Nicholas poured himself a brandy as he spoke. "Would you care for a drink?"

She shook her head, squaring her shoulders for a fight. If there was one thing in the world she would defend, it was her birthright as a Texan. "Texas is far from heathen, sir, though she did have a hard fight for independence. But as part of the United States, you have no right to speak of her so."

Nicholas tilted his head and gave her a strange look and she swore she was trapped. He then smiled and lifted his glass in salute. "Though Texas might be rough and tumble, she breeds the most beautiful and spirited of ladies. For that reason alone, I retract my disloyal comments." He took a sip of his drink before meeting her gaze with a quite serious look. "If you insist on returning to your city of Dallas, I will finance your trip and ask no more of you."

Jaci stood in silence, daring for one moment to believe she heard a wistful note in his voice. When his words registered, she had only one answer.

"I appreciate your offer, Nicholas, but no thanks. There's nothing in Dallas for me yet."

"Yet?" A frown creased his forehead.

"At this time," she hurried to correct herself. When would she quit making stupid mistakes?

Chapter Six

"Mr. Mason Edwardson and his daughter, Miss Lycinda," Selkirk intoned from the doorway, and the moment with Jaci vanished.

Nicholas would have liked a few more minutes with her before their guests arrived. He had an innate feeling she had made a slip of the tongue when they spoke of her origins, but he couldn't quite figure it out. He only recognized the flash of anxiety which crossed her face before Selkirk interrupted. With a sigh, he pasted on a smile and strolled toward his guests.

"Lycinda, it's always a pleasure when you grace my home." He lifted her hand and placed a kiss on the back. "Mason, good of you to come." He shook the older gentleman's hand.

Lycinda smiled demurely and swept him a curtsey. Always the lady, Nicholas thought idly before he glanced towards Jaci. She must have mistook his look, for she scurried towards the door.

"I'll leave you to your guests, Mr. Westbrooke." She whipped past him and he almost missed snagging her wrist to keep her from leaving.

"Oh, no, you don't," he whispered before adding aloud, "Nonsense, Miss Eastman. You must stay and allow me to introduce you." He tightened his grip as she tried unsuccessfully to get away.

"By all means, young lady, don't deprive us of your lovely company." Thomas Stillwell added from the doorway as he handed his coat to Selkirk and joined the group.

"Thomas, I didn't think you would make it." Nicholas greeted the doctor with enthusiasm. Perhaps things would remain manageable now. Even though they were close to the same age, Thomas had always been much more the social creature than Nicholas. "What happened to that assembly you planned to attend?"

"Alas, the Women's Christian Temperance Union decided not to allow any men at their meeting. Imagine! And with the outspoken Mrs. Annie Wittenmyer as their President, I fear we shall see all sorts of drastic measures being taken against the evils of liquor." Thomas finished with a flourish.

"She would be right to do so," Jaci spoke up, and then looked shocked that she had voiced her thoughts out loud.

Nicholas grinned and shook his head, adding outspoken to her list of attributes. Recalling his manners, he finished the introductions.

"I'm sorry, Miss Eastman. I was in the midst of introducing you. You remember Dr. Stillwell?" Nicholas nodded in Thomas's direction.

Thomas bowed slightly. "Very nice to see you up and around, Miss Eastman. You had us quite worried for a while."

Damn, Nicholas thought, not consciously wanting Lycinda or her father to know Jaci had been here for any length of time, or that she was anything other than a governess. He hurried on before Thomas said anything else.

"Mason, Lycinda, I would like you to meet Miss Jaci Eastman, Amanda's new governess." Lycinda's eyes widened slightly before she shuttered her gaze, but Mason openly scrutinized Jaci from head to toe, and back, like the vulture he was. Nicholas almost wished he had allowed her to leave when she wanted.

"I must compliment you on your taste, Nicholas." Mason managed to keep his voice low, but leered in Jaci's direction. "At least you thought to hire a young one this time." The older man's insinuations galled Nicholas, but he refused to be baited.

"Yes, she is very young, indeed," Lycinda added and Nicholas thought he heard a note of envy. Though Lycinda was truly lovely at the age of twenty-nine, Nicholas knew she worried about being considered on the shelf.

"Good evening, Mr. Edwardson. It's a pleasure to meet you. Miss Edwardson, you're spoken of quite — often — here at Wildwood." Jaci's soft drawl cast a spell over Nicholas, but he wondered at her words. How much did she know about his relationship with Lycinda?

"Can I get anyone a drink?" He moved towards the decanters set against the wall. Even if no one else wanted one, he needed a refresher.

"Thanks, my boy. I certainly need one. The roads are becoming quite a mess; took twice the time to get here. Don't see why you can't move to town and let your manager handle things here. Too damn far for my girl to have to go to see her intended, and it'll be too far later—"

"Papa, please." Lycinda interrupted her father's rather blunt remarks.

Nicholas felt his face and neck warm with embarrassment. In addition to being short, squat and balding, Mason Edwardson was an obnoxious bore. However, he was also the only banker who had enough clout to be able to help Wildwood in the days when his father had been financially unstable.

Even now, the man held notes on Wildwood, which Nicholas had used as collateral for Cameron's shipping venture five years ago. The spring races and yearling sale would clear his indebtedness, but until that time, Nicholas knew better than to alienate the man. Even so, his comments didn't rest easy.

He handed Mason a snifter of brandy, filled well past the half way mark. The banker became more tolerable only when he was sotted, so Nicholas might as well see to it. He then passed a stemmed glass of sherry to Lycinda.

"Miss Eastman?" he asked, even though he knew the answer before she spoke.

"No, thank you." She gave him a smile but her tone cut like a knife. When he glanced her way, he realized she understood all the references perfectly well. What a cad she must think him, taking advantage of her when he was intended for another.

"Perhaps Miss Eastman has other things to attend to — such as Amanda. That is what she's paid to do, is it not?" Lycinda's voice held a cattiness that surprised Nicholas.

"You are right." Jaci replied, a mischief-making twinkle in her eye. "But you will be delighted to know Mister Westbrooke has given permission for Amanda to dine with the adults tonight. As her governess, I must be present, also."

He glanced from one woman to the other. "Perhaps tonight wouldn't be the best time to start Amanda's lessons."

"Of course it would. What better way to learn than from several older people conversing." Jaci's gaze included all the occupants in the room, but lingered on Lycinda. She swept past him on the way to collect Amanda, leaving Lycinda open-mouthed and Thomas choking on his brandy.

"I never thought to see a cat fight at a horse breeder's," Thomas chuckled quietly behind Nicholas. When he turned to his friend, Thomas added softly. "I like a woman with spirit, and it appears Miss Eastman has quite a bit of it. I'm glad you kept her on as Amanda's governess. It will give me an excuse to come out more often." He lifted his glass in mock salute and Nicholas ground his teeth.

"Since when did you need an excuse to womanize, Thomas?" Nicholas questioned, hoping any sound of jealousy was covered in sarcasm. They had both done a fair share of skirt chasing in their younger years, until Nicholas had been jerked to an abrupt halt when his parents died and he inherited Wildwood.

He would have to warn Jaci about Thomas Stillwell, he thought. Only because she was his responsibility, he added to convince himself. He also knew full well he would eventually have to straighten out any mess caused by having Jaci in his house. From the sounds of Thomas's obvious humor and the looks exchanged by the two women, at least it would make dinner entertaining. Anything was better than listening to Mason complain about having to foreclose on another farmer.

* * *

Nicholas confessed to a slight disappointment, for both Lycinda and Jaci decided to behave and the meal was relatively uneventful. At least from all outward appearances.

Amanda had politely introduced herself and followed all the proper etiquette; speaking when spoken to, using the proper utensil, and not talking with her mouth full. Nicholas was pleased that Jaci had requested the child's presence, for Amanda glowed with happiness when Thomas asked her a question. At the moment, she was sharing her tale of Sir Lancelot and the kittens, to which Thomas laughed with encouragement.

Thomas seemed quite in his element entertaining all the ladies. It appeared his friend's gaze lingered overlong on Jaci whenever he answered a question she posed about his medical practice. And Jaci seemed to be asking a lot of questions.

He scrutinized his friend. What was it about the fair haired doctor that women found appealing? Was Jaci attracted to Thomas, or was she merely being polite? He scowled.

Since no one needed his guidance as host to keep the conversation flowing, he blocked it out and focused on the two lovely women who graced his dinner table.

There was a wholesome quality to Jaci that made her skin glow and her eyes sparkle with mischief. Her lush curves, though, had been created by the devil himself, enough to send any man's soul plummeting over the edge of control and desire. Her blonde hair was in direct contrast to Lycinda's dark curls.

She argued with him and had very outspoken ideas about Amanda's education; all of which did not lend themselves to being attributes of a fashionable young lady. She was anything but retiring, Nicholas thought, as Jaci laughed out loud at some remark Thomas made.

85

Yet every time she put her fork to her mouth, Nicholas swallowed convulsively, recalling the taste of her when they had kissed. Her dress, though demure, didn't conceal enough of her to make him quit thinking about the scene in the barn, her breasts heaving with exertion, glistening with sweat.

How in the world was he supposed to forget that she existed?

He would have to spend more time outside the house, or she would have to keep to the nursery. Either solution would not get her out of his mind.

His gaze moved to Lycinda, who also hung avidly on Thomas's every word, although she shot him a shy smile when she glanced up and caught him watching her. Her mother had raised her to be the ideal wife for a gentleman of his caliber. She was soft-spoken and retiring, and would never consider raising her voice to her husband.

Lycinda had competently run the Edwardson's home since her mother died ten years before, and he knew she had all the skills necessary for a lady of the manor. He found her attractive enough; petite in stature with dark hair and eyes. Her coloring would combine with his own to make beautiful children. Nicholas ached for a family and children of his own. So why had he become hesitant to proclaim himself and finally ask for her hand in marriage? Why did his groin ache with the memory of a single kiss shared with Jaci, and yet he could conjure up no similar feelings at the thought of making love to Lycinda.

It makes no difference, he told himself. Marriages were made for business reasons every day, and his would be no different. He must marry soon for the sake of Westbrooke tradition, since it appeared Cameron would never remarry. He was comfortable with Lycinda, and they had been friends for a long time. It seemed a reasonable enough basis to begin a marriage.

That reasoning, however, didn't eliminate the acute feeling of disappointment he experienced when Jaci excused herself and Amanda and told their guests good night. It took Thomas sliding his chair back to stand before

Nicholas broke from his musings. He jerked upright as Jaci stood.

"Good night, Uncle Nicholas. Thank you so much for a lovely evening." The five year old tried to sound grown up, but ruined the effect by grabbing his leg in a hug.

"If you will excuse me for a moment." Nicholas nodded to his guests as he scooped her up and kissed her cheek. He walked out the door of the dining room and over to the stairs.

"Thank you for coming to dine, Miss Westbrooke. It would please me immensely if you would share your company with me more often." He tried to remain solemn as he spoke to the now wiggling bundle in his arms.

Amanda giggled. "Oh, Uncle Nicholas, you sound funny." She hugged his neck and gave him a wet kiss. As he set her down on the first step, she asked, "Doesn't Miss Eastman look beautiful tonight?"

Nicholas turned to where Jaci had come up behind them. "Yes," he softly answered, his gaze capturing Jaci's. "Miss Eastman is by far the loveliest woman I know."

Her cheeks glowed pink with embarrassment and her lips were pursed as she tried not to smile, but the sparkle of her eyes gave her away. God, he wanted to kiss her.

"Nicholas, what do you say to a table of whist?" Thomas popped his head out the door to interrupt the moment.

Nicholas considered asking Jaci to join them, but knew it would not appear at all proper. Still, he hesitated before answering, trying to convey his feelings to her without speaking. She dropped her own gaze to the floor before he could read her intent.

"Yes, I'll be right there. Tell Selkirk we'll retire to the parlor for coffee. I believe he has a fire going." He gave Amanda one more kiss before he turned away. As he walked toward the parlor, the soft rustle of Jaci's dress and petticoats mixed with Amanda's chatter.

* * *

87

Jaci rushed up the stairs with Amanda, thinking she would die from heat stroke if she didn't get away from Nicholas. For a brief moment at the foot of the stairs, his look of seduction had seared her, and she had held her breath in dread — or anticipation?

When she thought back on the entire evening, she had been aware of his constant scrutiny, and although she had tried to ignore it, she had found herself glancing his way more and more as the meal progressed. His dark, almost brooding, gaze had shocked her with its intensity, making her recall the times when they had crossed the boundaries of employer-employee.

Only that morning, when she had exercised in the barn, she had become fully aware of his desire for her, and her body had reacted similarly. Regardless of what he had said about her not being a lady, his gaze told her that he wanted her.

The scary part about it — she wouldn't have stopped his advances. From what she read in his dark gaze, she had no doubt she would have gotten much more than she anticipated.

Amanda chatted gaily while Jaci readied her for bed, but she paid scant attention to the child's words until Lycinda Edwardson's name came up. From the very beginning, she had felt a stab of jealousy at her appearance in Nicholas's home. The gorgeous woman was tiny and dark-haired, and she reminded Jaci of a Barbie doll.

Jaci tucked a sleepy Amanda into bed, kissed her good night, and quietly closed her door. She kept reliving the meal, where the lovely Lycinda had eaten daintily, spoken only when spoken to, and smiled oh, so sweetly.

Damn, she swore silently, pulling her skirts up to keep from tripping as she stormed down the hall. She'd never get used to walking in these long dresses; would never begin to understand the customs that ruled the way nineteenth century women behaved and thought. Miss Edwardson, however, had no such problem and stood ready and able to do all that and more as Nicholas's bride. Jaci had seen how the woman gazed all sappy-eyed at him.

"Augh," she sputtered out loud, jerking the pins out of her hair as she stomped to her own room. "What did you expect?" she asked her mirror reflection. "You don't belong here, no matter who thought it a great joke to put you here. So you might as well face facts. Nicholas will marry Lycinda and she will live at Wildwood, no doubt tossing you out on your butt."

At the thought of leaving Wildwood, Jaci dropped to the vanity seat in tears. She had come to care for the residents of Wildwood. She had even learned how to relax and enjoy the slower pace of this century compared to the hectic life she had lived. It still amazed her sometimes that if something wasn't accomplished right on time, it was shrugged off and done later. After all, there are only so many hours in the day, Mrs. Jeffrey had recently said. And while Jaci had told herself that throughout her life, she had never been able to live by the credo. There had always been something that needed done.

As she struggled out of her dress and into her nightgown, she admitted that all her reasons for not wanting to leave Wildwood didn't have to do with the pace of living nor the staff. Amanda had become very dear to her; as had the child's uncle.

She used tongs to take several glowing coals from the fire and drop them into the long handled warming pan. She carefully walked the hot pan over to the bed and swept it back and forth over the sheets and coverlet to take away the chill.

She recalled how she had shivered each night when she climbed into bed before finally asking Molly for an electric blanket. That had certainly raised some questions. After a faltering explanation and some quickly conceived fantasy about the term because she had lived in the south, Molly told Jaci for the second time she was living in the wrong century. Of course, there wasn't any argument in that statement.

Recalling the story soothed her fears and as she snuggled beneath the mound of covers, she gave a sigh of resignation. There wasn't a whole lot she could do about the future — Lycinda's, or her own. The most she could hope for was that Nicholas would allow her to stay at Wildwood with Amanda after he married. She knew no other place in this world; no other way to sustain herself.

She drifted off to sleep, warmed by the fire. In her dreams, Nicholas did ask her to stay at Wildwood, but when she tried to recall the dream the next morning, it quickly dissipated. Had he wanted her as Amanda's governess, or in a totally different capacity? Her stomach lurched as all the possibilities crossed her mind, but at least for the time being, it gave her a feeling of belonging. She rose to greet the new day with more confidence.

* * *

Confidence which lasted only until breakfast, where Nicholas informed her, in no uncertain terms, that she would learn to ride a horse.

"I told you I didn't ride, and personally I don't care to learn." She stubbornly set her chin and drank her coffee.

"I can't believe you never learned to ride a horse. Everyone, man or woman, must know how to ride to survive."

"Not if you drove a Corsica," she mumbled under her breath.

"What did you say?"

She ducked her head, thinking fast. "I said I rode in a carriage."

"That's all fine and good, but it won't do. Everyone at Wildwood rides," he stated firmly. She turned to argue the point, but he continued. "Part of Amanda's education is learning to ride. As I believe we have already established, Miss Eastman, where Amanda goes, so goes her governess."

She scowled at him, but he went blithely on. "As long as you must be with her, you might as well ride. Besides, her instructor is quite capable of handling two pupils at once."

"And just who is Amanda's riding instructor?"

"Why, Uncle Nicholas, of course." Amanda clomped into the room, already dressed to ride. "No one can ride as best as him."

"As well as he," Jaci corrected automatically.

"Thank you. I'm glad you agree." Nicholas grinned at her remarks, knowing full well what she had intended. "Now Amanda, if you will take your governess up and get her clothes changed, I shall meet you both at the arena in fifteen minutes." He left no room to argue, turning on his heel and leaving Jaci with her mouth open.

Flabbergasted, she allowed Amanda to lead her upstairs, but when she chose a long dress with all the accompanying petticoats, Jaci drew the line.

"No, I think this will suffice." At the time Mrs. Sullivan made her clothes, no thought had been given to a riding habit. For now, she drew on a dark, chocolate colored dress with only one petticoat beneath, all the while thinking there was entirely too much material to allow her to climb on a horse. She knew her jeans, carefully hidden in the bottom of the armoire, would be more comfortable, but totally inappropriate for this venture.

With a sigh and some trepidation, she and Amanda walked to the arena. She dreaded getting up on some huge beast over which she had no control. All at once, an image streaked across her mind of the carousel horses — so well carved as to look real. Perhaps this was a test. She hadn't thought of it before, but maybe she needed a real horse to take her back in time, instead of a wooden one. That put an entirely different light on the activity, and Jaci's footsteps picked up considerably.

A nerve rattling hour later, Jaci didn't think she had the patience to stay atop this animal long enough to find out if it could return her to Dallas. The groom had helped her mount before disappearing, and Nicholas seemed more intent on instructing Amanda. He assumed she would follow along, but words like posting and collect the horse didn't mean anything to her.

In addition, the groom had given her a broken saddle. She had swung her leg over the saddle and finally straightened her skirts about her, only to find there wasn't a loop of any kind on the right side for her foot.

Nicholas finally decided she deserved some attention, and walked his magnificent black horse, Wind Dancer, over to her side. "Miss Eastman, you seem ill at ease."

"You might say that. I told you I didn't ride," She ground out the words as she gripped the horn at the front of the saddle and clutched the reins.

"It might help if you relaxed."

"Tell that to the horse. If it wouldn't keep fidgeting and bouncing around, maybe I could." As though the animal knew her thoughts, he sidestepped and pranced, bouncing against Nicholas's horse.

"Whoa, Sabet, whoa now," Nicholas spoke softly to the horse, reaching over to take the reins. Jaci quickly let go, glad to be done with it, but he wasn't done with her.

"No, you don't." Before she realized his intent, he swung a leg over his own horse and hopped on behind her. The horse fidgeted and snorted, but the minute Nicholas spoke again, it came to a complete and utter stop. Jaci still didn't release the horn.

"The horse can tell if you're afraid, so the first thing you must do is relax." His breath whispered against her ear, and she wondered how she could possibly relax with him that close to her. His arms came around her to handle the reins, one forearm brushing lightly against her breast.

"Then, you must—" he paused, his legs sliding forward slightly to bump her own. "Are you riding astride?" As though in disbelief, his right hand slid down her dress, squeezing and probing her leg.

She had thought there enough material in the dress to insulate every part of her body, but when his hand touched her, she felt the heat from his fingers. She jerked her leg, accidentally kicking the horse and again it jumped sideways. Nicholas immediately clutched her waist to keep her steady, and that was worse than his hand on her leg.

She stiffened an already straight spine, which brought her back in contact with his chest. She groaned; he chuckled in her ear.

"Miss Eastman, would you please relax and sit still for a moment?"

She gave a negative shake of her head. His nearness had her so unnerved she couldn't breathe, much less answer.

He chuckled again. "As lovely as I find you, and as much as I would love to kiss these delicate pink ears of yours, the back of a horse isn't exactly my choice for a rendezvous." Even as he said one thing, he did the exact opposite, his tongue flicking out to tickle the back lobe of her ear.

She groaned. In an involuntary movement, she wiggled her bottom back in the saddle. Her action brought her up tight against him and he reacted instinctively by scooting back. The horse apparently didn't like what either passenger was doing, and pranced forward. That left no horse beneath Nicholas and he tumbled off the back, fortunately letting go of Jaci when he did so.

"Oh, no." Still clutching the pommel, she swiveled this way and that, trying to see behind her to where he had fallen. The horse complied with her efforts and turned around, dropping his head to nuzzle Nicholas, who sat in the dirt.

Jaci tried to swing a leg over the saddle, wanting to get down and help him, but he held up a hand to stop her.

"Don't even attempt to dismount, Miss Eastman," he said with some chagrin. "You and your damned skirts would no doubt cause poor Sabet to bolt and run right straight over me."

She cringed. She liked it much better when he called her Jaci.

He picked himself up and dusted off his riding breeches, shaking his head in disbelief. Amanda, who had apparently felt left out of the skirmish, trotted her pony over to where they stood. "Are you all right, Uncle Nicholas? I don't think I've ever seen you thrown from a horse before."

He scowled. "I wasn't thrown. Miss Eastman pushed me."

Jaci sputtered. "I did not!"

"Yes, you did, and that's the end of it." He stood, hands on hips, like a petulant child, and regardless of his tone, Jaci laughed.

Amanda joined in the merriment. Jaci shook her head as she gazed down on him and laughed harder, tears escaping for no real reason. It just felt good to laugh.

She saw Nicholas wink at Amanda as he laughed, and she knew he wasn't mad at her. She started slightly when he reached for her, until she realized he intended to help her down from the horse. This was complicated somewhat from the fact that she didn't have both legs on the same side, as she now realized she should have.

Together, they stumbled before he righted her, his hands firm on her waist. "Miss Eastman, if you are always this clumsy, how on earth do you hope to teach Amanda the social graces?"

"I am not—" she started to argue before she glanced up and saw the twinkle in his eyes. She gave a sigh of pleasure; the release of pressure, both mental and physical, leaving her feeling exhilarating.

"It's because the horse has four feet. I can run quite well on my own two feet," she said without thinking.

Nicholas's hands tightened on her waist, and she remembered the one time he had seen her running. Then, as now, the tension between them had been a palatable force. Her eyes widened as she studied him, not sure how he would respond.

He stared at her for a moment, almost as though seeing something else. He cleared his throat and released her, gathering the reins of Sabet and Amanda's pony, Flower.

"Yes; well..." He stared off in space for another minute. "You won't have to worry about either my interrupting your run, or another riding lesson for a few days, anyway."

She felt acute disappointment at his words. While she preferred not riding, she liked his company.

"I must travel into the city on business, in preparation for the upcoming holidays." He didn't have to tell her where he went, but as he spoke, Jaci wondered why it seemed he sounded hesitant to go.

"Will you see Papa?" Amanda asked. The question surprised Jaci because Amanda never asked about, nor spoke of, her father. Although she called Nicholas by the title uncle, Jaci somewhat assumed the child looked to Nicholas as her father.

Nicholas ruffled the girl's curls. "I doubt it, Muffin. He left on a big ship for England, and I don't believe it will have returned yet." Jaci watched as Amanda's shoulders drooped. "But I will leave a message with the shipmaster to make sure he is home by Christmas."

Jaci wondered if he added that comment only for Amanda's sake, whereas he probably didn't believe his brother would come home for the holiday. It didn't appear to matter, for Amanda grinned and left the arena skipping well ahead of the adults. Jaci walked more slowly, for she already felt the muscles tightening in her backside and wondered if she would even be able to get out of bed tomorrow.

Chapter Seven

Nicholas wearily opened the door, glad to be back at Wildwood after a long week in the city. His business at the Philadelphia Exchange had taken longer than anticipated, but he felt good about the prospects for next spring's sales. Already, there had been inquiries about Wildwood yearlings.

Unfortunately, news from Westbrooke Shipping had not been as good. His dock master assured him all ships to and from England were running on schedule, but he couldn't insure that Cameron would arrive in time for the Yuletide holiday. Amanda would be crushed. Nicholas steamed, arguing to himself that although he loved his niece, she needed her father.

"Uncle Nicholas, you're not supposed to be home." A flurry of pink hurled itself at him.

"Hello, Muffin. I'm glad to see you, too." He reached down and lifted her high in the air, returning her kiss.

"Of course I'm glad to see you, but we didn't think you would be home until tomorrow."

"I'm sorry to be early. Shall I leave and return later?" He moved to put her down, but she tightened her arms around his neck.

"No," she squealed. "Since you are already here, you must stay. You can share our dinner because we decided to cook for ourselves."

"And who, exactly, is we?" Sniffing the air for signs of food, he walked through the house with his arms full of wiggling girl and pink ruffles.

"Miss Eastman cooked; and I helped."

He frowned. "It doesn't appear you're doing a very good job, judging by the smell." He wrinkled his nose at the odor, knowing nothing Delta had ever cooked smelled quite like it. "Besides, Amanda, you don't need to learn to cook, only to plan menus. You will always have a cook to take care of you."

He pushed through the kitchen doors, letting Amanda slide to the floor. His nostrils twitched at the strong, spicy smell. Amanda grabbed his sleeve and forced his attention back to her upturned face.

"No, Uncle Nicholas, you're wrong. Miss Eastman says a woman must be self...self?" her brow wrinkled in concentration. "Well, she said I must be able to take care of myself."

"Self-sufficient," Jaci softly supplied the missing word and Nicholas turned to where she stood by the large work table. She looked decidedly uncomfortable that Amanda had repeated her remarks to him, and for a moment Nicholas debated whether to call her on the carpet for filling his niece's head with such foolishness.

But only for a moment. She gave him a shy smile and he forgot everything except how lovely she looked. She used the back of one floured hand to brush her blond hair away from her flushed face. The blue of her gown added color to her appearance, even though her cheeks glowed already from the heat of the fire.

She had been the main reason for his rapid return to Wildwood this night, instead of waiting until morning. At the present time, he didn't dare voice what was growing in his heart, but the emotion continued to weave itself through the very fiber of his being. Soon; he cautioned himself to patience; soon.

From the doorway he watched as she and Amanda finished the concoction and placed the flat cooking sheet in the oven. She would make a marvelous mother, he thought, regardless of her unusual ideas about womanhood. Other pictures leapt to mind — Jaci with the kittens; Jaci holding Amanda on her lap and soothing a hurt; Jaci helping Molly to read. Visions of her were firmly planted in his brain and he couldn't erase them even in his sleep. Nor did he want to.

"Where's Delta?" He shook himself from his daydreams.

"Miss Eastman gave her the day off. She said she was working much too hard and didn't need to wait on us hand and foot," Amanda answered as she climbed onto his lap the minute he sat down on a stool.

"She what?" He frowned, shifting his gaze to Jaci, who refused to look at him but instead scrubbed at a spot on the table that was already clean. "Miss Eastman?"

Her shoulders scrunched towards her head at his tone. Yet before he said anything more, she slapped the rag down on the worktable, squared her shoulders and turned to him, hands on hips and eyes flashing.

"What?" The single word she uttered carried all the audacity of someone wanting to know why he questioned her.

Why, indeed? It was his home.

"Are you undermining my authority in my own household and turning my employees against me?"

"No, of course not. I simply think your employees deserve some time off."

"They get a day off. It is not your position to give them more than that." Her attitude implied he didn't treat his employees fairly, and that was far from the truth. He tended to be more generous than most.

"I do not need someone waiting on me all day long. When you are away on business, there's no reason why they must be on duty."

"I believe we've already discussed your interference with other's work, have we not?" He deposited Amanda on the stool and stood, feeling more in control of the situation when he towered over her.

"My interference?" Her voice rose an octave and her green eyes flashed dangerously. She stepped towards him as she spoke, each word accented by the swish of her skirts and the sway of her hips. In the midst of their argument, with her voiced raised and her dainty hands curled into fists, he wanted nothing more than to kiss her. He watched as the fire continued to smolder behind her thin control.

"Did you know Delta is sixty-eight years old? She has worked every day of her life since she was three. When she was a slave, she used to be up before the sun, starting fires in the rooms and carrying out chamber pots, for heaven's sake." Her eyes had filled with tears as she repeated Delta's past; a past Nicholas knew very well.

"Delta's not a slave anymore," he answered softly. "My grandfather brought his household up north with him, and my father freed them all — long before the war of dissension."

Apparently upset at her feminine outburst, Jaci wiped her eyes with the apron she wore and looked to the floor. "Yes, well, she still deserves a break."

Amanda interrupted at this point, and Nicholas didn't know whether the child did it purposely or not. It mattered not, for he didn't want to argue with Jaci.

"Is the pizza done, yet?"

"Oh, dear, I forgot." Jaci quickly turned and opened the door to the oven, reaching in to grab the baking sheet with only the thin cloth of her apron covering her hand.

"Ouch, Ouch!" She quickly dropped the pan onto the worktable and turned her back, but Nicholas was aware she had hurt herself.

Forgetting their argument, he rushed to where she fidgeted, shaking her burned hand rapidly in the air.

"Let me see." He took her wrist and turned her hand over, observing the red areas on the pads of her fingers, and a long red streak across her palm. "I don't think it'll blister."

"Can we eat?" Amanda didn't notice the grownups, more intent on the food, steaming from the center of the table.

"Go wash up. By the time you return, it should be cool enough," Jaci stated.

Even though he knew she was in pain, it surprised him to hear her answer Amanda in a normal tone of voice. The youngster immediately left to do as she was told. Well, at least one female in this group did so.

"Why did you do that? You knew it was hot," he chided, referring to grabbing the hot tray. He tugged her along to the sink where he pumped cool water and stuck her hand beneath the spout.

"I was mad; I didn't think. Ouch." Now that Amanda was out of the room, apparently she didn't feel the need to act quite so tough. She tried to jerk her stinging hand from beneath the water. He held on tighter. A tear glittered at the corner of her eye.

"Why won't you let someone take care of you? Why do you try so hard not to need anyone?" It was a question that had haunted him since she began working at Wildwood. With every action, she tried to prove her independence; her intention not to rely on anyone for anything.

More tears came. He gently wiped his thumb across her cheek, lost in the sparkling sea green of her eyes. He liked this soft, gentle side of her; the tender side that needed to be held and cared for. Before she decided once again to be in control, he took advantage.

Keeping her gaze captured in his, he shut off the water and gently patted dry her palm. Lifting her hand, he licked the pad of each finger before kissing across the tender red skin of her palm. His hot mouth continued to her wrist and the soft skin at the inside of her elbow.

Still holding her wrist, he tugged slightly and she swayed towards him; close enough for his lips to find hers. With a sigh, he released her wrist and wrapped his arms around her, pulling her the rest of the way towards surrender.

Nicholas's kiss was incredibly tender, and it scared Jaci to death. She didn't want to care for this man; didn't want to feel emotions she had buried long ago. It would only spell disaster. Yet even as she told herself she didn't care, she wound her arms around his neck and hung on tight.

His kisses tonight were different somehow; gentle, where before she had always had a sense of being devoured. He didn't clutch at her, but instead cradled her tenderly against him. The effect was more profound than ever. She ached with an incredible heaviness. She tried to step closer but he held her back; she opened her mouth for him to deepen the kiss, but instead he traced a path up to her ear where he sucked on her ear lobe.

A groan escaped and she felt her knees buckle. Was it the words he said, or his hot breath on her neck? Did it matter?

"Did you think of me when I was gone?" His tongue tickled her ear but the last thing she wanted to do was laugh. "Do you have any idea how much I want to—"

"Pizza, pizza!" Amanda's sing-song voice carried down the hall. "Pizza, pizza!" The chant echoed just outside the kitchen and Jaci felt the lack of Nicholas's warmth. She opened her eyes.

By the time Amanda entered the kitchen, Nicholas had managed to round the table and was leaning nonchalantly on the other side. She resented him for his attitude — how could he act unaffected?

Sucking in a deep breath, she mentally shook herself. That's why she didn't need anyone. But as she walked around the table to serve their dinner, she glanced once more at Nicholas. She found him staring at her with an almost painful expression. Her glance involuntarily slid downward and she realized he wasn't as unaffected as he wanted anyone to believe.

"Here, Uncle Nicholas." Amanda excitedly thrust a plate at him and Jaci watched his reaction.

"What is it?" His expression remained skeptical, and Jaci wondered what to say. She hadn't intended on explaining since he wasn't supposed to be home.

"Pizza, pizza." Amanda sang again, repeating the jingle Jaci had sung while they had made their bacon pizza.

It has taken some creativity to find all the ingredients to produce a semblance of Jaci's favorite food. It had sounded like a good idea at the time, but now, as she looked down at the bubbly goo with chunks of preserved tomato and bacon and onion atop a rather thick bread crust, she had her doubts.

Amanda didn't seem to mind. Nicholas looked askew as she picked it up with her fingers.

"Amanda."

She looked at him with her huge eyes, and Jaci laughed. Before she had a chance to explain, Amanda repeated to Nicholas what she had told the youngster earlier.

"It's a very modern food, Uncle Nicholas. You even get to eat it with your fingers." To show him how, she took a bite, the pizza sauce making a crooked smile across her face.

Nicholas glanced from his niece to Jaci, and she wondered if she was in trouble again. It seemed a never ending part of her existence. To her surprise, he winked at her as he followed Amanda's example and picked up a slice of pizza and began to eat.

Jaci almost cried. What was she going to do with him? She refused to put a name to the emotion that welled up inside as she watched the two of them eat. In the short time she had been here, she shouldn't feel the things she did, either towards Amanda or Nicholas. She had always been a private person, not free with her feelings, but these two made her feel so much a part of Wildwood and their existence here.

Yet she didn't exist here; at least not in the same sense. She kept reminding herself not to get involved; not to feel more than a passing fancy for the man sitting across from her. After all, if he married, he would be lost to her. And if she found a way back to Dallas and her own home? Too painful to contemplate, she forced the thought to the back of her mind and reached for a second slice of pizza.

"Pizza, huh?" He commented between bites. "It's not bad, I suppose, but it will never catch on as a meal."

* * *

November turned to December and still, little trace of winter marred the countryside. What snowfall they had, melted in the wake of warmer days. As long as weather permitted, Nicholas and his trainers ran the horses outside. When she had time, Jaci liked to stand at the white rail fence and watch the horses go through their paces.

Today was one such day and she tucked her shawl under her arms as she watched Nicholas. He stood inside the paddock, giving advice to a rider, then turning to speak in low tones to Mackey. She tilted her head sideways, recalling the day she had met the trainer.

Earlier that week, Nicholas had walked with her and Amanda out toward the barn. Amanda wanted to check on the kittens, which had grown and scattered over the weeks. She had finally managed to catch one and now cradled it in her arms.

"Mackey, come over here and meet Miss Eastman." Nicholas had called from behind her.

Her heart had catapulted into her throat as she turned quickly around. She momentarily lost her balance and fell into Nicholas.

Dear Lord, how did he know the carousel operator at State Fair Park? How would Mackey have ended up here, at Wildwood? But when her vision cleared at the sound of his voice, she realized it wasn't the same person at all.

"MacAdoo, do you remember Miss Eastman?"

"Howdy, ma'am. You look a right bit different, er, better, than you did the first time we met." He grabbed the hat off his head and twisted it in his hands.

She was still shaking, but managed to answer. "Good morning, Mr. MacAdoo. We've met before?"

"Yes, ma'am, the day you arrived, uh, in the horse pen?" He shrugged his stooped shoulders and smiled a half smile, as though he wasn't sure he should mention her circumstances.

That day seemed long ago to her. "Well, it's nice to meet you, Mr. MacAdoo."

"Call me Mackey; everybody does." The trainer grinned this time, showing crooked, tobacco stained teeth.

Mackey. Remembering that day now, she also recalled her acute disappointment at not being back in Dallas.

"Penny for your thoughts." Nicholas whispered close at hand and she jumped.

"You would owe me quite a bit of money if I actually made you pay every time you said that."

"Yes, but it might be worth my fortune to know what thoughts lurk behind the myriad expressions that cross your face when you think no one is looking." He came to stand beside her at the fence, one booted foot on the bottom rail, arms crossed on the top.

She searched wildly around for a safe topic, knowing full well she would never divulge what she had actually been thinking.

"Your horses are beautiful. You must be very proud of the tradition you have created." She spoke the truth, for even though she knew little about these animals, she realized they were exceptional. It reminded her of looking at art — a person might not know the period of a piece, or its worth, but it was still beautiful to behold.

"Not all the horses here were bred and foaled under the Wildwood name. Take Sabet, over there. He's not exactly your typical racehorse." He grinned as he answered and her breath caught.

He wore a jacket over a white shirt open at the collar, and she stared at the small vee of brown neck. All she would have to do is lean forward a little to kiss right there; right where his throat vibrated when he talked; when he swallowed.

She closed her eyes against the sight, thinking hard about anything else. "What about Sabet?" She recalled having ridden that horse — once.

"He's a gelding and not much of a racer, but I couldn't very well get rid of him after I won him."

"You won a horse?"

"That's how he got his name, Sabet. You know — 'It's a bet'? I won him from a drunk."

"You what?" She couldn't believe he would take advantage of someone that way. "Isn't that the least bit dishonorable; to bet with a drunk?"

104

He turned to study her for a minute and she wondered what he was thinking behind those glittering silver eyes.

"I don't know about Texas, but up here we take our horses, and our wagers, as seriously as we do our honor. Dishonor would come from not paying a wager, and any man who can't hold his liquor shouldn't be betting. Or he shouldn't be drinking." With that pronouncement, he walked away.

Honor. She still wasn't used to the strict code of conduct by which the men of this time period lived. The fact that they expected the women to abide by strange rules they created was even more of a mystery to her.

* * *

Jaci climbed into the carriage behind Amanda, who should have been exhausted, but instead chattered like a magpie.

"Did you see that elephant? And the giraffe? Oh, Miss Eastman, the zoo was the most magnificent thing I have ever seen."

Jaci grinned. Everything today had been magnificent. If it wasn't magnificent, it had been marvelous, the old standby word of the day. She would have to check the dictionary for a group of words not in the 'm' category.

The zoo had been a good idea, and she was glad they had come. Originally, Nicholas was supposed to accompany them, but a prospective buyer had dropped by unexpectedly. Not wanting to ruin Amanda's outing, he had allowed the coachman to drive them into Philadelphia, anyway.

Unlike zoos Jaci had frequented as a child, the Philadelphia Zoological Gardens in Fairmount Park kept most of the animals inside. They had spent the day wandering from building to building, stopping only briefly to eat at noon. As the day progressed, Jaci noticed a decided chill in the air, and now, as they loaded to return to Wildwood, she felt a snowflake drop onto her nose.

"We'd best be for home, Miss," the coachman said as he helped her into the carriage. "Looks to be some snow blowing in."

"Yes, you're right. Will you be warm enough up on the box?" At the coachman's strange look, she added, "Do you want my scarf?"

The man's eyes opened wider and she hoped she hadn't offended him in some way. Then he grinned and tipped his hat at her. "Thank you kindly, Miss, for thinking of me. It wouldn't be a bit honorable of me to take a scarf from a lady, now would it?" He closed the door behind her, and the carriage swayed as he climbed aboard.

Honestly, she thought, did every single man in this world worry about honor even over taking care of himself? She settled back on the seat as the carriage began to move. A slow smile lifted the corners of her mouth. In a way, it was nice to be fussed over and to have someone take care of her. Just a little.

Jaci had nodded off to sleep, Amanda curled up in the seat beside her, when the carriage lurched to the side. Along with the yelling and swearing by the coachman, the tilt of the carriage led her to assume a wheel had broken. When she was certain the vehicle had stopped and wouldn't turn over on them, she helped Amanda out the door. They stood by the side of the road while the driver paced back and forth.

"I can't go for help and leave you ladies alone." He came to stand before her, wringing his hands.

She opened her mouth to reply, but he resumed pacing, mumbling to himself. "I'll have to stay here until someone comes along to help."

Looking skyward as though for divine intervention, he gave a sigh. "Lordy, wouldn't you know it would decide to snow now. If I don't go for help, we'll very likely all freeze. If I do go, I'd be neglecting my duties to you ladies."

Jaci lifted the hood of her cloak as large, wet flakes fell with incredible speed. Not more than an hour ago, it had been rather mild. The man was right, though, about freezing if they didn't get home, but she didn't agree on their helpless condition. She was learning, however, that it did little good arguing with a man about honor and responsibility towards a woman. So, it appeared that left only one choice.

"I don't see the problem. If you have a jack and a spare, we can probably change it. It can't be any harder than a Corsica. "Amanda's giggle caught her attention and she glanced at the youngster, who held both hands over her mouth to suppress her mirth, but whose eyes danced with delight. Amanda wasn't even looking at her, but stared at the coachman. Jaci slowly turned back around, a horrid suspicion growing at the back of her mind.

The look on the coachman's face confirmed her worst fears — she had done it again. She felt her face flush with embarrassment as she fumbled for a motive behind her silly declaration.

"You don't carry a spare wheel, do you?" He shook his head. "Or a jack?" Amanda giggled again.

"My name be Jack, Miss."

"Oh." She now understood the reason behind Amanda's humor, and while she might think it funny, Jaci had the distinct impression Nicholas would not. And there was no doubt in her mind that he would find out.

Fortunately, within minutes, Doctor Stillwell happened along in his buggy. He and the coachman unharnessed the carriage horses and tied them behind his buggy. With some juggling, he managed to load Jaci, Amanda and the coachman into the small conveyance. They arrived at Wildwood cold and wrinkled, but safe, and Amanda had yet another adventure to share with her friends.

Jaci helped Amanda wash up and change while the doctor visited with Nicholas. Amanda ate her supper in the nursery, and was content to go to bed early, exhausted from the exciting day at the zoo. She cuddled beside the stuffed elephant Jaci had bought her and quickly fell to sleep.

Jaci changed her own clothes and descended the stairs to dine. The library door, only partially closed, didn't halt the flow of words as she came near. Nicholas's agitated voice, however, stopped her on the bottom stair. Her palms turned cold and clammy, and her stomach turned over rapidly. She sank down on the steps, not daring to move, and yet not wanting to hear any more of Nicholas's condemnation.

"It wasn't enough that she asked if he had a spare wheel and jack, but to imply she would change the carriage wheel herself? Whoever heard of a lady saying such things?" His voice sounded incredulous. "Every time I think she's adequately suited for this position, she does something very strange. Are you sure she's recovered from her head injury?"

The doctor laughed. "Personally, I like a woman with spunk. She's practical, at the very least, and not prone to the vapors over the inconvenience. I really don't see what you're upset about, Nicholas. I find Miss Eastman quite charming."

She had no idea why Doctor Stillwell rose to her defense; she had only known him briefly. She silently thanked him for supporting her, but gasped at his next words.

"I'll gladly take her off your hands, Nicholas. I am looking for a wife and she—"

"No." Nicholas's answer was swift and adamant.

Her earlier discomfort forgotten, she rose from the steps, ready to confront both men. Conflicting emotions rolled around in her stomach. She felt shock at Thomas Stillwell's declaration and annoyance at Nicholas's high-handed attitude. What right did he have to say another man couldn't be interested in her?

"Ah, is that the way the wind blows?" Doctor Stillwell's voice again held a hint of humor.

What did that mean? She wondered.

Nicholas replied. "Perhaps I simply meant that Miss Eastman will not be free until I marry. After all, I need someone to look after Amanda."

Now, what did that mean? Each additional sentence only confused her more, and she wondered if she wouldn't be better off breaking into their conversation before one of them said something she probably didn't want to hear.

"Of course, this conversation probably wouldn't be taking place if Cameron would accept responsibility for his daughter." Nicholas's voice came closer, but Jaci couldn't tear herself away from the banister to which she clung.

"Cameron still hasn't decided to be a father, has he? Perhaps one day. Well, hello, Miss Eastman. Have you come to join us for supper?" Doctor Stillwell's merry blue eyes twinkled as he smiled at her. She blushed, realizing he must know she had eavesdropped, however inadvertently.

In contrast, Nicholas scowled and his silver gaze flashed angrily in her direction. It appeared he was greatly disturbed by her earlier behavior. She never knew from day to day what he thought. If he kicked her out of his house, and Amanda's life, she would be lost. The world was not as she knew it. Impulsively, she lied, for she realized she didn't want Nicholas thinking poorly of her.

"I do apologize for my earlier behavior, gentlemen. You see, down south the roads are terribly rough and full of potholes."

"Potholes?" Nicholas questioned.

"Chuck holes; ruts? From the war, you know — the cannons?"

Nicholas cocked a brow in disbelief. The doctor stood there and grinned. This was not going well. She didn't want to compound her lie with too many facts about history she knew little about, but which these men had lived.

"Ah-hum. Anyway, the coachman began carrying an extra wheel, attached to the back of the carriage, in case one had a flat."

"A flat? How does a wooden wheel become flat?" From his tone, Jaci thought the handsome physician was enjoying her discomfort way too much. He reminded her of some of the macho males she had worked with in the past. However, unlike the century in which she grew up, here she felt at a definite disadvantage, if for no other reason than she didn't always understand the language.

"A break. I meant a break." Enough. They either believed her, or they didn't. She looked from one man to the other.

Thomas Stillwell's expression was easy to read. He thought her wonderful and would believe she could fly to the moon. The one who mattered, though Jaci hated to admit it, continued to scowl at her for several seconds before his silver gaze brightened, and the corner of his mouth lifted in a grin. "The south must have changed mightily after the war," he commented, offering her his arm. "They do seem to have acquired some strange customs, if Miss Eastman is a fair example."

As close to acceptance as she could expect, Jaci graciously took his arm. She returned his smile, falling into step beside him despite the long dress and dainty, backless slippers which still gave her difficulty when walking.

Chapter Eight

Winter had set in with a vengeance and the latest storm continued to blow, rattling the windows in the nursery. Perhaps if a person were born and raised in Pennsylvania, the winter weather wouldn't seem so bad. For Jaci, winter had always been a day or two of snow, perhaps a few weeks of temperatures in the freezing zone, but the rest of the time it was bearable, if not balmy.

She tucked her wool shawl closer around her as she stoked the fire. She shook her head, chuckling to herself. Not that long ago, she wouldn't have known how to build a fire, much less have adapted to all the odd inconveniences of her new way of life.

In an effort to learn about her environment and not appear out of place, she had volunteered to do everything from washing clothes in a tub to going to the spring house with newly churned butter. Well, she wouldn't be going to the spring house again any time soon. They could put the butter on the back porch and it would freeze.

She moved the toy box close to the fireplace and dumped the contents onto the thick rug. Amanda appeared content to build make-believe houses with her blocks. At times like this, Jaci wished she knew how to knit, for wool booties would help keep her feet warmer than the thick stockings she had donned this morning.

Curious, she bent down and retrieved a small carved animal. The miniature elephant had been sanded smooth and turned glossy from the natural oil in the wood. "Amanda, these are beautiful animals."

"I have two of each animal. And this boat they all went on long, long, ago so they wouldn't drown."

"Ah, yes. Noah's Ark," Jaci smiled as she answered. She handed the animal back to the little girl. In their studies, she hadn't thought to teach her any religion; she didn't know if it fell within the realm of her responsibilities. Besides, she wasn't sure if she believed in the Almighty anymore, and didn't think it would be fair to explain such concepts to an impressionable five year old.

She closed her eyes, not able to stop the memories that washed over her. Flashes of times when her family had attended church and Sunday school, and Jaci had believed in all those concepts of goodness and righteousness. That was before the accident, when the Good Lord had seen fit to take Jaci's mother away before she was done raising her two daughters. And Jaci, for one, still missed her terribly.

After the accident, she had refused foster care for herself and Mandy. Although Mandy was only twelve, Jaci was a legal eighteen. Now, as she wondered how Mandy was doing, she hoped she hadn't done her sister a disservice. By living together and taking charge, had she adequately prepared Mandy to be independent and self-reliant? She certainly hoped so, because it didn't appear she was headed home anytime soon.

She rubbed her hands along the arms of the rocking chair, the wood soothing beneath her fingers. She opened her eyes and looked around the room, for the first time actually studying the ornately carved wood furniture. It wasn't only Amanda's toy box, or all the wooden toys and blocks it contained. There seemed to be a uniqueness to most of the furnishings in the room.

"Amanda?"

"Huh?" The girl didn't look up. Her tongue stuck out slightly between two pink lips. Jaci watched as she studiously placed one block on another, then a third on top of that.

"Where did you get all your toys and furniture?" She thought of Gustav Dentzel, and knew Nicholas was good friends with the furniture maker.

"Uncle Nicholas made it."

"What?" That was impossible. Besides, she had been with him when he ordered the chest made for Amanda. The man had too much energy to spend such an amount of time carving little animals and fitting pieces of wood together to make a chest. Nicholas spent little time inside, even on the coldest days, and Jaci couldn't imagine that energy confined to a small woodworking shop.

Amanda added a fifth block to her growing tower before answering. "Uncle Nicholas did, too, make it. A long time ago he gave me these animals for my birthday."

Considering Amanda was only five, Jaci had to smile over her use of "a long time ago". Still, if Amanda said Nicholas made these things, she knew it was fact. She was impressed.

"Look, Miss Eastman, I made a sky scratcher." Amanda said with excitement, calling her attention back to the stack of blocks.

"That's skyscraper, Sweetie," she responded, smiling at Amanda's mispronouncement. Of course, she was happy that Nicholas didn't hear, for she wasn't sure the word was in existence at this time.

Jaci decided she might be warmer sitting on the floor beside Amanda. She gathered her skirts and slid off the rocker, crossing her legs Indian style beneath the piles of wool she wore. Idly, she stacked and unstacked blocks and other scraps of wood that Amanda used to create imaginary monsters. Without realizing it, Nicholas had provided his niece with the best learning tools possible — bits and pieces of wood — which allowed Amanda to stretch her imagination.

Jaci glanced down. While her mind had meandered, she had stuck small, notched sticks together to form what looked like an airplane with two wings. Idly, she moved her hand back and forth, making the little plane "fly."

"What's that?" Amanda scooted over and looked curiously at her creation. Jaci chewed on her bottom lip, wondering whether to talk to Amanda about airplanes. She wouldn't have to say anything about the date the Wright Brothers flew, which was another thirty years into the future. Perhaps the child would think of it as a legend, like the ones she had told her at other times.

The clock in the hallway chimed the hour. "I think I have a good nap time story for you," she said, struggling to get up from the floor without tripping on her skirts and throwing herself into the fire.

"Aw, do I have to take a nap?" Amanda argued, even though her eyes drooped and she yawned in the middle of speaking.

"If you want to hear the story of this, you do." Jaci flew the little airplane under her nose, turning and pretending to fly it over to the small bed on which Amanda slept. "Quickly pick up your toys, or there won't be time."

It took no time at all for Amanda to toss her toys back into the box and close the lid. Jaci helped her out of her dress and shoes and she scooted beneath the covers. She reached out and took the airplane and waved it back and forth as she had seen Jaci do.

"Does it make a noise, like the animals?"

"Yes, it does." Jaci scrunched up her face, trying to figure out how she would explain it. "It makes an engine noise."

Amanda looked at her blankly, so Jaci took her wrist and moved it back and forth in the motion of the plane, imitating the sound of an engine.

She sat on the edge of the bed and began her story. "Once upon a time, there were two brothers named Orville and Wilbur."

"Like Uncle Nicholas and my papa?"

"Yes, but these brothers owned a bicycle shop in Dayton, Ohio, instead of a horse farm."

"Bicycle? Molly saw one in Philadelphia and they're terribly dangerous and not at all the proper thing for a lady to ride." Amanda shook her head as she spoke and Jaci thought her much too wise for five years of age.

Deciding to hurry the story along, she said, "They also had a sister named Catherine."

"Like me," Amanda squealed. "I have Uncle Nicholas and papa. I'm not the sister, but it is close to the same, isn't it?" Before Jaci could answer, she continued, "Do they take care of her? Catherine, I mean?"

"Yes, of course, they take care of her, just like you. Now, if you're going to keep interrupting me, I won't be able to tell you the story of the airplane."

"Airplane. That's what it's called?"

Jaci sighed and Amanda got the message, settling back on the bed.

"Orville and Wilbur had a bicycle shop where they sold and fixed things, but they decided to build an airplane that they flew through the air."

"Why?" Amanda breathed the single word in wide-eyed awe. "How could they do that? Nothing flies."

"Birds do," Jaci answered. "You see, one day their father bought them a little toy. It was a bird that the boys wound up and the wings would flap and the toy would fly through the air."

"Oh, my." The very idea must have overwhelmed Amanda, for she laid there with her mouth open. Jaci decided not to go into a lot of particulars.

"The Wright Brothers studied hard and made little airplanes they called gliders before making a larger one. Finally, they put an engine on it and went to Kitty Hawk, North Carolina. They took turns flying through the air."

"What about their sister? What about Catherine?" Being a girl, the sister was more important to Amanda than the idea of flying through the air.

"Wilbur and Orville took Catherine for rides in the airplane. And when the boys got hurt flying their airplane, Catherine would help take care of them."

Amanda yawned and closed her eyes, her fingers still wrapped around the wooden plane. "It's nice to have somebody take care of you."

Jaci leaned forward and kissed her brow. "Yes, it definitely has its advantages."

Jaci tiptoed across the room, turning to the sleeping child as she pulled the door shut. Satisfied that she would sleep a few hours at least, she turned to go to the kitchen for coffee.

"Who are you?"

Jaci clamped a hand to her mouth to keep from screaming. Pure reflex brought her other hand up to push against Nicholas's shoulder. "Good Lord, you scared me to death."

"Answer me." He grabbed her extended hand tightly.

"Sh." She put a finger to her lips and walked down the hall away from Amanda's door. Since Nicholas clutched her wrist, she figured he'd follow.

He did, but when he thought they had gone far enough, he pulled her to a halt.

"Miss Eastman, I couldn't help overhearing your story. I can certainly appreciate the legends you have recited before to my niece. And while such stories don't have any basis in fact, they are somewhat understandable. This time, however, I must question telling her a story of such outlandish proportions. Flying ships, indeed."

She jerked her hand out of his grip, both angered at his highhandedness and slightly frightened that he had heard a story about the future. She would have to bluff her way out of it.

"It was only a make-believe story about something that might happen in the future. Maybe someday we'll fly—" At his look of outright disbelief, she thought again. There must be something.

"You don't recall the story of Icarus and Daedalus?" Were those the names of the Greek mythology characters? She noticed his hesitation and breathed a little sigh of relief. Still, he squinted at her with suspicion.

"What about balloons — gas balloons?" She was grasping at straws.

"Do you perhaps refer to the Confederate's attempt to construct a spy balloon during the war? The myriad display of the ladies' silk ball gowns, sewn together to make a balloon which was captured before they hauled it a mile up river?" For a man who espoused the fact that the war was over, she thought his tone held quite a bit of northern arrogance.

She tried to change the subject. "Yes, well, it doesn't matter. It was simply a story."

"Ah, Miss Eastman, but it does matter. A balloon is a far cry from a machine that flies through the air with a motor attached."

She had begun to hate it when he called her Miss Eastman. It always meant she was in trouble.

Looking up, she found his gaze intent on her face, as though trying to see inside her head to where her memories hid. She stared at him, hoping he would accept the story; and her. She couldn't be that lucky.

"Who are you?" he asked again, slowly shaking his head in disbelief.

He has asked her that question before, and each time she had answered with less and less information. After all, he didn't believe her, anyway. The first time she had said she was from the future, he had accused her of being addlebrained. What good would it do to explain?

"I just am." She looked at him sadly. In the three months she had lived in Wildwood, she had come to care about its occupants — all of them, and yet she still didn't understand the significance she played in this household. Was she to spend the rest of her life here, baby-sitting his niece, growing old in a world still very foreign to her?

She didn't wait for him to dismiss her. She turned and hurried to her own room, quietly closing the door behind her. She didn't want to forget who she was, nor the world from which she had come. Yet every time she let a little bit escape through stories to Amanda, she got caught. How was she to keep her memories alive?

* * *

Jaci should have known that walking away wouldn't end their discussion if Nicholas deemed it incomplete. This morning when Molly came to her room and said Mister Westbrooke requested her presence, she realized she had only postponed the inevitable.

117

As she walked downstairs to the study, she tried to come up with a logical explanation for the stories she told Amanda. However, there was nothing logical about motorized flying machines in an era where the word horsepower was taken literally.

Nicholas bid her enter when she knocked on the door, and he immediately rose from his chair. He looked quite handsome, his dark hair pulled back and the gray streaks adding to his sophisticated appearance. In the warmth created by a glowing fire, he had forgone his jacket, his shirt sleeves rolled up to reveal strong arms, lightly sprinkled with dark hair. His casual attire added to his charm, and to her nervousness.

"Miss Eastman, how pleasant of you to pay me this visit." He motioned her towards the chairs by the fire.

"You requested my presence."

"Ah, yes, but of late I seem to be ignored in my own house when the need suits." He grinned at her, and she couldn't help but smile back.

She seated herself, gracefully sliding back from the edge until she came to rest against the velvet of the cushion. He appeared to be in a good mood, and she sincerely hoped that was a good omen. She'd soon find out. "I thought you were going to call me Jaci?"

"I believe I did say that at one point, didn't I?" He had seated himself across from her, propping one booted foot over the other knee, his fingers steepled in front of his lips. He had such a look of concentration that Jaci soon began to squirm, feeling like a bug under a magnifying glass.

"You and I have had some lively debates, have we not?" he asked, his expression not varying or giving anything away.

She didn't know whether he was mad, upset, or merely curious. Until she determined the exact direction of this conversation, she decided to answer with a simple, "Yes."

"While your stories to Amanda are creative, I hesitate to have her head full of nonsense like Indians in the sky and now flying machines."

She straightened. So that was the topic of conversation today. Perhaps it was time to see exactly how open-minded Mister Nicholas Westbrooke was. "What if they're not nonsense?"

"Come now. I know there have been attempts, but no one has ever created a motorized flying machine. Are you telling me that the Wright brothers have done so? Why haven't I heard about it?"

"Not have done so. They will do it." She spoke barely above a whisper, but he sprang on her words.

"You're saying it will happen in the future. You're speaking again about being from the future?" His voice rose.

She sat with head bowed, staring at her fingers entwined in her lap. She wouldn't lie, but she sincerely hoped he would drop this particular discussion. There was nothing she could do about her origins, and nothing he could do about getting her back there. She didn't want him mad enough to send her away from Wildwood.

Nicholas stood and began to pace in front of the fireplace. His next words caught her totally by surprise. "Let me play the devil's advocate for a moment. I don't believe you, mind, but just suppose—"

She jerked her head up to stare at him.

"Suppose you are from the future. Why don't you invent a way to get yourself back? I mean, surely there are things you have in your time which we have not been blessed with yet."

His sarcasm wasn't lost on her. If she could, perhaps she should invent something that would put him in his proper place. However, not only did she not have the knowledge to invent anything; not even fast speed film, and photography was her love; but what if she should somehow change the course of history? What if — she voiced her thoughts.

"If I invented something early, or somehow altered events that made an impact on history, it might change my own history as well. I mean, suppose whatever I did somehow altered the history of Texas, and because I

119

messed with things here, I wasn't born when I actually was. I wouldn't exist then — in the future — so how could I slip back through time and end up here?"

As she spoke, Nicholas had come to stand in front of her, hands locked behind him and an incredible look on his face. She grimaced. "This is very confusing. Does it make any sense at all?"

"Somehow, I understand what you're saying, and that worries me no end." His high brow wrinkled as he frowned.

"So, what happens now?"

"I am still not convinced that what you say is true." When she started to protest, he held up a hand. "I said I understood your confusion, but whether such a concept as time travel could actually be accomplished or not—" He shrugged those eloquent shoulders and shook his head, his hair picking up highlights from the fire. "I think that blow to the head you received when you landed among my horses did more damage than we thought."

Jaci's shoulders sagged in defeat, and relief. Actually, she thought it would be better all around if he continued to think that. Hearing Selkirk outside the door, she decided it would be a good time to escape.

"I believe Selkirk needs to visit with you. I'll leave you to your manly things." She scooted past him and headed for the door.

"Jaci?"

She stopped and turned.

"Try to stick to less fanciful topics with Amanda. She has far too much imagination as it is."

She smiled, for although he had made a statement, his tone of voice implied he was seeking her permission.

"Of course." She would give in this time, for it seemed the easier path to take.

* * *

Not more than a week went by before Jaci and Nicholas were at it again, this time over Amanda's studies. Even though the child was only five, Jaci wanted to teach her math and science as well as reading.

They were arguing in the study, and Nicholas remained standing in front of his desk. Jaci had noticed, as a gentleman, he always rose when she came into the room and would remain standing until she sat. Today, to spite him, she refused to sit down and instead paced back and forth. The more she tried to make him understand the importance of her position, the more stubborn he became.

"I see no reason to clutter her brain with nonsense," he countered her latest argument, crossing his arms over his chest.

"You know arithmetic, and the science of husbandry. Does that over tax your brain cells?"

"I'm a man. It's different."

"Of all the egotistical, chauvinistic—" she sputtered to a stop when Nicholas began to laugh. "What is so funny?"

"Do you know how absolutely adorable you are when you're angry?" He grinned in response to her startled expression. A lock of hair fell over his forehead, and her stomach tied in knots.

She threw up her hands in despair. "I can't reason with you." He took a step toward her and she fled.

Her confrontations with Nicholas were getting more heated by the day. Every time she had a conversation with him, his silver eyes seemed to cut to her very soul, exposing her secrets and disarming her defenses with his charm. Everyone said he was supposed to marry Miss Edwardson, but he didn't appear to be of the same intent. Why else would he make such idiotic comments? Every time he said something sweet, like calling her adorable, she fell deeper under his spell.

Not getting involved should have been easy, for she had been raised in a world of feminine freedom. She had no use for a chauvinistic male with an ego the size of Texas and no understanding of independent women. Then why did her heart flutter every time he said her name? Why did

121

she ache for those times their paths crossed? How come her dreams and all waking thoughts were invaded by his presence, and why he didn't kiss her again?

"Oh, Mandy, how I wish you were here to guide me," Jaci sighed dejectedly as she wandered back to her room. Her sister, the romantic, had been the one to know the ins and outs of the dating world. Such things had always been furthest from Jaci's mind.

"Why are you always talking to someone named Mandy?" Amanda had followed her into the room, and regardless of Jaci's wish for solitude, the youngster hopped onto the bed, pink skirts bunched up around her making her look like one of the roses in the garden.

Abandoning any sense of decorum, Jaci fell face first onto the bed beside her, crossing her arms under her head as she turned and gazed at the pixie.

"Mandy is my sister."

"A sister? How old is she; where is she; can she come and play with me?" She bounced on the bed as she jabbered questions faster than Jaci could absorb.

Jaci quickly turned her head to hide the unbidden tears that sprang forth. Amanda's inquisitiveness reminded her of Mandy at that age. Her throat constricted.

"Well?" Amanda didn't seem likely to give up, and waited impatiently for Jaci to answer. To stall for time, she pulled the child into the curve of her body, nestling her cap of springy curls under her chin so the child wouldn't see the tears which still blurred her vision.

"Mandy is a few years younger than I am, so she's much too old to play. Besides, she lives very, very far away." She struggled to keep her voice steady. "Her real name is the same as yours. When we were both very small, I called her 'my Mandy' because I thought she belonged just to me."

Amanda squirmed and wiggled before coming to rest once again against Jaci. "I wish they would call me Mandy, instead of A-manda." She stressed the `A' as though it were an entire name of its own.

Jaci smiled.

"You can call me Mandy, if you like. I mean, since you don't have your sister here to get us mixed up and all."

"But your uncle wouldn't like it, would he?" It seemed Nicholas was forever on her mind.

"Well, no. He probably would not." She stopped, and Jaci wondered what her mischievous little mind was cooking up now. "But you could call me that, when we're alone." She tilted her head back to look up at Jaci with eyes that held wisdom beyond her five years. "Maybe then you wouldn't be lonely for the real Mandy."

Jaci was glad the child snuggled down against the soft mattress and didn't see the stream of tears that washed down her face. Silently she sent a wish across the centuries. "Oh, Mandy. If I had to leave you, at least someone saw fit to drop me into a loving household." She hugged Amanda closer and cried herself to sleep, hoping Mandy managed to survive without her.

Hours later, when Amanda didn't come to the library to bid him good-night, Nicholas went in search of her. He asked all the servants and looked in all the rooms. At length he stood in front of Jaci's door. Should he disturb her to inquire about his niece?

She had left in a huff after their latest discussion, and he wondered if she was still angry with him. Her wild ideas and fanciful stories were beyond believing, and her unconventional ways set his teeth grinding. Yet he admired the way she stood up to him. He usually intimidated the most stalwart man at the Philadelphia Exchange, but Jaci wouldn't back down if she thought she was right.

Added to her stubbornness was her beauty, which was heightened when her green eyes flashed and her cheeks flushed. For some reason, she didn't appear to like it when he openly admired her beauty. Of course, because it bothered her, he quite frequently deliberately baited her.

His second knock was not answered, and his brow furrowed in concern. How odd that both of them appeared to be missing at the same time. Using his concern as an excuse, he opened the door and glanced into the room, illuminated only by the moonlight streaming in through the tall windows.

He clearly saw a shape on the bed, and when he moved closer, discovered his niece curled up in Jaci's arms. For a moment, he contented himself to gaze down at the two of them. In sleep, Jaci looked soft and delicate, much like the lady he knew her to be. Gone were the spark filled eyes and the proud defiance in her voice. He smiled as he thought to savor the peace, knowing full well it would last only as long as she got her own way.

He had promised himself he'd wait until after the holidays to make his intentions known. It would not be fair to pursue Jaci until Lycinda had been set free from any contract, unintentional or not. Yet each time Jaci and he spoke; each day as her scent lingered in the upper hall when he came down for breakfast, he found it harder and harder to keep his resolution.

He wanted to kiss her and he ached to hold her in an embrace all night long, but only after they had exhausted themselves making love. December couldn't fly by fast enough. He didn't know how long his aching body could resist the temptation her mere presence caused.

He shifted his gaze to Amanda, happy and secure, embraced in loving arms. Whatever peccadilloes Jaci might claim, she appeared to be good for Amanda.

A sigh of frustration escaped as he gently tugged off two pairs of slippers and covered the sleeping beauties with a quilt. As he quietly shut the door, he thought back to the first days that Jaci resided at Wildwood. At that time, he would have allowed her to stay if only for Amanda's sake, for the child needed the gentler influence of a woman.

Now, he had very specific purposes of his own for keeping her bound to Wildwood. Regardless of how he had initially fought it, he had fallen in love with her. He wondered how many rounds he and the unconventional Miss Eastman would have to go before they both gave in to the mysterious forces that drew them together.

Chapter Nine

Jaci walked downstairs after leaving Amanda with Molly for the afternoon. As much as she had come to love the child, the hours when the maid watched her were precious.

"Is our little hellion down for a nap?" Nicholas spoke as he walked out of the study.

Startled, she stopped on the bottom step. Though Nicholas worked at Wildwood, he stayed busy outside or in the arena, and she rarely saw him during the day. Lately, though, she had found herself trying to catch a glimpse of him out the window as he trained horses or spoke to a groom. Even with snow on the ground, the horses were trained outside whenever the wind-chill was bearable.

"Hello. Are you there?" He teased as he smiled.

Her heart melted a little more than it had the last time he smiled at her, which meant it was a puddle somewhere. Each day it became harder to remember she didn't belong here. And every day found her falling a little more for the silver-eyed, horse breeder.

"I'm sorry; my thoughts were elsewhere." She returned his smile, hoping he would stay and visit with her. Regardless of their arguments about everything from education to women's rights, she liked discussing things with him. Then she realized he was buttoning his coat. "Are you going somewhere?"

"I'm off for a ride, actually, to scare up some wild birds for Delta. Would you care to join me? The weather's tolerable, for December."

Because Amanda loved her pony, Flower, and always wanted to ride, Jaci had forced herself to ride more after her initial disaster. She had finally begun to like the activity, although she didn't have much style. Now she hesitated.

"You mean ride outside; away from the barn and arena?" She blushed when Nicholas laughed outright.

"Yes, I am allowed off the grounds, and you are allowed out without your chaperone."

"Without my, oh, you mean Amanda."

Nicholas nodded. "Do you trust me to see you back in one piece?"

The question sounded innocuous enough, but she heard the caress behind it. She glanced up. Eyes the color of hazy smoke, yet with a flicker of fire, met her gaze. Her stomach turned, her heart thumped, and she swore a little groan escaped.

If he noticed, he was too much the gentleman to comment. Besides, maybe she was reading too much into his comment. The only way to find out, she reasoned with herself, was to take him up on his offer.

"I'd be delighted to ride with you, but I do need warmer clothes."

He slapped his hand with his gloves, his smile widening. "Wonderful. I shall see to the horses while you change. I'll collect you at the front steps."

* * *

Their ride took them to the northern edge of his property where trees and shrubs created a dense forest and windbreak. The snow cover wasn't deep and the horses had no trouble moving along the trail which ran parallel to the thicker part of the woods.

Jaci had bundled up with extra wool stockings and her fur lined cloak, and now was glad she had. Even though the sun reflected brightly off the snow, the air was cold.

"We'll leave the horses here and walk," Nicholas spoke as he dismounted and moved around to help her.

As she dismounted, her foot slipped and she came crashing down at him, knocking them both against his horse. The horse stood steady and Nicholas grabbed her around the waist to balance them both.

"Oops, I still have something to learn." She clutched the lapels of his coat. His arms circled her and she felt suddenly very warm and secure, despite the cold December day.

"Perhaps there was ice on the sole of your boot," he whispered the excuse for her.

When she glanced up, his gaze told her he didn't care how she had ended up in his arms. Standing among acres of frozen white lace covering the trees, the horses blocking the wind, Jaci felt she belonged to another world. That thought brought a smile to her lips as he bent his head to kiss her.

His breath was warm, quickly heating her chilly lips as he slanted his mouth across hers. She felt his hands tighten at her waist as he pulled her closer.

"Oh...my," she sighed when he released her from his kiss. His eyes were intense, burning into her own, branding her heart with his desire.

His breathing was ragged and it took long seconds before he spoke. "Damn. I—"

Jaci stopped his words with a mittened hand. "I don't want to hear you apologize yet again for kissing me. If you regret it, why do you continue to do it every time we're alone?"

He didn't release her, even as he denied her charges. "I don't kiss you every time," he hesitated, "just, almost every time. And it's not entirely my fault. I can't seem to help myself when I'm around you."

In all honesty, she couldn't blame him for she was equally at fault. She dreamed about him at night; dark, exotic dreams full of marvelous sex and happily-ever-after. Now, she leaned up on tip-toes for him to kiss her again.

Without hesitation, he granted her unspoken request, his kiss hard and hot, vibrant and deliciously wicked. His lips cajoled hers to open and their tongues dueled for possession. Yet as he pulled her against him, she felt he held something back.

What would it take for him to completely lose control? Even as she secretly wished for that moment, she wondered if she would lose her soul to him if he should take her beyond the first steps of passion. For once, it seemed the right thing to do.

"Nicholas," she breathed his name in the frosty air, clinging to him as he kissed a path down her chin to her neck. She leaned back as he fumbled for the buttons of her cloak, aching with anticipation. He jerked at her jacket, gloved hands unable to work the fasteners.

Before she could help, he released her and ripped off his gloves, flinging them to the snow. Seconds later, his warm hands slid around her stomach between her wool jacket and her blouse. Dissatisfying as it was, it would have to do, for his mouth captured hers again and desire consumed her thoughts.

He grasped her mittened hands in his and raised them to the side of her head to rest against the saddle. It was to his credit that he had trained the horse well, for it shifted only slightly when he pushed her up against its side.

She recalled the last time they'd kissed. For whatever reasons, his honor always got in the way of complete surrender; a surrender she desired more each day.

She spoke, her voice husky with desire. "I want you. I think I've wanted you for a long time." She leaned forward to kiss his chin. "I fully accept the consequences of my actions...all of them."

Nicholas surprised her with the harshness of his answer. Moaning out loud, he kissed her again, this time nipping her lip and sucking the very life's breath out of her. His chest pushed against her breasts and his hips ground against her skirt. The warm clothes she had carefully donned were now a hindrance.

Still holding her hands captive, he kissed a heated path down her throat. When his hot mouth covered her breast, she groaned from the sheer pleasure that shot through her. Even through the silk of her blouse and underthings, she felt his teeth graze her nipple. She tried to jerk her hands free but he refused to release her, pulling her hands even higher, which in turned thrust her breasts forward to his reach.

"Dear heavens," she gasped, wondering how they might possibly stay warm making love in the snow. It never occurred to her that they wouldn't. In fact, she thought she would simply die if they didn't. "Please, Nicholas."

"Sh, sh," he whispered against her mouth, merriment twinkling in his eyes now, for he apparently found humor in her pleading.

She didn't care. When he kissed the corner of her lips, she swiveled her head to capture his mouth, leaning into his kiss and refusing to release him. A soul-baring hunger stripped her of any pretense. She wanted him. She craved him like an addict after drugs.

"Dear God, woman, what have you done to me?" His ragged whisper touched her heart as his hot breath fanned her cheeks. He leaned his forehead against hers, squeezing tight on her hands which were still pinioned against the horse. She tried to kiss him again, but he tilted his head out of her reach. His eyes were closed and she couldn't read his thoughts until he gave a sad shake of his head.

"Damn you, Nicholas, don't do this to me again." Her threat was without venom, for she knew the struggle he fought. At the same time, she cried out for him to appease the passionate hunger he had created.

"Would you have me come to you, stripped of my honor?" He released her hands and stepped back. When he brought his head up and met her gaze, she saw the torment their passion caused him.

"I would have you any way I can." She took a step towards him, but he put up a hand to still her. Lightly, he caressed her cheek, his hand still warm against her cold skin.

"Sweet, sweet Jaci, how I adore you."

"Then, why?"

"It is difficult to explain, for women don't see the world the way men do. My honor is my bond — my mark for all of mankind to see and accept. To take you would take my honor, also."

129

Jaci fumed. "Well, if that's not — what does that make me, practically begging you for it?" Tears blurred her vision and she swiped a hand angrily across her eyes. "Do you think me cheap and dishonorable for acting this way; for wanting you as I do?"

He gathered her in his arms, tucking her under his chin and cradling her head in his large palm. "Sweet, merciful heavens, don't ever think that. A man would have to be a fool to think ill of what you offer, or to think less of you for offering it. Every man alive dreams of a woman aching for his touch; crying out as he loves her."

She felt a shudder race through him and was sadly comforted by the thought that he ached as badly as she did. He continued to hold her, rocking in a gently soothing motion.

"But what about you, Nicholas? You speak in general terms, but not of yourself."

She couldn't have misread him. It was impossible for him not to want her as desperately as she needed him. Need. She had told herself all her life that she would never need anyone again; never depend on anyone for her happiness. Now here she stood, in the arms of a handsome, caring man, craving his touch and needing his affection. She felt him sigh, and wondered at his thoughts.

"I won't pretend not to care, sweetheart, but you must have patience. There are things to be resolved yet, before I am free to speak my mind." He loosened his hold and tilted her chin up with one hand. A gentle kiss on the nose was offered with a weak smile.

She started to protest when a gunshot echoed in the distance. She jumped, but Nicholas didn't appear too concerned.

"Must be old Henry, the gamekeeper." He released her to pull his gun from the saddle sheath.

She needed closure to their discussion, but apparently he didn't. While she still ached for his touch, he conversed on an entirely different subject.

"With the preparations Delta and Mrs. Jeffrey are making, we'll need much more food than normal. Henry must be out hunting."

"If you have a gamekeeper, why are you hunting? And what preparations are you talking about?"

"I enjoy the challenge; you know, man against the elements." He grinned at her and she shook her head at yet another sign of the chauvinistic society in which she had been tossed.

"What preparations?" she repeated.

"The party. Have you and Amanda gotten Molly to sew you new dresses?"

She had forgotten about the party. Besides, she didn't want another dress. "You have been too generous already. I can't possibly ever repay you. I won't accept more."

"Nonsense." He began to walk.

She trotted to catch up with his longer strides. She felt unsettled, but Nicholas didn't appear affected. She would simply have to wait until things calmed down after the holidays. If she had to hog-tie him, she would find out exactly what he felt for her.

"If you don't care for the blue, Molly can find another fabric to suit you." He shrugged, sounding like a disappointed little boy.

"I do like the velvet, but surely members of your staff don't dress quite so elegantly," she hesitated, then continued, "or even go to parties."

He frowned at her before answering. "We're not in town and don't stand on quite the formality. Besides, Amanda is family and where Amanda goes—"

"—so goes her governess," she finished the statement with a laugh.

"Good, that's settled." At the same time he spoke, he raised his gun to a shoulder, sighted and fired. A pheasant fell to the ground not thirty yards from them. "Are you going to bird-dog for me?"

"I thought that was Sir Lancelot's job."

The corners of his mouth lifted. "Alas, he was not brave enough to venture out with me."

131

Still struggling with her emotions, Jaci took in his devastating smile and said, "It appears Sir Lancelot is a lot smarter than I am."

* * *

Jaci and Amanda spent the day helping Mrs. Jeffrey and the entire staff decorate the ballroom for the Wildwood Christmas party. Garlands of fresh cut greenery draped the doorways, mantels and windows, caught at the corners with bright red ribbon. A huge Christmas tree stood against the wall halfway between one end and the other. It had no lights like modern trees, but instead had fragile glass balls and tiny fabric bows tied to the branches.

Glancing around the enormous room, Jaci wondered why she hadn't ventured in here before now. Mrs. Jeffrey told her it wasn't used much, since the family living quarters were, for the most part, on the west side of the house. The housekeeper went on to say when Nicholas's parents were alive, the ballroom was constantly overflowing, as Mrs. Westbrooke loved to entertain and often had guests up for weekend house parties.

She tried to imagine the house full of people. A large partition unfolded to separate the ballroom from the formal dining area on the north end. Now, the accordion type door was pushed back to allow guests to mingle along the dance floor, or take time to eat at the buffet table which had been set up in the spacious dining room.

Amanda had informed her that ice sculptures were being carved in the ice house; horses, of course, and they would decorate the table. The dance was still several days off, but Mrs. Jeffrey was leaving nothing to chance and had the maids and house staff hopping. Even Mr. Selkirk was seen polishing silver in the kitchen.

"Aren't you excited?" Amanda quizzed her as they turned their decorating efforts to the family parlor across the foyer from the ballroom.

"Oh, yes." She responded automatically for the hundredth time.

"I peeked at your dress today. Molly almost has it done and it is divine."

She smiled. Amanda always picked adjectives that were larger than life — magnificent, marvelous, and now divine. Idly, she twisted a strand of hair. She had been letting it grow and it was far longer than she'd ever worn it, but she planned to curl it and wear it up for the dance. She wondered if Nicholas would like it. Actually, she wondered if Nicholas would like her.

Her thoughts turned to the creation Molly had sewn to her specifications. Did she have the nerve to wear it? The dress draped off bare shoulders and down the back, leaving her back almost bare. After the conversation she and Nicholas had in the grove, she had decided seduction was the name of the game. Come hell or high water, she would make him lose control and do something.

She brought her thoughts back to the present. As she lifted Amanda to hang the mistletoe over the doorway to the parlor. Amanda giggled as Jaci told her about the mistletoe tradition.

That evening, she read to Amanda by the fire, waiting for Nicholas to return from town. When he spoke from the doorway, his voice startled her, the masculine timbre sending shivers down her spine. She drew a steadying breath as she stood and gazed at his handsome countenance.

"Hello, ladies, and how was your day?" His arms were crossed over his chest, the black evening coat he wore stretched taut across his wide shoulders. Matching black trousers clung to his muscular thighs; one shiny boot kicked in front of the other in a casual pose.

Amanda quickly forgot her ladylike manners as she flew across the room and launched herself into her uncle's arms. Nicholas effortlessly caught and swung her high. He grinned as he hugged her close, and Amanda planted a wet, smacking kiss on his cheek.

"Hey, Muffin, what was that for? I've only been gone for the day."

"You're standing 'neath the mistletoe, and that means all the ladies in the room get to kiss you." When he quirked a brow in disbelief, she nodded her head to emphasize her point.

"What are you talking about?"

She pointed overhead at the string of green leaves hanging from the doorjamb. "It's a tra...tra..." Amanda turned to Jaci for help, looking quite angelic when compared to her tall, scowling uncle.

"Tradition," she supplied the missing word.

"Yes, that's it. Mistletoe is a tradition. Miss Eastman says so." As she talked, Amanda tugged on Nicholas's neck, apparently trying to pull him into the room even though she was well off the ground and couldn't budge him if he wasn't inclined to move.

Nicholas's eyes gleamed as he strolled towards her. Too late, Jaci realized she should have been more specific about the tradition.

"The tradition states that all the ladies have to kiss me?" His grin was infectious, and even though she should know better, she found herself smiling in return. By this time, the two of them were very close to where Jaci stood by the fire, and she wasn't sure if the heat from the flames or her own wayward thoughts brought a blush to her cheeks.

"Well, I—"

"Now that I think on it, this tradition is familiar. And I'm sure it is intended for everyone present." His smile melted her bones; his silver gaze seared through her like an electric shock to her heart. He lowered Amanda to the floor, his gaze never leaving Jaci's.

She tried to swallow, but the lump in her throat prohibited any response to his silent request. Request? More like a demand for compliance, and Jaci felt her will to resist evaporate in the heat of his gaze.

Sighing in defeat, she decided to get it done. A quick peck on the cheek would redeem her in Amanda's eyes and yet keep her from getting too close to the source of her discomfort. Besides, every time they kissed, they got carried away, and she didn't want Amanda witness to that.

She lightly placed her hands on his lapels, leaned forward on tiptoes and closed her eyes as her lips puckered toward his cheek. At the last possible moment, she felt him turn, and her lips were captured by his. Hot, liquid fire raced through her and she swayed. His large hands captured her shoulders to steady her, but he refused to release her from what should have been a brotherly kiss on the cheek.

When he finally lifted his head, his hands still held her close as he whispered against her heated skin. "That is definitely a worthwhile tradition. Are there others that would interest me?"

She couldn't think with him standing so close, and said the first thing that came to mind, not realizing the consequences of her words. "We used to hang our stockings by the mantel on Christmas Eve."

His brows shot up in surprise and his grip tightened on her arms. She felt his heart hammering beneath her fingers, still flattened against his chest.

"Ah, I shall definitely be close at hand on the Eve; in case you need help removing your stocking."

She blushed hotter; her legs tingled as though his hands were already beneath her skirts removing the silk. Luckily, Amanda decided she had been ignored quite long enough and took that moment to tug on Jaci's skirt.

"Uncle Nicholas, Miss Eastman. Why are you still kissing? You're not standing under the mistletoe now." With the naturally short attention span of a youngster, she quickly changed to another subject of interest. "Uncle Nicholas, did you bring Papa home with you? Will he be here by Christmas?"

It broke Jaci's heart to hear Amanda's request, and from the look on Nicholas's face, she knew Cameron would probably not make it home for the holidays. She didn't understand why he would rather captain sea-going vessels than live at Wildwood with the rest of the family.

135

She did, however, fully understand Amanda's wish for her father to be home for the holidays.

She closed her eyes to keep the tears from falling, a flood of Christmas memories forming behind her eyes. If only Mandy was here, she wished. Her heart pounded as she realized she had wished her sister to Wildwood, instead of herself back to her own time in Texas.

Chapter Ten

Nicholas choked on his champagne when Jaci entered the Wildwood ballroom. Her hair, pulled back from her face into little ringlets, capped the proud tilt of her head and exposed her slender throat. She had chosen the blue velvet after all, and it set off her coloring to perfection.

He didn't know who had designed the dress, but it broke every rule of fashion. Soft velvet hugged her curves, the draped material cascading down her back while leaving most of it bare. The only acknowledgment to propriety was a bow in place of a bustle and the long train which was standard on women's evening attire.

Now, he quizzed her as they danced. "While I personally applaud your choice of style, doesn't your dress somewhat inhibit your movement?" To test his theory, he danced her into a graceful turn, his own steps sure; his hold tightening when he felt her miss a step.

She leaned into him, her soft breasts brushing against his chest. He whispered into her soft, blonde curls, "On second thought, perhaps the style has more merit than first appears."

She recovered her step, but he didn't loosen his hold. "It's not the dress at all, though I thank you for noticing. I happen to have two left feet when it comes to dancing." She chattered gaily. "As for the dress, the only concession to style I would allow is the train, though why it's necessary is beyond me. All I've done the entire night is carry it around by this little loop." She wiggled her wrist, and his gaze moved from the soft circle of velvet on her wrist up her gloved arm to a practically bare shoulder. A shoulder he longed to caress with his lips.

"You do have good taste, Nicholas, for I like the blue velvet you chose." She paused then added, "It's very soft against my skin."

This time, it was Nicholas who missed a step. Jaci, however, looked at him with such wide-eyed innocence, he thought he must have misunderstood. But then she smiled, and her lips taunted him and her gaze seduced him as surely as her dress had when she first stepped into the room.

At times like this, he questioned her appearance at Wildwood. She didn't dress or act like any woman of his acquaintance. Her outspoken attitude put her in a class by herself. He knew nothing about her, and the Pinkerton man checking her background still had no leads. Perhaps he should be more hesitant, but somehow from the moment she had appeared with her soft southern drawl and wide eyes, he had been captivated.

The music's tempo increased, and although she appeared hesitant over the intricate steps, she laughed brightly as he turned her round and round again.

"You are like no other lady I have ever known."

Her smile deepened. "Perhaps I'm simply a scandalous woman."

Normally, he held his own in any conversation, but the sexual bantering with Jaci taxed his logic to the extreme, not to mention his libido. "Perhaps I should keep you behind locked doors to make sure tongues don't wag."

She shook her head and clicked her tongue. Her eyes glittered in merriment. "Whatever would your fiancée think, having a kept woman in your house?"

He scowled. "I don't have a fiancée, officially, but if I did, perhaps I would choose to keep the woman, and not the fiancée."

Her eyes widened at his pronouncement and he was pleased to see he had shocked her. Damn, but he wanted to tell her; wanted to get it out in the open and finished. "Listen, Jaci, we must talk. There are things—"

"Good evening, Miss Eastman; Nicholas."

Nicholas turned to the sound of Thomas's voice and inwardly groaned to see that he had Lycinda on his arm.

"Since the music has ended and another dance about to begin, I thought I would request the pleasure of Miss Eastman's company. Do you mind?"

Though Thomas asked the question, Nicholas knew there was but one response. "Of course not."

He handed Jaci over with a bow and circled Lycinda's waist as the music began. Unfortunate timing, for the orchestra played another slow tune, which meant he would have to make conversation. He opened his mouth to comment on her appearance, but she never gave him the chance.

"Really, Nicholas, I don't say much about how you handle things," Lycinda stated as soon as the music began, "at least not yet."

"But?" He knew there was more.

"It's not at all proper for a governess to attend a party of this sort. It's simply not done."

"Why not? Amanda is present as well. I didn't realize new social rules were in play, Lycinda, but since this is my home, I don't believe it concerns anyone else." His tone had an edge of steel which caused Lycinda to lower her gaze. He hoped that would be the end of it. She had never questioned him before, and he didn't like having to defend his actions.

When she glanced at him again, the demure look was back, and for some reason, that made him edgy. He understood why at her next comment.

"Papa thinks spring would be a good time for a wedding — before your sale and all the races, you know."

Nicholas had a mental flash of Mason Edwardson counting the prize money as each race was won and then keeping it all while he sat by and watched. Or worse, that something would happen to Nicholas and the greedy bastard would take over Wildwood on behalf of Lycinda, his grieving daughter. Both pictures were too horrid to contemplate.

"I've been meaning to speak with you about that," he stated.

"Yes?" Her voice held a note of hopefulness

He surveyed all the neighbors, friends and acquaintances who had come to his home for a festive party. He winked at Amanda, who enthusiastically waved from Thomas's side as he danced her around the floor. His gaze found Jaci, talking to George Eastman and sipping a crystal glass of punch. She laughed at something the man said and Nicholas's gut twisted.

Lycinda lightly tapped his shoulder, reminding him of her presence. "You were saying, Nicholas?"

"I think it's something we'd best leave for discussion until after the holidays." Appropriately, the music ended at that precise moment and he was excused from explaining further.

He escorted Lycinda to the edge of the dance floor, leaving her with her father. As he made his way across the room, pausing often to visit with friends, he inconspicuously looked for Jaci. Before he reached her, he saw her eyes widen and face turn ashen at something George Eastman said. She bit her lip as she gathered her skirts and turned away, hurrying out the wide door to the foyer.

Nicholas cut behind the enormous Christmas tree, bumping into a servant with a laden tray before making his way out the furthest exit. Once out of the ballroom, he turned this way and that trying to locate her. "Did you see which way Miss Eastman went?" He questioned a servant.

The young woman shrugged, and Nicholas took off down the hall. He'd have to do it the hard way and search room to room.

* * *

Jaci paced back and forth in the dark library, unable to focus on anything. Stopping before the small secretary in one corner, she tried to strike a match to light the lamp, but her hands shook far too hard. She rubbed her hands up and down her arms trying to get warm. No fire had been lit in this room since the festivities were to be held in the ballroom and adjoining dining room.

She quit pacing and took a steadying breath, closing her eyes. The door remained slightly ajar, but the music muted the many conversations from across the giant foyer.

Oh, God, what had she done? She couldn't believe it when Thomas had introduced her to the famous, or soon-to-be famous, young George Eastman. In every photography course she had taken, his name had continually cropped up, being synonymous with Eastman Kodak.

They spoke of photography, and their identical last names, but she had found it an extremely taxing situation. She wanted to talk about high speed film and developing processes that he hadn't invented yet. She finally settled for asking questions but giving little information away for fear she might tell too much. In the course of their conversation, he mentioned a wife and baby daughter.

"I'd love to meet them some day," Jaci had responded politely.

"Alas, my wife doesn't socialize anymore; not since poor Richelle's death." A shadow had crossed his face, as a fist suddenly squeezed the life out of Jaci's heart.

"I'm...I'm sorry. Your daughter; her name was Richelle?" At his nod, she had swallowed, praying the answer to her next question would not give credence to the terror she had felt welling up inside. "When did she die?"

"This past October fourteenth."

Oh, dear God. She had squeezed her eyes shut for a moment, before excusing herself to dash out of the ballroom.

Now, as she stood in the library, which was cold and silent as a tomb, she wondered how it had happened. It didn't make any sense at all, yet it made every sense in the world. Richelle Eastman had died on the exact day Jaci had been thrown through time.

"What are you doing here in the dark?" Nicholas' voice made her turn to where his shadow loomed across the floor when light spilled from the doorway.

"Nicholas." She ran to him, flinging herself at his solid bulk, knowing he would help her understand what had happened. He was, after all, a very rational man, not given to imagination and fantasy.

"Whoa, wait a moment. I can't see a thing." He kept her tucked in the crook of his arm as he led her over to the secretary. With one hand, he expertly struck a match and lit the lamp — the lamp she couldn't light earlier.

He turned her around, ducking his head to see her more clearly. "I saw you speaking with George Eastman. What did he say that upset you so?"

She gave him a watery smile, not sure if she wanted to share her thoughts with him now. After all, since he didn't believe she came from a different time, how was she to explain?

"George's baby daughter died in October, on the exact same day I appeared at Wildwood. And it's all my fault."

"What? That's nonsense," he chided. "You didn't even know his baby. What was her name?"

Jaci looked at him in anguish. "Richelle. She had the same name as me."

He shook his head in disbelief. "There are more than two people in this world with Eastman as a last name."

"Jaci Richelle Eastman," she countered, tears welling up despite her efforts to blink them away.

Nicholas had moved away from her during the course of their conversation, and now he stood, arms crossed and legs braced, in the center of the room. He had swung the door shut when he had entered the library and the only illumination was from the lamp. Shadows played off his high cheekbones and broad shoulders, and she thought again about the fluke which had landed her literally at his feet.

If her assumption about George Eastman's daughter was true — that one person died when another passed through time — then she couldn't continue hoping to ever return to her own time. Not if it meant someone else had to die.

Looking at the man across the room, she didn't think she would mind staying at Wildwood, if she had him by her side. As though her thoughts were transparent, he smiled at her and crooked his finger.

Without hesitation, she moved into his arms. Instead of kissing her senseless, which she would have preferred over thinking too much, he simply held her. She laid her head against his chest to hear the steady beat of his heart. His arms securely pinned her to him.

"Sweet, sweet Jaci. Why must you try so hard to explain everything? Life is full of unusual coincidences. Is it not enough that you are here, with me, at Wildwood? Do you have to dissect every word a person says, every action taken, trying to discover hidden motives? You're simply overwrought with the emotion of the party and all." He patted her back and she knew that although his tone was gentle and loving, he didn't understand.

At that moment, she almost saw things from his point of view. The cold reality of her own life had left little room for faith. She had questioned actions, and with good cause, knowing some of the deviants living in Texas. But here in 1874, words were taken at face value, and as he had pointed out to her on numerous occasions, words were taken as truth.

He tilted her chin up. "Will you return to the party?"

"I must see to Amanda."

"Amanda has already been taken up to bed; exhausted, I might add." His humor touched Jaci's heart.

"It would be best if I retire, too." She couldn't bear his kindness. She knew her eyes were probably red from crying, and the thought of conversing with anyone else at this point was beyond reason for her.

"I'm afraid I'm not as lucky as you. As host, I won't see my bed until the last guest has gone. It is probably fortunate I don't decide to do this more than once a year." He let her go and moved to extinguish the lamp.

He walked her to the bottom of the stairs where she told him good night. She had stepped onto the first stair when his hand at her elbow stopped her.

"Soon, Jaci, very soon. Will you allow me a little more time?" She didn't know to what he referred, but his voice begged her for this moment.

"It seems I have nothing but time, Nicholas. I don't suppose it will hurt to grant you some. Good night." She didn't wait for a response but walked up the stairs and down the hall to her room, the orchestra music fading behind her.

She had never felt so alone in all her life. Even when her parents had died, she had Mandy and her friends to see her through difficulties. Here at Wildwood, there was no one. Oh, Nicholas had given her a job, and she had a roof over her head, but she couldn't talk to anyone about her problem because no one understood. All her training and experience, all her hard fought independence and self-esteem meant nothing in this century.

He was probably downstairs right now, dancing Lycinda around the floor, smiling and laughing, while Jaci cried inside. Why did she feel jealous? It wasn't as though she had any claim to the handsome man.

Her stomach rolled and her head pounded with conflicting and mismatched thoughts and emotions. She rushed behind the privacy screen and dropped to her knees, retching into the chamber pot. She hated herself for being weak; hated this century for all the inconveniences like the lack of modern plumbing and having to wear so many clothes that her stomach ached by the end of the day.

She sobbed as she tore at her clothes, wanting to be shed of anything that reminded her she didn't belong here, even as she secretly wished she did belong. She longed for the right to fight for Nicholas and show him how she felt.

She had teased him tonight; bantered with him on a sexual plane which men and women used in courting. He had responded, too, as she knew he would. Yet, as always, he held something back. He spoke of patience and desire in the same breath, which only confused her.

Stripped naked, she crawled into her bed, pulling the coverlet under her chin and feeling miserably sorry for herself. The practical, down to earth side of her that always ruled kept saying to make the best of her situation. There was little she could do about getting back to her own world.

Battling that practical side, however, was a new emotional core and it had created a different ache and need inside. For years, she had kept her emotions buried deep, for she didn't want to experience again the hurt or pain she had felt at her parents' deaths. Now, she knew her emotions hadn't departed, but she wondered if she really wanted them functioning again.

During most of her adult life, she had held to the convention that if she couldn't photograph something, it didn't exist. That maxim had kept her from feeling disappointment when her various romantic flings had fallen by the wayside; when boyfriends had disappeared and stopped calling. She kept telling herself love didn't exist. Now, even as she repeated the mantra, she recognized it for what it was — an attempt at self-preservation.

Her mother had loved her husband and her children. But Jaci's father hadn't loved them; he had merely tolerated them. In the end, her mother's love hadn't been enough to stop him from drinking, or from driving the car off a cliff. At that time, when she was eighteen, Jaci had sworn an oath not to love because it meant being dependent on another human being for happiness and in the end, like her mother, she would only be hurt. It had taken a trip to another century for her to realize she needed love and acceptance in her life. She needed to be pampered and held and cared for, instead of always being the one to do the caring. And now that she realized it, the ache was all the more real to know that she couldn't have any of it.

* * *

The Wildwood Ball had been the first in what began an entire stream of holiday parties. Because of the distance into town, Amanda and Jaci didn't accompany Nicholas, and many times, he didn't return until the next day.

She knew without being told that propriety dictated his moves in town and it wouldn't have been proper for him to take her. Besides, she was certain he kept Lycinda Edwardson company during those long, cold nights in the city.

Today, however, he had informed her at breakfast that she would accompany him into town to finish whatever shopping she had for Christmas, and to help him with his. Now, bundled up in wool and covered with fur lap robes with warming bricks at her feet, she silently sat across from him. The carriage wheels crunched on the snow as the driver kept the horses trotting at a good clip.

It had surprised her that the snow didn't stop the activity around Wildwood. For some reason, she had assumed everything would come to a stand-still without snow removal equipment. Such was not the case, and the number of trips into town by Nicholas and his people had created a fairly packed road. Of course, there were other residences further west, and some closer to the city than Wildwood. All had access to the same main road.

She studied the man across from her as he gazed out the windows. He looked tired. Each time he blinked, his eyes drooped a little more. She smiled. Some things never changed, regardless in which century you lived. Too many parties apparently were taking their toll.

"Why don't you live in Philadelphia, as Mr. Edwardson suggested, and leave the horse training to your managers? It would be educationally advantageous for Amanda, and so much more convenient for your business." She blushed when she realized how her comment must sound.

He turned his gaze from the passing scenery back to her and his eyes twinkled with laughter. Even so, the creases on his handsome face were deep, and she longed to soothe them away. "It is only during this hectic time of the year that the ride becomes interminable; and some of that is of my own making. Besides, I wouldn't choose to live in such a crowded metropolis, nor would I subject Amanda to that rabble as she grows up."

146

Crowded; rabble? Jaci almost laughed outright. What in heaven's name would he think of Philly in the twenty-first century?

The carriage came to a stop in town. Nicholas hesitated when she requested he drop her off alone.

"I'm only going to the few shops along this street," she pointed, "and they're right across from the City Tavern. I'll meet you there at noon. Besides, I have things to buy which I don't need you to see."

"Still, a lady shouldn't parade around town unescorted."

"It's broad daylight, Nicholas." She stepped out of the carriage and lifted the hood of her cloak. "I'll see you in an hour." Stepping up on the boardwalk, she waited until the carriage rolled out of sight.

Actually, she didn't have any shopping to do, but enjoyed strolling down the sidewalk, peeking in the windows. Since it wasn't her responsibility to maintain supplies at the estate, she rarely came into town. Life at Wildwood was pretty self-contained. Given the fact all the employees also lived right there, it was rare when she considered herself alone.

She enjoyed the company of the employees, Amanda and Nicholas, but every once in a while, she craved solitude. As a freelance photographer, she'd go to work alone, listen to the radio station she chose, and many times spend the entire day by herself. And that was just fine; most of the time. So, even though walking down the streets in 1874 Philadelphia might not qualify for being alone, it was as close as she could get for now.

* * *

Later, as she and Nicholas finished their meal of the most delicious chicken pie Jaci had ever tasted, Gustav Dentzel entered City Tavern. Nicholas waved him over to join them for a mug of hot cider.

147

"You remember Miss Eastman?" Nicholas asked by way of reintroducing her.

"*Guten Tag*, Nicholas, *und die schönes Fraülein mit goldene Haare*." He nodded and smiled at her.

"Hello. I'm sorry, but I don't speak German."

Nicholas interpreted. "He said good day to me and the woman with noodles for brains."

Her mouth dropped open, her gaze shifting between the men. Mr. Dentzel looked somewhat confused, but Nicholas began to laugh.

"I must learn to speak the English better," Mr. Dentzel stammered. "I do not think young Nicholas told you truth."

It occurred to her that Nicholas was teasing, which was a surprise, given his propensity to be rather somber. She patted the older man's hand, knowing that what she was about to say would have Nicholas guessing at her background again.

"That's quite alright, Mr. Dentzel. There is a story from Kansas where a scarecrow had only straw for brains, and the Wizard still granted him a wish."

As she expected, Nicholas immediately snatched the bait. "What scarecrow? I thought you said you came from Dallas?"

She casually sipped her cider, remarking to the wood carver how good it tasted on a cold day. When she glanced over at Nicholas, she merely batted her eyes and gave him a slight smile. Noodles for brains — I think not.

* * *

Nicholas promised Gustav that he would stop by presently to pick up Amanda's chest, so it was a surprise when the carriage stopped before a stately home on the other side of town.

"Don't we have to stop at Mr. Dentzel's?" She questioned as he handed her down from the carriage.

"I promised some friends that I would make an appearance at a recital this afternoon. Since misery loves company, I brought you along." He grinned at her and Jaci knew she had been had.

"You're very good at this game, you know." She issued the back-handed compliment as they walked up the steps.

"Ah, but it pleases me to know that you are learning. Very fast comeback at the Tavern; very fast." He chuckled and she shook her head, his infectious humor seeping into her.

Jaci actually enjoyed the afternoon. Nancy Schaffer was a wonderful hostess, and spent considerable time introducing Jaci to everyone as "a dear friend", instead of "the governess", or worse yet, "Nicholas's employee." She wasn't sure what Nancy knew about her relationship at Wildwood, but she appreciated her tact.

Somewhere in the middle of the afternoon, she realized Nicholas wasn't in the room. When she asked about him, Nancy waved away her concern.

"I have no doubt several of the men have disappeared, either to another room for some cards, or out of the house entirely. I'm sure my own dear Michael would have done the same, if he weren't already at court."

She continued, "As much as I would like to instill some culture into this backward city in which we live, it appears I have little luck in that direction. You must, however, have Nicholas take you to the Academy of Music, our opera house. They do the most delightful performances." Nancy left her to visit with other guests, and Jaci contented herself to wander around the room admiring the art.

Later, she stood by the parlor window, staring out at the lengthening shadows. Nicholas still hadn't appeared to claim her when Mrs. Schaffer returned from seeing the last of her guests out the door.

"It was a marvelous recital." Jaci felt she should make conversation.

"Come, dear, sit by the fire. Yes, Jenny does have a wonderful voice. She wants to study music next year, but I'm afraid her father may try to marry her off." The older woman gestured to a seat by the fire, giving a small silver bell a ring.

While she ordered tea from the maid, Jaci studied her host a little closer. She was soft spoken and unassuming. Her sparkling eyes seemed to know more than she was telling. Jaci had grown accustom to the clothes and the speech of this period, but still felt awkward at times, and hoped she hadn't given away some hint that she didn't belong.

"Who won the election — Reagan or Carter?"

"Reagan, by a landslide," Jaci responded automatically, then gasped. Her gaze darted around the room, her heart pounded, as though police would suddenly appear out of the woodwork to arrest her for being a fraud. "Dear God, you know. How?" A hundred questions raced through her mind as the other woman sat there and smiled.

"Mrs. Schaffer?"

"Please, call me Nancy."

"Nancy, it is so good to have someone to talk to; to be myself, if only for a few minutes, without saying something untoward. But, how did you know I was from...later?" She finished in a whisper after a maid poured tea.

Nancy sipped her tea before answering. Jaci's hands were shaking too badly to pick up the porcelain cup.

"You have that panicky look. I still remember it, even though it's been ten years or more. And, you walk as though you have on Levi's."

It suddenly dawned on Jaci that if Nancy knew she was from another century, then Nancy, herself, must be a time traveler.

"Why?" The single word spoke volumes.

"It's my understanding from others with whom I've spoken, that, while it doesn't have to be catastrophic, there is always a reason for us to be here."

"Us? You mean there are others?"

150

She smiled. "A few. You see, it seems there is a need for some to cross time to find that one person with whom they belong."

Jaci thought of Nicholas; his arrogant manner and chauvinistic attitude, and the fact that he was to marry. He couldn't possibly be the reason she had come back. She voiced her opinion.

"Your reason may not be apparent yet, but there will be one," Nancy Schaffer assured her.

Jaci said, "Perhaps I was sent to help prevent a war or something. I'm not at all good at history. I—"

"We are definitely not here to change history, except on a very personal level. Did you know you'll have a chance to return to your own time?"

Jaci's stomach lurched. "Did you?"

Nancy's smile was radiant this time. "Oh, yes, but by that time, Michael was so attached to me, I couldn't possibly leave him." Her eyes revealed her love, and when Jaci turned, she found Michael Schaffer just entering the room.

She knew her time was limited. "What can I do? How will I know?" She wanted to know when she would go back, the sooner the better, before she fell too deep to get out.

Nancy lowered her voice. "It's not something we can speak of openly. You will know. I wish you luck. Perhaps I will see you again, after we return from England."

Their privacy was gone as Michael Schaffer stopped at his wife's side. He nodded slightly at Jaci, then immediately turned to his wife, his gaze softening. Nancy stood and glided into his embrace with no thought to any other presence in the room.

"Did it go well in court?" she asked as she smoothed his suit collar down.

"No. It looks as though we'll lose, so we'll have to appeal."

"And the brief; how is it coming?"

"Slow." As he spoke, his hand dropped casually to her waist to draw her closer.

"Is Frederick the only one working on it?"

"Yes, well—" He cleared his throat and Jaci wondered if it were some secret he didn't dare discuss in front of her.

"Oh, dear. " As though just recalling her presence, Nancy turned. "I'd like you to meet someone."

Michael was a lawyer, Jaci realized from their conversation. As Nancy formally introduced them, she thought she would dislike having him for an adversary in a court of law. He was about Nicholas's size, but he had a presence about him that intimidated her. Formidable was the word that came to mind. Thick brows bunched over piercing blue eyes as he acknowledged his wife's introduction, and Jaci felt he saw right through her fraudulent shell.

His face transformed, however, when his gaze went back to Nancy, and Jaci felt their love as a tangible presence in the room. She had never been interested in photographing people, but this once she wished she had her camera to try to capture their essence.

She turned, anxious to leave. She wasn't the least comfortable intruding on the intimacy they shared. Besides, she needed time to digest the recent discoveries Nancy had shared with her.

Fortunately, Nicholas entered the room at that moment, carrying her wrap. She looked at him with different eyes. Was he the reason she had traversed time? Nicholas, the most self-sufficient, independent, and responsible person she had ever met? Somehow she doubted it.

Michael and Nancy Schaffer walked them to the door, wishing them a happy holiday, and promising to visit Wildwood when they returned from England, which was Michael's original home.

Jaci felt a moment of panic. After all, she had only learned she was not alone in this complicated world, and now Nancy was leaving. She squeezed the other woman's offered hand and whispered, "Call me."

* * *

"Call me?" Michael repeated as the carriage rolled out of sight. He bent his gray head to kiss his darling wife's ear. "Don't tell me she's one, too?"

"I'm afraid so," Nancy sighed.

"Does Nicholas know about her problem?"

"Not yet."

"I'd better warn him. I doubt he has the same agreeable disposition as I do to handle it." Michael pulled his wife back into the house and shut the door.

"Yes, as I recall, you handled things quite well. You only carried on about it for two months. And no, you will not tell Nicholas that Jaci's a time traveler, though I doubt he'd believe you, anyway. You know it's something they have to work out themselves. Besides, I'm not so sure she wants to stay."

She turned in Michael's arms and kissed his chin. "I'm very thankful I met you before my window in time appeared again. I can only hope that Jaci will come to understand her reason for being here before she loses the chance to be happy; and to be loved."

* * *

"Call me? Whatever does that mean?" Nicholas echoed Michael's words as they rode away in the carriage.

Jaci felt a strange elation over discovering she wasn't alone any more, but she thanked the lack of lighting in the carriage so he couldn't clearly see her face. "Isn't that what you say to someone when you want to visit? You know, calling cards and all that sort of thing?"

He sighed; the same sound of resignation he used every time she said something unbelievable. "I suppose one might say that, although it is more proper to issue a written invitation." He paused before adding. "You do have a strange way of speaking."

153

She shrugged, already lost in thought. She went over every single word she and Nancy had shared; looking for some hint that would tell her when she would return to Dallas. She contemplated the handsome man sitting across from her in the carriage. She clutched her hands, hot and sweaty inside her gloves. Did she even want to return to Dallas?

Chapter Eleven

"'Twas the night before Christmas, and all through the house, not a creature was stirring...'" Jaci recited her favorite holiday poem as she tucked Amanda into bed.

"I want to stay up," the five year old complained, even as she rubbed tired eyes.

They had already celebrated a full day — gift giving with the servants; a marvelous dinner of turkey with oyster stuffing and all the trimmings; and singing as the Yule log was lit.

"If you stay up, Santa won't visit, and we won't get to take that sleigh ride your Uncle promised."

"I know," Amanda said on a sigh as her eyes drifted closed. Jaci bent to kiss her forehead, and then blew out the light on the night table.

Silently, she descended the stairs to the main floor, took her wrap from the hook and bundled up. Hoping not to disturb anyone, she let herself out into the night.

In the rush of getting ready for Christmas, she had pushed aside her conversation with Nancy Schaffer. Always, though, in the back corner of her mind, she had hoped to be home with her sister at Christmas. Even if her practical side said it was not to be. If, as Nancy assured her, she would know her purpose and recognize her window to return, she could do little but wait.

The air froze in her lungs as she inhaled. Snow swirled about her boots and tried to sneak past the fur that lined her cloak and hood. She couldn't stay out long; she'd freeze even with the layers of wool she wore and the benefits of her fur lined muff. For a few minutes, though, she wanted to feel open space around her, even if the gray, snow-laden skies of Pennsylvania weren't the wide-open blue that Texas boasted.

"I imagine this isn't the kind of winter you've had in the past." Nicholas voiced her very thoughts from behind her, and immediately Jaci felt warmer.

His features were somewhat obscured by the night and the fact that the fur fringing her face softened her gaze. She raised a hand to slip her hood back to see him better, but he reached out to stop her, his touch warm on her wrist.

"Don't; you'll catch cold." He settled her hood back in place, but his fingers lingered on her cheek. She tilted her face towards his warmth.

"Why so sad? Christmas should be a time of joy and laughter."

"I miss..." she began, tears choking her reply. She gave a slight shake of her head and turned away.

"Jaci." He enfolded her in his arms as he whispered her name. She didn't object as he pulled her back against his chest. They stood in silence among the swirling snowflakes and midnight sky.

He hugged her tighter, and she felt the stirrings of desire. No, it wasn't desire she felt. The warmth spreading through her chest and surrounding her heart was more than desire; something much deeper and more lasting. Nicholas had slowly infiltrated her heart with his smile and had quietly unearthed her strongest feelings with his gentleness and caring. Jaci, the cynic, had come to realize that love did exist.

Oh, please, don't let me love this man. It wouldn't be fair to him, and I would die when it came time to leave.

"Do you know how right this feels — to have you here at Wildwood?" He whispered close to her ear.

"Amanda is a sweetheart, and I appreciate the fact you let me stay as her governess. I don't know that I ever thanked you for that."

He turned her in his arms and tilted her chin with a finger. Even in the dim light from the house, she saw the silver glitter of his gaze.

"You know good and well it's not Amanda's care to which I refer."

Of course she knew; but it wouldn't do any good to admit it.

"Jaci, I love you."

"No, no you don't." She covered his mouth with her hand, hoping to block the words, but they hovered between them and Nicholas didn't appear to want them back. "You don't know anything about me; we argue constantly and I don't do what I'm told." She glanced back and forth, anywhere but at his face, looking for more excuses.

"And that's one of the reasons I love you." He pulled her closer, their hips meshing.

Panic welled in her chest. She didn't love him; she didn't; and it wasn't fair of him to love her. "You love Lycinda."

"No," he said, shaking his head.

"You're supposed to marry her. Her father said so."

"No." He grinned at her; that silly, little boy grin that lit his eyes and made her heart melt.

"You can't. I can't." She said with dejection as she twisted out of his grip and stepped away from his embrace.

"Why not?"

Damn, he was persistent.

"I already told you. You don't know—"

"I know that you're lovely and stubborn and spirited and argumentative at times. I also know you love Amanda as much as I do and usually your arguments are on her behalf." He paused, and she wondered if he wanted her to argue with him now.

"There's more to me than that; things you can't even begin to imagine." It wasn't simply that she came from a different century. She couldn't allow him to love her when she didn't know what was to become of her.

"Then tell me your secret so we can get on with our lives."

"I...I can't." She rushed towards the door, aching for his touch but knowing it unfair to take what he offered when she couldn't give in return. As she hurried inside, his words echoed behind her.

"I love you, Jaci Eastman. I won't give up!"

Jaci slept fitfully that night, dreaming of Nicholas and declarations of love. "If only...if only..." she mumbled in her sleep.

"Wake up, wake up, it's Christmas day!" Amanda bounced on her bed and her eyes flew open. In that short space of time between sleeping and waking, she was back in her bed in Dallas; Mandy clamoring at her to wake up and see what Santa brought. As she scooted out of bed, her bare feet hitting the cold, wood floors, she sent a silent wish for a Merry Christmas across the century to her sister.

"Okay, okay, Amanda. Merry Christmas to you, too." She hugged the little girl before heading for the privacy screen. "You might as well wake your uncle up, and I'll meet you downstairs in a few minutes."

As soon as Amanda left, Jaci washed her hands and face in the water provided in the pitcher. Glancing at her reflection in the mirror as she brushed her hair, she decided she needed to dress before going downstairs. Her puffy eyes looked bad enough; there was no reason for Nicholas to see her in her nightgown and robe.

Nicholas. What was she going to do about him? Jaci's hands fumbled with dress buttons as she recalled their conversation last night. I love you. His words warmed her heart and gave her goose bumps at the same time.

She had wanted to seduce him; she still did, but lust was different from love. Besides, that was before she had found out there would be a window for her to return to Dallas. Now? She didn't know what she wanted.

"Miss Eastman?" Amanda's voice came from down the hall and Jaci closed her mind to the might-have-beens and descended the stairs with a Christmas smile on her face.

There were more presents under the tree than had been there last night. Jaci wondered when Nicholas had time to shop.

"Merry Christmas to you," he said softly as he handed her a cup of coffee on a delicate china saucer.

"Thank you," she returned, taking the coffee and letting her gaze linger over his appearance. His hair was pulled back, as always, but he had dressed casually in tailored slacks and a shirt open at the throat, covered with a satin, smoking-style jacket. His face was clean shaven, the creases around his mouth deepening as he smiled. She realized she was staring.

"You can have your heart's wish, you know. All you have to do is ask." He leaned close to whisper.

"I don't...I wasn't..." Jaci sputtered.

He laughed and left her standing in the middle of the parlor. She took a gulp of coffee. The nerve of that man — to think she was staring at him because she wanted him. Even if she did, it was very impolite of him to notice.

She settled in a chair close to the fire as Amanda passed out her gifts. She had drawn pictures for her uncle and Jaci — a horse for him and a field of flowers for Jaci. When Jaci asked who the two little girls were in the middle of the flowers, Amanda whispered, "Me and Mandy," and Jaci cried.

Nicholas insisted Jaci pass out her presents next and leave his for last. Self-consciously, she handed him a small wrapped package. Amanda had already claimed her larger box in which Jaci had wrapped a riding habit and a jaunty little hat. She squealed excitedly when she opened the lid.

Jaci had agonized over what to buy Nicholas. She knew the rules governing gift buying must be radically different here than in her time. To tell the truth, even after living under the same roof as he for the past three months, she didn't know his tastes, except in brandy, which she refused to purchase.

"The Gilded Age," he read the title out loud when he unwrapped the book. "This is Twain's newest treatise on the ruin of mankind, isn't it?"

"You've read it," Jaci stated, disappointed.

"No, I haven't. Thomas mentioned last week how hilariously Twain wrote, but I've had little time to read." He smiled in thanks. "This will make a most welcome addition to my library."

"Now open Uncle Nicholas' present," Amanda interrupted as she shoved a package into Jaci's lap.

As she opened her present, Nicholas got up and slid a wooden chest from behind the tree. She recognized the trunk which Nicholas had consigned Gustav Dentzel to make for Amanda. When Nicholas saw her watching him, he put a finger to his lips, his eyes twinkling.

She glanced down at the box in her lap. On a bed of soft satin lay a miniature carousel horse, cast in silver. "Oh, my," she breathed as she lifted the delicate piece from its cushion. The carving was intricate, every detail revealed in the lines and etching in the metal.

"It's a music box," Nicholas supplied.

Jaci wound the figurine and set it on the table at the side of the chair. A tinkling melody, reminiscent of the waltz she remembered dancing at the Wildwood ball, floated about the room as the carousel horse gracefully turned on its center pole.

Tears blurred her vision as she glanced up at Nicholas. "Thank you; it's beautiful." The words seemed inadequate to express what she felt at that moment.

His smile, dazzling and heartwarming, completed her Christmas.

"Now, Muffin, it's time for your big present." He turned his attention to Amanda, and Jaci sat back to watch. However, his next words caught her off guard. "Your papa sent a message to the Shipmaster to say how sorry he was to miss Christmas, and he sent along this chest for you to put all your treasures in."

Amanda squealed in delight when she opened the lid to find a pretty rag doll waiting for her hug. "I knew Papa wouldn't forget. Did he say when he would be home?" She raced to Nicholas and gave him a hug.

"Soon, Muffin. He'll be home soon." He returned her hug, but his gaze connected with Jaci's over the top of Amanda's head.

She slowly shook her head when he winked at her. She smiled in return, silently mouthing the words, "You are wonderful," letting him know she knew the truth and understood.

* * *

Sleigh bells jingled as the horse pranced across the hard packed snow. Amanda giggled when Jaci sang a song she called "Jingle Bells", and Nicholas felt content with his world. He hadn't declared himself to Jaci again; he didn't want to pressure her. It didn't bother him at all that she denied his love. The wonder in the kisses they had shared told a different story.

He lightly touched the reins to the back of the horse, clicking softly under his breath, relaxing to enjoy the winter scenery. Brown tufts of grass still showed sporadically, waving stiffly in the cold air. A continuously, curving set of parallel lines from previous sleigh rudders cut through the snow on the side of the hill. Those would disappear fast enough if another storm came through. The silence of a winter snow was overwhelming. As much power as the swirling masses of moisture contained, the white flakes bombarded everything in sight without a sound.

His musings were cut off when Jaci spoke, her thoughts reflecting his own. "The stark contrast between the pristine snow and dark bark of those bare trees makes me wish for my camera. I'd love to capture the beauty of Wildwood in photographs."

"You take pictures?" He vaguely recalled her comments about being a photographer.

"Yes," she sighed, "I did at one time. My idol was Ansel Adams. He took the most beautiful pictures — the

161

contrasts were vivid — and yet he only used black and white film."

"What other kind is there?" He didn't know much about photography, but he did know it had progressed beyond the brownish tones of a daguerreotype.

She appeared taken back by his question, but shook her head and simply stated, "Never mind. Tell me about Wildwood."

"My family has been here three generations. Grandfather tried farming, but decided breeding horses was a lot less work. He invested a tremendous amount of money purchasing the best thoroughbreds available anywhere in the world. My father continued that tradition, as have I."

"Your house and arenas and track all look well-tended."

"Breeding horses, either for show or racing, involves much more than the animals. It takes skilled people and good facilities. The birthing stalls are. . .well, never mind." He flashed her a grin. "You'll have to excuse me. When I speak of Wildwood, I tend to forget myself."

"You have every reason to be proud. It's beautiful."

He did feel pride, not only in his home, but in Jaci, for she saw the hidden beauty of Wildwood as well as he did.

"Wildwood does tend to be isolated. We have no neighbors for miles around, and as you have probably ascertained, I'm not much for entertaining. In the winter, trips into the city become even less frequent."

She responded as he hoped she would, although she couldn't have realized how important her answer was to him. "I don't mind the solitude. I never was much of a socialite."

He clicked the horse into a trot for home, feeling good about his decision. He had no doubts that Jaci would marry him, though she might need convincing. He loved the lady sitting on the seat beside him, and knew she had intense feelings, too. He intended to explore those feelings more fully once he had released Lycinda from any obligation.

"I must go to Philadelphia," he said without preamble. The sooner the better, he added to himself. "Tomorrow."

"But Uncle Nicholas, you promised to take us ice skating. You even got me new skates for Christmas, 'member?"

Nicholas sighed. "You're right, Muffin. I'll go to Philadelphia the day after."

* * *

The day dawned crystal clear, and as promised, Nicholas bundled Amanda, Jaci, and Molly beneath blankets and furs in the sleigh, allowing Amanda to sit up front with him. At the last minute, Sir Lancelot jumped into the sleigh and snuggled down at Amanda's feet.

"Go on with you now; scat." Molly tried to shoo the dog away, but Amanda protested, hugging the dog around the neck.

"He's an Irish Setter, isn't he?" Jaci asked. "Aren't they hunting dogs?"

"Well, Sir Lancelot here isn't much of a hunter." Nicholas playfully reached down to scratch behind the dog's ear. "Unless you count hunting for a scrap off Amanda's plate." Sir Lancelot whined as though in protest and everyone laughed.

The single horse had no trouble pulling the sleigh across the hard packed snow on the lane, and Nicholas assured them the pond lay close enough to the road that they wouldn't have far to walk. Immediately upon arriving at the pond, he gathered enough wood to start a small fire should they get chilled while skating.

While Molly helped Amanda put on her skates, Jaci struggled with her own, swatting aside petticoats and heavy velvet skirts. "It was much easier in pants and a sweater," she mumbled under her breath, wondering how on earth she would ever stand up, much less skate across the frozen pond.

"What's that, Miss?" The ever vigilant Molly lifted her head from lacing Amanda's skates.

"Never mind. It's of no consequence." Jaci stopped in the middle of knotting the second skate. Dear me, I'm even beginning to talk like them.

Her thoughts were immediately diverted when Amanda squealed. She straightened her skirts carefully around her legs as she watched the child glide out onto the ice, her cheeks rosy with cold and excitement. For such a young child, she skated exceptionally well, and Jaci assumed it was the circumstances.

At Wildwood, the pond was always available in winter, and cost nothing. By contrast, she and Mandy used to go to the indoor rink at the Galleria, paying for the privilege of skating for an hour or two. Because of that, the opportunity hadn't come along very often.

"Miss Eastman, perhaps you would stay warmer if you got off that log and moved about."

She glanced up sharply as a shadow crossed her vision. Nicholas, handsome as always in his greatcoat and wool trousers, extended a hand to her.

She wondered when she had fallen in love with him. The words didn't surprise her today, even though two days ago she had protested such an idea. Deep in her heart, she had already known the truth. She shook her head in wonder.

For most of her adult life, she had tried to avoid macho males who wanted to run her life, and yet here she was, stuck in the wrong century with just such a man. And the problem? She didn't seem to mind it.

Nicholas had a magnetic personality which drew others to him, herself included, and his smile was enough to make a girl faint, or swoon, or whatever they did in 1874. He had a terrific sense of humor, talked to her intelligently and not in a condescending manner, and seemed to value her as an individual. Of course, when they argued, it was as violent as the thunderstorms that shook the earth, but even their fights had sent shivers of excitement through her.

So what's the problem? She asked herself. Aside from the fact that she didn't belong here and didn't know how long she would stay? She shook her head to clear it as she allowed him to pull her out onto the ice, deciding today wasn't made for worrying.

"You're much more graceful on skates than the back of a horse," he teased as he skated in front of her.

Her skirts billowed out about her, but she found they didn't inhibit her movements like she thought they would.

Nicholas was showing off by tipping forward, one foot lifted behind him in the air. She pushed him, catching him off balance. He wobbled and fell on his fanny.

"Alas, it's too bad you're not. Do you always end up on your as...derriere?" She stood in front of him to judge his reaction.

His grin was infectious, and she threw back her head and laughed, tossing all her dire thoughts to the wind. She turned and skated away, but he quickly caught up with her.

"Here, try this," he challenged as he expertly turned in front of her, capturing her hands in his and resting one of them on his shoulder. With no apparent effort on his part, he skated backwards while guiding her into the steps of a waltz. Though awkward at first, she soon found she actually did move more gracefully on skates with all her petticoats than she did on dry land. She began to hum a tune in time to their movements.

"I cannot figure you, Jaci. You have no apparent skills; you have said yourself you were not reared in any of the womanly arts. Yet you adapt to almost any task set before you — cooking, teaching Amanda, riding; even dancing on ice. However do you manage?"

He spun her in a graceful circle, his movements bringing her closer. She knew they could only have a relationship based on honesty, and her newly awakened love made her reckless. She flashed him an impish grin as she answered his question. "Television."

"What?"

She had to clutch his shoulder tightly to keep from tumbling when he jerked her tight against him. She had tried to explain before, but he always refused to listen; forever falling back on that age-old male doctrine that women didn't know what they were talking about.

165

"Television. It's a machine that shows moving pictures to educate. You know, I watch the cooking shows on PBS, ice skating at the Olympics, and all the old movies on Saturday nights."

He stopped abruptly and she slammed into his hard chest. She curled her fingers around the lapels of his coat before bringing her gaze up to the silver gleam of his eyes.

"I think we have had this conversation before." Puffs of frosty air punctuated his remarks. "I wonder perhaps if you will ever fully recover from your original injury. I doubt you would still spout nonsense about magic boxes and flying machines if you had." He had not let her go; his arms circled her in a cocoon of warmth; his breath only adding to the heat of her blush.

Did he feel the electricity like she did; the need to touch him even when she knew she shouldn't? She tilted her head back, her gaze taking in the wayward lock of black hair falling across his forehead, the gray at the temples that only enhanced his appearance. When she shrugged negligently to relieve the tension, he grinned, his full sensuous lips parting to reveal straight white teeth. She lightly tugged on his lapels to bring him closer.

As often as they had kissed recently, she should have been prepared. Even so, it amazed her at how quickly passion ignited in his gaze. His lips swiftly descended to hers, capturing the breath from her body and bathing her in warmth. She had always laughed at her sister's description of jolts of electricity from a simple kiss, but now she realized it could happen — it was happening.

The buzzing in her head reminded her of the accident at the carousel, and she wondered if she would open her eyes and be back in Dallas. Perhaps becoming involved with a man from the wrong century was what she needed to return to her own time.

When the pressure on her spine and mouth lessened and she opened her eyes, however, she found Nicholas staring strangely at her. Her mittened fingers shook as they touched her mouth, still tender from his kiss; her heart pounded a rhythm too fast to count. She had remained in

166

Nicholas's time. Tears stung her eyes as she realized she was immensely glad she had not been transported.

"Uncle Nicholas, Miss Eastman — watch!" Amanda called for their attention and she didn't have time to dwell on her mixed up emotions.

She did notice that Molly, who preferred not to skate, sat by the fire, her gaze carefully averted. Even so, Jaci blushed. She didn't know how her actions looked to Molly. With a sigh, she switched her thoughts and attention to Amanda, who was turning tiny circles further out on the pond.

"Be careful, Muffin," Nicholas called to his niece, ever mindful of their safety. Jaci heard the yearning in his voice, and knew he thought of Amanda as his own daughter.

"Oh, Uncle Nicholas, you know I am. Don't be an old fuddy-duddy."

Suddenly her scream rent the still morning. Horrified, Jaci watched as, in slow motion, Amanda began to sink through the ice.

"Amanda!" Nicholas bellowed a denial even as he raced toward the hole that had swallowed his niece. Jaci scrambled after him, her heart in her throat and her breath coming in short gasps.

Nicholas fell forward and slid the last several feet as he reached for Amanda. He paid no attention to the popping and hissing, but before her eyes, the ice cracked open further around the hole. She stopped well away from the turbulence, realizing she would do no good if she, too, fell through the thin sheet covering this part of the pond.

She watched, terrified, as Nicholas snatched Amanda from the jagged edges of the ice. Although time stretched interminably, he had reacted quickly and it was actually only seconds before he clutched a wet Amanda to his chest. He jerked his coat off and wrapped it around the little girl.

"Hurry, Nicholas, we must get her dried off," Jaci yelled as Amanda coughed and wheezed, shivering violently. He struggled to his feet, but as he began to skate forward, an ominous crackling vibrated around them. Jaci reached out as the ice gave way with a mighty groan.

Nicholas threw Amanda forward, and Jaci grabbed at her. Together, they fell backward, Amanda's wet dress and petticoats causing her to weigh twice as much as normal. She bundled the girl in her arms, scooting backwards on her fanny, digging the ends of her skate blades into the ice to give her traction. She scrambled around at the edge of the pond, keeping her gaze focused on Amanda's breathing.

Sir Lancelot yipped, racing around in a tight circle by Jaci, trying to get closer to Amanda.

"Miss Eastman, Mister Westbrooke — he's..." White faced, Molly pointed.

Jaci turned to scan the broken surface of the pond. Where was Nicholas? Where?

"Nicholas!" Even as she screeched his name, she thrust Amanda into Molly's arms and scrambled back onto the icy surface. Sir Lancelot whined, grabbing a mouthful of her skirts and pulling, trying to keep her from leaving the bank. The pond was literally falling to pieces, and huge cracks now crisscrossed the surface. Suddenly Nicholas's head appeared from where he had fallen through another weak spot.

"Sir Lancelot, go for help, now!" The dog only raced back and forth between Jaci and Amanda, whining and yipping.

"Sir Lancelot." Amanda's hoarse whisper stopped the dog in its tracks. "Go." She pointed towards the house and the dog raced off, this time barking loudly.

"Wrap Amanda in a blanket and get her to the house! I have to help Nicholas!" Jaci flung the words over her shoulder as she stepped further out onto the ice.

"Oh, Miss," Molly wailed, "I can't drive a horse. I swear—"

"Molly, you can do it. You can do whatever it takes to fetch help for Mister Westbrooke. Do you want him to—" She caught a glimpse of Amanda's petrified face and didn't finish the sentence. Her thoughts must have transmitted themselves to Molly, however, for the girl hustled Amanda into the sleigh and grabbed the reins. The harness bells jangled as the horse trotted away, and Jaci sent a silent prayer for help to arrive before it was too late.

Regardless of the thin areas, the cracks, the threat of falling in herself, Jaci inched toward Nicholas. When she skated as close as she dared, she dropped to her knees and scooted forward on her fanny. For once, she was thankful for all her petticoats as they insulated her against the cold.

Nicholas had dragged himself part way out of the icy water, his fingers digging into the ice. His face was taut with strain; eyes closed with the effort she knew it took to hold on.

"Nicholas, I'm here. Tell me what to do." Her voice quivered. Further crackling echoed across the frosty air, and a vision flashed across her mind of her own dying. Though she might long to return to her own time, she didn't want to die to do it. Nor did she want the man she loved to die. "Grab my hand. Let me pull you out." She flattened out on her stomach and reached a hand to his.

"Get back." His words hissed, as cold as the icy water in which he struggled. Though his words were only whispered, the ice cracked further, and she saw his gaze flash wildly around them.

"No, I won't leave. I can help, I know I can. I'm stronger than I look." She pleaded, "Nicholas, please."

He didn't answer. She glanced around for something to use to help them, but the few loose pieces of wood had been thrown on the fire. Just then, she saw a wagon appear across the far side of the pond. Too far away for the bundled figures to be recognized clearly, she thought it must be the twins.

"Toby! Travis! Help!" Even as she yelled, she felt the ice vibrate beneath her, and realized her mistake before Nicholas said anything.

"Don't...yell," he gasped, and she could only wonder at how cold he must be. She had no idea how long someone could stay in the icy cold water and survive; nor even how much time had already passed. But she did know the longer he stayed submerged, the less were his chances.

"If my yelling will crack this whole damn pond, I'll do it. Then you can walk out of the water instead of me dragging you up from the bottom." She didn't know where she had the strength or determination to sass him at a time like this, but it did bring forth a watery smile, and for that she was glad. She glanced back to the far side where the boys had whipped the horse into a canter, the wagon bouncing precariously over the frozen trail.

"God, I wish I had a telephone." The thought came unbidden to her tongue, but when she glanced guiltily at Nicholas, she noted his eyes were closed and he appeared to be sleeping. Sleeping? She knew that was the worst thing for someone in the cold. She shook his arm and urgently called his name. Every movement she made caused the ice to quiver, and it was only by chance that it didn't give way.

"Jaci?" His voice was weak, but he was aware of her presence and Jaci took that as a good sign. "What is a telephone?"

Oh, dear, now she had done it. He had little patience for her stories of what he called imaginary misfortunes of her still rattled mind. But she had to do something, so she started talking. She voiced what she hoped were the most incredulous of all inventions. Anything to keep him alert.

"Where I come from, we have telephones, and telegraphs, and television. There are also satellites that fly through space...and videotape machines. If I had a video camera, I'd take pictures of how ridiculous you look..." She wanted to keep it light, but she sobbed, and fresh tears froze on her cheeks the moment they fell. She cautiously released one of his arms and raised her hand to his wet hair to brush it back from his forehead. God, he was so cold.

"Pictures? We have pictures. You know George Eastman..." His voice, already weak, faded until only a puff of white frost indicated he still breathed. His head lay sideways on one arm, his skin deathly pale. Jaci caressed his cheek with her hand, which she had removed from her mitten since it was wet anyway.

"No, silly. Moving pictures, not photographs." The ice beneath her cracked again, and she clutched his arm with both hands.

"Let me go, Jaci." Defeat and resignation edged his words. "Just let go and save yourself. This...ice won't hold..." His eyes had been glazed but focused on her face. They now closed, the lids blue with cold, eyelashes spiked with ice crystals.

"No!" Her anguished cry of denial echoed against the silence of the woods.

In that single moment before his eyes closed, Jaci realized why Nicholas had always looked familiar. Those very same silver eyes had stared out at her from the glossy paper of a photograph; one she had taken at the carousel. That night in her dark room, what seemed like years ago instead of only months, Nicholas Westbrooke had cried out to her in pain; begging her for something that, at the time, she couldn't identify.

Now, she understood. She had met her destiny and nothing she did would change that. Regardless of what Nancy Schaffer said, Jaci knew she did have a purpose for being here. She had come to save Nicholas.

Over the sound of her sobs, she heard someone call her name. She turned her head as far as she dared without releasing Nicholas, and saw Toby and Travis at the near edge of the pond.

Toby cautiously walked out onto the ice. When it popped beneath his weight, he looked helplessly at Jaci.

"Throw me the rope, Toby. I'll get it around him. Get the wagon ready to move." She knew the longer they waited, the higher the danger to Nicholas. Even now, his breath was extremely shallow and his arms shook beneath her grip. He had lost consciousness, and she dared not let loose of him for fear he would sink beneath the surface.

It took Toby two attempts to get the rope close enough that she didn't have to let go of Nicholas to reach it. Her own limbs were numb with cold, and she prayed she could make the rope secure enough to bring Nicholas out of the water. She knew she couldn't hold him if he started to slip.

Her hands shook with fear as she tied the rope around him and yelled at Travis to start pulling.

The hardest part was yet to come, for as the rope became taut, Nicholas's clothes hooked on the ice. Instead of pulling him up out of the water, they only succeeded in breaking more ice around him. She rapidly scooted back before she yelled at the twins to pull quickly enough to jerk Nicholas above the ice and out of the water.

Once they reached shore, she scrambled to her feet as Mackey and one of the stable boys came running down the hill. Together, the men lifted Nicholas from the frozen ground. Toby whipped the horse into motion as soon as they were all in the wagon. She removed her skates while Mackey piled warm blankets around Nicholas's shaking body. Even so, his skin was blue with cold, and he mumbled incoherently. When Mackey started rubbing Nicholas's arms beneath the blanket, she cried out.

"Don't do that!" At Mackey's look of surprise, she softened her tone. "Rubbing his skin is the worst thing you can do. It will damage the nerves." Mackey's incredulous expression said he doubted her word. She knew, however, from location shoots she had done, the effects of frostbite and exposure. How was she to make him understand?

"We need to keep him warm, and once we get back to the house, we'll bring his body temperature up gradually. Too great a temperature change will shock his system."

"What about pneumonia?" Mackey was clearly concerned about his employer's condition, but she couldn't reassure him. She wasn't a doctor.

Instead she asked, "How's Amanda?"

"I'm not sure. That mangy dog raced into the yard barking and grabbing my pant leg, and then here came Molly, driving that horse hell bent—" He cleared his throat. "Well, I imagine Mrs. Jeffrey's got her bundled up in bed already. She didn't stay in the water too long, did she?"

"No, not as long as Nicholas," Jaci whispered. The old trainer's gaze returned to Nicholas's face. Her thoughts paralleled his, for she knew he wondered, too, how long was too long in the freezing water?

Chapter Twelve

Jaci wouldn't go to her own room to change until she had been reassured that Dr. Stillwell had been summoned. She told Selkirk to get Nicholas's clothes off as soon as possible, and what to do until the doctor arrived. Even so, chaos reigned by the time she entered the room.

Toby and Travis were hovering at the foot of the bed, twisting their caps and shuffling their feet. Selkirk fluffed the pillow beneath Nicholas's unconscious head, straightened the covers, and fluffed the pillow again.

Feisty Mrs. Jeffrey was arguing with Mackey, who said they should massage Nicholas's legs like they did the horses.

"Miss Eastman said cold water towels, and that's what we shall do until the doctor gets here." She yelled at the crusty old trainer as she removed a towel from Nicholas's leg and replaced it with another.

Jaci was happy to see someone carrying out her instructions, although she had no idea if it would help. She only knew what wouldn't, and that was hot water and rubbing. She seemed to recall that too drastic of temperature changes for frostbite was like getting the bends when scuba diving.

It had been more peaceful in Amanda's room when she stopped to check on the child, but then, Amanda wasn't in danger of losing her life. Nicholas had grabbed her so quickly she hadn't had much time to catch cold. Molly sat with her to make sure a fever didn't develop, but Jaci felt Amanda was in fairly good shape. Unlike Nicholas, who had been willing to sacrifice his life for his niece's.

She moved quickly to the side of the bed, placing her hand on top of Selkirk's. The butler jerked, but when she met his gaze, she saw how troubled he was. "He'll be alright, but we have to let him rest." Selkirk appeared relieved someone had taken charge, for he nodded and left the side of the bed to take up a vigil by the twins.

"How's he doing?" She asked Mrs. Jeffrey.

"He'd be a lot better if everyone would leave him be." Even though her words were crusty, the housekeeper's voice trembled.

"Has someone gone for Dr. Stillwell?"

"Yes, Miss," Toby answered, "but with the icy roads, it may be awhile."

She looked from face to face. Nicholas commanded respect and loyalty from his employees, and now she saw the true concern they felt for him. It appeared he was much more than these people's source of income. What would they do if —

No. She refused to even think of any other possibility other than his full recovery. But Mrs. Jeffrey was right. They needed to let him rest.

"You may all go. Mrs. Jeffrey and I will tend to Mr. Westbrooke." She turned back to help, but when she heard no movement behind her, she glanced up again. Everyone stood exactly where they had before. She sighed. She would have to speak to Nicholas about granting his employees some free thinking and independence.

"Selkirk, please go downstairs and tell Delta to make some coffee; and tea for Mrs. Jeffrey. Oh, and a light broth for when Mr. Westbrooke comes around." Without hesitation, Selkirk turned and left to do as she asked.

"Toby and Travis. I'm sure there are chores to be finished this afternoon. Mr. Westbrooke will want you to take care of his horses." The twins seemed glad that someone had given them a direction to follow.

"Mackey?" What was she to do with the trainer?

"Yes, Miss. I can take a hint. I'll see to the boys. You let me know when the boss comes 'round." He patted her shoulder as he left.

"Thanks, Mackey. You always were a friend," she said, realizing she was speaking of both the Mackey's in her life. Briefly she wondered how the twenty-first century Mackey fared.

Once the room had cleared, she took a closer look at Nicholas. He had some color in his face, but dark circles framed his eyes, and his skin felt clammy to the touch. With no need for words, she continued helping Mrs. Jeffrey change towels every few minutes.

Over the course of the next hours, they gradually raised Nicholas's skin temperature. He never stirred beneath their ministrations, and she frequently checked his breathing and heart rate. While wiping his face with a cool cloth, she thought she saw him flinch, and hoped it was a good sign. But when she changed the dressings on his legs a little later, she pinched his skin right above the knee and he never twitched a muscle.

Horrid thoughts whirled through her mind and her stomach churned. What would happen to him if all their efforts were too late? How would she feel if Nicholas lost the use of his legs; or lost his legs altogether?

How would he feel? The thought put the final touches on her already upset stomach and she rushed over to the screened area and threw up in the chamber pot.

"What the hell happened? How is he?" Jaci heard Thomas Stillwell's voice even over the sound of her own dry heaves. She dropped to her knees. There was nothing left to come up, but still she couldn't quit gagging.

A cool hand slid across her forehead; another rubbed her back. Thomas's soothing voice reached her. "Take a deep breath now. Come on; that's a girl."

Between breaths, she gasped, "Help Nicholas."

"Nicholas is breathing normally; you are not. Since he's unconscious, there's not a lot I can do at the moment."

She had managed to get her stomach under control, and turned and slid the rest of the way down the wall. She turned watery eyes up to the doctor.

"Besides, you sounded like you were in much worse shape." He smiled at her and she felt a little better — until she thought of Nicholas lying over on the bed.

"Oh, Dr. Stillwell, what can we do? You have to save him." She started sobbing and the hiccups began.

"I will certainly do what I can for Nicholas, but if you come down ill, who will help Amanda, or Nicholas, through this crisis?" This time, the doctor gave her a stern look, and she knew he was right.

She nodded her head several times in agreement, and held her breath to stop the hiccups. When the doctor held out a hand, she took it and he pulled her to her feet. Together they walked over to the bed.

"Mrs. Jeffrey explained briefly what happened. Do you have any idea how long Nicholas was in the water?" Thomas became very professional as he asked questions and probed Nicholas's legs.

For the first time since the accident, she actually became aware that Nicholas wore only a night shirt, his legs bare, the covers thrown back. Even when she had been tending him, she hadn't thought about anything except making him well. She blushed now as she watched Thomas examine him. After all, they were Nicholas's bare legs.

"Miss Eastman?"

"Mm? Call me Jaci." She answered automatically.

"Well, all right. You don't appear embarrassed being at a man's sick bed, so I assume you will help Mrs. Jeffrey take care of Nicholas?" His words were hesitant, but she heard neither acquiescence or condemnation in his voice.

"I'll do whatever needs to be done." She felt stronger now that the doctor was here, although he had yet to comment on Nicholas's condition. "Will he be all right?"

Thomas shook his head. "I don't know. We have much to learn about the human body. Just when we learn to diagnose, some poor specimen betrays us and dies, or survives, despite our best efforts." He gave her a weak smile, but she saw the grave concern for his friend in his gaze.

"You appear to have some skill at nursing, as his skin feels normal to the touch. The nerves below the surface are another matter, and may take time to recover from such trauma. I have no doubt, though, that he'll develop a fever, in which case you might need Mackey or Selkirk to help keep him in bed."

He snapped his bag shut. "I'll leave some medication. We won't know what damage was done until he wakes up and tells us." Handing her a bottle, he turned back to his friend, placing his palm on his chest once more. "Get well, my friend. I'll have to think hard to come up with something that can possibly outdo you on this one."

Jaci didn't understand the significance in his remarks, but panicked when she realized he was leaving. "Don't go! What will happen if he does get a fever? How long before we know something?" The idea of taking care of Nicholas; the idea of not being capable of doing so; quickly overwhelmed her.

"You and Mrs. Jeffrey will do fine. Many a time she's had to take care of Nicholas and me when we got into trouble well over our heads." He smiled at the older woman who once again hovered over the still form on the bed. "Besides, there's little more I can do for now, and I have an anxious lady and a most worried husband waiting for the delivery of their first child. Where Nicholas is in little danger of further damage, George's trials have only begun."

"I'll walk you down the stairs." She needed to move; needed a breath of fresh air.

"Someone must get word to his brother, Cameron," she stated at the door, although she was actually thinking that someone in the family needed to be here to be in charge.

"I took care of that before I came out. The minute Sam came to my house, I sent a servant down to the dock master. If he's not already on the way back, they'll track him down and relay a message as fast as possible."

Night had fallen by the time she bid the doctor good-bye. She walked out to the kitchen and helped Delta prepare a tray which she took back upstairs to Nicholas's bedroom.

"Any change?" She questioned Mrs. Jeffrey as she set the tray on the small table by the window.

The housekeeper shook her head.

"Here; have something to eat." Jaci set out two bowls of soup and a plate of fresh bread.

177

With a tired sigh, Mrs. Jeffrey sat down at the table with Jaci. "How does something like this happen?" The woman shook her head sadly.

Jaci reached over and patted her hand. Sounding more confident than she felt, she said, "He'll come around, as hard headed and feisty as ever."

* * *

She lived to regret her words when, three days later, they were still fighting Nicholas as his fever raged. He would be calm, though unconscious, for hours at a time, before suddenly flinging the covers aside. His eyes would be open as he ranted and raved about anything and everything but he didn't see her, and no amount of soothing words stopped his rampage.

After the third such episode, one of the men always remained close, either in the room or right down the hall, for neither Jaci nor Mrs. Jeffrey could hold Nicholas down when he decided otherwise. She doubted he would have hurt either of them, but she knew he didn't realize what was happening.

He did, however, seem calmer when she sat with him, speaking in a soft voice, though her words didn't always make sense even to her. After one such fever episode, she noticed that no matter how much he thrashed about the bed, he wasn't moving his legs. It was only his upper body that moved.

"I'm not at all sure the cause," Thomas frowned in answer when she asked him about it on his visit. He poked and prodded along Nicholas's leg, then lightly ran his finger up the sole of his foot. Not one toe curled in response. "His legs are normal in color and warm to the touch. I no longer fear gangrene, but until he becomes conscious, I can't tell you more."

For Jaci, that meant waiting, however long it took. Amanda came to keep her company, but the poor child grew so sad seeing her uncle lay helpless on the bed that Jaci tried to find other things to keep her occupied. While she sat with Nicholas, Molly would play with Amanda, Mackey took her for horse rides in the barn, and the twins even rounded up the kittens and brought them up to the house one afternoon.

If Jaci wasn't with Nicholas, she spent time with Amanda, reassuring her that her uncle would be fine; that it wasn't her fault, and that her father was on the way home. What little sleep she managed came from exhaustion when she would unintentionally fall asleep in the chair by Nicholas's bed or on the couch by the fire in his room.

Tonight, she dreamed that he was finally awake and fully recovered. He called her name and she ran to him, hugging him in a tight embrace and kissing him with abandon. Other sounds intruded, but she blocked them from her mind in her joy to have him back with her. It took her fatigued mind long minutes to realize that she no longer dreamed, and that the noises came from across the room where Nicholas lay.

Scrambling to her feet, she rushed to the side of his bed to find his eyes open. He struggled to sit up, but when she reached forward to prop him up with more pillows, he pushed her away.

"Leave me." His voice, harsh from disuse, grated on her already frayed nerves.

"No, you need me."

"I don't need anyone. Besides, you haven't seemed especially blessed in any of the other domestic areas. When did you learn the art of healing, and how the hell do you expect to help me?"

"You're feverish," she commented, reaching out to touch his brow. He grabbed her wrist and squeezed.

"Get out!"

She knew it was the pain and fever talking. She didn't know if he had tried to move his legs. She assumed he had and was having difficulty. That would explain his tantrum, and she simply refused to listen.

Mandy had called her plenty of names when punished for wrongdoing, and she found that to be a good parent you had to be consistent and tough skinned. She decided she would have to treat Nicholas the same way.

In a no-nonsense manner, she moved back by the bed and straightened the bed covers and poured him fresh water. She felt him watch her and her hands shook.

He was right; she knew nothing about taking care of a sick person. All she had ever done was pick up the phone and call their family doctor, but no one here wanted to be in charge. Selkirk and Mrs. Jeffrey both looked to Nicholas anytime something went wrong. Now, until he was better, he would have to put up with her.

She moved to the hearth and started to add a log to the fire.

"Don't. It's hotter than hell in here now. Do you want to burn the house down?"

She turned back to him and noticed he had thrown the covers off and his face now looked flushed. She moved to his side and wet a cloth with cool water. He fought against her placing it on his forehead, then finally gave a ragged sigh of resignation and threw an arm over his eyes to shut her from his vision.

His action reminded Jaci of hide and seek with Amanda. She had stood in a corner as plain as day and covered her eyes with her hands, thinking if she couldn't see Jaci, then Jaci couldn't find her. Now, she was sure Nicholas thought the same although she didn't understand why he was so determined to hide from her help.

She changed the cloth on his forehead. "Does that feel better? When I'm sick, I know—"

"You don't know anything about it." His hot breath fanned her cheeks as his anger swept across the short distance between them. Flashing silver eyes, the color of a storm cloud, defied her to tell him different.

"You're right; I don't know how you're feeling right now. But I do know about the little boy who peed on his mother's flowers because he had heard his father say the ground was too piss-poor to grow anything." His eyes

180

widened at her language, and the fact she knew this about him, but she still saw the anger.

She wouldn't let up. "I also know about the young boy who took a whipping for his little brother when he left the gate open and the horses got out."

"Why are you doing this?" He choked out the question; his anguish tugging at her heart.

"I want to know where that spunky boy is — the one who could bear anything for his family. Where's the man with a smile for everyone, who treats Amanda with the love of a father; the one who embraces life? Where is he?" she demanded.

There was a long silence as Nicholas glared down at his legs, lying uncovered on the bed, not a muscle moving in either of them. He raised his gaze to her, the anger so intense Jaci took a step back.

"He drowned in that pond."

Nicholas turned his head to the wall, and Jaci knew she would not reach him now. She watched in silence as his eyes drifted closed and his breathing shallowed. At least this time it would be a natural sleep; a sleep that would make him well — she prayed.

* * *

Loud cursing followed the crash of shattering glass. Shaking her head in resignation, Jaci started up the stairs.

"This has got to stop," she muttered to herself. It had been over a week since the accident, and Nicholas wasn't improving. He still couldn't move his legs, and each day he became more surly. To a point, she didn't blame him, but he didn't have to take it out on the staff.

As she reached the door to his room, Selkirk came out, carrying a dustpan with shards of broken glass piled high. The smell of whiskey was strong. That was another problem she supposed she would have to deal with, since no one else appeared capable of taking charge.

181

"I'm sorry, miss," Selkirk said, shaking his gray head. He seemed to have aged in the past week and she knew Nicholas's illness was taking its toll. Selkirk was the only one Nicholas would allow near him to tend to his personal needs, but at the same time he verbally abused the poor man.

"None of this is your fault, Selkirk, so please quit saying you're sorry." She straightened her back and decided that, regardless of circumstances, she would have to make Nicholas see reason. After all, what could he do; fire her? And even if he did, he couldn't enforce his dictates. Perhaps that would make him mad enough to get well. She grimaced at the unpleasantness she was sure awaited her behind the door.

Patting the butler's arm, she cautioned him. "No matter what you hear in the next few minutes, do not come up here." At his attempt to interrupt, she repeated herself. "Don't come up, do you understand?" She captured his gaze and held it. Only after he nodded his head in agreement did she release his arm from the death grip she had.

Pasting a smile on her face, she pushed open the door and entered the lion's den. "Nicholas, you must stop badgering the help. Poor Molly and Mrs. Jeffrey won't even come up here anymore. What's to happen if Selkirk decides to remain in the kitchen with everyone else?" She chattered gaily as she crossed to the windows and pulled back the curtains, letting in the wintry morning light. She didn't look at him yet, for she knew if she did, her resolve would weaken. The sight of him lying helpless on the bed always did that.

"Get out." Two hostile words were all she got in return.

"You know I won't do that." Although it might appear improper, Jaci was the only one Nicholas allowed to touch him, even though she knew he hated every minute of exercise she provided because it continued to bruise his ego. He yelled and cursed at everyone from the lowest stable lad to Selkirk. If he told them to get out, they obeyed, for he was still the master of his household. She simply refused to pay any attention.

"You're letting your hair grow." The unexpected comment, couched in softer tones than his usual bellow, spun her around.

She gasped at how rough he looked. His face had become much more lean, his cheekbones more prominent, his silvery eyes deeper set. A dark shadow of a beard covered most of his lower face. Apparently he hadn't allowed Selkirk to shave him before he had thrown his tantrum.

"You are too," she commented, for his hair looked as wild as the north wind and quite as unruly. Yes, she thought, it was definitely time to take charge.

She stopped at the wardrobe and grabbed a clean nightshirt. "Here, put this on while I get the lotion." She handed him the shirt, but instead of taking it, he grabbed her wrist, pulling her closer. Her heart beat faster.

"Why don't you put it on for me?" In other circumstances, she would have gladly complied, but his voice wasn't seductive. It was a sneer, and she knew he only tested her.

She twisted her wrist out of his grip. "For starters, you need to begin to take care of yourself. You're perfectly capable of doing so." She turned her back on him and moved to the dresser to retrieve the lotion she used when she massaged his legs. She took her time, not wanting to turn around when he was naked, and not knowing if he would even change.

"You can turn around, Miss Eastman. I am clothed enough not to offend your delicate sensibilities." The sneer continued and she sadly shook her head. This would no doubt be a lot harder than she anticipated.

He had the clean shirt on. "I'm glad you decided to cooperate." She moved to the side of the bed, poured some lotion on her hands, and began to massage his calves.

This had been a ritual since the accident. Dr. Stillwell didn't understand why Nicholas couldn't use his legs, since they had returned to normal for all outward appearances.

183

Jaci knew muscles would atrophy from lack of use and she suggested physical therapy until he walked again. Both she and the doctor agreed on this, even over Nicholas's shouting that he wouldn't lay around while she, or anyone else, touched him.

He had laid there, though, for there was no way to get away from her. Hostile and silent, she felt the heat of his glare on her back as she massaged his legs. Some days, the physical contact was more than she could bear, for regardless of his present condition, his closeness still caused an emotional upheaval to her system. She had fallen in love with him, and the fact that he couldn't presently walk made no difference; she still loved him.

She continued his therapy, hoping one of these days he would fight back, pushing his foot against her palm, jerking his leg away from her touch. But he did not.

When she reached across him to work on the other leg, she heard his sharp intake of breath. At least he was feeling something, she thought, but didn't dare sneak a peek at him, until she heard the clink of glass.

She paused in her ministrations and turned to find him staring at her breasts, a drink in his hand. In one gulp, he downed the glass of whiskey and reached to pour another.

"You don't need that," she stated calmly.

"You don't know what I need, Miss Eastman," he returned, bringing the glass to his lips, his gaze searing her from hip to shoulder. "And if you did, would you give it to me? Would you crawl into bed with a cripple?"

Jaci gasped at the harsh words cutting into her like a knife. She began to wonder if she were strong enough to deal with this situation after all. Yet when she looked beyond the cynicism, was there anything more vulnerable than a man whose very essence of living had been stripped from him?

"I would come to bed with you, Nicholas, because of the man I grew to...care about," she spoke gently, her gaze caressing his face, looking for some sign of softening.

There was none. He simply poured himself another drink and slowly drank it, his gaze steady on her face as though challenging her.

She had learned the hard way to survive, and she now had a strength of purpose which did not waver. She walked up to the head of the bed and took the drink glass from his hand. "How can I make you understand?" She began quietly. "It's all right to depend on someone else. As far as the other is concerned, it can take more than an accident to keep you from being a man."

"Well, aren't you the eternal optimist. Does it not occur to you that I will never walk again?" He shouted at her, though she stood only a foot from him.

"I've learned over the years that some things can't be changed, and you have to learn to live with them."

"Aha."

"However," she stressed the word, "in other cases, you must make the most of your opportunities, and answer the challenges set before you." She thought back to her parents' deaths, when she felt the world had collapsed beneath her. She had pulled through, however, and she knew in her heart that Nicholas could, too, if only he would help himself.

She glanced around the chamber, where the drapes had been pulled shut constantly unless she was here, and where the smell of whiskey overwhelmed her. It appeared at the moment that Nicholas did not want to adjust, nor did he want to face the world he had known. She would have to think of a plan to capture his attention and make him quit feeling sorry for himself.

Gentleness hadn't worked; pleading hadn't caused him to relent. She pursed her lips and settled her hands on her hips as she surveyed the bedroom. Her eyes lit on what she needed, and she marched over to the corner, snagging the handle of a basket which set near the desk. Turning it upside-down, she emptied the magazines onto the desk.

"What are you doing?" She thought she detected a hint of anxiety in his voice.

Good.

She marched over to the mantel and began depositing into the basket the bottles of liquor which Selkirk had brought up.

"Leave those be."

She ignored him. "You're going to be a lonely old man unless you quit drinking and talk to someone. Unless you admit you need help, more than your legs will shrivel up and die." They were the hardest words she had even spoken, and it took determination not to choke on the anguish she felt building inside. But someone had to make him see reason, and so far, no one had.

She snagged the last bottle off his bedside table before he realized her intent, but she didn't move fast enough to keep him from grabbing her wrist.

"Give it back."

"No." She would not relent; she wouldn't.

"Please?"

She looked him straight in the eyes and held her ground. "My father drank himself into an early grave and took my mother with him. I'm not about to let you do the same."

He released her arm and flopped back onto the pillows. "Look at me. What difference does it make?" Despair edged his words, and Jaci fought against it for him since he wouldn't fight his own battles.

"What difference? Look at Amanda. What will become of her?"

"I can't help her now; not like I am." He turned his head to the wall, breaking eye contact.

Her anger flared. "You idiot. You've got to talk to her."

He wouldn't answer.

"You can't ignore the problem. You may not want to deal with it, but you can't run away."

"Bad choice of words." He fired back at her.

"You know what I mean. Talk to her. Tell her it's not her you're mad at. It's not her fault."

His head snapped up, eyes wide. "What are you talking about?"

"Amanda blames herself for your condition. If you would quit wallowing in self-pity and think about her—"

"She'd be better off without an uncle who can't walk."

"Is that what you think?" She practically screeched. "She doesn't love you because you have all your legs and arms and fingers and toes. She loves you because you love her."

"What do you want from me?" He bellowed and she swore she saw tears in his eyes before he again averted his gaze.

"I want you to try. Living's a Helluva lot harder than dying." She touched a hand to his shoulder, and though he didn't jerk away from her touch, she felt a tremor run through him. I love you, Nicholas, she thought, but knew better than to say the words out loud, for he would accuse her of pity.

She blindly made her way to the door, trying one last time to make him understand. "What happened to those words you shouted at me Christmas Eve? Where's the man who yelled, 'I won't give up'."

"Go away." His words were full of pain and desperation and Jaci's heart broke.

Chapter Thirteen

Nicholas swore as Jaci ran from the room, slamming the door behind her. She apparently refused to see him for what he had become — a useless cripple. Everything he was; the very essence of his being, revolved around his ability to stand tall and to speak with business associates eye to eye. He couldn't train his horses and make deals while flat on his back or from a cripple's chair. And he couldn't love her.

He watched dust motes dance along the sunlight which streamed in past the open curtains, bathing him in sunshine. Damn her! She had taken his drink, which was the one thing that transported him into a world without heartache. He longed to remain in that dark void where sunlight and happiness didn't pierce, for surely that's what had happened to his soul.

How could he explain how he felt, when he didn't understand himself? Never in his life had he been this useless. He turned his head away from the light. He wouldn't cry — tears were for women and children. God knew Jaci, Amanda and the rest of the female household had shed enough for him over the past weeks. And little good it had done. Didn't they think he would walk if he were able?

His eyes burned, and he squeezed them shut, refusing to let the tears fall. Grown men didn't weep. God, how he longed to belong to that world again.

Only Selkirk knew of the intense, secret struggles he fought. Time after time, he demanded his legs move him out of bed and to the chamber pot. By Nicholas's command, Selkirk would stand stoically by, even as he cursed him and the world. At the very last second, when he either accepted the butler's help or embarrassed himself on the bed linens, Selkirk would silently assist him.

Now, he feigned sleep when Selkirk came in with his luncheon, preferring not to eat. He would even forgo his whiskey, because in order to get a new supply, he would have to interact with the man and ask for it. It was bad enough he lay helpless in this bed; he would not beg. The butler quietly set the tray on the table within reach and left. But he, too, left the damnable drapes open.

* * *

Even after Nicholas's tirade, Jaci continued to tell herself it was because of the fever, or the drink, that he said the things he did. She had to make herself believe that, or most certainly she would fall apart.

She glanced around the kitchen table where several of the staff and she and Amanda had gathered for lunch. Somehow, she had been given charge of keeping everyone else from collapsing under the strain of Nicholas's illness.

Of course, no one actually needed to be told what to do; they had been doing it for years. But cook still needed someone to check the menus, and Mrs. Jeffrey liked to know that she and the housemaids such as Molly were continuing on the right track with a little praise for their hard work. Without wanting or asking for the responsibility, Jaci had been thrust into the role of Mistress of the Manor.

She watched as Selkirk entered the kitchen to visit in whispers with Delta before coming over to the table. Nicholas rang for Selkirk several times a day, but the butler never gave any indication of what the two of them discussed. Normally, Jaci would assume it didn't pertain to the running of the household, and she didn't question him. After her recent argument with Nicholas, though, she felt she needed to say something.

"Did Mr. Westbrooke eat?" At her question, Selkirk shook his head and poured himself a cup of tea. She glanced at Amanda, whose face mirrored her own concern,

189

and decided it wouldn't do to discuss too much in front of the child. Nicholas still refused to see her and it was devastating the little girl.

"Amanda, be a sweetheart and help Delta with the dishes, would you?" Without a question, the child left the table to help Cook.

"You didn't take him another bottle of whiskey, did you?" Jaci whispered to Selkirk. "It's imperative that he—"

"I understand your reasons for taking away his bottles, miss," the butler answered. "I simply don't know that will make a difference." Poor Selkirk appeared to have aged much more than anyone else, and again she wondered what it was that Nicholas saw fit only to tell this man.

"What does Nicholas say to you all those times you go up there alone?" She asked what she thought was a simple question, but Selkirk's face turned red and he tipped over his chair in his hurry to leave the table.

"Nothing, Miss, nothing at all."

She wouldn't take that for an answer. She grabbed the sleeve of his coat before he got far. "Selkirk, you sit down here and tell me what's going on. Don't you think all of us want to help him get well?" She gestured to the rest of the staff, all avidly staring at him with wide eyes.

"I can't do that, Miss." His tone was remorseful.

"Can't; or won't?" Jaci challenged him.

Selkirk's gaze bounced rapidly around the room, never settling anywhere, and definitely not on her.

"Please?" she pleaded, for suddenly her heart pounded and she felt somehow this man held the key to Nicholas's life.

He jerked his head towards the door, and without a word, she followed him into the hall, away from the other servants. Heaven only knew that the servant's grapevine would have the news soon enough, but apparently Selkirk kept his own counsel because no gossip had reached her yet.

"It has to do with his...bodily functions," he whispered, his face turning redder by the minute.

She scrunched up her face. "I don't understand."

He sighed, staring at the wall off to the side of her head, refusing to look at her. "Miss, this is exceedingly embarrassing. I cannot begin to explain something like this to a lady."

Her eyebrows flew up as understanding dawned. "Oh, my, I never thought...but you say he rings for you when he needs to go to the bathroom?" Loud bells were going off in her head, and her heart had begun to beat faster at the possibilities.

"Miss, really..."

She grabbed the butler by the lapels, determined to get him to tell her. "Don't clam up on me, now, Selkirk. If he knows he needs to go, he feels something in his lower body." When she saw the look of awareness on his face, she released her hold on his jacket. Patting it smooth, a gigantic smile came to her.

"And if he feels that particular sensation, his nerves are healing and he should be able to walk." She turned away and headed for the stairs. "This is great; this is incredible. Oh, Nicholas is going to be so happy—"

"Miss?" Selkirk stopped her progress. "It's a most embarrassing situation. I wouldn't suggest that you bring it up to Mr. Westbrooke."

"Nonsense, Selkirk. It's time things got back to normal around here." She lifted her skirts to race up the stairs, the butler groaning behind her.

* * *

"Will you not leave me with one ounce of dignity, woman?" Nicholas yelled at her.

Jaci couldn't believe he wasn't at all happy with her diagnosis. "I believe you have bruised nerves, and they're beginning to heal. That's why you feel the need to go to the toilet."

Dead silence greeted her statement. Then, in a deadly soft voice, Nicholas ground out, "I do not need you hovering over me. Get out."

His words effectively doused her spirits, for though he had yelled at her before, it never had quite the effect of his soft spoken words. The glass of water she had poured slid from her shaking fingers and shattered on the floor.

"You don't mean that," she whispered.

"Of course I mean it. Now leave."

She looked deep into stormy eyes no longer glazed with fever. She recognized fear and desperation, but that was no reason to speak to her with such loathing. His words tore at her heart and with a cry, she turned and fled.

"Nicholas, that's certainly no way to talk to a lady," Thomas accused as he entered the bedroom. She couldn't greet the doctor, but instead turned her head to the side as she brushed past him on the way out the door.

Thomas found her later, after his examination of Nicholas. She had curled up in the window seat in the parlor, still crying her eyes out.

"I can take you to town, if you wish. You can stay with me." His invitation was issued quietly, and it took her a moment to realize exactly what he meant. She gave him a watery smile as he stood uncertain in the middle of the room.

She slowly shook her head. "I can't leave him, though I thank you very much."

Thomas frowned, his fair features such a contrast to Nicholas's dark looks. There was much to be admired in both men, but she feared her heart belonged to only one.

"You would rather stay here while he rants and raves and curses at you?" The good doctor's brows came together over piercing eyes, but something in his voice made her reconsider what she thought were his motives.

"Does he mean it; all those hateful words?" She almost choked on the words, recalling the anguish in Nicholas's voice at the time.

Thomas came over to the window seat and sat, taking one of her hands in his large, warm ones. "Right now,

Nicholas hates everything about his world. He dislikes you, and me, because we can walk, and he hates himself because he can't."

"But that's so unfair. I love him." She flung herself into his arms, comforted by the strength she felt there. How easily it had been to come to depend on others in this world.

Thomas's smile was gentle as he set her from him. "I thought as much, and am happy for Nicholas. It might be the one thing that can make him want to live again. Right now, he doesn't consider himself a man."

She shook her head. "What do you mean? Because he can't walk doesn't make him less of a man." Jaci knew many handicapped individuals, and while a few remained hostile to the rest of the world, most lived productive lives.

"It's more than walking, though that is a very large part of it. It's..." Thomas shifted his gaze.

"Do you mean 'bodily functions'?" She mimicked Selkirk's voice. In the midst of chaos, all these very proper men couldn't speak of such things. In other circumstances, she would have laughed. "Selkirk told me about that and I think it's a good sign. If he feels the urge to do that, he may soon feel sensations all down his legs."

"You may be right on that note, and we should hope for the best. Still, there are other things to consider."

She looked at the doctor; this man who no doubt had seen everything there was to see on both man and woman. He wouldn't meet her gaze. "Are you talking about sex?"

Thomas blushed clear to his sandy eyebrows. This time, she did laugh; she couldn't help it.

"Haven't you ever delivered a baby, Doctor?"

"Of course I have."

"Well, sex is what created babies in the first place. I see nothing embarrassing about two people consummating their love for each other." She paused. "Are you saying you don't think Nicholas can make love?"

Thomas had to clear his throat before he answered. When he looked at her, she saw deep humor in the twinkle of his eyes. "You have quite a unique outlook and I think

Nicholas is very fortunate to have found you. I sincerely hope he doesn't throw it all away. If anyone can make him feel like a man again, in any or all ways, I believe it will be you." He bent near and kissed her cheek, and she knew how fortunate both she and Nicholas were to have him as a friend.

* * *

As soon as breakfast was over the next day, Jaci summoned Mackey and Selkirk to the study where she explained her plan.

Mackey shook his head. "I don't know, Miss. I dare say he'll steam real good if you do that."

"Mackey, he's steaming now. What will make the difference? Besides, look at the view from this window." She scurried over to the drapes and threw them wide. "He can wake up to the sun shining in the window and see his horses from his bed. What could be better?"

She turned to face the men, firm in her conviction. "Nicholas needs to be with people. He can not remain upstairs shut away any longer; nor will I allow him to do so. Spring will be here in another month and I know it will make a difference." At the continued reluctance she saw on the men's faces, she added the *coup d'état*. "You put me in charge; now you will reap the benefits of that decision. I expect the changes to be made by the end of the day."

Though the feeling of power made her head light, her stomach twisted nervously as the morning slid by. She deliberately stayed upstairs with Amanda most of the afternoon, trying to get the child to study. Eventually, they both gave up. Here was yet another reason Nicholas had to get well.

Amanda refused to learn her lessons, and Mackey said she hadn't been to the stables much since the accident. Every time Jaci helped her dress, it seemed her little shifts hung looser on her shoulders. As far as Jaci knew, Nicholas still hadn't seen Amanda. Well, all that was about to change.

Jaci had dreamed about the accident again last night. Each time that happened, the revelation came to her that Nicholas had crossed the century to show up in her photographs. To her, that meant something, and she refused to give up on him.

She prepared a special tray for him that night, telling Delta she would take it up herself. Selkirk and Mackey were the only people who knew the plan, and she wanted to leave it at that. She didn't want anyone else getting into trouble, and she had no doubt there would be some.

Nicholas scowled at her when she came into his bedroom. The lamps had already been lit and the drapes drawn, even though there was about an hour of daylight left. Smiling sweetly, she set the tray on Nicholas's lap and stuffed another pillow behind his back.

She didn't comment on the darkness, nor the fact that he apparently hadn't let Selkirk shave him today. Since the accident, more often than not he would let his beard grow for days at a time before either he or Selkirk would shave it. Jaci frowned, but said nothing, leaving him to eat in solitude.

She didn't venture back for two hours, and when she entered the room this time, she immediately rang for the servants. The dinner tray had fallen to the floor, the dishes scattered from the impact. Nicholas lay sideways on the bed, still as a post.

Selkirk appeared by her side. "You didn't do him in, did you, miss?" His voice sounded quite shaky.

"No, of course not." Even so, Jaci reached out to check for Nicholas's pulse. He hadn't moved a muscle, and she really did hope she hadn't given him too much of the sleeping draught Thomas had originally left. "The drug will make him sleep soundly, so he won't argue with us when we move him. By the time he wakes up, he'll be in his new room downstairs. What can he do? Climb out of bed and walk back up here?"

The butler gasped, and she supposed her dark humor didn't set well. When Mackey entered, the two men hoisted Nicholas up and carried him downstairs to the study-turned-bedroom.

She dismissed the men once they had Nicholas comfortably tucked into bed. She opened the drapes and allowed the moonlight to filter through the glass. The night was clear and she saw a horse or two in the paddock. Because she knew he couldn't hear her, except perhaps in his deepest subconscious mind, she spoke from her heart.

"Nicholas, I hope you realize I'm doing this for your own good." She walked quietly back to the bed and sat down on the edge beside him. She took his hand and caressed the back. "I love you dearly, and am terrified of losing you. You must begin to understand that I'll love you forever. I want to see you well and on your feet again, but even if you never take another step, it won't stop my feelings for you."

She bent forward and placed a soft kiss on his brow. "I didn't want to fall in love with you. I now know what Nancy Schaffer meant, and I never thought it would happen to me."

She studied his profile. In sleep, the worry lines were gone; the downward slope of his mouth had softened. Perhaps he was having happier dreams than his day-to-day life inspired. She hoped so. Only the new day would tell whether her latest attempt to goad him into living would work.

* * *

"Sel-l-l-kirk!" The bellow ricocheted off the walls, and if the servants hadn't already been up, they most certainly would have risen in a hurry.

"Oh, dear, here it comes." The gray-haired man commented as he and Jaci looked at each other over coffee.

"Well, at least we won't have any trouble hearing him from now on," she said wryly, not at all sure, in the morning light, that they had done the right thing. Unable to allow Selkirk to take the blame, she shadowed the man down the hall as he entered the study. Back against the wall, she scooted forward to overhear their conversation; feeling guilty, but not guilty enough to stop listening.

"What in the hell is going on? How did I get here?" The bellow hadn't softened, even though Selkirk was now inside the same room.

"Miss thought you'd be more comfortable—"

"Who?"

"Miss Eastman, sir. She thought it would do your spirits good to be among your family on the ground floor, and to see your horses." Jaci heard the scratch of the curtains being drawn open further.

"The only thing that will help my spirits is a bottle of spirits. And draw the damn drapes!" Nicholas's voice had become so belligerent that Jaci almost stepped inside.

"I'm sorry, sir, but Miss Eastman says no more booze." Apparently Selkirk could hold his own.

"Booze?"

"Her word, sir, but I believe it means spirits."

"Miss Eastman, Miss Eastman. Who the hell put her in charge? Isn't this my house, anymore?"

"Yes, sir, but while you're recovering, Miss Eastman has taken over; so to speak, sir."

"Well, get Miss Eastman in here." There was a pause, and Jaci longed to see what was transpiring.

"Now!" The single word was hollered. Jaci's head scrunched into her shoulders.

"Yes, sir." Selkirk's voice was quite near, and when he appeared at the doorway, a wide grin split his usually stern features.

In a conspiring voice, he whispered, "Come," and headed down the hall towards the kitchen. Jaci quickly followed. Once they were out of hearing distance, he turned, the smile still in place.

"By Jove, it's good to see him show some spirit. He hoisted himself up on the bed, and for a moment, I actually thought he would jump up and come after me."

For the first time in days, Jaci laughed. It appeared things would get better. She took Nicholas his breakfast as a peace offering. He scowled at her but didn't bluster, and she refused to be intimidated. Calmly she explained that moving him was for his own good; the sunshine was for his own good, and getting well was for his own good.

"I'll come back when you're in a better mood," she ended her speech as she put his breakfast tray on his lap.

"That'll be a cold day in hell," he countered, but she took heart that he didn't sound nearly as belligerent as usual.

* * *

"Good day, sir. We're all very glad you've made it home." Selkirk's voice drifted into the parlor from the front door, and Jaci wondered to whom he spoke. Thomas wasn't expected, and she knew of no one else who had indicated they would come visiting.

Sitting in front of the fireplace, she looked up from the game of checkers she and Amanda were playing. A gasp escaped as a man entered the parlor. "Nicholas? How on earth?"

Amanda squealed and jumped up, running across the room. "Papa!" She grabbed the man's leg in a hug and wouldn't let go.

The man stood there, awkward and seemingly not knowing what to do with the child who clung to his person. He clumsily reached down to pat her head.

So this is Cameron, the prodigal brother, thought Jaci. He looked just like Nicholas.

Dark hair fringed a tan face, his eyes the same silvery color. Upon closer scrutiny, she realized he was shorter than Nicholas, and gray had yet to tip his hair.

"Amanda, where are your manners?" she softly chided the child.

Amanda peeked around the edges of Cameron's coat, not in the least bothered by the fact that her own papa didn't toss her into the air as Nicholas did upon his return from business. She looked at Jaci, puckered her lips and shrugged her shoulders.

Jaci sighed and shook her head, trying to gracefully untangle her legs and rise from the floor.

"Allow me." Cameron had moved across the room to help her.

"Thank you." She suddenly felt shy, not at all sure how to respond to this man. After all, he was family, albeit absentee, and she was only an employee.

"My brother; where is he; how is he?" Even as he spoke, Cameron doffed his greatcoat and hat, handing them to Selkirk, who had followed him into the room. "Amanda, stop." He curtly acknowledged the child's tug on his pant leg.

Jaci immediately sprang to the little girl's defense. Gently, she untangled her from her father's leg and lifted her close. Kissing her cheek, she whispered softly to her, but shot daggers at the man. "Don't worry, sweetheart, your papa is tired from his trip. I'm sure that's the only reason he would speak so."

The man had the good grace to look properly chastised. "I'm...I'm sorry, Muffin."

"Don't call me that," Amanda retorted, though her words were muffled as she hid her face in the curve of Jaci's neck. "Uncle Nicholas is the only one who can call me that."

Cameron looked taken back and somewhat embarrassed. Perhaps she should work on him as long as he was home. He might be more receptive to change than his brother. But the thought of taking on any more dysfunctional family challenges drained her of strength, but she managed a weak smile of welcome.

"Good day, Cameron. I am Jaci Eastman, Amanda's governess. Your brother is resting comfortably, but we did move him to the study. If you would like to see him, I'm sure he's awake. Even if he isn't, see him anyway, because he should be awake. Selkirk can show you the way."

Cameron looked quite startled that anyone would speak about his brother that way. She figured she would have to explain her behavior eventually, knowing the younger brother had no idea what the household staff had been through during the past month.

"I need to put Amanda down for a nap. You are welcome to speak with your brother, and I shall see you at dinner." As Amanda clung to her neck, she realized she looked forward to setting Cameron Westbrooke down and explaining quite a few things to the errant young man.

Chapter Fourteen

Nicholas heard Jaci's comments, since no one saw fit to close his door and allow him any privacy. His life was no longer his own, and Cameron's appearance only confirmed that. They needn't have summoned Cameron. During all their years growing up, and even after they reached adulthood, Nicholas had been the one to fix things, not Cam. What was his younger brother supposed to do now except make Nicholas feel more guilty at the idea of having another person around whom he couldn't support?

"Nicholas?" The timid query came from near the door, and Nicholas's heart ached at the sound of that voice.

His eyes stung and his arms longed to clasp his brother close. Still, he feigned sleep when Cameron whispered his name, because he couldn't force himself to face the little brother who had always looked up to him.

At least in this instance, someone gave him a little respect. The door closed quietly and he was left alone again.

* * *

Nicholas might have known his peace wouldn't last. Instead of Jaci bringing him breakfast as she had done practically every day since his accident, this morning Cameron hoisted the tray. With the efficiency of a military sergeant, Cam deposited the tray on the table by the bed, marched to the curtains and flung them open, and turned to face Nicholas, hands on hips. He squinted against the bright sunshine.

"My God, man, you look horrendous." Whereas last night Cameron's voice had Nicholas longing for his attention, this morning he could as well do without his false cheerfulness.

"Close the curtain, Cam."

"No; can't be done. Miss Eastman says sunshine is good for the soul."

Nicholas groaned. Did everyone on this entire earth quote Jaci Eastman? Of course they did; he'd been hearing it for weeks.

Cameron sauntered back towards the bed, catching up the breakfast tray. "Here, scoot yourself up so you can eat this while it's hot. I brought two cups; thought I'd join you for a cup of coffee."

Nicholas raised a brow and started to argue, but knowing he hadn't won in more days than he could count, decided against it. Besides, the aromas coming from the covered dish were too tempting. Using the strength of his arms, he pulled against the headboard, dragging his body into a more upright position.

Cameron set the tray in his lap, grabbed a cup and poured them both coffee, before sitting in a side chair and propping his booted feet on the bed.

"Are you quite comfortable?" Nicholas groused.

"Actually, no, I would be more comfortable at the breakfast table. But since you're in here and refuse to come out, I guess this will do — for awhile." Cameron never looked at Nicholas the whole time he was talking, and Nicholas wondered where he got the bravado to speak so. Cameron had always been quiet; not shy, exactly — just not aggressive.

He decided his brother's comments didn't warrant a response, at least not until he ate. Regardless of his outlook on life at the moment, he couldn't resist Delta's cooking.

After he had appeased the worst of his appetite, he asked around a mouthful of eggs and ham. "Why aren't you at the shipyards?"

"You know we have effective managers in place. The last two years have even shown a profit." Cameron hesitated. "I only spend my time there to...forget."

Even through his own pain, Nicholas understood Cameron's inability to cope with the loss of Sarah, his wife. Still, it made him feel more of a cripple, knowing that Cameron had only come home because Nicholas could no longer handle Wildwood. He scowled at the thought.

"Miss Eastman and I had quite a nice visit last evening over dinner." Cameron changed the subject. "Wherever did you find her?"

"She more or less fell at my feet." Nicholas replied sarcastically.

Cam sighed. "The women always did that around you. I don't see why, especially considering your rather surly disposition and disheveled appearance."

Nicholas finished chewing the eggs and ham before he answered. "If you came home simply to harass me, you can leave on the next ship out of harbor. I already get all the badgering I can take from the lowest servant right up to your inestimable Miss Eastman."

Cameron set aside his cup and began pacing. A frown replaced the normal smile on his brother's face. And still, Nicholas egged him on. "What's this? The care-free, never responsible Cameron Westbrooke with a studious look upon his face. This must be dire."

"Damn it, Nick, why are you doing this?"

"Doing what?"

Cameron's hands gestured hopelessly. "Being obnoxious; a bore." He paused. "Giving up." His hands dropped to his sides and he stood there, looking at Nicholas with the same expression he had when their parents had died. Fix it, his gaze pleaded. You're my big brother and you can make it all better.

Nicholas looked away, unable to answer. Did he have the strength to change? Did he have the courage?

* * *

"Uncle Nicholas?" The words were soft and tentative. When he turned his head to the door, he saw Amanda; eyes full of tears and a lip that trembled even as she tried to make it stop.

No matter what else in the world had gone awry, Amanda was surely not to blame, and Nicholas cursed himself for excluding her. Jaci's words echoed in his head — She thinks the accident is her fault.

He opened his arms wide and without hesitation, Amanda raced across the huge room and flung herself at him. The poor child sobbed against his chest as he held her tight, soothing her with a stroke of his big hand to her back.

His catharsis was quieter, for it wasn't manly to cry, but the tears silently coursing down his cheeks were nevertheless cleansing.

"Papa's home." She sniffled once she had cried herself out.

"So I've heard, Muffin. He did come to see me, you know." He wiped her eyes with a corner of the sheet.

She wiggled around until she was seated cross-legged on the bed. Nicholas flinched when she accidentally kicked him with the toe of her shoe, and thought Mrs. Jeffrey would have a fit if she knew the youngster had her shoes on the bed. It made no difference, though, for in the joy surrounding the precocious five year old, nothing else mattered.

He had forgotten how much energy Amanda had and how happily she embraced life. As he watched her face light up over an explanation of Sir Lancelot and the kittens, "again", she had said, he felt the tightness in his chest loosen and begin to fall away.

"At first, Papa wouldn't let me go to the barn for the kittens. He said it was too cold and too far away and I was too little." She made a face and gave a huge sigh.

"Aren't the two of you getting along?"

She gave him a mournful look, her lips pursed as she shrugged her shoulders. "He doesn't know how to play."

Suddenly she gave a gasp of delight, crawling around on the bed, jostling everything. When she got as close as possible to his face, she put one small hand one each of his cheeks and looked him right in the eyes. "You can teach him, Uncle Nicholas. He's a very nice papa, I suppose, but he's got to lighten up."

He was sure his face registered surprise at her choice of words. Lighten up? A phrase like that could only have come from Miss Eastman.

"I will speak to him about it, Muffin. I am sorry it's taken so long for me to understand, and I hope you will forgive me."

Amanda gave him a big hug. "Oh, Uncle Nicholas, I don't have to forgive you; I love you."

* * *

Nicholas didn't realize the extent of his healing, at least the emotional side, until he accidentally overheard Cameron visiting with Jaci. The weather had turned unusually nice, and the two of them were walking outside. As was her penchant of late, she had opened his window slightly when she had brought in his breakfast. Nicholas didn't consider it eavesdropping; he certainly couldn't help but overhear considering his inability to get up and close the window.

"Why does she say that?" Cameron asked.

"Say what?" Jaci returned, and Nicholas debated for a moment to whom they referred.

"I love you, Papa. How can she love me?" Cam's voice sounded anguished, and Nicholas began to understand that his brother wanted Amanda after all; he simply didn't know how to go about it. "I haven't seen her a dozen times since her birth."

"A child's love is unconditional, Cameron. She loves you, and Nicholas, because you are her family, not because of what you give her or how much attention you show her." Although Jaci discussed Amanda, there was a wistful note in her voice. "She may crave that attention, but she doesn't need it to love you. Love appears to be something that, once given, can't be retracted or even re-channeled."

"Is that the case with you?" Cameron asked the question, but suddenly the answer was very important to Nicholas, and he leaned forward in bed to hear her reply. Unfortunately, they were walking away from the windows, and he only caught snatches of the rest of the conversation.

"Right now, Nicholas is belligerent and far from giving, but — love — unconditional. It's no wonder I steered clear — love — desperately."

He laid back against the pillows. His heart pounded hard enough to make his head ache. He was frustrated at not hearing all of what she had to say, but told himself it didn't matter. He had no right now, to ask her to love him, but how had she fallen in love with Cameron so fast, if in fact, that was their topic of discussion?

He thought over her words to Cameron, and wondered if love was as absolute for adults as it was for children. He felt an ache in the region of his heart, wishing for a happier world, where Jaci was his as he had wanted, and that he was whole.

If nothing else good had come from his accident, though, at least Cam was beginning to understand Amanda. It was time the two of them learned to be a family. He thought about never having children; babies to bounce on his knee and watch grow into adults to carry on the legacy of Wildwood. He groaned with the intensity of a stirring deep in his groin. He hated the fact that he still thought like a man and inwardly felt like a man, but couldn't perform like one.

* * *

Jaci appeared at his bedside as usual the next day. Nicholas had wondered that, with Cameron home, perhaps she would find his brother more appealing. Of course, there was also the fact that he had two good legs. However, when he asked where Cam was, Jaci absentmindedly waved off in the distance, mumbling something about the stables.

He continued studying her as she began his therapy, rubbing the muscles of his legs until he knew her hands had to ache with the constant effort. Instead of chatting gaily, as was her want, she remained unusually quiet.

"Why so quiet? Did you use all your words with Cameron out in the garden yesterday?" He hadn't meant to let that slip but jealousy made his words biting. "Do you find Cameron handsome; appealing in a manly way?" He girded himself for her answer. After all, he had no right to keep her from finding happiness.

She looked at him at last, but her expression wasn't that of someone in love. Shadows circled her eyes, their vibrant emerald color somewhat dulled. When her shoulders sagged as though in defeat, he suddenly realized how tired she must be. He mentally kicked himself for adding to her workload and taking his frustrations out on her.

"You look tired."

She gave a little sigh as she put the cork back into the bottle of lotion and placed it on the table by his bed. "I am. Amanda has a slight cold, and fussed most of the night. Molly tried to get her to sleep, but she would have no one but me." She yawned quite loudly, and Nicholas suppressed a smile. "When I rocked her, she finally slept, but I didn't."

"You should rest, instead of worrying about me."

She looked at him with surprise, as though disbelieving he would tell her not to work hard. "You're right."

Before he had time to react, she crawled right over him and into his bed.

"What on earth?" he exclaimed.

She snuggled down with her buttocks right next to his hips, yawning loudly. "If I return to my room, they will find me." She didn't need to explain who she meant.

After he got over his initial shock, he settled back against the headboard and contented himself to watch her sleep. A warmth spread through him. He swore he felt it from his heart clear down to his toes, which was, of course, impossible. What a difference she had made in his life. From the moment she had stumbled into his horse pen, she had turned his world topsy-turvy. He reached over and tucked a strand of hair behind her ear, pausing his movement to caress her cheek. She was letting her hair grow, he noticed, although it remained shorter than any woman he knew. Yet it wasn't her physical appearance that made her special. She had a strange outlook on life, and the stories she told Amanda were preposterous. He probably should worry, but oddly enough he didn't.

He recalled her peculiar comments about something called television and satellites while he clung to life at the pond. Was it delirium from the cold? Had she actually spoken of making moving pictures and flying through the air? He scrutinized her, trying to see something different, perhaps a mystic appeal. He actually considered for a moment that she might — perhaps that was why —

No, he dismissed the thought. No one traveled through time.

He lay in his bed, content for the first time in ages with Jaci beside him. He would doze only to awaken when she moved her hips, or an elbow, poking him in the side or the hip. Late in the afternoon, Selkirk came in to see to his needs, but Nicholas waved him away with a smile. Though the butler raised an eyebrow at the two of them in bed, he said not a word. Nicholas wondered exactly how many seconds it would take for that news to reach the rest of the staff.

As the sun began to set, he glanced out the window to where his horses raced about the paddock. Wind Dancer pranced, commanding the most attention, and indeed the mares did seem to stop and take notice of him. Nicholas smiled, for inside Wildwood, unlike the paddock, the females appeared to be in control rather than the males.

Even in her sleep, Jaci must have sensed his thoughts, for she rolled over one last time and awakened. She shot straight up in the bed, glancing wildly around as she brushed her hair from her eyes.

"Oh, my heavens. What did I do?" Her wide, green gaze met his and her cheeks blushed a delightful rosy pink. Obviously embarrassed, she bounded out of bed, at least not crawling over him this time.

"I do hope you feel quite rested. Do you know you toss around quite a lot when you sleep?"

"I do not," she huffed as she flounced to the door.

"And you snore," he couldn't resist adding.

She turned sideways to look at him, her mouth gapping open. "I most certainly do not."

He watched her quickly disappear and for the first time since his accident, he laughed outright. If the prickly Miss Eastman meant to stay around Wildwood, she had better get used to being teased.

His horses caught his attention again, and this time when he looked, his thoughts took a different turn. Amanda had told him that Miss Eastman had said he had to fight back to get better. Of course, everyone in the house quoted Miss Eastman, including Cameron, but it appeared to Nicholas, now that he had gotten past his initial bitterness, that perhaps she was right. She seemed to adjust, no matter the circumstances, and he supposed for the interest and welfare of his niece, and Wildwood, he must do the same.

However, if the inordinately stubborn female thought to rearrange his life without his permission, she had better think again. He rang for Selkirk. By the time the butler appeared, Nicholas already had a drawing of what he needed from Mackey.

Selkirk dryly asked what kind of mess Nicholas planned on making with the wood and tools he ordered, and Nicholas grinned.

"Quite a large mess, Selkirk. I trust you'll take that news back to all concerned?

Chapter Fifteen

Jaci smiled as she exited Nicholas's room. She had no idea what he was carving out of the wood Mackey and Sam had hauled into the study last week. She didn't care, either, for at least he had decided to do something. The first day it happened, she had hollered about the wood shavings scattered across the floor. The second day, an even bigger mess had appeared. She nagged again and he simply grinned at her. It was then she realized the game he played.

He had very little control over his life at the moment. No doubt this was one way of getting back at her for taking charge. The more she hollered, the larger mess he made. It was childish, to be sure, but she decided to play along, for it was good to see him sitting in a chair instead of lying on his bed. In the event he never did walk again, carving would serve him well and allow him to find a usefulness for his life.

Of course, she hadn't given up on his walking, for she saw evidence every day that his nerves responded to her therapy. Sometimes, she swore a muscle twitched, or that his toes curled in response to her massage. Whenever she mentioned it, though, he would become agitated, she soon kept quiet. It seemed if he couldn't jump out of bed and run as fast as Wind Dancer, he wouldn't acknowledge any change.

She deposited his breakfast tray in the kitchen. Her smile stayed in place, for she knew in her heart that he would get well. Then, he would decide he loved her after all, and they would live happily ever after. She almost laughed outright, for her attitude had taken quite a turn over the past several months. She didn't mind, for love did that to a person.

Her thoughts were interrupted by the sound of voices. Selkirk was speaking to someone — a female. Jaci hurried toward the front of the house, rounding the staircase as a skirt disappeared into the parlor.

"Selkirk, who just arrived?"

"Miss Edwardson." The butler responded, but appeared a little out of sorts.

Her heart started pounding. Lycinda. It had been months since she had thought of the woman Nicholas was supposed to marry. The woman who hadn't even shown up to find out how he fared. She instinctively lowered her voice. "What's she doing here?"

"I don't know, Miss. It's not my place to ask. I put her in the parlor for the moment. I wasn't sure if she should go to the study, since it is now Mr. Westbrooke's bedroom."

"Well, she can't see him." Jaci squared her shoulders, ready for a fight.

"Excuse me?" Selkirk looked at her askew.

She paced back and forth. "I won't have her upsetting Nicholas." She actually didn't know whether that would happen. She only knew that Nicholas didn't need anyone else in his life for whom he felt responsible, but unable to help at the moment. "Oh, where is Cameron when I need him?" she muttered to herself before grabbing Selkirk's arm.

"Stall her." She grabbed her cloak and flew out the front door, hoping Cameron was by the track and not clear down at the barn.

The warmer weather had begun melting the snow, and she tried sidestepping the puddles, for her slippers weren't the kind of shoes to wear outdoors, even on fair days. She finally gave up, grabbed her skirts high and walked in a straight line, regardless of the water.

Her gaze darted back and forth, looking for Nicholas's brother, but her mind was back at the house, trying to guess what would happen. She envisioned Lycinda, remorseful and sympathetic about the accident and Nicholas marrying her out of gratitude. Jealousy bit, and Jaci decided Lycinda had come instead to demand Nicholas fulfill his obligation and marry her, but all the woman really wanted was his money and Wildwood.

She stopped and turned in a circle. Not finding Cameron anywhere within her vision, she started back to the house. Lycinda's arrival at this particular time might cause irreversible damage, crushing Nicholas's fragile ego, right when he had begun to think himself capable again. She was not about to let that happen.

Her foot slipped coming up the steps and she had just recovered her balance when the door opened and Lycinda hurried out. The other woman didn't acknowledge her presence, but Jaci saw her watery eyes and evidence of crying on her face. She watched as Lycinda climbed into her carriage and the driver whipped the horses into action. The carriage rumbled down the drive and out of sight.

Great. All her work; all the energy she had spent getting Nicholas to take hold of life again. If Lycinda left in tears, Jaci had no doubts that Nicholas was in just as fine a mood. She kicked off her slippers and tossed her cloak at the rack, determined to get to the bottom of their conversation as quickly as possible. There was no sense letting him brood too much.

She entered the study to find the curtains closed and Nicholas back in bed. He hadn't spent a day in bed all week. It must be worse than she imagined.

She got right to the point. "What did Lycinda say?"

"Nothing; get out."

She jerked open the curtains. "Don't even think about starting that with me again." She turned back to him, but he faced the wall and she couldn't read his expression.

"Nicholas, talk to me." She didn't touch him. His body was taut and she knew he would only pull away.

He still wouldn't look at her as he spoke, his voice anguished, even though he tried to sound nonchalant. "Who would want to be saddled with a husband who can't make lo. . .fulfill his duties to sire offspring?"

"She broke up with you?" That was one scene she hadn't contemplated.

Nicholas scoffed. "It seems the lady wants a whole man for her husband, not an invalid."

"Well, it's her loss," Jaci stated emphatically. "She doesn't deserve such a man as you."

"And what kind of woman would?"

"I don't understand. You are a good, kind, loving person, and soon you'll be well and on your feet again—"

"That seemed to be the other part of the lady's dilemma." Nicholas interrupted her as he dragged himself upright. She saw the anger in his eyes, and wondered if perhaps it was a good sign, rather than bad, that he was showing some spirit. "Apparently Miss Edwardson's father is very concerned for my health."

From the insinuation in his voice, she knew his words weren't to be taken at face value. "What is that supposed to mean?"

"If I can't be on my feet, Wildwood horses won't be trained to win races, and Wildwood studs won't breed colts to sell." He wouldn't look her in the eye, trying to preserve some of his dignity. "Since Lycinda's father holds bank notes to this place, it might very well be the end of Wildwood."

"We'll see about that." She was livid and marched right over to the door, intent on seeing justice done. Nobody was going to take Nicholas's home away.

"Ironic, isn't it?" His voice caught her attention. She turned back. "Lycinda beat me to the punch by breaking our engagement. Although I was going at it for entirely different...well, never mind. It doesn't matter now."

"You mean you don't love me anymore?" Jaci knew she pushed him, but felt they had reached a real turning point in his recovery.

"I never meant to say that. It makes no difference now."

"Like hell," she muttered as she slammed out the door, plans already racing around in her head. They had not come this far to have Nicholas give up on himself, and her.

* * *

That evening, Jaci had Cameron take Nicholas's dinner to him with explicit instructions that he discuss the horse racing and breeding aspects of Wildwood. If they were to keep Wildwood profitable, Nicholas's work would have to continue until he could see to it himself.

In the meantime, she visited with Mackey and Selkirk about a different project. Mackey started shaking his head the moment he entered the parlor.

"What is it, Mackey? I haven't even told you what we're going to do." She questioned the old trainer.

"Doesn't make no difference, Miss, if you'll pardon my saying so. Your schemes tend to raise the roof right off this place." He doffed his hat and stood there twisting it in his big hands, clearly uncomfortable in the formal sitting room.

"Mackey, would I do anything to upset — well, never mind; of course I would — but it's for his own good."

Both Selkirk and Mackey groaned at this, but she proceeded to lay out the plans for her newest project to help Nicholas. Both men left the room shaking their heads, but assuring her they would do as she wanted.

Now, it was up to her. That night, she soaked in a warm bath in front of the fire in her room, daydreaming about the plot she has concocted. If Nicholas thought to roll over and ignore her, he had another thought coming.

She had refused all her life to give her heart away, and now that she had, she wasn't about to let any man stomp on it. She chewed her bottom lip. Was Nicholas ready for her latest scheme? What if she were wrong?

* * *

"Lady, I told you to get out."

Jaci smiled as she quietly locked the door. Nicholas called her Lady in that peculiar tone of voice when he was

214

super mad; when Jaci, or even Miss Eastman, just didn't convey his scorn at her interference.

"Nicholas, I can help you, if you will only let me." She slowly approached the bed where he lay, pillows propped behind his back. She thought they had been making progress, but he looked so lost. A man who was used to being in control and active couldn't confine his spirit to a bed. That fact was quite evident today.

His hair was in wild array; the curls at his nape and falling across his forehead much longer than fashionable. The bed covers were tangled, and she wondered if he fought battles even in his dreams.

She quietly set the overturned chair upright; further evidence that he had tried to get out of bed. She didn't care if he dragged himself clear across the room. It meant he was trying, and that meant her assumptions were correct.

You would think he'd give up telling her to leave him alone, because she always ignored him. They had the same argument almost every afternoon when she entered his room. Why did nineteenth century men think they had to dominate everyone and everything? Why couldn't they accept the fact that sometimes they needed someone else; as much as that someone needed them?

That was the crux of the matter. As much as she hated to admit it, she needed Nicholas, and had fallen in love with him. Her gaze came up and locked with stormy gray eyes.

The battle they fought always ended the same. He would tell her to get out; she would stay, wordlessly massaging his legs and exercising the muscles. He would glower at her, but she wouldn't leave; and he wouldn't admit that he liked having her there.

Now, she was tired of the stalemate, and decided to press the issue. Her feelings were mixed. She wanted him and felt, despite his verbal abuse, that he wanted her, too. What if she pushed him and he didn't respond; or didn't find her desirable enough to make the effort? She didn't know what would hurt worse — her feminine ego, or his sense of manliness. She was willing to take the chance. Was it fair of her not to ask him to do the same?

Nicholas squirmed beneath her scrutiny. She gazed at him differently today. Something in her eyes, in her walk, signaled a change in her. "What mad scheme do you plan to torture me with today?" Although he wore trousers and a shirt, he still felt undressed beneath her green-eyed gaze.

Under normal circumstances, he wouldn't have felt the least bit embarrassed at having a beautiful woman alone in his bedchambers. Under normal circumstances, he would have been seducing her. But these were not normal times, and he was no longer a normal man.

He concentrated on her face, on the blonde hair hanging loosely around her shoulders. Her full lips curved into a smile as her gaze caught his.

"Let's try something different today. Let me help you." She unbuttoned his shirt, pulled it off and slid her hands under his shoulders. Heat shot through him, tingling his nerve endings and accelerating his breathing.

"I doubt this is a wise idea." Why had his voice cracked?

"Of course it is. Since you're not getting the exercise you need, we should be working on all your muscles, not just your legs."

He protested. "I've been up every day, using my arms and hands to carve."

"That's not enough," she stated, continuing to push him until he was on his stomach.

Rolling him over had put him in the middle of the bed, too far away for her to further aggravate him, Nicholas thought. He pushed himself up on his elbows as she pulled the pillows out from under him, curious as to what she would do now. He watched her frown in concentration, her gaze moving from the edge of the bed to him and back. Then she shrugged, kicked off her shoes, and climbed onto the bed beside him.

The bed bounced beneath their combined weights and his breathing quickened. "What in the name of all that's holy are you doing?"

216

She giggled at him. "I would say that I'm trying to seduce you, but you might get frightened and run off. Let's say I'm testing to see if your bed is softer than mine. I might want to oust you from the master chamber."

"That's not funny in the least." The comment was muffled as her jiggling caused his elbows to slip and his face ended up flat against the mattress.

"What — the part about taking your bed?" She paused, her voice dropping to a husky whisper, "or the part about seducing you?"

He groaned and decided not to fight it, for her hands were already working their magic. Today, though, her fingers slowly moved down his neck and across his shoulders, instead of massaging his legs. Again and again her nimble fingers probed and squeezed his bunched muscles, gradually working down along his spine.

Nicholas was in agony. Never in his life had he wanted a woman as much as Jaci made him want her; and there was nothing to be done about it. Her hands did crazy things to his mind, making him imagine the wonder to be discovered in each other's arms. As her hands scorched a path down his back, a deep ache began in his groin; or so he imagined.

His entire body jerked as she straddled his back. "Jaci," the sound was a moan when he felt her heat through the thin cloth separating them.

"I can't properly continue your therapy from your side. It's not as comfortable." The throaty whisper came close to his ear, followed by a soft gasp as her breasts came in contact with his bare back.

He felt her breathing increase, as did his, and he was afraid to move for fear the ecstasy would go away. He wondered if she had any idea what she was doing to him. His answer came with her whispered plea.

"Nicholas, I need you. I want you." Incredibly sweet kisses began behind his ear. Her hot lips traced a path along his neck to his shoulder before trailing down his bare back.

Her chest continued to press against his back and her buttocks slid further down his body. Tears formed as he tried to find the words to deny her something they both wanted. Why was she doing this to him; why was she tormenting him?

Suddenly angry at his inability to be a man, he pushed himself over, toppling her onto the bed beside him. Keeping his back to her, he tried to control his voice as he spoke.

"If you are, for some unknown reason, trying to humiliate me, you have succeeded quite well, Miss Eastman." He felt the bed move as she righted herself. He jerked his arm away from her touch.

"No; you have it wrong. Why would I—"

"You know I am only half a man. Why would you purposely try to seduce me?" His voice and mind accused her, even though he desperately wanted what she offered.

This time she practically screamed. "No, that's not true!"

He flopped onto his back, turning his head to pin her with an icy stare. "I have no feelings in my legs, for God's sake."

Regardless of his tone of voice, it appeared she wouldn't relent. She knelt on the bed beside him, but didn't physically touch him as she spoke. Instead, her gaze caressed him, and her sultry words wove a web of seduction around them.

"Nicholas, it's your legs that don't work, not your entire body. I know you have feelings — feelings a man has for a woman. Why would you deny yourself?" She slid her fingers to the tiny buttons at her throat, slowly undoing one after the other as her words continued.

"You have done something to me. I can't define it, but I want it to continue. When I'm around you, I get these funny feelings — here," she slid her palms over her breasts, and Nicholas swore he saw her nipples peak, "—and here." Her hands slid to where the core of her womanhood lay beneath the layers of clothing.

He stared, mouth dry, as her fingers went back to unbuttoning, revealing a lacy camisole beneath the bright fabric of her dress. Hot streaks of pleasure-pain shot from his chest to his lower abdomen. He glanced down to find his body reacting hot and strong to her essence. It hadn't been his imagination. He closed his eyes, still unsure of his ability to please a woman without the use of his legs.

"I...can't...make love to you." It was an anguished whisper.

"Then let me make love to you."

His eyes flew open, settling on her full breasts, revealed beneath her open blouse and the thin silk of her camisole. Feeling as if he floated in a dream, Nicholas reached up to lightly trace the lacy edge of the fabric. She inhaled sharply at his touch, but she didn't back off. Instead, she bent closer, allowing him a clear view of her breasts.

Passion burst rapidly as he pulled her into his arms, his fingers twining in her hair. Hungrily, his mouth found hers, forcing her lips apart as his tongue invaded to taste her sweetness. She moaned in response, deepening the kiss. Frantic that time would run out before she knew him completely, her hands slid over his chest, firm beneath her fingers and coarse with hair.

Reluctantly releasing his mouth, she followed the curve of his chin, dropping kisses as she went. She paused at his throat, feeling the erratic beat of his pulse, pounding in rhythm with her own. As his hands caressed her back, she licked his flat nipple until it became a hard pebble against her tongue.

She knew a certain exhilaration as her hand slid beneath the loose band of his trousers to the smooth, taut skin of his hips. She felt wild — free of the restraints that had always kept her from wanting to feel like a woman. Her heart raced as Nicholas groaned.

She was positive now that her effect on him was exactly what he did to her. As he continued to caress her back, she felt loved, and cherished.

Nicholas's desire rose to the breaking point. He wished she were naked, so she could feel his lips on her skin the same way her lips branded him. Incredibly, by allowing her to be the aggressor, his senses were heightened to the point where he was sure he felt fire clear down to his toes.

She moved quickly out of his arms and he opened his eyes to see her standing, right in the middle of his bed. He searched her face, hoping he would not see regret. Instead, her green eyes twinkled as she slowly removed her blouse and camisole, exposing creamy skin to his view. He struggled to sit up, his palms itching to feel the skin she exposed.

She stepped out of reach, shaking her head as her lips curved into a sensuous smile. "Lie back, Nicholas. Remember, I'm in charge."

He expelled a ragged breath, but did as she asked. His gaze followed her as she unbuttoned her skirt, letting it drop to the coverlet along with her petticoats. Sure that he would die before she finished, his breath caught as the ties to her pantalets came undone. He tried to swallow around the lump in his throat when she boldly slid the white cotton down over slim hips, first revealing a flat stomach, then the dark triangle of her womanhood.

She got in a hurry when it came to his trousers, quickly sliding them down his legs and tossing them to the floor. He didn't mind at all. Dropping to her knees beside him, she rubbed her breasts against the coarse texture of his chest as she began kissing her way back to his chin.

He grabbed her arms, dragging her up the length of him until his lips captured hers, reveling in the pleasure she caused. Every place their bodies touched, fire ignited, racing along nerve endings until he thought he would be consumed in the blaze.

She arched her back and he greedily took what she offered, sucking one rosy nipple into his mouth while his hand gently caressed the other. Her moans told him what he wanted to know. As he transferred his attentions to the other breast, she spread her legs, straddling his hips and pushing back until her buttocks rubbed against his manhood. His moans immediately mingled with hers.

Unable to deny either of them the passion that had been ignited, he lifted her, slowly bringing her down on him until their hips again touched. She arched her back, sitting erect, causing him to plunge deep within her. Her gasp vibrated the still air.

He was enraptured with the beauty that had taken him by storm, refusing to leave him alone until thoughts of her consumed him. He focused on the rise and fall of her breasts as she moved. She brought her hands up to the nape of her neck, then higher, causing her honey blonde hair to pile atop her head, then tendrils cascaded down, giving her a totally wanton look. The movement caused her nipples to jut outward, begging for his touch. He reached up, capturing the pert tips between his thumb and forefinger. As she began to move her hips up and down, he surrendered completely to her sweet seduction, reveling in the hot pressure deep in his groin.

Nicholas's hands on her breasts shot currents of fire through Jaci, pooling in a hot core in the center of her being. As she increased the rhythm of her hips, she marveled at the feeling of oneness that the act of making love created. Although he couldn't lift his hips off the bed, they were in perfect rhythm.

The contractions began deep within her and surged so strong and so quickly she panicked. She opened her eyes, not wanting to climax before him. He met her gaze straight on, delving within her to her very soul. She couldn't give voice to her thought, for emotion choked her, but he sensed her need.

"Now, sweetness." He grabbed her hips, lifting her faster, increasing the friction between them.

Her cries mingled with his as together they flew to the highest peak where there were no physical limitations; there were only incredible feelings. Tingling sensations raced along her spine, down her legs to her toes, causing her to jerk against him.

She collapsed against his chest, not wanting the feelings to end. She kissed the dampness away at his throat. She reached up, trailing a finger across his closed eyes before tracing the outline of his lips. She looked at him in question when his hands gently touched her shoulders as though he were trying to push her away.

"Am I too heavy for you?" she teased, not wanting to give up her comfortable position nor the wonder of having him still inside her.

"No. It's just that..." He hesitated.

She felt suddenly embarrassed, lying naked on top a man, especially when she thought back to how brazen she had been to seduce him. Rolling over, she gathered her clothes to dress. To say that she was confused would be an understatement. She would have to get away from him in order to properly think through what had happened.

Nicholas was having a hard time reconciling his current emotional state. Sated passion, something he thought never to feel again, warred with his inability to provide what every woman wanted — a strong, fit man. He knew he wasn't reacting as he should, yet couldn't help himself. When Jaci moved to dress, he had to wonder if she regretted what had taken place. Foreboding thoughts caused him to lash out in anger.

"Is it your habit to give yourself so freely to a man?" He knew his sarcasm stung because she stiffened, but refused to look at him as she continued to dress.

"It is normally considered that a woman will save herself for the marriage bed," he added, his shattered ego taunting her.

She finally looked at him, anger flashing deep in her gaze. "But, of course, you would use that nineteenth century male logic on me. Does that mean you're asking me to marry you?"

"Of course not." Although denial immediately leaped to his tongue, he contemplated the idea as he watched her finish fastening her skirt. A sudden thought struck him. "Marriage may not be a bad idea, since you may already be impregnated. It wouldn't have to be forever. After the birth of my child, you can continue with your own life — go back to where you're from. I shall even pay you for your services."

She jerked as though he had slapped her. "You bastard. You're no better than any other man I've met. You all think what you offer is so wonderful."

Nicholas saw tears well up, but she continued to yell at him. "Well, let me tell you something — I don't need you. There is more to life than sewing, cooking, and being a brood mare." She spun around, racing for the door, never once glancing back at him.

He watched her flee, feeling like the bastard she labeled him. Why had he acted like such an incredible heel? In the darkest corner of his mind, he knew why. The thought of her making love to him out of pity was impossible to bear. So he had shamed her, turning the beautiful rapture they had shared into something sordid.

He fell back against the pillows, berating himself. The jovial attitude he had always had; that which had even carried him through his parents' deaths; had deserted him after the accident. For months, all he wanted to do was stay in that gray world which was totally void of feelings because it blocked his heart against disappointment.

But no, Jaci would have none of it. She had brought Cameron back; had forced Nicholas to face his limitations, and had even beset him with Amanda, who was impossible to resist.

Damn her! She had made him start feeling again.

He covered his eyes with one arm, trying to blot out the image of her body on his. No amount of concentration erased the ache he felt as he remembered the touch of her hands; the butterfly soft kisses she bestowed over his entire body.

Chapter Sixteen

Several days passed, and Nicholas didn't see Jaci at all. He knew she shunned him because of his cruel words, and he didn't blame her. He had done a lot of soul searching and chastised himself mightily for his self-pity. Now, as he gazed out the window from his lonely bed, he hoped he had an opportunity to tell her how wrong he had been.

A commotion at the door brought his attention around as Jaci appeared in his bedroom, followed by Tom and Sam, two of his stable boys. They carried a wood contraption consisting of two parallel bars attached about three feet above a flat base.

As he sat in stunned silence, she ignored him completely, instead motioning the boys over to the foot of the bed. He wondered what she had in mind to torture him with today.

"Put it right here, if you please. That's fine. Thank you for your help." She gave the two boys a gracious smile, quietly dismissing them.

They looked skeptically from her to Nicholas, but he simply shrugged. He had no more idea than they as to what she intended. He glanced from the contraption to her, aware for the first time of the strange attire she wore, some of which looked suspiciously like his.

Jaci blushed under his scrutiny. "I put on my old pants because I knew I'd have to work with you myself. I hope you don't mind that I borrowed one of your shirts." The cuffs of his shirt were rolled up and the tails knotted at her slim waist.

Hell, no, he didn't mind. The open collar exposed her lovely neck and her fanny looked enticing in the strange blue trousers that looked a size too small.

As for himself, he had awakened this morning with a renewed determination to make things right. He had Selkirk trim his hair and shave the whiskers from his face. The two of them had struggled getting his good trousers on and his lips had quirked in amusement when he recalled how fast Jaci had gotten them off that single blissful night.

Now, he waited for her to speak, but she stood there watching him, uncertain, worrying her bottom lip with her teeth. He realized he would have to take the initiative; but by rights he should, for it was he who had put them in this awkward position in the first place.

He kept his gaze fixed on Jaci's face as he pushed his legs around until he sat on the bed as he would a chair, his legs dangling over the edge. Her eyes widened with his efforts and he was pleased to see her impressed. Perhaps the rest of what he had to do wouldn't be as unmanageable as he imagined.

"Though it pains my gentlemanly honor, I cannot stand in your presence as I should for what I am about to say." He cleared his throat, not having realized how difficult this would be without pacing to collect his thoughts.

She didn't say anything, but waved away his concern with a flick of her wrist. He continued before he lost his nerve.

"I want to apologize—"

She shook her head but he held up a hand to stop her from interrupting. "No, I must apologize for my behavior. I was a rude, obnoxious bore and don't deserve the precious gift you granted me. I blamed you for giving me that which I wanted all along, perhaps because I felt I no longer deserved it." He shrugged. "I don't know." He searched for the right words to tell her how he felt. Yet he held back his innermost feelings because; well, because he couldn't ask her to love an invalid.

"As much as I have fought against it, you showed me how to feel again. That became both a pleasure and a pain, but regardless, I had no right to speak so badly to you. You would never—" he paused, not able to understand her reaction. "What now?"

Jaci stood, exactly where she had begun, trembling from head to foot. She lifted a hand to her mouth to still its trembling while tears streamed down her cheeks. The whole time he spoke, she slowly shook her head from side to side. Nicholas didn't know if that meant she didn't believe him, or wouldn't listen to any more of his apology.

She didn't give him time to debate the issue. Instead, she launched herself at him, knocking him backward onto the bed, sobbing into his shoulder.

"A simple I don't believe you would have been much easier to take, I think," he commented, still not entirely sure what her reaction meant.

She placed her hands to the side of his head, raising her gaze to study him, eyes flickering as though searching his soul. She gave him a dazzling smile as she again shook her head in consternation. "Did anyone ever tell you that you talk too much?"

She punctuated her remark with a kiss and Nicholas knew ecstasy. Pure and simple, and for that brief time, nothing else mattered. He didn't dwell on his inability to walk, the future of Wildwood, or anything or anyone else in the world except his precious Jaci. Once again he was stuck with the dilemma of not being able to ask her to marry him, for his future was still uncertain. But even that didn't seem quite as important at present.

Jaci smothered him with kisses, instead of concentrating on his mouth as he would have preferred. In her exuberance, he felt them slide off the edge of the bed. With a thunk, they landed in a heap on the floor just as Selkirk brought in Nicholas's morning coffee.

Selkirk didn't look the least bit surprised. "You haven't tried to do him in again, have you, miss?" the butler asked with the most pained expression.

Jaci giggled close to Nicholas's ear before she turned to answer. "No, Selkirk, you needn't worry. But we are going to make sure he walks again, aren't we?"

The butler looked at the contraption Jaci had ordered brought into the study, then back at Nicholas. "If you say so, miss." Not a muscle twitched as he lowered the tray to the table and took his leave.

She scrambled off him to fetch them coffee.

"Ouch," he yelped. In her haste, she jabbed a knee in his thigh.

"What?" Her head jerked back around.

"Regardless of what you told Selkirk, I do believe you're trying to get back at me. You just kneed me in the leg." His words registered in his own mind at the same time her mouth dropped open.

She scrambled back, straddling his legs and coming nose to nose with him. "Did you hear what you just said?" she practically screeched.

"It's my legs that don't work, not my ears." Even as he reprimanded her, he felt his grin widen.

She hugged him, kissed him twice, and hugged him again. "Not any more, Nicholas. You can't use that excuse any more. We are going to have you walking in no time."

* * *

Now time began to stretch forever as Jaci worked with Nicholas. He understood the concept of using the parallel bars to support himself, but in the beginning he employed only his upper body and simply dragged his legs along.

"Concentrate," she emphasized for what seemed the hundredth time.

"I am concentrating." He sounded like a spoiled child. She had to remind herself that talking, and walking along side as he struggled, was the easy part.

She placed her hand over his on the smooth wood of the bar. He stopped, relaxing his grip somewhat. They had discovered that his legs would support him when he finally stood erect, and she chose to believe that a good sign.

Nicholas had stated that standing did little good unless they wanted to give him a handful of cigars and prop him in a corner like the wooden Indian outside a general store. Jaci thought the return of his sense of humor an even better sign of his recovery.

Now, he lifted his gaze to hers. She saw determination and it gave her strength. It was good to know that he was fighting now, instead of giving up.

"You have enough strength in your shoulders and hands, you can go back and forth on these bars all day, using only your arms," she spoke softly, trying to choose the right words that would encourage, not discourage. "But the idea of the parallel bars is for support, while you make your legs move. That's what I meant."

Nicholas sighed, releasing the bar with one hand and leaning against the one closest to her. He gently brushed a finger across her cheek, tucking her hair behind her ear. She turned her head to kiss his hand, but he had replaced it on the bars. "Stand down at the end where I can see you and have something to walk toward," he stated without looking at her.

She did as she was told, moving between the two bars at the very end. In the days they had been working together, there had been no repeat performance of their lovemaking. Even though apologies had been made, Jaci was scared to death to initiate anything, for fear it would again damage his ego.

He had never mentioned it again, either, and although he touched her sometimes, like now, it wasn't enough. She watched as he slowly shuffled one foot in front of the other, wobbling constantly as though his legs belonged to someone else and he had no feel for what they would do. She watched his hands grip the railing and remembered how their callused palms had caressed her skin.

She wanted more. While he struggled and forced his legs to move, she struggled with a plan to seduce him, again. That's what it would take, she was sure. She would need to find the right moment when he felt secure enough with himself not to reject her offer. That would be too devastating for both of them.

* * *

Jaci sat at the crest of a small hill, watching the activity in the horse track off in the distance. The day was gorgeous — cloudless, warm, with a soft March breeze ruffling the leaves on the trees. Instead of enjoying the pleasures of nature, though, she remained lost in thought.

It wasn't often, anymore, that she thought of her other life, as she referred to Dallas in the twenty-first century. Sometimes, however, when it was hard to understand her significance here, she thought she'd be better off back there. She still believed Nicholas was her reason for being here, but she wondered if she did him any good.

"Hello, care for some company?" Cameron's voice broke into her musings, and Jaci turned as he rode up.

"Have I told you how much I appreciate you being here?" she asked with a smile as he plopped down beside her.

"Only every day — sometimes several times a day." He grinned back at her.

Cameron fit in so well at Wildwood, she didn't understand why he didn't stay. He and Amanda had formed a bond, and often he would teach her lessons as Jaci continued working with Nicholas. She wondered, though, how much learning took place, for she often saw them out under the trees playing tag.

When he wasn't with his daughter, he worked with Mackey and the trainers. Cameron didn't think there would be any problem having the horses ready for the spring races, and she hoped he was right. But would Cameron Westbrooke's name be enough to promote Wildwood?

She shook off her daydreams. It wouldn't matter, because Nicholas would be at the races; she would see to it.

"What is it, Jaci? What's bothering you?"

"I don't understand. He's getting better. I mean, he can stand and is beginning to walk, but yet he's not the same as before the accident." She sighed, deciding to get it all out in the open. "I love him, Cameron, but he won't accept that. What am I going to do?"

Cameron pulled up a long blade of grass, chewing it silently before answering. "It took me a long time to realize how important family is. Even though I was only two years younger than Nick when our parents died, I looked up to him to take care of things. And he did. When Sarah died, it was impossible to fix, so I left.

"I didn't want anything to do with family, because too many people I loved had died." He shrugged. "I guess I thought that if I left my baby and Nicholas, I was helping protect them — from myself. I can't believe how much I've missed by not being here. Amanda is such a delight — Nicholas has done well by her."

"Yes, but he's not her father, and Amanda has enough love for both of you."

"True." Cameron shook his shoulders as though to dislodge a ghost and turned twinkling eyes to her. "But we haven't solved your problem. What are we to do with that mule-headed brother of mine?"

She shrugged. "I don't know. Sometimes he gets so agitated when I walk into the room. He even made some comment about standing up to apologize—" She broke off when Cameron started laughing.

"It's his breeding. A gentleman always stands when a lady enters the room. Even though he can't, and has every reason not to, it still rubs him wrong."

"That's the most ridiculous thing I've ever heard."

"It may seem that way to you, but Nicholas has to re-establish himself in his world. He must reaffirm his honor and himself as a man."

She shook her head. "I swear. What is it about you men and your honor and manhood? There's nothing wrong with Nicholas in that department. He sets my blood on fire with his kisses, and he certainly had no trouble making love."

"Jaci." Cameron blushed as red as a tomato.

"Oh, for Pete's sake, Cameron. You men go around bragging about screw. . .sowing your wild oats, but I'm not supposed to know about those things?" Jaci realized she probably ventured into forbidden territory, but doubted

Cameron would repeat this discussion, given how embarrassed he looked.

"You're a lady. Ladies don't know about things like that." He defended her, even though she didn't need it.

"There's a lot of things I know, Cam. Perhaps someday, I'll enlighten you."

Cameron glanced skyward as a slight drizzle began. She thought he looked relieved to have something else to talk about. "Come. It won't do Amanda or Nicholas any good if you get ill."

She arched her eyebrow and grinned. "Why, Cameron Westbrooke, you'd better watch out. You sound like Mrs. Jeffrey." She gave him her hand to pull her up, and together they walked back down the hill.

* * *

Nicholas surveyed his carving with a critical eye. His gaze flowed along the lines of the horse from fetlock to tail. He smiled, his hand caressing the hard apple wood he had selected. Once, he had thought building furniture and carving carousel animals would be his life's work. At the age of eighteen, he had rebelled against his father's authority and had gone to work for Gustav Dentzel. There, he had discovered the magic of bringing a piece of wood alive in form and shape with his hands. Over the years, he had forgotten about that magic.

After he sanded the rough edges and added detail, he would paint the four foot replica of Wind Dancer and place it on a permanent pedestal. He hadn't carved it with the intention of giving it to Dentzel for one of his carousels, although he heard they were fast becoming a favorite amusement ride.

No, this horse would be his gift to Jaci. He wanted to add, if only to himself, that it would be a wedding present, but he was afraid to project that far into the future. Right now, it was enough that she stuck with him, day after day, forcing him to take hold of his life and concentrate on the task of walking again.

He recalled how she had looked, standing at the other end of the parallel bars, worrying her lip with her teeth. Even though each step he took had brought him closer to her, those steps had felt like a thousand needles jabbing his legs at once. His legs bore his weight, but as he forced the muscles to work, they twitched and rebelled so strongly, the pain sometimes caused brief blackouts. Every time he stopped, even for a minute, she would encourage him, and he didn't have the heart to deny her.

So he had kept at it; forcing his legs to move along the wood base, his hands tightly gripping the railings, until he came to the end where she stood. God, how he had wanted to kiss her. She had given him the most glorious smile, and the pain had slipped away. In its place, an intense pleasure coursed through him from his head to his toes, along with an incredible desire to make love to her.

Instead, he had turned around within the confines of the bars and shuffled back to the edge of his bed. Nicholas Westbrooke, who until recently had thought himself a man among men, was afraid of a slip of a woman. Even though she had accepted his apology for his boorish behavior the last time, he was hesitant to touch her again. He didn't think he could bear her rejection, and he didn't want her to accept him out of pity. Until he knew what direction his life would take, he decided to keep her at a distance, no matter how difficult that decision.

He concluded his inner conversation as he finished carving the notch that would hold the real leather reins. Jaci would soon arrive with his lunch, and he didn't want her to see the carousel horse until it was finished.

"Hello. It's a lovely day out. We should see about getting you outside."

He turned at the sound of her voice, her smile reaching him across the room. She tilted her head, trying to see around him to his work. He bent over the arm of his chair and reached for the drop cloth.

"What's that? Is this your big secret project?" She teased him, moving quickly across the room. She stood across from him, lunch tray in hand, staring at his carving. He held his breath in anticipation of her response. He had wanted to surprise her, but now he hoped she at least liked it.

"Why, Nicholas, it's beautiful. It looks like a carousel horse." As she said the words, he watched her eyes widen and her breath catch. The tray slid from her hands and crashed to the floor.

Unable to reach her, he sat helplessly as the color drained from her face and she began to tremble. "Jaci, what is it?" He pushed himself up, for a moment forgetting, and fell against the arm of the chair. The wooden horse stood between them, effectively blocking his ability to reach out to her.

She backed away, a shaking hand pressed against her lips.

"Jaci, talk to me." Her acute reaction to his carving scared him.

"It's the carousel horse."

"Well, yes, I'm glad to see it at least resembles that from which I modeled it," he said, trying to tease her out of her fright.

"No, I mean it's the carousel horse — the one in the photograph." Her voice quivered. With jerky steps, she backed away from the horse as though it were a ghost.

He shook his head in confusion. "I don't understand. What photograph?"

"Huh?" Her eyebrows bunched together, her gaze searching his.

"What photograph are you talking about?" Her behavior frightened him, but he didn't know what to do other than get her to talk.

This time her face transformed, registering recognition instead of shock. "Of course, the picture." She turned and raced from the room. He heard her steps as she ran up the stairs.

He gazed from the empty doorway back to the horse he had been carving. It most definitely had been a surprise, but she hadn't reacted with joy as he'd anticipated. He reached for the bell cord to ring for Selkirk to clean up the luncheon mess scattered across the floor.

"Here, here, look at this," Jaci spoke as she rushed back in, digging through some sort of bag. She came to stand beside his chair, but he noticed she carefully avoided looking at the almost completed wooden horse.

She quickly unfolded a paper and shoved it into his hands. "Look. There's a picture of you, and this horse." Still without looking, she pointed behind her to the accused statue.

He surveyed the paper, which did contain a horse. He wasn't at all convinced that a person stood behind it; the shape was shadowy and blurred, at best. "It is a painted miniature of a horse similar—"

"It's not a painting, it's a photograph — a colored photograph."

He scrutinized the picture more carefully. "It's a very good likeness — how did they get the detail?"

"Nicholas!" Her screech effectively caught his attention. "Look at the horse, Nicholas. This horse," she thumped the picture for emphasis, "and your carving are identical. How is that possible?"

He did as she requested and studied the picture. Suddenly his breath caught. "Dear God, it's true."

"I told you it was the same horse."

He shook his head at her comment. "No, this." He pointed to a corner of the picture and she bent close to see the spot. "It's the airplane you told Amanda about." He looked up at her, his voice incredulous. "I thought you were making it up — that you had a vivid imagination."

She knelt beside his chair as he continued to stare at the picture. He tried to convince himself that it was a flaw in the paper; that in folding and unfolding this photograph, she had scratched it somehow. But the more he studied it, the clearer it became. Against the blue of the sky was a large object suspended in the air — an airplane flying across the sky.

She confirmed it. "I hadn't noticed the airplane before. When I took the pictures and developed them, I was only concerned with the carousel horses, and how this image had ruined the photo session." Again, she pointed to a spot behind the horse.

Her wild stories were true. The photograph convinced him. Through some fluke in nature, Jaci had been thrown back to Wildwood from somewhere in the future. All her comments; all the times she hadn't understood their culture, came flooding back to him. She had made references to Dallas as though it were a large metropolis, when the town had only existed some thirty years. She had cooked food he had never before tasted; and had created stories and taught Amanda things that had no bearing on anything within his realm of knowledge.

"Nicholas, I know how hard this is to believe. It was just as hard for me to understand when I first got here. But it did happen." She dug into the strange bag. "Here; look at these." She identified the objects as she dropped them into his lap. "A roll of high speed film, a plastic credit card; car keys. How else would you explain these?"

"We have keys," Nicholas answered the only possible part of the question. "It's logical to assume somewhere across the United States these other objects might exist." He said the words, but he didn't believe them. He believed her, even though his very logical self said such a thing as time travel was impossible. He fingered the smooth canister that she said contained film. He ran his thumb over the raised letters which spelled her name on a calling card. No, she had called it a credit card.

"What use does this have?"

"It's a credit card. I use it to pay for things, instead of money."

"Instead of money? You mean you don't have currency?" He turned the card over and over in his hand.

"Yes, we do, but this is used instead of writing a check against the money in a bank account."

"Well, there you have it. It's not new for we have letters of credit from banks now." He shrugged off what she said.

She got up and began to pace. She waved a hand in the air, and he thought she looked delightful all flustered and confused. He tried to see her as he had the first day she appeared — wearing strange clothes and covered in mud. He tried to imagine her in some future world. He shook his head. The Jaci Eastman he knew, regardless of where she had come from, was the soft, feminine creature who now strolled back and forth across his study.

"There's got to be an explanation you'll understand," she muttered as she passed him.

Even though he didn't think he wanted to know, he asked anyway. "When do you live?"

"In 2015," she whispered.

"I'm long since dead." The wonder of it all struck him.

"And I have yet to be born in 1875. How do you explain it?"

He shook his head, neither wanting nor having an explanation. "I don't need an explanation. Some things are not meant to be explained — like lightning and storms and death and disease. Some things you simply have to accept on faith." Although he realized he was taking a chance by giving voice to his emotions, he felt it necessary to make her understand. "It doesn't matter. All that matters is that you are here with me now. I need you here with me."

His words stopped her in her tracks. She turned a slow circle until she faced him, the silent wooden horse now separating them. Her gaze searched his face and he hoped she realized how sincere he was — how desperately he still loved her.

"I can't ask you to give up your life for me. I can't make a commitment to you right now, but I hope you realize how I feel."

She stood still as a statue, staring, and Nicholas wondered if she had heard any of what he said. Here he had almost declared himself, and she wasn't even listening.

"You have to quit carving this horse. You have to stop right now." She sprang into action, rushing over to the table which stood near his carving. Snatching the lunch tray from the floor, she began scooping his carving tools onto the surface.

Nicholas reached out and grabbed her wrist, bringing her movements to a halt. "Jaci, stop; what are you doing?"

When she turned, tears streamed down her face. Her hand trembled as she touched the horse, turning it around to face the same way as the photograph.

"Look at the picture, Nicholas. The pose and position of the head and tail; the legs you have carved. You had never seen this photo before, and yet it's exactly the same as this carving you're doing in 1875. But I took the picture in 2015. Remember when you took me to Mr. Dentzel's that first time and you thought I was crazy because I was looking for a particular carousel horse?"

"Well, not crazy, maybe." He wanted to tease her out of her mood, for her words were scaring him. Deep down in the pit of his stomach a knot had formed, growing larger with each statement she made. He wanted to stop what she said, for somehow he sensed where her words would lead.

"This was the horse I was looking for, even though you hadn't made it yet." She moaned softly and put both hands to her head as though in pain. "Oh, this doesn't make any sense at all, but please, I beg you, quit carving it. If you finish, somehow it will bring the process full circle, and that might very well send me back to my own time."

Even as she said the words, he denied them in his mind. It was too incredible an idea to comprehend. He looked at the other things she had carried in her bag, yet decided to pursue a different reasoning. "I had forgotten about your feelings when you first came here," he said. "As I recall, you kept saying you wanted to go back to Dallas. I simply didn't understand exactly what you meant."He watched her face as he carefully made his next statement. "Perhaps if, as you say, the carousel horse will transport you back to your Dallas, I should finish it posthaste." He was only testing her, a knot of fear almost causing his heart to stop beating.

"No!" She cried.

"Whyever not?" He was taunting her and he knew it. But he wanted to know; had to have her confession of what she felt for him. He wondered if it wasn't more crucial to his recovery than the use of his legs.

Her gaze met his, but she quickly looked aside, refusing to give away too much. "Because. . ." she began.

"Why, Jaci? What would make the difference, if I did finish the horse and if it did, by some miracle, send you back?"

"Because, maybe I don't want to go back yet. Maybe there's some purpose for my being here that I haven't thought of yet." She shrugged her answer, but Nicholas knew she held back, afraid to commit; just as he had. For now, her words were enough. He breathed easier.

"A purpose for being here? Other than to cause havoc with my life, you mean?" He grinned at her.

"That's not funny," she weakly protested.

He dumped the odds and ends of her bag onto the tray with his carving tools. He held out his hand. "Come here."

She faltered and he wondered if she was afraid to touch him for fear he, or she, would disappear. "You're safe; you'll see." He gestured with his hand.

Tentatively, she raised her hand to his, the touch of her fingers against his palm lighter than butterfly wings. His fingers closed around her slim hand and he tugged her to him, pulling her down onto his lap. He wouldn't allow her to hesitate. One arm curled about her waist to hold her close. He reached up with the other hand and tilted her chin.

"A promise," he whispered as he kissed her soft lips. "My pledge." He kissed her again, tenderly, for he wanted her to ache for him as he did for her. "Regardless of some phenomena which might have happened to bring you to me, this is real." A third time, he touched his lips to hers. "We are real."

Chapter Seventeen

"It's only three weeks. Do you think the horses will be ready?" Cameron asked.

Nicholas scowled as Jaci entered the study and she knew it wasn't because Cameron discussed plans for a pre-season race at Wildwood.

"Please, don't get up on my account," she said with a smile, and Nicholas immediately relaxed. She recognized it as a man thing, and even when she considered it stupid in the extreme, her statement helped him retain his honor.

She set the coffee service down, pleased to see him sitting behind his desk. Although she helped him with his therapy, she knew he still needed assistance getting around, especially to the bathroom, but she never saw him at those times. As intimate as they had become, he still wouldn't allow her that familiarity. She listened to their conversation as she poured coffee. Nicholas hadn't been happy with her, or Cameron, when they informed him they had organized a pre-season race and bar-b-que on Amanda's birthday. That was why neither had told him until the invitations had been issued, both to other horse breeders and to friends and neighbors. Mackey had help make up a list, Mrs. Jeffrey and Delta had come up with the outdoor menu, and the entire staff was pitching in to get the grounds ready for the spring event.

It did her heart good to see everyone working hard, and knew they did it for Nicholas. Rumors were flying about his miraculous recovery, and although she sometimes felt their progress was slow, Nicholas called it interminable. Still, she supposed it could be viewed a miracle.

Nicholas looked up from his book work. "Well, since you and Miss Eastman decided to sponsor this fiasco, should it make any difference whether I'm in attendance?"

Cameron hopped up from his chair. "Of course it does, Nick. The Wildwood name is yours; the horses are yours. The whole idea of having a race was to get you to—"

"Cameron, don't you have something to do?" Jaci interrupted, not wanting him to tell Nicholas that they had planned a race, hoping it would be the enticement he needed to walk again. She knew, with the man's pride, that he wouldn't accept their interference in that way. Besides, telling him wasn't going to be necessary.

Nicholas was getting better each day. She noticed the way his hands gripped the exercise bars; more relaxed and not white knuckled as before. At the same time, she knew he was frustrated at not being able to walk without help.

She ushered Cameron out the door with whispered instructions to keep Amanda busy and not to return the rest of the day. She had decided Nicholas needed further prodding in his efforts to walk without using the exercise bars.

A mischievous smile on her face, she quietly closed the door behind the younger brother, turning the key in the lock. She leaned her back against the door surveying Nicholas, who chose to ignore her at the moment and remained engrossed with his ledgers.

The walking bars, as he referred to them, were situated at the end of his bed, stretching a good ten feet towards the desk, but still leaving another ten feet of open territory. Since Nicholas was already at his desk, she couldn't hope that he could walk the distance back to the bars.

She stepped to the side, tilting her head to see behind the desk to the chair on which he sat. The study floor, like the other downstairs rooms, was hardwood and Nicholas's desk chair sat on a small rug. So, that's how they did it. Given the shiny surface of the floor, she bet the rug allowed Selkirk to push Nicholas around the room. Very clever, and just the trick she needed.

She reached over his shoulder to remove the pen from his hand. "It's time for your workout." She tried to keep her voice nonchalant, but it quivered in anticipation. Startled, he turned to look at her as she pulled the chair away from the desk. As she thought — it moved easily across the smooth floor. She gave him no time to protest as she scooted him over to the end of the bed, turned the chair in a complete circle — twice, simply for the fun of it — and stepped away.

"You can get yourself up to the bars from there. I'll move to the other end where you can see me while you walk that way." As she spoke, she backed up very, very slowly, never taking her eyes off him. She didn't dare do anything until she knew he would complete the exercise. As promised, she stood near one end when he pulled himself up and slowly moved in-between the bars.

Nicholas kept his eyes focused on his feet, as if staring at them would insure that they moved. Jaci let him begin before she called to him. Her hands were at the neckline of her shirtwaist, unbuttoning the row of fasteners.

"Nicholas?" she spoke his name softly to get his attention.

When he raised his head, she slid the blouse off one shoulder. His gaze hardened and his steps faltered. She feared he would fall, but he shuffled his feet back under him and stopped, never taking his gaze from her bare shoulder.

"You can do that," she nodded to the exercise bars, "while I do this." She pulled her blouse out from her skirt and slid it the rest of the way off, dropping it to the floor. She ran the tip of her tongue over her teeth, seductively enticing him with every gesture. Her fingers unhooked her skirt, pushing it provocatively down her hips as she swayed from side to side.

Her actions galvanized him, and his feet began moving again. With each piece of clothing she removed, his steps seemed to quicken. Perspiration broke out on his forehead; his lips were edged with white as he concentrated on making his feet move.

They were no more than four feet apart — her with only stockings and chemise on; him at the end of the exercise bars. She knew he wanted her; saw the evidence of his passion in the way his chest heaved in exertion and anticipation. Would he take a chance?

Her gaze locked with his, seducing him, telling him of her need. She slid a finger in her mouth, and then traced her lips, gliding across her chin and down her throat to the edge of her chemise. His gaze never left the path her finger traveled.

He licked his lips, leaned forward, and hesitated. She felt a moment of remorse — had she pushed too hard? She held her breath as he tentatively took a step beyond the bars. One step after the other, bringing him closer to her. She didn't move; didn't reach out her hands to make the distance shorter because she knew he needed to do this by himself.

One more step and he clutched her shoulders. She winced slightly under the pressure, but stayed erect.

"Nicholas, you're marvelous." Her soft words seemed to break his concentration because he grabbed her around the waist as he fell, twisting so she landed on top.

"Oh, my God, I'm sorry," she squealed, bracing herself above him with her arms, quickly scanning his face to see if he was in pain.

"It's all right." His voice was full of laughter as his hands brushed her hair back from her face. "I'm all right," he said in awe. He pulled her head down, brushing his lips across hers. The exercises were forgotten; the pain forgotten in the glory of their physical awareness of each other.

"I must have you." His ragged plea caught her by surprise and her heart beat faster.

Yes. It was what she wanted; what she dreamed about every night. Still, she hesitated. Her eyes surveyed the hard floor; a small throw rug was all that had cushioned their fall.

"Here?" she questioned even as the ache within her grew.

"Here; now." Nicholas's voice was urgent; his hands already sliding up her bare legs beneath her knee length chemise. "You started this, and I must see it through to completion."

They hadn't spoken about that first experience, nor touched since in an intimate way. Were his feelings genuine? She searched his face, wanting to see more than lust; or desperation. What she saw in his deep pewter gaze was adoration and passion, and she wanted to weep.

Instead, she kissed him with abandon, letting the excitement and intense heat flow through her body and into his. He clutched her tightly and managed to turn over, nestling his hips between her legs. He wasted no time in foreplay, but it didn't matter. She wanted him as desperately. Only when he surged within her did she feel complete, and she wrapped her legs around his waist as he began, awkwardly at first, to move his hips in the rhythm she ached for.

Their lovemaking was intense, and she wanted to draw him into herself and never let go. He was glorious, rising above her on the strength of his arms, face taut with pleasure. His hips danced erotically with hers and soon sent her spiraling upward to the stars. Her climax quickly swept her away, but with an intensity only born from love

When he collapsed against her, his head tucked in the crook of her neck, she cried. Sobs racked her, shaking her shoulders and causing her head to pound. She loved him so much! How would she bear it if she were now transported? How was she to live without this proud, stubborn, magnificent man who had taught her how to love? She cried harder.

"Sh, sh, sweetheart. I'm okay; I'm really all right." He tried to reassure her, assuming mistakenly that she cried because they had fallen, or because he might be in pain. He rolled to the side, still rocking her gently against his hard body.

He began to apologize. "I'm sorry I was in such a hurry. I could easily blame you for enticing me, but even if I had made the overture, I don't think I could have gone slowly." He kissed the top of her head. "I wanted you so damn bad!" She felt the shake of his head against her hair.

"You do something incredible to me." She murmured against his chest, calming now but unable to untangle herself. She felt his chest shake, and it took a minute to realize he was laughing. Almost too sated to response, she managed only a weak, "What's so funny?"

"I find it incredibly amusing that a man of my demeanor and age would make love to a woman on a hard, wooden floor, especially when a bed is easily within reach." He gave a big sigh, which Jaci assumed was male pride and satisfaction. "Not only that I would, but did with such great intensity and lack of control." His last statement made Jaci feel every inch a woman, and very pleased to be his woman.

He released his hold and she sat cross-legged beside him as he struggled to pull his trousers back up. They hadn't even managed to get properly undressed.

"One of these days, we are going to make love standing up." Nicholas's words caught her totally by surprise.

She had to grin as she asked, "Is that a promise?"

"No, that's my sacred pledge to you." His gaze was intent, and her stomach clutched with desire. Her heart swelled with love for this man who made her forget everything except how wonderful it felt to be in his arms.

* * *

Selkirk called them to dinner, and Jaci, Amanda and Cameron proceeded to the morning room. Jaci had long since abandoned the formal dining room for their meals. Before Cameron had returned, she and Amanda had often eaten in the kitchen.

The morning room, located past the study on the way to the kitchen, was small and intimate, even though the table easily sat twelve. It was of easy access for the kitchen staff, too. Before they sat, Jaci pulled the drapes back to let in what remained of the daylight. The dusky hues of sunset shimmered through the newly leafed trees.

"I'm glad spring is here; it makes such a difference from the dreary winter cold and early darkness." She made the comment as Cameron held her chair and seated her to the right of the head of the table. He took a seat to the left of head, with Amanda on his left. An unspoken observance since Cameron had arrived was that Nicholas would someday sit again at the head of the table. Until then, his chair remained vacant.

"I'm glad it's spring because my birthday's soon," Amanda chimed in, grinning from ear to ear as her father pulled out her chair, also. She had matured far beyond her five years over the past several months, but once in a while, the child in her emerged again. Jaci wished there were other children around for her to play with, for every child needed peers to establish themselves in the world. They didn't need to act like adults in an adult world all the time.

"Papa has said maybe I can have a new pony for my birthday, but I don't want one. I love Flower and he's the only horse — what's that?" Amanda interrupted her statement with the question.

"What's what?" Jaci returned, but in the silence following her question, she heard the noise, too.

Thunk — pause — thunk — pause. It sounded like wood hitting wood, but not as though someone was wielding a hammer. She turned towards the noise, for she had her back to the door, when Amanda squealed and Cameron let out a curse.

A cane in his right hand and his left hand clutching Selkirk's shoulder, Nicholas walked slowly into the morning room. His right leg was noticeably weaker than the left, and each time he moved it forward, the cane struck the floor with considerable force.

He hadn't made it far into the room before Amanda shot out of her chair and raced around the end of the table. If it hadn't been for Selkirk's steadying presence, she would have knocked Nicholas to the ground when she barreled into him, grabbing his legs with both chubby arms and hanging on tight.

"Whoa, Muffin. It'll be a while yet before I can swing you into the air like old times."

"I don't care. I love you, Uncle Nicholas. Miss Eastman and Papa said you would walk before the races because you wouldn't want to miss them."

"Oh, they did, did they?" Nicholas rejoined.

Jaci flushed guiltily as Nicholas shot her a glance, but in her elation over seeing him walk alone, she didn't care if he thought their tactics underhanded.

Cameron had joined his daughter, replacing Selkirk to give Nicholas a steady shoulder as they advanced towards the table. Jaci stood at her chair and gapped. He looked devilishly handsome in his dark suit and white shirt, the silver threads of his hair only adding to his appeal. He was clean shaven and his strong jaw tightened in determination as he made slow progress.

She knew he had been getting better, but the few steps she had witnessed were nowhere near the accomplishment of walking from the study to the morning room. Her eyes narrowed thoughtfully as Nicholas moved past her to the head of the table. "I think you've been practicing without me," she accused lightly.

Nicholas gave her a smile, nodding for her to be seated. Not until she had done so, did he drop into his chair, laying his cane on the floor beside him. "Some things can be done alone, while others need constant supervision," he whispered just for her.

She felt her face flush and she sincerely hoped Cameron didn't read the innuendo in his brother's words, but apparently he was busy getting Amanda seated.

Amanda chatted throughout dinner and Jaci was happy to let her. She ate little, stirring her food around on her plate, her gaze constantly sliding to Nicholas. It was hard to believe he had walked on his own and sat there eating with them instead of in his room. It made her stomach spasm and her head pound. Did his recovery mean she was no longer needed here at Wildwood?

246

"The race is on my birthday, Uncle Nicholas. And Miss Eastman says we'll have a big-be-quick for dinner."

"Bar-b-que, Sweetie," she corrected gently, pulling her thoughts back to the present.

"Although I wasn't in favor of a race in the beginning, perhaps it would be a good time to sell off several horses," Nicholas murmured as he sipped his wine.

"There's no need to worry about the note payments, Nick." Cameron looked adamant. "The ships are making good time and should be back in port by the end of June, laden with goods that will sell promptly. It isn't necessary to sell off any Wildwood stock—"

"That's beside the point, isn't it, Cameron?" Nicholas's voice, unusually harsh, commanded silence.

Jaci didn't understand. "Why not use the horses for stud, instead—"

"Excuse me?" Nicholas exploded, and when she looked at him, his gaze shifted quickly to Amanda and back.

Still, she shrugged, used to having clear spoken conversations. "Talk to me."

"A gentleman doesn't speak about such things in the presence of ladies, especially those of tender years." Again his gaze sliced to Amanda.

"Would it make any difference if Amanda weren't here?" She refused to let the subject drop.

"Miss Eastman, that's enough. I'll not have my dinner interrupted by useless questions."

For some reason, Nicholas was terribly agitated, and she wondered if they would have to allow him to re-establish himself again, now that he was walking. This male-ego thing was getting more than a little wearing. Perhaps it was time to do something about that, too.

She smiled sweetly. "Amanda, sweet, would you please excuse us? You may take your dessert in your room. Your papa will even join you, won't you?" Her gaze silently implored Cameron to help. "Mr. Westbrooke and I need to talk."

Amanda thought it a great treat to be allowed dessert away from the table, and Cameron seemed more than happy to comply with Jaci's wishes, much to Nicholas's consternation. Being a man, his brother should have stayed here to support him.

His thoughts were lost as his gaze followed Jaci. She escorted Cameron and his daughter to the door, quietly closing it behind them. He heard the key scrape in the lock.

Nicholas's heart did a little flip-flop at the thought of being locked in a room with Jaci. He tried to recall his anger at her interference, but her hips swayed and the silk of her gown rustled and he knew he was lost.

"Why do you have to sell the horses, Nicholas? Why not use profits from Cameron's shipping business?" Though she interrogated him, her voice caressed him and her gaze seduced him.

"It's a matter of honor, Jaci. I made the loans, not Cameron, and I have a duty to repay them."

"But you did it for Cameron; for your family. Isn't it all right for family to help now?"

He leaned back in his chair, content to drink in her beauty. She had worn her hair up tonight, but little pieces escaped her bun and softened the lines of her face. Her gown, of palest green, shimmered around her.

He had apparently incited her ire, for her bosom heaved with indignation. He wished, rather fervently, for her beautiful breasts to spill out of the low neckline. His thoughts prompted him to wonder how quickly irritation turned to passion, and he decided to find out.

"I told you, it's a matter of honor — something you apparently know little about." He ended this sentence in a teasing voice.

"How can you say that?"

"You stripped me of my honor when you took advantage of me. I was flat on my back; helpless—"

"You wanted it, too." Her eyes sparked and he recognized the look she had worn yesterday when they made love. "Admit it," she demanded, her eyes alive, and he had her right where he wanted her.

"No," he denied. "A gentleman would never admit he needed a woman."

She shrieked at him, hurrying her movements from the end of the table until she stood directly behind his chair. Having pushed her over the edge, and now not sure that was a good move, he turned, trying to keep her in his sights.

She jerked his chair out from the table, and then marched around to face him again. Before he could plan his strategy, she hiked up her dress and climbed onto his lap, her face only inches from his. "Admit it — you need me."

"No, I would never allow you that kind of power over me." He continued to tease her, loving every minute of it as the sexual tension in the room rose. His body heat hovered near the melting point each time she squirmed on his lap. Suddenly she stilled, staring at him with a wide-eyed gaze that made his heart trip with passion.

"You're the one who taught me passion, Nicholas, and how to feel. Now are you going to deny what you feel? What is part of us?"

He groaned his answer, pulling her close to thoroughly kiss her. She allowed him freedom to explore her mouth with his tongue, and the taste of her sent his senses spiraling. He kissed a trail of heat down her throat to the swell of her breasts.

He wanted to make love to her again, for yesterday seemed a lifetime ago. She curled her fingers in his hair, gently massaging his neck and he scoured his brain for an answer to his incredible need. When she wiggled her fanny against his groin, he thought he'd explode.

"Tell me you don't need me," she whispered in his ear, her tongue darting in and out, taunting him.

"Jaci, quit. You're driving me crazy."

She gave him a siren's smile. With her tongue caught between her teeth, she scooted back, reaching down to quickly unbutton his trousers. His manhood sprang free, throbbing with need.

To his surprise and delight, she shifted her dress around, holding it up with one hand while the other hand caressed his length before allowing herself to slide down onto him. Nicholas closed his eyes, the sensations coursing through him so strong and pure he hoped he survived their impact. She moved quickly, and he realized she was as frantic as he to reach the pinnacle of satisfaction.

"I swear you're a witch," he murmured as he licked along the tops of her breasts. Her movements increased, carrying him swiftly toward fulfillment.

She clutched his shoulders and threw her head back, her face a mask of pure sensual pleasure. Nicholas thought he had never seen her more beautiful.

"Not...a witch," she panted, "just from another...century."

He was on the brink of climax as he heard her words, and realized it didn't matter at all. He burst asunder, the impact of their coupling so intense he thought he could have been transported to another time.

* * *

"I can't believe I did that," Jaci gasped against his neck long minutes later.

"To what are you referring — seducing me, or screaming my name in the throes of passion?" He was quite pleased with himself, and with Jaci, though he would hesitate to openly admit he liked her brazen behavior.

"Oh, no, did I really scream?" She pushed her face closer to him, as though burying herself against discovery. Her breath against his hot skin was enough to start his passions rising once again.

He had to chuckle at her chagrin. "Actually, I doubt they heard you past the kitchen."

She groaned.

"There is something to be said for you being from the future and more free with your feelings, but I do hope you never decide to attack me in public." He had tried not to think about her origins. Sometimes, however, her attitudes, like towards sex, were foreign to his experience with women, he couldn't help but recall she had come to him across more than one hundred years of time.

She finally lifted her head. He held his gaze steady as she searched his face, and he hoped whatever she wished to find would appear for her.

"Do you regret our relationship, Nicholas?"

He adamantly shook his head. "Though I must admit I don't understand it, I most definitely don't have any regrets. And while I will most probably wish I had kept my mouth closed, I find myself curious as to what a woman from 2008 expects in a relationship."

She ticked her reasons off quickly, and he knew his eyes grew wider with wonder at each of her words. "Independence. There has to be a giving as well as taking — fifty-fifty. And trust — that's most important. Oh, and women are very capable of having ideas, and those ideas have the right to be tried." She paused to breathe, and he thought she looked very sure of herself.

"Fifty-fifty? It sounds as though you want to be a man." He slid his hands down the smooth curve of her back. "That would be a terrible waste, you know."

"Not a man, just equal; a partnership."

"I suppose next you'll tell me you want the right to vote for our government officials."

"That, too." She grinned at him. "What about you?"

He had no trouble telling her exactly what he thought. "A nineteenth century man takes care of what's his."

She quirked a brow at him and pursed her lips.

"Let me rephrase," he gave in with a sigh. "I treasure any gift given to me. I protect those who have been magically placed in my care." He kissed her nose lightly. "But, I do live by a code that demands honor, loyalty and fidelity. Can you accept that?"

"And does the fidelity thing work both ways?"

He knew what she was asking, and wondered what history had written about men of his era. Instead of answering directly, he questioned her, not knowing what standards she had lived by. "Would I have any reason to be unfaithful?"

"No." Her answer was swift. Then her golden brows came together in a frown. "I have to behave according to today's standards?"

"Absolutely. No arguing or questioning my authority in front of others." On this, he would not yield.

She leaned forward, her breasts on the verge of spilling out of her gown. Her lips met his in a feathery kiss; once, twice. As he was inclined to deepen the kiss, she pulled back. "So I can't be aggressive?" she asked.

"Well, I didn't say that."

"But if I'm to behave and obey perfectly by these standards, mustn't I also be demure and submissive, and definitely not take an active role in lovemaking?" She wiggled her bottom and he yielded — quickly and completely.

"I suppose there are a few customs we can begin a century early." She tickled his ear with her tongue and he sighed. "Ah, yes, definitely a few."

Chapter Eighteen

Jaci remained content on Nicholas's lap, sighing softly as he rubbed her back. She felt his breath against her hair as he gently kissed the top of her head. She knew she would love him forever. A shiver sliced through her — almost a premonition — and she jerked upright.

"Are you cold?" He rubbed her arms. "I can ring for Molly to bring you a wrap — but I'd rather not." His gaze — a sexy, liquid silver — caressed her, and she smiled, wishing never to move away from his embrace. "We should move to the parlor where there's a fire," he added, his voice reluctant. She shifted slightly on his lap, and he groaned. "But I'd rather not."

"Mmmm." She gave him no more answer than that. For long, lovely minutes, they sat in complete silence. Nicholas continued to rub her back. Her heart and soul were filled with warmth; a soothing peace she had never experienced before.

He finally let out a heavy sigh and set her away from him. Jaci looked up in question.

"I think it must be time to retire to another room. Selkirk is knocking from the other side of the door, and I'm afraid it may be opened any moment now." His voice was fringed with humor.

"Oh, dear, if they did hear me—" Her voice trailed off, too embarrassed to finish her thought.

This time, he laughed out loud as he set her on her feet and smoothed down her gown. "I was only teasing you earlier."

"I didn't yell?"

He reached down and grabbed his cane, slowly pushing himself to his feet. "Oh, you were quite vocal, all right, but I doubt your moans reached past these walls."

She tried to look indignant, but she was pleased with Nicholas's recovery and their lovemaking, so she simply shook her head and grinned. He took her elbow and led her from the room

As they moved down the hall, she felt the increased pressure of his grip, and she realized he wasn't as strong yet as he would like to think. Without words, she moved his arm around her shoulders to bear more of his weight.

When they reached the parlor, she had to allow him to seat her first, though she knew he was worn out. He stood for a moment by the fire, seemingly lost in thought, and she began to fidget.

He cleared his throat and turned to face her, leaning heavily on his cane. "We need to talk."

Oh, dear. She didn't want him bringing up any heavy conversation topics tonight. Even though she loved him dearly, she knew their passion was all there could be. She wouldn't ask for a commitment, not with her existence here so tenuous. Frantically, she tried to think of a change of subject, but he continued.

"I am still a cripple," he began, his gaze shifting away from her face, "and not yet capable of providing—"

"Providing what?" she interrupted, not allowing him to demean himself. "Nothing about your physical self keeps you from caring for the people who live at Wildwood. Why do you give so much to others and not want happiness for yourself?"

He looked totally taken back by her words. "How can you say that? I've done nothing but take from you and Cameron — from everyone — since the accident."

She jumped up and stood directly in front of him, placing her hands on either side of his face. She gazed steadily into his eyes and longed to tell him how very much she loved him. Yet in his present state of mind, she wondered if it would only create another imaginary burden for him to carry

His left hand raised, clasping hers as he turned and kissed her palm. "You must know how I feel," he sighed, "but I have commitments — debts to be paid." His eyes hardened as he gazed off into the distance. "Mason Edwardson holds the notes to Wildwood, and would like nothing better than to take what is mine."

"Even though you were once engaged to his daughter?" She didn't understand the lack of loyalty.

He snorted. "Perhaps because of that relationship, he is more determined than ever."

She huffed with indignation. "Well, we'll have to make sure he doesn't succeed. How much will it take?"

"I must raise two thousand dollars by the first of June to satisfy the mortgage."

"Oh, is that all?"

He looked as though she had sprouted another head. "Good God, woman, don't you have any concept of the value of a dollar?"

"Well, of course, I do; I think." She recalled what she had learned about the cost of items here in 1875 and realized money didn't have the same value when compared to what she would have made for a photo shoot. She damned herself for not paying closer attention in history class. If there were something she could invent with knowledge of the future, even if it would change history, she would do it for Nicholas's sake.

The only thing that came to mind was the Kentucky Derby. According to what Cameron had told her, bets were placed at the county races, but only friendly wagers, and not the kind of money they needed. Though she didn't know what kind of money the Derby would garner for the winner, she intended to find out.

She smiled, sure in her love and in her course of action. "We shall enter Wind Dancer in the Kentucky Derby and with the winnings, you can pay off your debts."

He scowled. "The Kentucky Derby? I have never heard of it."

She shirked. Did the Derby exist yet? If not, perhaps she would put a bug in someone's ear and they would create it. "It's a marvelously grand horse race held at Churchill Downs, and we are going to win it."

She heard Cameron speaking to Selkirk outside the door and decided now was a good time to say good night. She reached up on tiptoes and kissed him. "I will write them tonight and find out the date of the race." She tried to hide her excitement, and only hoped her knowledge of the future was yet another reason she had been sent here.

* * *

"You have done well, Herr Nicholas," the old wood carver stated, running his hands over the satin surface of the horse Nicholas had carved.

Nicholas had met Gustav Dentzel in the barn before the other guests began to arrive. After everything he had learned, he couldn't bring himself to complete the carousel animal for Jaci, and yet he knew in his heart it must be finished.

"Take the horse, Gustav, for one of your carousels. But I would ask that you paint it midnight black."

"*Nein!* Black is no color for so beautiful a creature." Gustav shook his head.

"Come." Nicholas led his friend to the barn entrance, pointing to where Wind Dancer pranced inside the paddock. "Have you ever seen a more magnificent animal? Please, friend, paint the horse black, for it is Wind Dancer, and also my dreams of the future."

His chest constricted with fear for what might happen when Jaci saw the wooden horse again, but he also knew they had to bring the story full circle. He had stared at her photograph until his eyes crossed, and nothing changed the fact that she had taken a picture of this very carving. However, when she came back in time, with the picture, he hadn't created the carousel horse yet.

He had tried, and failed, to logically plot the course of their relationship and what had happened. It always began with his discovery of her beauty beneath the mud from his horse pens, and ended with her passionate response to his lovemaking. It came back to that every time. He loved her; he was sure she loved him, and all the rest seemed inconsequential. He had to put his faith in their love; and pray that it was enough for the task ahead.

* * *

Jaci's gaze found Nicholas slowly walking up from the barn with Mr. Dentzel. Theirs was a strange relationship, considering the differences in their ages. Looking around at the assembled guests, however, it didn't appear Nicholas's age interfered with doing business and associating with any generation.

A frown replaced her smile as she observed the two. Adamant, Nicholas waved his arm in a wide arc towards the horses, and Dentzel shook his head. Soon, the wood carver nodded, shook Nicholas's hand, and turned towards the shade of the gazebo. Jaci wondered what that had been about.

She continued watching from the porch as Nicholas brushed the hair back from his forehead. He was casually dressed, white shirt with sleeves rolled up, snug trousers tucked into knee high riding boots. He was still thinner than before the accident, but he was eating well. When he turned, she knew his gaze followed the horses as they warmed up on the track. Nicholas hadn't been training, and he most definitely wasn't racing today, but he still had a lead rope dangling from his back pocket.

"Nice buns," she mumbled under her breath.

"What you need, Miss Eastman?" Delta asked as she stepped past her, platters of food in her arms.

Jaci laughed and offered to help the cook carry things out to the huge tables that had been constructed out of boards and sawhorses and placed under the trees. Her last glance of Nicholas found him approaching Wind Dancer. He leaned on his cane only slightly now. It was good to see him able to work with his horses, and be outside. In those few minutes, she fell in love with him all over again.

Chuckling to herself, she turned away from the track to finish the preparations for the bar-b-que. Guests had started arriving early that morning. The house was full of women, visiting and embroidering, as their husbands mingled around the track, good naturedly joking and placing wagers.

She had been amazed at the number of children spilling from the carriages as they arrived. If she had known, she would have invited them over long before this to play with Amanda. All the little girls had squealed with delight when Amanda had whispered there were kittens in the barn. In a flurry of rainbow colored dresses and petticoats, they had raced away to find them, Sir Lancelot barking happily at their heels.

The afternoon swept past with incredible speed, and she enjoyed herself immensely. She had effortlessly slipped into the role of hostess, making sure guests had plenty of food and drink, seeing to shady porch chairs for the older matrons, and privacy for a few young mothers in need of nursing their babies. To her surprise, none of Nicholas's neighbors appeared to find her role the least bit unusual. Their focus, instead, seemed to be on Nicholas's remarkable recovery.

Cameron, of course, claimed his share of attention from the young ladies. She hoped he would find someone he to love, now that he had rediscovered that emotion and enjoyed being a father.

She sighed as she looked around the happy scene. Everyone looked at peace; serene and comfortable, and she suddenly realized that she was, too. There was nothing more she needed in this life than what she had found at Wildwood.

"Makes you wonder why the world didn't stay this way, doesn't it?" The question was whispered softly from behind, and Jaci turned to see Nancy Schaffer, prettily decked out in a candy striped dress and jaunty hat.

"Nancy, how wonderful that you're back." She hugged her friend. "How was your stay in England?"

"Michael's relatives are stuffy beyond bearing, but we survived. As you have?" Nancy replied, and Jaci saw all the unspoken questions in her gaze.

Their last conversation flashed through her mind and she recalled Nancy's indication that Jaci would have a choice to stay in this century or return to her own. But she had also said Jaci wasn't here to change history, and on that she had to disagree. Saving Nicholas from drowning; realizing the implications of the photograph; all led Jaci to believe she did have some divine reason for being here.

As for a choice, Jaci hoped Nancy was wrong, because she didn't want to contemplate choosing between Nicholas and anything else. She tried to decide how much to tell Nancy, but was interrupted by Amanda.

"Miss Eastman, the races are about to begin." The little girl tugged on her skirt and Jaci knew the moment was lost.

Nancy patted her arm and smiled. "There's nothing you need tell me that isn't clearly written on your face. Despite what I've heard about Nicholas's accident, it appears everything is working out." Nancy's husband came, nodded to Jaci, and took his wife by the elbow to lead her to the race track. It was just as well, for Jaci didn't want to contemplate the future right now.

Everyone was caught up in the festive air of the races, and for the next few hours, she didn't worry about anything else. Nicholas was truly in his element. He held the attention of the entire audience as he announced the races, each consisting of only four horses to prevent injuries on the track. After all, this was only a friendly neighborhood race, and no one wanted their horse hurt before the official race season began.

She watched him more than the horses, for he continually amazed her with his commanding presence. His friends appeared not to consider his slight limp a problem, and as they walked along the fence, she saw several who slowed to match their pace to his. He would listen avidly to each of the owners, and quite often, she was sure the handshakes they shared were business deals, not friendly greetings. That was how business was done, and she knew Nicholas reveled in it.

At one point, as the next set of horses were being brought onto the track, his gaze caught hers. Across the span of the yard, she felt drawn to him. What was he trying to tell her — that he loved her? She wished suddenly that they were alone. She took several steps toward him, hoping for one or two minutes of privacy.

Before she reached him, Lycinda glided up to his side, laying her hand possessively on his arm. Jaci watched as he bent his head in deference to Lycinda's petite size, listening avidly to her words. At one point he even threw his head back in a laugh, and her heart broke.

Had Lycinda decided, now that he was well, that she had made a mistake in breaking up with him? He appeared to pay rapt attention to what she said. Had his feelings for his former fiancée re-emerged; was that the commitment he had referred to? She bit her bottom lip as it trembled.

How could she, a simple governess with no skills, compete with someone as exquisite as Lycinda? She watched him, ever the gentleman, lead Lycinda back to her father as the race began.

Jaci always felt she didn't belong to this world, no matter what passions she and Nicholas had shared. Now she asked herself if she had the right to fight for his love. Had she learned enough about living in this century to combat Lycinda's innate charm?

The sun continued to shine brightly on the crowd at Wildwood, and the food and drink continued to be consumed. Laughter rang out across the meadow, but she spent the rest of the afternoon lost in her own thoughts. By the time the last race was run, she had made her decision.

* * *

Darkness gradually descended, but the numerous lamps and lanterns kept the night at bay, and the revelry continued well past midnight. A dance floor had been constructed by laying large, flat boards together by the gazebo, and no one seemed to mind that it wasn't a formal affair. In fact, Jaci felt people were relaxed and enjoyed themselves much more this way. She laughed and waved as Amanda hollered at her, swinging around on her papa's arm.

She eyed Nicholas warily as he crossed the yard, taking another drink from a passing servant. He was drinking too much, again, but she knew better than to say anything. Perhaps he was merely celebrating being able to walk among his neighbors.

"Good evening, Miss Eastman; Stillwell." Nicholas nodded at Thomas, who still stood at her side after the dance was finished.

She wondered about the gleam in Nicholas's pewter eyes. They hadn't spoken since the races; since she had seen him with Lycinda. Was he acting strangely, or did she just perceive it that way? Surely he wouldn't tell her, in front of Thomas, that he didn't want her anymore? Deciding to let him take the initiative in the conversation, she merely inclined her head in greeting.

"Nicholas, it's good to see you up and about. You've made a remarkable recovery." Thomas sounded rather formal, as though he, too, felt leery of Nicholas's attitude.

"Yes, I have indeed. In fact, my recovery is so complete, I've come to claim—" his eyes twinkled, and Jaci held her breath, "—a dance. You don't mind, do you, Stillwell?" Without waiting for an answer, he handed his cane and empty glass to Thomas, whisking Jaci onto the wooden dance floor.

She couldn't prevent the reprimand from leaving her lips. "You were rather rude to Thomas. I'd suggest you not drink too much and behave with a little more—"

He whirled her around so fast she didn't complete her sentence. His hand on her back brought her closer to his chest. "Thomas, is it now? My, how familiar." His tone was irritated and Jaci looked up to see his flinty gaze focused on the doctor, anger manifesting itself in the set lines of his mouth. Suddenly, it dawned on her that he was jealous. Well, how about that. Perhaps there was hope for Jaci's fragile heart after all.

"Yes, Thomas." She had the delightful urge to needle him. "He's become a good friend, and he enjoys my company." As she spoke, his arm tightened on her back. She wondered if she had pushed him too far when he suddenly faltered, his leg turning unexpectedly under him. He clutched momentarily at her and she automatically stiffened her back to support him.

"You're not completely recovered. Why did you insist on dancing?" All thoughts of jealousy evaporated as she tried to maintain their balance without alerting anyone to the problem.

"It is not considered good form for a man to show weakness. I thought you realized that by now." His face grimaced with pain, and her heart melted.

Men. Why did they think they had to be so macho? Without thinking, she said, "Let me get you over to Thomas and he can take a look at you."

Luckily, they were at the edge of the dance floor where the lantern light waned, and no one saw him hesitate. Several emotions crossed his features; possession remained in the wake of the rest. "It is said in some cultures that when a person saves another's life, they are bound together until the debt can be repaid." His husky voice and smoky gaze mesmerized her. "Since I have yet to repay you, Miss Eastman, you are not free to see anyone else. You are not free at all."

Instead of a threat, his words brought her unaccountable joy, yet she didn't feel it the right place to voice her own feelings of love. "And how long do you intend to stay in my debt, Mr. Westbrooke?"

He pulled her tight against him, and she felt the heat of his male essence. Her heart jumped and fire coiled in her very center. The music ended and they stopped dancing. He bowed low over her hand, and then raised his gaze to hers.

"For a very, very, long time."

* * *

Early the next morning, Nicholas stood at the track railing, a heavy mist doing nothing to dispel the heat still ravishing his body since his conversation with Jaci last evening. He had longed for the crowds of people to vanish and the lanterns to be doused. All he had wanted to do was lay her down in the soft grass and make exquisite love to her. But it hadn't happened, and he had spent the remainder of the evening with an intense ache in his belly.

He knew his remarks about Thomas were uncalled for, but he wanted her to know that she belonged to him. It had nearly done him in to see her speaking with the doctor. As soon as he was completely well; as soon as the debts were paid—

"He's magnificent," she breathed, her words drifting to him as her scent tantalized his senses. She came to his side, holding his hand on top of the cane, her energy seeping into him as it always did to waylay his fears and force him to seek the future.

As though Wind Dancer knew she complimented him, he raced around the track, mane and tail flying, hooves striking the hard packed dirt with a staccato beat. Nicholas shifted his weight off his weak right leg. He well remembered how it felt with the wind in his face, the horse's muscles bunching beneath his legs.

"You can do it, Nicholas, you can." She read his thoughts. He hadn't ridden since the accident, but now his heart beat as hard and rapidly as the pounding of the horse's hooves. A vision formed of the two of them racing far away from everything threatening. It would be him and her, making love as thunderously wild as his stallion's speed, as enduring as the land over which they raced.

"Come with me?" he asked, taking her hand and leading her to the stable.

It didn't take long to have the horses saddled, and now he raced ahead of her to the top of the hill. For a moment, Jaci paused her smaller horse, taking in the splendor of seeing him ride again, but also the beauty of the land, still so virgin compared to her time.

Dots of darker green interrupted the bright color where rows of cedar covered the hillside. White swirls across the sky collided with brilliant azure blue. She shaded her eyes. Tiny droplets of water shimmered on the leaves of the nearby trees. Everything flowed, bright and new, and the photographer in her longed to capture the moment.

Nicholas sat, laughing at the world around him, hair blowing in the wind. He flung his arms wide. "I never thought I'd ride again; never thought Wind Dancer and I would see this scene. What can I do to repay you for giving this back to me?"

"Love me," she answered softly.

He shook his head, his eyes dancing. "That's not what I meant. What can I give you in compensation?"

Joking, and yet not, Jaci said, "Your heart."

Nicholas swung his leg over the saddle and slid to the ground, long strides eating the distance to her side. As he spoke, he reached up and circled her waist, pulling her from the horse. "My darling Miss Eastman, you already have my heart; have had it for quite some time."

"Then make love to me, Nicholas."

Without another word, he took her hand and led her up the hill, gently laying her down on the lush grass. With exquisite tenderness, he showed her exactly what love was and how much she meant to him. For all the past times when their passion had ruled their minds and they had raced to the edge and leaped, this time he refused to let her control the pace.

He worshipped every inch of her body with hands and lips and heated gaze, reducing her to a trembling mass of nerve endings. Even when he covered her with his body and entered her, it was with a gentleness more erotic than anything she had experienced in his arms before.

"I love you, Jaci, more than life itself. Your softness, your giving, your heart have kept me alive when I would have rather ended it all." His fevered words made her heart soar. "If you will have me for your husband, I will spend the rest of eternity pleasing you," he kissed her ear, "and loving you."

His passionate words sent Jaci spiraling over the edge and Nicholas followed, their climaxes fusing them together even as they burst into pieces. As she drifted back to earth, she cried for all that had been, and for all that could never be. For in that moment, she knew it wouldn't be fair to him if she stayed

Chapter Nineteen

Cold rain, carried by a gusting wind, splashed across the porch. The drastic change in temperature from the warm afternoon caused Jaci to shiver and pull her cloak tighter around her. She hadn't packed all her clothes, taking only what she considered essential for escape. Now, she shifted uneasily as she lifted her bag, hesitating to step from the warm, sheltering manor into the wet darkness. The moment she left Wildwood, she knew she would be swallowed up by the night and her life irrevocably changed.

She reached behind her to pull the door closed but it was jerked out of her hand, causing her to stumble backward. To maintain her balance, she dropped her bag and clutched the first solid object within reach — a warm, very hard body.

"What the hell do you think you're doing?" Rough hands grabbed her arms; an even rougher voice shouted at her over the wind.

She let go of Nicholas's shirt front and stepped back. He released her, but remained solidly in the oak doorway, his height blocking most of the light that streamed from the hall. She couldn't make out his features, but his voice held anger, and something not quite definable.

Last night, Nicholas had the servants move his bed back upstairs, and had invited her to share it with him. Like a fool, she had agreed, and it had made leaving all the harder. Now she struggled to get her equilibrium, and to figure a way out of this dilemma. To shift his attention, she questioned him. "It's the middle of the night. Why aren't you still sleeping?"

"Better question — why are you leaving?" He hadn't moved except to cross his arms on his chest, making him all the more formidable. Shadows played across his stern face.

"I'm...ah," She looked at the bag by her feet. "Who told you?"

"Lady, if there is staff in a household, there are no secrets. Now, I ask you again; why?" Lightning flashed and thunder shook the boards of the porch where she stood, as though nature, too, took Nicholas's side against her.

The wind picked up, whipping her hair across her face. She brushed it out of her eyes, shouting over the rain. "You don't understand. I have to go. I have no place here." It was breaking her heart to deny the love she had once thought she would never know.

"What do you mean?" He shouted back at her. "Your place is with me." She shook her head and his face fell. Frown lines deepened across his forehead; his shoulders sagged. More softly, he stated, "I thought you were happy here."

"I was — I am. Don't make this harder than it already is." She was crying and she sounded like an old movie. He held out his arms, but she knew she couldn't touch him. If she did, she'd never leave.

"I thought I was frightened when I couldn't walk," he said. "I was helpless, unable to provide for Amanda and my staff. But I didn't know what fear was until I woke up and you were gone."

She sobbed harder. "I can't stay. Don't you see?"

His arms dropped to his sides, hands clinched. "All I see is you running away. What happened to the woman who defied me at every turn; who fought my battles for me and made me fight? Where's the woman who wouldn't give up?"

"It's not the same," she argued, yet not wanting their last moments together to end in a fight.

"Why isn't it the same? Because you're from another century?" He waved a hand in the air as though that were the least of the considerations. "It doesn't matter. There's no difference if you're from 2015 or from Richmond, Virginia — you're mine. And regardless of your futuristic logic, I know you want to belong to me; to belong here at Wildwood. So tell me why?"

"Because...because I love you, damn it! And that's not fair to you. I don't know how long I can stay here. What if I disappear without warning?" Her confession was cut short as he grabbed her close. He broke into a glorious smile just before he kissed her, stripping her of all rational thought. His kiss was totally possessive, and yet she detected an underlying current of tenderness that she hadn't felt before.

Gently, he brushed wet tendrils of hair away from her face as he gazed into her eyes. "God, you don't know how long I've waited to hear you say that. I have loved you since before the accident, but I couldn't ask you to love a cripple, a man—" This time, his comments were cut off as she returned his kiss, her tongue tracing the fullness of his lips, memorizing their texture and their taste.

The small brocade satchel remained unattended on the porch as he swept her into his arms and carried her inside. He limped only slightly, but when she requested he put her down, his lips silenced her protests.

He didn't make it back to the bedroom, but instead deposited Jaci on the edge of his desk in the study. She began to shiver violently from the rain, and he swore under his breath as he jerked her sodden cloak off and flung it to the floor.

"If I had any doubts that you were not of this world, I have them no more, for you have pushed me to unnatural heights of anguish and anger this night." As he spoke, he continued removing her clothes, and she wasn't sure if it was because they were wet, or because he was angry and not thinking.

She sucked in her breath as he gently brushed the swell of her breasts above her bra. He raised his gaze to hers, speaking only in a whisper. "These are the clothes you wore the day you arrived. You actually were going to leave me?"

She touched her fingers to his lips. "Sh," she shook her head in answer. He looked so forlorn. "I love you so much, Nicholas, but is it enough?"

"We will make it so," he answered, his lips once again pressing hers, compelling her to give all of herself into his safe keeping. Without reservation, she finally conceded.

Somewhere in the heat of their passion, she quit shivering and quit worrying about the future. She concentrated only on his love. His touch roused all her nerve endings to the pinnacle of sensitivity. He lifted her from the edge of the desk and in seconds her jeans were stripped from her legs.

Her lycra running shorts stuck to her like a second skin, and he hesitated before removing them. He tilted his head to the side as though not sure what they were, and then shrugged. She guessed it didn't matter, as long as they were off.

Once he had her naked, he gently lifted her back on the desk and removed his own clothes. She watched, ever fascinated by the play of muscles across his chest, the strong hands which were always gentle with her. She sucked in her breath at his nakedness, for no matter how often they had made love, he still caused her heart to quicken.

He stood before her, magnificent and proud, no cane supporting him, and her heart wept. How much longer would she have — how many days, or hours, before she was no longer needed and would be sent back?

If those were the rules.

Nicholas gently spread her legs and stepped between them. When his chest touched her breasts, her nipples stiffened and she felt on fire.

"Remember my promise?" he whispered against her mouth, kissing the corners, before trailing his tongue along her lips. She opened to his unspoken request and he deepened the kiss. Instead of satisfying her desire, he only fueled the fire. She ran her hands up his chest, stopping momentarily at his nipples before circling his neck to hold him tight.

"Do you remember?" he asked her again.

"I don't need a promise, Nicholas, I only need you. Please, take me to bed." She was breathing heavy and wondered if she could hold off the ache which meant she was near climax. She wasn't ready for these exquisite feelings to end.

"You are a hard woman, Jaci Eastman, not to remember my promise. A man's promise is his bond." His breath came in short gasps as he entered her in a single stroke. He made love to her with a rhythm so intense she wondered they didn't disintegrate from the heat. She clung to his shoulders, her bottom resting on the desk, her legs locked around his back to prevent him from leaving her as he moved faster.

"Nicholas," she gasped as she climaxed, the contractions cresting in wave after wave of sensation. When she thought the sweetness could not get better, he cried out her name.

He pulled her off the desk and anchored her against him. His hands supported her as he slowly turned in a circle, and the climax she thought finished kept tumbling over and over within her.

In that glorious moment of completion, she did recall the promise he had given her. A silly promise, really, under ordinary circumstances. And yet, their love was anything but ordinary. He had promised one day to make love to her standing up.

* * *

The clattering of the train's wheels against the track woke Jaci from the few minutes of fitful sleep she had tried to capture. Her cheeks flushed as she straightened in her seat, hoping no one on the train noticed the way her breath had caught. She prayed she hadn't moaned in her sleep.

She turned her face to the window, watching the scenery go by, but her mind returned again to that night in Nicholas's study. Even after she had admitted that she recalled his promise, he hadn't let her go. No, they had remained in the study the rest of the long night. As the

270

thunder rolled outside, they had made love again and again, but not one time lying down.

As dawn lightened the sky, he had asked her to marry him. Actually, he had demanded. She had tried to warn him, reminding him she didn't know the rules by which they played this time travel game, but he wouldn't listen. She smiled as she recalled his mention of the honorable thing; how she owed it to him since she already badgered him like a wife; already shared his life like a wife, and would forever have his undying love — like a wife. She had finally relented, under one condition — Wind Dancer had to win the Kentucky Derby.

Even that hadn't deterred Nicholas, and so here they were, on a southbound train for Louisville, and the very first Run for the Roses.

When she had written a very generic letter to the race secretary in charge of the Kentucky Derby at Churchill Downs in Louisville back in March, she had no idea whether the race even existed. In the meantime, Nicholas had continued to train Wind Dancer, stating he was the fastest thoroughbred on the continent and she had better be picking out a wedding dress.

The letter had come the first week in April from a Col. Meriwether Lewis Clark, who appeared quite pleased that they had heard about his race as far north as Philadelphia. He explained in his letter that the facilities, only recently named Churchill Downs in honor of a relative on whose land the track had been built, would be the site of the first race of this kind on May seventeenth. They were only allowing fifteen horses to race, they had to be three-year-olds, and Col. Clark insured them a slot in the field.

He closed the letter by issuing a personal invitation to visit him while they were in Louisville. He indicated a curiosity as to how they had found out about the race and all the particulars that only a few people in Kentucky had known. She grimaced at that notion, but Nicholas laughed, assuring her that the questions would disappear in the wake of Wind Dancer's performance.

She shook off her daydreams and rose from the hard train bench, hoping for a moment of fresh air. There were apparently no rules on these early trains about smoking, spitting tobacco, or even drinking, and after the hours and hours they had been riding, she needed to get away from all the male passengers.

When they had first boarded in Philadelphia, Jaci had been excited. She had never ridden a train, even Amtrak, and the idea of riding an authentic, 1875 locomotive thrilled her, but that had been days ago. They had debarked overnight only once, in Charleston, Virginia, and she had sighed in relief to see the soft feather mattress at the hotel.

Mackey had stayed at the stable with the horses, for they had brought both Wind Dancer and Sabet. Nicholas felt that Wind Dancer would fare better with a stable mate on this long journey. Tom and Sam had stayed with Mackey; the two stable boys responsible for exercising the horses whenever the train stopped for fuel or water. Sam would also ride Wind Dancer in the race.

As the train kept up steam and headed westward, Jaci's stomach knotted as tightly as her hands clutched the rail which ran around the small platform between cars. She had dreaded leaving Wildwood and Amanda. It was the first time she had been away for an extended period since her arrival in this century. She almost felt Amanda was an anchor in this century, without which she would disappear. Nicholas kept reminding her it was not a person, but the carousel animal that threatened their love, and even that could no longer hurt them.

Anxious to reassure herself, she continued through the passenger cars until she reached the freight car, especially designed to stable the horses on this long trip. An associate of Nicholas's had provided the special car, at no little expense, to insure the Wildwood horses arrived in Louisville safely. The man had brooked no argument, stating that Pennsylvania must be represented at this southern race in style. Nicholas's horses rode in more comfort than did some of the passengers.

She sniffed when she entered the compartment. The sweet smell of hay and alfalfa assailed her nostrils, and the horses whinnied softly in greeting. She had already seen the boys, herded by Mackey, go towards the passenger compartment with the food hamper she had packed. That guaranteed Nicholas remained alone with the horses.

Not that she wanted to seduce him or anything. A smile touched her lips. They spent more time making love on anything other than a bed, but it wasn't the physical act of making love that she needed right now. What she needed most was simply the touch of his hand, and to curl into his warmth — anything to let her know that what they shared was real.

How she managed to keep from waking him, she'd never know, but when she came around the edge of the furthest stall, Nicholas remained sleeping, sprawled on the hay. She stared at his cherished features, searing yet another imprint on her brain for later — when she no longer had his closeness. She gradually became aware of his slight snore; something she hadn't noticed before. It caused her to smile.

She hugged herself, wondering when her dreams would evaporate. Each new wonder in their relationship also brought pain and fear of ending. She had thought when she saved him from drowning that would open her window to return to Dallas. Afterwards, she considered his ability to walk again to be the point at which he didn't need her and she'd go back. Now, each new day brought joy at having time to spend with him, and a building fear that it would be their last day together.

She didn't know the rules and there was no way to predict when it would happen. All the times she thought a window would open hadn't, and now she prayed it wouldn't. Perhaps she was the one time traveler they forgot about and she could simply live her life. Perhaps...

Should she wake him? She needed him desperately at that moment. Her skin longed for his touch; her soul craved his comfort, but he looked so peaceful. His hair had come loose from its tie and lay in wild array, yet it made him look more youthful. He had loosened his tie and unbuttoned his vest, and his coat hung from a nail by Wind Dancer's stall.

"Are you going to stand there all night and stare at me, or come over here where I can touch you?" His sleepy voice caressed her, and even over the racket of the train's wheels against the track, she heard the longing. Her own ache grew; she needed him to take away her fear.

Hip to hip, she fitted herself against him, regardless of the straw and wrinkles she knew she'd have. She tucked her shoulder under his arm, laid her head on his chest, and wrapped an arm across his waist. Still not satisfied, she draped a leg over his.

"Are you staking your claim?" He teased, but she didn't feel like laughing.

"Aren't you scared at all, Nicholas?" she whispered, afraid to raise her voice for fear of shattering the fragile dream she had woven around them.

"Of what — losing Wildwood?" He shrugged. "No, I feel very confident Wind Dancer will win and the money will pay off the debts." She felt him turn and place a kiss on top her head. "Thanks to your knowledge of the Kentucky Derby."

That wasn't what she meant. "What about — what about us?"

He laughed aloud at that. "Why, Miss Eastman, have you forgotten your promise already?"

She turned to rest her chin on his chest. "Nicholas, I haven't forgotten one second of all the time I've been at Wildwood. But don't you see — what if I don't stay?"

He pressed a finger to her lips. "Sh, I won't listen to that."

"But—"

"Do you love me, Jaci?"

She didn't know where he headed, but answered immediately. "You know I do."

"How much?"

"With my life," she stated emphatically.

He dragged her across him until they were nose to nose.

"Then why do you question? You must have faith, sweetheart."

"Nicholas, some fluke brought me through time to you. How do we know that a fluke won't send me back? And what might that be? And—"

He kissed her to silence and she let him. She needed to know he loved her; she needed comfort. As always, he didn't disappoint her. His kiss expressed his passion and his need, but also his confidence in their love.

* * *

The ensuing days proved hectic, and they kept Jaci's mind off her troubles. They stabled Wind Dancer and Sabet at Churchill Downs upon their arrival in Louisville. Nicholas took time to make sure his horses suffered no ill effects from the long journey before he allowed himself to enjoy the hospitality of the hotel. Sam, Tom and Mackey would stay in quarters at the track.

Scheduled workout times were available so only a few of the fifteen horses were on the track at any one time. Nicholas always attended when Wind Dancer ran and Jaci usually accompanied him. There was a festive atmosphere around the Downs which soon infected both of them.

She was singularly impressed when they meet Col. Meriwether Lewis Clark, whose vision inspired the creation of this race. She longed to tell him how his race track would take on a mystic status, both for Churchill Downs itself, and for the city and residents of Louisville, but she knew no one would believe her.

Col. Clark singled Nicholas and her out one night at dinner to express his enthusiasm over their attendance at the Downs. "I never imagined word of this race would reach as far north as Philadelphia; at least not this first year." They shared a secret smile at the man's obvious pride in his accomplishment.

"Yes, I was most impressed with the Epsom Derby and St. Leger, both of which are English classics, you know." He smiled at Jaci, but she knew he only sought to impress Nicholas with his horse racing knowledge. "I decided to model my races after those, for I want to stimulate interest in thoroughbred racing."

He lowered his voice as though to impart a secret. "I even imported pari-mutuel machines developed by a French colleague named Pierre Oller. Perhaps you might care to make a wager?" Nicholas had merely inclined his head without actually acquiescing.

Throughout the week before the race, Nicholas and Jaci rubbed shoulders with the elite of Louisville and Kentucky at various dinners and balls. Even though this was the first race at this track, the participants were going to make sure it was a race everyone remembered.

May seventeenth, race day, dawned sunny and cool. Nicholas had bought Jaci a new dress and hat especially for this day, but it took some time for her to dress. Her stomach refused to allow her to eat breakfast, and now, fifteen minutes before they had to leave, she still felt like throwing up.

Nicholas paced, giving her as much time as he dared before they had to leave, but she realized he didn't know quite what to do with her. Finally, her stomach settled enough for her to be comfortable and they departed, taking a carriage from the hotel to the outskirts of town. The grandstands were filling fast, but each owner had a box reserved right at the front of the track. The mile and a half race would be over in less than five minutes, so Col. Clark made sure his guests had plenty to entertain themselves prior to the start of the race.

The stables were off limits except for owners, but the grandstand area had a restaurant buffet and lounge for the ladies that were designed to keep them out of the sun. Nicholas left Jaci to see to last minute preparations with

Wind Dancer. She nervously reached for a glass of champagne, scanning the crowd over the rim of her glass.

No one from Philadelphia was here and she considered that good; and bad. It would have been nice for Nicholas to have friends and family around, but again, what if things didn't end up like they wanted? What if. . .? She gulped down the champagne and reached for another glass. It was fortuitous that Nicholas returned when he did, otherwise she would have gotten quite drunk.

"The race is almost ready to begin," he said from behind her and she turned to greet him. He didn't look the least anxious, and she wished she had his attitude. "Would you like to place a wager on the outcome of this race?" As he spoke, he led her over to one side of the grandstands.

His eyes widened when she pulled a roll of bills from her purse. "I think I must pay you too well."

"This certainly isn't my money." At his look, she continued quickly. "Cameron, and Thomas, and even Mrs. Jeffrey gave me some and if you don't think I've been paranoid about someone robbing me since we left Philly, well, let me tell you." As she chattered non-stop, she gave the man behind the barred window all her money. When he asked which horse she wanted to bet on, it momentarily threw her off balance.

"Wind Dancer, of course." She then realized the poor man didn't know she stood by Nicholas Westbrooke, owner of Wind Dancer and Wildwood. She continued her conversation with Nicholas. "I'm very happy to get rid of it."

"Are you implying you won't get anything back?" He raised a brow in question.

"Of course not, but with everyone's winnings and the winner's purse, we'll have to get a bank draft."

He grinned. "You're that confident Wind Dancer will win? Do you know something I don't?" He took her elbow and guided her through the crowd to the box they had been assigned.

She felt surprised he would ask. "Heavens, no. If I recalled that much history, I would have invented something quicker, or closer to home."

He laughed. "We'll simply have to take our chances, won't we?" When they entered the box, a gentleman already there stood and doffed his hat.

"Jaci, may I present, uh, Mr. Christopher Stein. Mr. Stein, this is my betrothed, Miss Jaci Eastman. Thank you for joining us."

Mr. Stein didn't speak, but bowed slightly and gave her a cryptic smile. Jaci would have spoken to draw him out, but a trumpet blared at the same time thunder rumbled.

She glanced skyward. "When did the clouds come?" Her stomach plummeted; she didn't contemplate rain. "Can Wind Dancer run as fast in the rain?"

"What?" Nicholas asked, preoccupied with the field of horses.

She pointed skyward and Nicholas looked up, forehead wrinkling. "I usually don't run him on a wet track, for fear of injury. Perhaps the rain will hold off." His gaze went back to the track, where several skittish horses were being held by their trainers.

Thunder rumbled again, almost in defiance of Nicholas's words. Col. Clark, impervious to the weather, stood at the front of the grandstand and greeted his guests, the owners and all the visitors who had come that day — an estimated ten thousand people, he said. A murmur of approval rippled through the crowd, followed by a round of applause.

The horses were quieted at the gate. The trainers removed blindfolds as needed, and left the thoroughbreds in the hands of the jockeys. His red and black silks shimmering in the sun, Sam looked very confident on Wind Dancer's back. Jaci saw his lips move as he quietly spoke to the horse.

The starter's pistol cracked in the silence, launching both the horses and the audience into action. Surging up from her seat, she yelled along with other spectators for their favorites. Nicholas didn't shout, but when she grabbed his hand in her exuberance, he returned her tight hold.

The thundering of hooves couldn't be differentiated from the rumbling in the increasingly dark sky and it wasn't until Wind Dancer crossed the finish line that she realized it had begun to rain. But it didn't matter. Nicholas caught her around the waist, swinging her in a circle and enthusiastically kissing her.

"He won! He actually did it!" He released control of his emotions now and shouted along with the rest of the crowd. Regardless of who stood near, he cupped her cheeks and kissed her with passion. "I love you, Mrs. Westbrooke."

Her breath caught. In the excitement of winning, she had forgotten her pledge. "But I'm not," she protested.

"Soon to be corrected." He turned her around to face the gentleman who had shared their box. "The Reverend Christopher Stein."

Her mouth dropped open as her gaze traveled back to Nicholas. He smiled at her and her heart melted, as it did every time he looked at her.

Despite the rain, she reached up and circled his neck. Pulling his head down, she whispered against his lips. "I love you, Nicholas Westbrooke. I'm scared to death about what might happen, but I love you too much to stop now." Her kiss would have gone on indefinitely, but Reverend Stein interrupted.

"Would I be out of line, sir, if I suggested seeking shelter?"

Jaci began to giggle when Nicholas seemed disinclined to stop licking the moisture from her lips. It was pouring now, and she saw the beautiful feathers from her hat drooping in front of her eyes. When she pushed against his chest, he gave in with a sigh.

Hand in hand, they raced to the stables and out of the rain. The crowd had followed the horses as the trainers also sought shelter for the animals in their charge. She and Nicholas found Mackey and Wind Dancer surrounded.

Col. Clark found a way to rise above the crowd and called for attention. "Though I had no control over the weather, I do most sincerely apologize, especially to our fair ladies." He doffed his hat and bowed as low as his perch on the stall partition would allow.

"I'm pleased, however, with this, our first Kentucky Derby." Applause followed. He raised his hands for silence. "Mr. Westbrooke, are you among us?"

Nicholas raised his hand in affirmation, and after giving Jaci's shoulders a squeeze, he worked his way to the front of the crowd. Before even acknowledging Col. Clark, he ran his hand down Wind Dancer's muzzle, congratulating Sam and slapping Mackey on the back. Finally, he allowed the Colonel his attention.

"It is with great pleasure that I award Wind Dancer, of Wildwood Stables, our garland of roses!" As the blanket of red flowers was looped over Wind Dancer's neck he shook his head as though very well aware of the fine job he had done. "And to his owner, Nicholas Westbrooke of Philadelphia, Pennsylvania, this bank draft in the amount of two thousand eight hundred fifty dollars." Applause and cheering erupted wildly as Nicholas accepted his winnings.

At least now Nicholas had the money to pay the mortgage and insure Wildwood's success. Jaci shivered, the heat of excitement giving way to cold from the rain seeping through her wet clothes. She rubbed her arms to warm herself, wondering where she could hide and dry off, when Nicholas's words caught her attention.

"I thank you for your good wishes," he profusely stated, "and I invite you all to stay right here while the Reverend Stein marries me to the lovely Jaci Eastman."

A cheer arose. It wasn't the wedding Jaci would have planned for herself, if she had ever actually dreamed of marrying. The smell of hay and wet horses replaced the scent of flowers, and the only music came from soft whinnies. But none of that mattered when Nicholas gazed into her eyes and pledged his love through all time.

Nicholas somehow managed to have a bath ready for her when they got back to the hotel. He deposited her with a kiss and a promise to return soon. He had told the men they would have rooms in the hotel that night, and promised to share a drink with them.

She experienced a twinge of disappointment but shrugged it off, knowing he would return quickly. It was her wedding night and she shivered in anticipation as she sank deeper into the tub. No matter what had gone before, she was married now.

"Mrs. Nicholas Westbrooke," she whispered as she turned the wide gold band on her finger.

"And how delightful Mrs. Westbrooke looks, all slick and naked in that tub of water." Nicholas leaned over from behind and kissed her nose.

"How did you get in?" She didn't even jump, for Nicholas was always sneaking up on her, and she had somehow come to expect it ever since he had started walking again.

"I told the desk clerk I wanted to ravish the lovely lady in room 108 and he gave me a key — with a grin." While he spoke, he began peeling his wet clothes off, for it still poured outside.

Jaci pretended not to notice, but her body hummed with desire. He sat and jerked off his boots and socks, wiggling his toes, and Jaci even found his feet sexy.

"Do you mind?" He asked as his pants dropped to the floor.

"Huh? Mind what?" She had no idea what he asked for his naked body claimed all her attention.

"Mind if I ravish you?"

She raised her gaze to his. "Not if you do it very, very, slow."

With a growl, he reached down and scooped her out of the tub. She squealed, grabbing him around the neck. Seconds later, water splashed from the oversized tub as he sat down with her on his lap.

"How strange. I wondered why this tub was much larger than the one back home." She murmured as he began kissing her neck.

"Don't women of the future share their baths?" His soapy hand slid over her breast.

"I didn't take baths; I showered."

He quirked a brow.

She tried to explain, which was difficult given the movement of his hands. "It's a nozzle high on the wall, in an enclosed area, like a closet. The water comes out a spray, and you stand up to wash."

He nuzzled the sensitive area behind her ear. "Novel invention, but it doesn't sound very relaxing," he pulled her down against his chest, "nor as cozy."

She wiggled her bottom against him and was delighted with his response. "And your point is?" She teased him.

"My point, darling Mrs. Westbrooke, is that no matter what else changes through the years; no matter what marvelous wonders are invented; one thing will always remain constant." He turned her in his arms and kissed her deeply. "My love for you will endure through all eternity."

Epilogue

Menlo Park, New Jersey — 1879

"You must think us dreadfully boring, being awed by such inventions as were in the exhibit. After all, I'm sure you've known about Edison's light bulb and phonograph for some time," Nicholas commented as they left the exhibition hall and walked into the bright afternoon.

"Of course I know about them, but since I've been here, I've come to appreciate the simpler life. I only wish I had the wherewithal to do the inventing. Imagine what I could show them."

"Jaci—" He shook his head in warning, for they had decided on their wedding night that she would do nothing which might irrevocably change history.

"Well, it's marvelous to see Amanda's eyes light up at all the new wonders she'll have in her lifetime. I can't wait until she hits her teens and has access to Bell's telephone. Now that Cameron has decided to stay in Philly and let others drive his ships, she can have a house full of modern conveniences."

"Pilot, dear, not drive," Nicholas corrected gently.

"Sorry. Speaking of pilots, they didn't have an airplane in the exhibit hall, now did they?"

"I warn you," Nicholas reprimanded, but his eyes twinkled.

"Papa! Penny, Papa, penny." Four year old Cassandra came racing at her father and Nicholas scooped her high above his head, spinning her around in a circle. Jaci smiled as she remembered him doing the same to Amanda years ago. Now, ten year old Amanda followed in Cassandra's wake at a much more sedate pace.

Nicholas tweaked his daughter's nose. "What does my precious Cassie want with a penny?"

As Cassie tweaked her papa's nose in turn, Jaci laughed, her hand sliding over her slightly rounded stomach. She had never expected to find happiness in a marriage, much less the incredible bliss she still experienced in Nicholas's arms. Though Amanda was like their own child, she would soon be leaving to live with Cameron and attend school in the city. God had blessed them with Cassandra, and now she was pregnant with another. This time, she hoped for a son for Nicholas, to carry on the Westbrooke tradition. Not that Cassandra wouldn't be capable, but Jaci longed to see her do something extraordinary — like become the first woman pilot, or President.

For now, her attention turned to where Cassandra pointed. "Me want to ride horsies, like Papa's."

If Nicholas's free hand hadn't already been holding Jaci's elbow, he probably wouldn't have been able to stop her from falling. As it was, he had to juggle her and Cassandra. However, she couldn't stop the dizziness, nor the incredible sense of déjà vu that twisted like a knife in her heart.

"Nicholas." Her voice came out a strangled whisper. She managed to keep from collapsing into a ruffled puddle, but leaned heavily on Nicholas as they stood in the middle of a busy walkway.

Straight ahead, not more than a hundred feet, a carousel glimmered, its horses and menagerie animals chasing each other round and round the platform. It wasn't hard to pick out the lead horse, for he rose high above the rest, his mane and tail flying, one leg raised as he proudly stepped forward in all his midnight glory.

"It's your horse." Her voice was urgent. All the ghosts from hell had risen up and fluttered very close by.

Nicholas steadied her as he set Cassandra down and asked Amanda to watch her. He turned to her, and she frantically searched his face for the reassurance she needed. He didn't fail her; just as he hadn't any time before. His shoulders back, his feet braced, he exuded confidence. But it was his gaze that held her, for in his sweet, silver eyes she saw love — enough to last a lifetime and beyond.

"That horse is our destiny, Jaci. I promise you it will be all right." He took her hand and stepped toward the carousel. She jerked back. He turned, taking her chin in his hand and forcing her to focus only on him. "Do you love me, Jaci Westbrooke?"

"Yes, you know I do." Her answer was automatic.

He grinned at her rapid response. It was a game they played, whenever she became over-anxious about her fate. "How much?"

"With my life," she answered, and saw his love shining in his gaze. A great burden of worry seemed to lift from her shoulders.

Nicholas lifted Cassandra to one hip, took Jaci's hand in his and began walking towards the carousel. "Then trust me."

Jaci grabbed Amanda's hand. She felt she needed all the anchors she could manage.

When the carousel stopped, a group of riders got off. Nicholas sat Cassandra on his replica of Wind Dancer and gathered Jaci and Amanda close. Jaci kept her gaze focused on Nicholas, holding her breath each time the platform jiggled.

"I thank God daily for seeing fit to send you to me," Nicholas told her quietly, "and believe me, our love will surmount any obstacle."

He held out his hand and when she placed her hand in his, encircling Cassandra, their fingers brushed the mane of the horse. An electric shock raced up Jaci's arm, but she remained next to her husband.

Before the carousel began to move, a photographer called for their attention. Nicholas and Jaci laughed together, their daughter squealing in delight over riding her papa's horsie, and the photographer's camera flashed.

* * *

Dallas, Texas — present day

"We didn't find anything, Miss Eastman. Witnesses said it looked as if your sister dropped down into the middle section of the carousel to help the old man."

Mandy Eastman shook her head in disbelief. "I don't understand. You mean she simply disappeared?"

"We've put out a missing person report," the detective explained. "It's the strangest, damn thing. I guess the gears on that merry-go-round weren't adjusted right or something. Apparently once the children got off and the operator fell against the lever, it spun so fast some of the poles actually bent outward with the centrifugal force. But, that doesn't help you any, does it? We'll check back at the park later today and see if anything's been reported."

The police detective turned to leave. "Oh, I almost forgot. Your sister's camera was still at the scene. It must have been set on an automatic timer, because the roll of film had been completed used. I took the liberty of having the film developed, for clues, but didn't find anything out of the ordinary. Just photos of the carousel and some people."

Mandy thought it odd that the detective said there were people in the pictures, because Jaci had wanted only the horses for her magazine layout. However, she thanked the police and closed the door behind them.

It had been five days since her sister's disappearance, and nothing was known. Wearily she sat down on the couch, opening the envelope and spilling the pictures out on the coffee table. She smiled at the sight of the horses, seemingly so alive through her sister's photographic ability.

One picture caught her eye, and when she picked it up, she gasped, for here was the horse she clearly recalled from earlier photos Jaci had taken. There was a blur of some sort behind the horse, and Mandy quickly shuffled through the other pictures looking for something similar. When she found it, she began to cry.

Standing behind the magnificent, black carousel horse was the man Jaci had originally photographed. Through her tears, Mandy saw Jaci standing beside him, their hands clasped around a darling little girl; another girl next to them. A smile touched her lips as she looked lovingly at her sister.

It was no wonder the police hadn't recognized her picture. Her face was older, reminding Mandy of a faded photograph she had of their mother. Jaci's hair was longer, worn in a bun no less, and she had on ruffles and lace that Mandy swore she'd never wear today. It was the expression on Jaci's face, though, that set Mandy's heart to rest.

The police would take their time to determine exactly what had happened that day at the carousel. To Mandy though, it no longer mattered. For whatever reasons there might be, her sister had found true love. From the look on her face, they were indeed living happily ever after.

The End

Author's Note

The first Kentucky Derby actually was run on May 17, 1875. I tried to stay as close to the truth as possible, but of course had to allow Wind Dancer to win because Jaci had promised to marry Nicholas.

Aristides won the race that day, ridden by Oliver Lewis. Aristides's owner, H.P. McGrath, received the purse of $2,850.

The Kentucky Derby has been held consecutively every year since 1875, and although it is now on the first Saturday of May, it has been run on every day of the week except Sunday. Originally a mile and a half, it was changed to the current one and a quarter miles in 1896.

Barbara Baldwin books also published by
Books We Love

Lost Knight of Arabia
Prospecting for Love
If Wishes Were Magic

Barbara was born in California and now resides in the Midwest. She loves to travel and explore new places, which usually means each of her novels is set in a different locale. She has been published in formats from poetry and short stories to full-length fiction. She wrote and co-produced a documentary on state history which won state and national awards, but she really loves writing romance, whether it be contemporary, historical or time travel. Just for fun, each year she writes a Christmas short story for family and friends—some heartfelt and others whimsical — but always a gift from her heart. She has an MA in Communication, has taught at the college level and has made over 100 presentations at state and national conferences. She also loves to create art through pottery and fused glass, candles, baskets and quilts. Visit her website at http://www.authorsden.com/barbarajbaldwin.

www.ingramcontent.com/pod-product-compliance
Lightning Source LLC
Chambersburg PA
CBHW020949260626
47169CB00006B/1889